SHIELD MAIDEN

21ST CENTURY SIRENS

T STEDMAN

SHIELD MAIDEN

Website www.tstedman.com

Cover Art
by
Anna Dittmann

Print edition
ISBN 978-0-9933098-3-0
Edited by
Helen Williams &
Nicky Jeans

This edition published: February 2015

THE ROYAL FAMILIES

OF ATLANTIS

Dubonnetti
Bonaci
Santalini
Florianna

Of Murrtaine
Borge

PROLOGUE

*S*hinto Temple, just outside Higashi Village, Northern Okinawa, Japan, twelve years previously

"THAT'S IT, Snow-san, feel the air current under your fingers," Sensei Daichi said, as he mirrored her slow movements.

He stopped what he was doing and circled the eight-year-old's body, crouched low, back straight, swaying her arms in a gentle wave while she carried out her slow-motion Kata.

"See … feel … hear … smell. Use all your senses to feed your mind, Snow-san."

"I hear the birds, Sensei," little Isla said, smiling with her eyes tightly closed.

Sensei Daichi silently and swiftly moved to the opposite side of her and she instantly adjusted her stance to the direction he had gone.

Like lightning, he lunged at her with his hand. She dodged her head sideways by a hair's-breadth and countered with a kick that he caught in his hand and held it so she wobbled to remain upright.

"Quicker, Snow-san. Never leave yourself vulnerable." Sensei Daichi let her little bare foot go and moved slowly, turning around her again while she continued with her Kata. "What do you feel, Snow-san?"

She thought for a moment as she continued to slice the air slowly with her arms. "I feel the wind from the north of the village, Sensei."

Very carefully, Sensei Daichi lifted a staff from the ground and struck at Isla's shin to take the leg from under her. She jumped and leapt away, then resumed her stance and Kata again.

"And what can you see, Snow-san?"

"I see the pineapple trees and flowing rivers of Kyushu, Sensei."

"That is good, Snow-san. Your place of peace will be with you always, no matter what trials you face."

Isla was a little troubled at the thought. What trials could she possibly face? Her life here in Higashi was tranquil and happy.

Just as her concentration wandered, she realized that the lesson hadn't ended when she felt a tentacle of mental pressure from Sensei creep through her first barrier of consciousness. Quickly, she sent up a grille and refused him entry.

"Work on your mental blocks, Snow-san. Never leave your pathways open. Your mind is your sanctuary; if you guard it well, it will always be your retreat."

She felt disappointed that she had fallen down on such a basic part of her training.

"Open your eyes, Snow-san, and come and sit."

Isla stood up straight and padded over to the cushions in

reds and oranges arranged at the end of the open-sided temple. She crossed her legs and rested her arms on her thighs.

The elderly sensei joined her, his old bones complaining as he lowered himself down to sit opposite her. "Tomorrow we leave this place, Snow-san."

Surprise and fear flickered across her face. She had lived here at the temple ever since she could remember and loved the sensei dearly, like a father. "Where are we to go, Sensei?" she asked cautiously.

"For the next chapter of your destiny, we journey to America."

Her eyes went wide. "Are you coming with me, Sensei?"

"It is my destiny to stay with you as long as I live, Snow-san."

She smiled, relieved. *Maybe it will be like an adventure.* She would have hated to be parted from the elderly monk.

"You must stop that, Snow-san," he reprimanded.

Her face fell. "Stop what, Sensei?"

"You reveal your heart on your face." Despite his stern words, he looked kindly at her. "A smile, a look of love or longing, you give yourself away. An enemy has control when they know what you love."

Isla stared at him, thinking that he was talking more in riddles than usual today.

"You cannot trust everyone as you can here at the temple, Snow-san."

"But how will I know who I can trust, Sensei?"

"You will not know, but your heart will tell you eventually. A great destiny awaits you, Snow-san. You will marry and he will be like you in many ways ... one of our people. He will be of the sea."

Her heart beat wildly. That was what her heart wanted

more than anything. She'd spied on the courting young women of the village. To find a boy just like her would be a dream come true.

THE NEXT DAY, the two of them gathered their few belongings; they didn't own much, having no need of material possessions at the temple, and made the journey from Okinawa to Kadena, the military base where a plane would take them to a facility in Montana, USA.

The journey was long and tiring, but eventually they landed and walked down the steps of the plane. Isla held the sensei's hand. He must have felt a little of what she felt as he allowed it.

The place smelled funny to her. No smells of ripe pineapple or fragrant flowers. They entered the building, which was grey and square like a large box – a far cry from the ornate red wooden buildings of home. A tall, grey, distinguished-looking gentleman met them with two large soldiers in uniform. He bowed and Sensei bowed after in greeting, so Isla did the same. He smiled at her.

"Good day, Sensei. Welcome to America. I am Duke Ormond Delissi. We met many years ago; eight to be exact," he said in an accent like he was singing, and smiled at Isla again.

"I remember it well, as if it were yesterday," her sensei answered.

"Welcome, Isla," the duke said directly to her.

She bowed again, as regally as she could.

The duke seemed amused. "Come, I will escort you to your new home. I hope you will be happy here, even though it is only temporary."

He led them into a small meeting room where two men in suits met them. Apart from the two soldiers that accompanied them, there didn't seem to be anyone else in the building.

The duke introduced them as Special Agents assigned to her care; *whatever they were*. Everything felt overwhelming and strange.

"Is there anything you wish to ask me before I go, Isla?"

She grasped Sensei's hand tighter than ever and looked up at him, then back at the duke. "When do I get to go home?" She knew it was a question that she shouldn't have asked, but she guessed it was her last opportunity and he seemed such a kindly man.

The duke smiled apologetically at her. "Not for a few years yet and then you will meet your family," he said brightly.

Hiding her disappointment wasn't easy. That was a very long time before she could go back to Japan.

Before Isla knew it, the duke bowed again and took his leave. She would wait another ten long years before she met him again. The question of how much he knew of what went on in that room after he left would never be far from her thoughts.

EVERYTHING WENT quiet except for the ticking of a large plastic clock on the wall. She would never forget it. There were no clocks in the temple. It came to symbolize the time her life ended. The clock became the rhythm of her life. Light and shade, loud and soft, happy and sad, love and hate, they all faded into mediocrity.

Two loud pops were all it took to change everything. Her sensei doubled over and collapsed on the floor. Her shock was so profound that she didn't move a muscle. She didn't cry. She looked straight ahead of her while the two soldiers dragged his body away.

The two men who'd met them walked forward. One of their mouths moved, but she didn't understand or hear what he said. It was as though someone had turned off the sound.

Never show what you love. Never show what you love, she repeated like a mantra.

utskirts of Milan, Italy, four years previously

Isla sat, dressed completely in black, in the SUV parked in the narrow lane.

"Now, Isla, you go in over the wall, across the field and over the perimeter fence. There are dogs … here." Her handler, Christophe, passed her a small bag of cubed meat. "Follow the plans I showed you. You have them memorized?"

She nodded.

"You disable the alarm here." He pointed at the sheet of paper open over her lap. "You go up the servants' staircase and along the landing. You will know the door. You will feel it. That is the door you must enter. That is the person you must eliminate. Are we clear?"

She nodded. It was nothing unusual, except the part about knowing the door. That was strange. She didn't have any more time to give it much thought before Christophe looked at his watch. "Thirty minutes, that's all you have before contingency action is taken."

"Okay." She wasn't sure what contingency action was yet; she'd never tested it out, but she suspected it had something to do with the implant she had in her neck. In it was a lethal dose of venom, making it impossible for her to run or make an escape. She opened the door quietly and slipped outside into the night.

"Thirty minutes," Christophe reminded her as the door closed and she bounded over the wall.

A short sprint across the field and she was at the perimeter fence. A quick assessment showed nothing too taxing, no barbed wire or electricity. She took two steps back and leapt up, grabbing the top, swinging a leg and over she went, landing softly on her feet in a crouch.

She ran low in the direction of the large rustic villa. Almost there and she heard the growl. A sleek black Doberman baring its teeth and drooling, two more were creeping up alongside it.

Quickly, she flashed a picture directly to their minds of a fierce dog gnashing its teeth. It stopped them dead with a yelp. She took out the bag of meat from her utility belt and spread the cubes on the floor. They were soon eating the meat laced with something to knock them out.

Creeping slowly around the walls of the house, she found her way to the back, where the pantry was situated. She cut a hole in the gauze in the small window and climbed inside. The beeping told her she had ten seconds to disable the alarm. It was tucked away between a wall and the freezer. She quickly snipped the two wires inside the box and the beeping stopped.

She looked at her watch. Only four minutes had passed. She breathed and quickly thought of the countryside of Kyushu and the soft summer breezes that blew through the leaves of the pineapples. As always, her pulse slowed and she breathed easier, continuing her progress through the house, taking the route just as Christophe said.

Today, her objective was to kill a son of the Florianna

family. She never asked why; that wasn't her concern. Sometimes she was sent into a situation to steal or to place surveillance equipment – it varied.

Briefly, she wondered what this person had done, but then reminded herself that there were worse things than dying, like living this half-life she lived, for instance. The only thing that kept her going was her sensei's promise that one day she would meet her husband – someone just like her.

The landing stretched ahead of her at the top of the stairs with doors on either side. Slowly, she made her way with her eyes closed, feeling her way and branching out with her mind. Her small black dance slippers made no sound at all.

She faltered. *What was that?* Her throat felt like it was closing up. She looked at her watch. Only six minutes had gone. It couldn't be the implant. She shook her head. Perspiration beaded on her forehead and top lip.

Just get it over with. Do the job and get out.

Her hand went to the brass doorknob and she stealthily entered the room. The small bedside lamp was on, creating an orange glow. She could have done with it being dark really; her night vision was excellent and she would rather not let her victim see her.

Slowly, she made her way to the lump under the sheet on the bed. At three-thirty in the morning, it was little surprise that the target was sleeping. Her vision blurred momentarily. She shook her head to clear it, then made her way to the bed, pulling her large hunting knife from its holster strapped around her torso. Her speciality was assassination at close quarters.

Isla halted at the bottom of the bed and her eyes tracked up the sleeping body. He was lying on his back. Just a sheet covered him to the waist.

Silent and as light as a cat, she crawled onto the bed.

Nearer and nearer, even managing to put a leg over his sleeping form until she straddled him, edging slowly forward to put the knife close to his neck for the kill stroke, swift and painless.

It was unclear what distracted her, the beautiful coffee-dark skin stretched over the muscled physique, calmly moving up and down with soft breaths. Or was it the swirls and arcs in black ink that reminded her so much of the monks from her childhood?

Her eyes scanned up to his face. Like a statue, the hard lines and angles of his jaw and cheekbones begged to be touched. His hair was so black it shone blue in the light.

She had an overwhelming urge to touch him; more than that, she wanted to put her lips next to his skin to smell and taste it. Her reaction baffled her; never had she had such a physical reaction to anyone in her life before. Her pulse was racing, something she had full control over as a rule.

The impulse was irresistible and she palmed her knife in the other hand and ever so slowly reached out the tips of her fingers towards the beautiful face.

His eyes slowly opened.

MALLEVEN HAD TURNED up the previous afternoon for a prearranged rendezvous with his cousin, Cesaré Florianna. They were supposed to be going out together to celebrate finishing their training with his uncle and sowing their wild oats before they both went off to Cambridge.

Cesaré had got sidetracked and not come home at all last night. Malleven would bet his life on him being with a woman; he was like a dog in heat. He wasn't too bothered. Cesaré's oldest brother, Sandro, had told him to sleep in his bed as the guest rooms were being refurbished.

He'd always been a light sleeper, but was even more so the

more practised he got in the black arts and increased his knowledge of the evil that lurked when you slept and were unaware. So when the slight click of the door tapped in his subconscious, his brain tripped awake.

Malleven decided to lie still and wait till whoever it was came close to striking range. He was a master in meditation and so he slowed his heart rate down to give no indication that he was awake.

Excitement bubbled up in him when he felt someone very light and skilled in the art of stealth creep up onto his bed. The audacity astounded him. The urge to take a peek was almost overwhelming. And when they straddled him without transferring any weight onto him, the blood surged to his cock as he thought of the games he would play with this would-be assassin before he killed them. The wait was all the more erotic when he felt their eyes rake over his semi-naked body, then inch closer to his neck before pausing again.

He was just about to flip them over to dominate them when a wave of nausea hit him and his eyes swam as he opened them slowly and rested them on the most beautiful female he had ever seen. Her blonde hair was scraped back from her pale-cream face and her large staring eyes were the colour of clearest water.

She didn't move to action either. In fact, when he relaxed under her, she slowly rested her suspended weight onto him and they studied each other.

"You'd better do something with that knife, before I do something to you."

She didn't answer, but a beautiful blush entered her pale cheeks.

Malleven couldn't help but move his eyes to the huge knife she held in her left hand. Slowly, he moved his arm to take it from her loose fingers and dropped it over the edge of the bed.

"Tell me, is it me or the owner of the room you have come to kill?" his Italian voice purred. He was intrigued. She was too skilled to be merely a jealous or spurned girlfriend. This was no ordinary woman; in fact, a quick assessment told him she was little more than a teenager.

A micro expression and he noticed it. "Ah, Cesaré … well, his loss is my gain," he said, quietly.

His brilliant mind was quickly working out and doing the maths. *Why would someone be trying to kill his cousin? Was it possible? Could she be one of the fabled Sirens they all awaited and searched for? Blast, his divining ring that could have identified her was in bits at home while he used it for his experiments. With five Sirens in the world, one for a prince in each of the five families, a Human or another family's plot to kill Atlantean princes was highly likely; they all sought the upper hand.*

What better assassin than a Siren? His strong physical reaction to her, despite taking Elixir, was suspicious even without his ring.

His hands were holding both of hers. "Why did you hesitate? I doubt you have had that problem before?" He yanked her closer to his face.

She hitched a breath when she found her face was within inches of his, but didn't struggle.

Malleven had a Siren in his bed, the object of his wildest dreams, and there was no way she was going to escape, not until he allowed her.

HE WAS PULLING her closer to his mouth and all she could do was shift her eyes from it to his eyes and back again. *What power was this? Why couldn't she just kill him like so many targets before? She got the assignment, did the training and got the job done.* Something this time had stopped her. *But this wasn't the one, he'd just told her so... that meant this guy wasn't the target.*

She would just have to go back to her handler and tell him she had to abort the mission.

As she'd been running things through her head, he had continued to pull her closer until her mouth was nearly on his. She could feel his hot breath. Despite her training, her heart rate was hammering, and she was hot – so hot.

"Your body heats for me," he said, right next to her mouth. His voice rumbled through his chest, pressed against her breasts.

Yes, it did heat right from the centre of her – at her core. Between her legs, she ached. *What was wrong with her?* It was as though she would combust at any moment. And yet she didn't want to hurt him. She wanted to be pressed closely like this. Interaction with her was forbidden; her only contact was with her handler. "Touch me …" she whispered.

No sooner were the words out of her mouth than he covered it with his own and she was crushed against his body. His arms came around her back and into her hair and he pulled her to him.

It was sensation overload. His mouth moved against hers until his tongue pushed against her closed lips and entered – more than that, he invaded her mouth as if he owned it.

It felt like every inch of him was in contact and moved against her. His arms pinned her tightly, but his hands roamed her back, then ventured down to her buttocks, where he kneaded and massaged. Every sensation was like a blissful pain that shot straight to her womb and pooled between her legs. And when he moved his fingers lower and felt her inner thigh through her tight leggings and touched the heat of her, she dissolved into him.

My god, she panted. It was impossible to breathe. He seemed to sense her weakness and adeptly rolled her over and was on top of her before she knew it. He deepened the kiss and pushed his hips into her parted legs so she could feel him hard against her, moving in a steady rhythm. He had her helplessly pinned, but it was good. "So good," she moaned. Her cheeks were on fire.

His mouth left hers and he lifted his head. "You are too hot. Do they keep you in the water?"

Isla nodded. "Some of the time." She could have told him that at the age of eight, she'd been held under water to the point of drowning to see if she could breathe the water, but that felt irrelevant at that moment. She was feverish and delirious and unable to lie still. All she wanted was to feel relief.

She groaned as his weight left her and her eyes followed his beautiful naked body as he left the bed. A dark, dangerous Adonis covered in the markings she remembered so well. His huge erection was standing proud of his body; she couldn't take her eyes from it. The first she had ever seen and it didn't scare her in the slightest.

He went over to a dressing table where there was a collection of bottles of various colours and sizes, looked at the labels of a few and chose two. Then he picked up a glass and poured the two together, took a couple of sips and came back to the bed. "Here, drink this."

Isla sat up and looked at it warily. *Could it kill her? No, he had drunk some.*

"Here, take it. I want to fuck you, not kill you … even though I should."

Her face went a darker shade of crimson with his words. She wasn't worldly, but she wasn't stupid. She could deduce what he intended to do, and her heart sped even faster. Her hand reached out to the glass, whether it was a good idea or not, she took it and knocked it back.

"Good … When will they expect you back?"

"Straightaway," she whispered. "They are parked a couple of kilometres away. I was allocated thirty minutes." She glanced down at her watch. "No more than twenty minutes left."

When she looked back at him, his eyes bored into hers shrewdly. "You have never been touched?"

She stared at him, shook her head and lowered her eyes.

"We'd better make it count then."

And he pushed her back against the pillows and joined her on the bed again so half of his weight rested on her. She found she was powerless to resist his touch.

Whatever he had given her was working as she could feel herself cooling down. However, she had no time to acclimatize as he rolled back on top of her, unclipped her knife holster and whipped her black jersey up over her head.

She held her breath as he gently lowered the strap on her black bra low enough to expose the top of her breast so he could kiss down her neck and down to the soft, plump flesh. Then he pulled the triangle down and placed his mouth over her tight peak. He toyed with it between his lips and his teeth and drew it deeply into his mouth as he sucked. The sensation drove her wild and she found her own hips moving into his in rhythm. He moved his head, nipping and kissing to give the same attention to the other breast.

Her body was melting, her womb contracting and she needed something so badly. She couldn't bear it. "You're killing me," she moaned.

She felt him grin, her nipple still in his mouth. "I promise I won't hurt you … not unless you want me to?" And he lifted his body slightly and pulled down her leggings and, without warning or permission, her knickers came off as well until she lay completely naked before him.

His eyes grazed over her as she lay there, relaxed. She felt no shame, not only because she had been prodded and poked by doctors and scientists since she was eight years old, but this was different. Her eyes felt lazy and were half shut, but every nerve-ending was alive and buzzing. It was the first time she had felt alive in a long while.

When his mouth came down on hers again, she was ready and opened straightaway for him, swirling her tongue with his. He growled his approval. "You learn quickly … I like that." And his hand stroked down her body. It meandered and teased until it reached the soft curls between her legs. "What is your name?" he breathed, next to her lips.

"Isla … Isla Snow," she gasped.

"My snowflake," he whispered. "Open your legs and let me touch you."

It wasn't a request for permission and she opened them slightly.

He smiled down at her, looking her deep in the eyes while his fingers probed and stroked her delicate folds.

Isla gazed up at him, her breathing ragged. She realized that his eyes weren't black at all, but the deepest blue she'd ever seen. She groaned again as he circled his finger, gathering her wetness, travelling from her tight bud down to her entrance and pushing a little at a time. She found herself panting for more.

When two of his fingers entered her, he smothered her cries with his mouth. She thought he was killing her, her heart raced so. He gave her little respite as he travelled with his mouth down her body, hovering over each breast to lavish them with attention and went on further until his tongue pushed between her legs.

He pulled her leg up so her foot was flat on the bed for better access and continued to circle and lap with his tongue while he touched her deeply with his fingers. Just as she thought she would die, he came back up her body and stared into her eyes as if deciding on something. "You will bleed if I fuck you, Isla … will your handler know?"

Isla was breathing hard, insane with a need she didn't

understand. *God, she needed him to do something.* "Yes, but I don't care ... Please ... Please help me?" It was an exquisite torture.

He said no more but moved quickly and plunged his mouth to her core and sucked the little bud into his mouth, rolling his tongue over and over it.

She called out, "Help me..." not able to contain it any longer. Heat radiated to her lips, chest, core and down her legs to her toes in a wonderful explosion. She found herself pushing her hips up to meet his mouth as he worked her with his tongue, wringing every last sensation out of her. Just when she could bear it no more, he plunged his tongue into her and pushed and lapped until she screamed.

His kissing slowed to a gentle licking until he nipped her thigh and crept back up her body to reach her face. He leaned up on an elbow and pushed her wayward hair out of her eyes and mouth.

Isla gazed up at him, not yet able to speak; her chest still rising and falling with exertion. "What have you done to me?" she whispered, eventually.

He smiled down at her with satisfaction. "Your first orgasm, Snowflake."

"I thought you were going to fuck me?"

He laughed out loud.

MALLEVEN LOOKED DOWN into Isla's beautiful, flushed face, completely satiated with her release. He'd made the decision not to fuck her, as he didn't want her handler to find out she had been deflowered and endanger her position. And he guessed she was a little too young, not that he didn't want to.

It was in that instant that his plans crystallized in his mind. The stars had told him Sirens were on the earth in this generation. It had always been an ambition to take one as his, but now he knew where to find one when he was ready. Besides, this one needed to be with her people; she would die if they continued to cage her like an animal.

The appearance of Sirens marked the dawn of a new Atlantean Kingdom and he suspected the Human governments must have been trying to ruin it before it began. There were five Sirens, each destined to mate with a prince from one of the five royal families. Fleetingly, he wondered if this one were for his – the Florianna.

The first prince to find his fated Siren would be king. Despite being too minor a prince to be officially recognised as king, no matter what he did, he would obtain all five. He wasn't exactly sure how yet, but he would make it his life's work, as with them all, no one could challenge him, Human or Atlantean alike.

"Do you know what you are, Isla?" he asked, pulling her up and off the bed to stand up.

"I know I am not like other women."

Malleven led her to the small adjoining bathroom and switched on the shower, careful not to wet her hair or use any strong-smelling soap. He washed her, taking special care between her legs.

It wasn't that he was a particularly caring male, but he was safeguarding his investment and following a hunch. He groaned his approval as he watched her black bands begin to emerge all over her body. He twirled her around to study them. "Ah, Isla, simply stunning." Then he turned her back to face him and put his own dark-brown arm next to hers, and watched as her eyes went wide when she realized that similar bands were appearing all over him.

Her hands rubbed over them, over his chest and he allowed it, smiling, turning to show her his back. "You see, Isla, we are the same. You should be with your people, you should be with me." To seal it like an oath, he pulled her to him and kissed her.

"Can I stay with you now?"

Malleven smiled at her. She delighted him in her naivety. "No, Snowflake. It is too soon, and you are too young."

Her eyes fell, but he pulled her chin back up with his finger.

"I will die there," she said, with a resigned hopelessness.

He turned off the shower, wrapped her in a towel and another around his waist. Then he gathered up her things. Hard by nature, he couldn't understand the knot he felt in his chest for the first time. It simply wasn't logical. He usually preferred males anyway.

Soon she was dressed, and the last thing he passed her was her hunting knife. "I am glad you weren't hasty with this." He was teasing, but his voice remained stern.

She wiped her eyes quickly with her hand.

He didn't fully understand the compulsion but pulled her to him. "Listen to me, Snowflake, I will do all in my power to set you free so you can be with me, okay?"

She nodded, like a child placated. "I'll be waiting."

Quickly, he grabbed her wrist. "Shit, are you overdue?"

She glanced at her watch anxiously. "Well over ten minutes."

"What will they do?"

Her hand went to her neck. "I'm not sure. I have an implant."

"Poison?"

"Yes, I think so."

Malleven closed his eyes and searched her aura for any impurities. Nothing. He opened his eyes again. "There is nothing yet ... You must go, Snowflake, but I cannot leave you with your memories, I daren't for fear they will extract them and learn of me."

A look of dismay crossed her face. "What? I won't remember you … tonight?"

He shook his head ruefully. "It won't be for long. I will restore them, I promise."

She swallowed and slowly looked into his eyes. He put the gentlest touch on each of her temples, with his thumbs at the centre of her forehead. "Wait …"

He paused.

"You didn't tell me your name?"

He relaxed and smiled. "Malleven … my name is Malleven." And he concentrated and centered his energy. His hand waved across her eyes. "Go," he said, surprisingly reluctant. He watched her slip out of the door and back the way she came.

ROUGH HANDS GRABBED her waist as she went feet first through the pantry window. She almost yelped. She was spun round on landing, with her knife already in hand. "Christophe?" she breathed.

"Where the fuck were you? You've been gone nearly an hour."

She paused for a second as an image of a beautiful, dark male slammed into her brain, then went as quickly as it came. "The target wasn't home. I had to hide in a cupboard; the family awoke."

"Come on, let's get out of here."

She ran with him to the perimeter fence, but was aware of his suspicious eyes on her the whole time as they walked briskly across the field back to the parked car.

It had been a close shave, for what she was unsure, but she would work it out when she got back to the facility and privacy.

CHAPTER 2

Tia Storm, New York, present day

Dante Dubonnetti, the king, sauntered into the New York bar with two of his water nymphs. It was late, he was tired and his nerves were shot, knowing he was going to have the confrontation with Tia – his wife – that had been a long time coming. He dreaded it and welcomed it in equal measure; after all, it had been almost a year since he'd seen her.

He couldn't believe that she had been back for weeks and still hadn't presented him with his two children. No, she and Jay (his best friend), who were bound and also had a child together, had been shacked up in Barbados playing happy fucking families while he waited. Enough was enough.

His nymphs linked arms with him on either side. They were a welcome distraction, as he had no emotional attachment to them and that suited him just fine, given his total preoccupation with Tia Storm, his Siren and most compatible mate in the world. He couldn't handle any more complications in his life. They were perfectly happy receiving only physical gratification, allowing him to forget Tia and Jay, if only for a short time.

Dante paused at the entrance of the VIP bar. A quick scan and he knew the place was full of Santalinis; another Atlantean royal family, otherwise known as the Honourable Guard, or special forces of the race. *At least they were well guarded and not taking risks.*

It didn't take long for his eyes to home in on the objects of his impromptu visit. Across the bar, Jay was sitting on a barstool with Tia standing facing him between his knees, her arms around his neck, passing ice cubes between their mouths. Every now and then, she would laugh, tossing back her head and Jay would lean forward and kiss her exposed throat with cold lips.

Dante swallowed at the intimacy of it. It was their private time together and they were completely oblivious to him. The glimpse into their world did nothing to improve the place he was at. He was dog-tired. The bond he and Tia shared needed replenishing, necessary every few months and it was way overdue. Jay, on the other hand, was the picture of health, having received the gift of Tia's spirit, no doubt, every time they made love. He gritted his teeth and resolved to stick to the reason of his visit.

Just at that moment, Tia glanced across the L-shaped bar and saw him. It was inevitable that she would sense him there. Their bond would forever make it so.

Quickly, she whispered an excuse to Jay and scurried off to escape him before he could approach. Dante took a breath and walked slowly over to Jay, his friend and brother, whom he loved almost as much as Tia.

Jay swivelled around on his stool as he spotted him walking over. Stepping down, he pulled Dante into an embrace as soon as he got close enough.

Dante clapped his back and kissed his friend's shoulder, getting a grip on his emotions.

"Dante!" Jay said, pleased to see him.

"Jay, man, how ya doing?"

"Good." Jay was already assessing the two water babes he had with him, and raised his eyebrows at him for an intro.

"This is Anthea and Elisse," Dante said, grinning.

Jay nodded, smiling, straightaway getting their appeal. Dante had already told him about them. He leaned towards them and kissed them both on the cheek.

"She's avoiding me?" Dante said, in sad resignation.

"I told her she can't keep it up," Jay said.

"Will you entertain these two for five minutes, Jay? I must speak with her."

"Sure." Although he shook his head, knowing the drill. Shit was going to get ugly.

Dante left Jay and strode across the room to a corridor that led out to the cloakroom and loos. Feeling with his bond, although now weak, it didn't take him long to track her to a dead end with a fire escape chained shut.

He came up behind her while she faced the door, shaking the handle in frustration. She was like a naughty child facing the corner. "Tia."

She shook her head and refused to reply.

"Tia … you will speak to me. Turn around." He was just inches away now, breathing down on the top of her head. "Turn around and look at me, Tia."

"No."

"No? … What childishness is this? Don't make me have to force you … I expect you to present my children to me, and re-pledge. I've given you plenty of space and you fuck me off like this, Tia … I've only got so much patience … Look. At. Me!"

She turned around into the shadow of his body, her eyes still looking at the floor.

He put his forefinger under her chin and gently pulled her face up to look into his eyes. "You think avoiding me is going to help, Tia? It is impossible … we get sick … we're trapped."

All the while he spoke, his lips travelled down the side of her face, his eyes closed while he breathed in her wonderful scent he'd missed for so long.

"No!" she shouted and ducked under his arm, walking purposefully back to the VIP lounge where she'd left Jay.

Dante sagged in defeat and wearily followed her, knowing what she would find. He stopped right behind her at the threshold of the room and rested his hands on her shoulders. There, as he expected, was Jay with a girl draped either side of him, preening, caressing, and whispering in his ear, while he sat on the stool she'd left him on. He let her have a good few moments to get the full impact of the view.

He felt her shoulders rise and fall with her expanding diaphragm as her anger built, then watched as she flew at the group at the bar.

No introductions were made before Tia grabbed the redhead by the hair and flung her sideways. Screaming at the other, she backhanded her, sending her reeling, but the momentum of the strike made her spin and stumble and she was grabbed around her middle and gripped tight while her arms and legs flailed and kicked. Several of the guards surrounded them, including Keenan, her sister's mate, but none of them could do a thing to intervene with Dante there – the king.

Struggling and scratching, she ripped at the familiar heavily tattooed arms holding her like a vice.

Dante gently touched her forehead, stilling her with his mental energy. It took a lot of effort, not just because he was weak at the moment, but he hated seeing her hurt. *Easy,* he projected straight to her mind so no one else could hear. *Stop this nonsense, Tia ... Relax.*

She visibly relaxed and flopped her head back against Jay's chest and neck.

When Dante was satisfied that the fight had gone out of her, he addressed Jay. "She will come straight to Ireland, and she will bring my children to be presented to me and pledge as she is meant to."

Jay's face remained impassive, as if he'd been expecting the showdown. "I'll bring her."

"Good." Dante sighed and inclined his head for the two nymphs, who were straightening themselves out, to follow him, then he walked out.

Fuck, his heart was beating. She always forced him into these fucking confrontations. But for what little he expected of her, she would comply.

Tia slid down Jay's body when he released her, confident that her brain had tripped back online.

Slowly, she turned with clenched fists ready to pummel Jay's chest, but as she lifted them to strike, he grabbed her wrists fast. "Pack it in, Tia," he said, low and deliberate. "Save that shit for Dante."

She gave him the filthiest of looks, pulled out of his grip and flounced off to the exit. Not caring whether she had an escort or not, she rushed out into the street. Their limo was waiting. She got in and shifted to the furthest corner, as far away from Jay as possible, when he followed and slipped into the back seat.

Her head leaned on the window and she watched everyone begin to leave the club and get into their cars. Keenan and Lacy (her sister) went to another car, despite travelling there with them, probably to give them some space.

Reeve, another of the guards, got in next to Jay, as they weren't allowed to travel without security, making the atmosphere doubly awkward.

While they travelled in silence, she scowled over at Jay periodically.

Jay remained infuriatingly silent until eventually he turned his attention to her. "I don't know why you let him play you like that, Tia."

She was quiet for a beat. "What?" she said, flabbergasted. "I just wanted us to be happy, just me, you and the kids." She felt wounded. *She was fighting for them for fuck's sake.*

"You can't blame him for wanting to see his kids," Jay said.

She glared at him and fumed. *How did all this fucking end up her fault? He was the one standing there with girls draped all over him.*

"You can't see how he set that situation up?" Jay continued.

Tia frowned in confusion – everything had happened so fast. "I couldn't bear seeing those bitches all over you," she said quietly, glancing over at Reeve, who was politely looking the other way out of the window.

"But it's okay for Dante?" Jay said, looking back at her with raised eyebrows.

Again, she was taken aback. "He can do what he likes … it's up to him." *It wasn't the same at all.*

Jay gave her his best sardonic look. "Look, I know Dante more than any other person alive."

"So?" she responded, feeling her blood begin to boil.

"He knows you are punishing him for his other women."

"What?" she demanded, feeling slapped. Her eyes widened in disbelief, then looked down and wondered how a nice evening could have suddenly gone so pear-shaped.

Jay shook his head and smiled. "He knew you were a tinderbox waiting to be lit … he lit the fuse and you reacted perfectly."

She looked down at her restless hands, intertwining them in her lap. *No... No, he was wrong ... surely.* "What was he to gain from it, apart from the obvious – causing trouble between us?"

Jay smiled at her patronizingly again. "He knows me better than that, Tia."

She stared back at him for a few moments. "What then?"

"He got to punish you with the very thing you are punishing him for …"

"So what are you saying?" she said, knowing he hadn't said everything.

Jay took a deep breath. "He got to show you I'm no saint."

JAY TOOK no pleasure in being so blunt. It was blindingly obvious that she genuinely didn't understand why she reacted the way she did. Unfortunately, her naivety made her really easy to play.

With his final words, he watched her visibly shrink and retract into herself. *Fuck*, it felt like kicking a puppy. He hated himself sometimes, but Christian Dubonnetti's parting words had continued to go round and round in his head ever since he'd heard them; *he wouldn't be able to help himself, he'd destroy Dante, and Tia would hate him for it.* No, he had to find a way to get out and away from them all. He'd gone over and over it; it was the only thing he could do.

Her voice dragged his attention back.

"I'm sorry, Jay," she said, wearily.

Ah, fuck. "For what?" he said, a little too angrily.

"For everything … I'll take them to him tomorrow."

Jay was left staring at her a long time after she'd stopped

speaking, trying to fathom her while she looked out of the window. The woman who had unconsciously dragged him out of the shithole of faceless, mindless sex with countless women and a festering legacy from his childhood, one from which he could never escape. And Christian Dubonnetti had known. Knew he was tainted and would contaminate and ruin all who he came into contact with.

The nymphs tonight, they may not have been human, but what they represented was commonplace to him, and Dante knew him well, that he could never run from his past.

Unfortunately, Tia didn't. Not that side of him, anyway. And it wouldn't be long until it raised its ugly head and shattered her white knight illusion of him. So Dante was right to show her, because for all his faults – and there were many – Dante loved her to distraction, and whether she cared to admit it or not, she loved Dante too, and they belonged together.

Jay memorized every line and contour of her beautiful face, the face he'd never forget when he left her.

CHAPTER 3

op-security marine study facility, Key Largo, Florida, two years previously

Isla had waited for two years for Malleven to come and save her from her living nightmare. In the beginning, she'd just gotten flashes of memory from that night; mere glimpses. Then, over time, her strong mind had re-found the neural pathways and worked the whole thing out. Now her memory was totally restored.

The man named Malleven had duped her as she was so young and naive, molested her and covered his tracks by trying to wipe her mind of the incident. Then sent her back to her miserable life, none the wiser to anything having happened – or so he thought. But because of her early telepathy training, he'd only managed to scramble, not wipe, her mind and after a short while she'd pieced it all together. He probably never intended to come back for her at all.

Now she just simmered.

Originally, the thought of meeting someone of her species, a male she could marry, was the sole thing that kept her going. Now it was a stone-cold determination to escape but, above all, to feel nothing for anyone. Malleven had firmly and finally closed the lid on any ideas of foolish emotion for her.

Still stuck with her implant, her options for the time being were limited, but she wasn't inactive. Every night, when her handler thought she slept, she used her mind to interfere with the surveillance camera in her sparsely decorated room and would search and plan escape routes around the study facility where she was imprisoned.

Over the two years, she had memorized every door code, every lift access and every computer ID. She knew every walkway and every corridor. She had acquainted herself with every member of staff who'd left, retired, was new, or temporary, and their shift patterns.

Everything was in readiness. For what? She wasn't sure yet, but when it came, she would know and she would take her chances or die trying.

Recently, and purely by accident, she had discovered a floor she never knew existed, a level below the one the deepest lift went to. It intrigued her as it was on the furthestmost reaches of the campus, almost at the sea's edge, and no one ever went there.

Tonight, she planned to investigate and had stolen a universal swipe card from one of her guards for the purpose. She was convinced that something really top secret must be kept there, as it was so remote. Tonight was going to be momentous, she could feel it.

ISLA WENT THROUGH EXACTLY the same routine as she did every night. She worked out, completed the half-speed Kata her sensei had taught her to relax and centre herself, ate a light meal of fish and vegetables, and lay in her cot to sleep.

She waited for two agonizingly slow hours to make sure

her security guards took for granted that she would be asleep, and be playing cards and watching TV rather than concentrating on the monitor connected to the camera in her room.

She centered her mental energy on it and watched as the wisp of smoke drifted up, showing that it had shorted. Then she crept to her door, clicked the lock to the mechanism on the outside and ran, quietly as a cat, along the corridor to the far reaches of the campus.

Isla dodged every camera, and the ones she couldn't she fuzzed. She went down in several lifts and through many airlocks until she came to the building that was of interest to her. Down to the level below the basement she had never been to.

When she came out of the stairwell, the lighting was dim. It wasn't an issue for her as her eyes worked better in poor light, as her pupils were over-dilated from spending long periods underwater. In fact, her eyesight in daylight was poor.

The whole place was damp, suggesting that an aquatic animal was stored here. *But what?* She daren't imagine. It was so top secret she wondered what experiments were carried out on the poor thing.

Isla continued down the bare grey corridor, lit by dull emergency lighting at intervals along the ceiling. The sound of water dripping from a leak somewhere echoed and every so often, she could swear she heard a splash.

She broke into a jog and headed to the furthest corner. That was the direction the noise and her instinct called her.

Eventually, she slowed down towards the end of a corridor where the walls were joined by plate glass. She cupped her face up against it to see inside. It looked like a large pool enclosure, much the same as she'd seen in maga-zines that would house penguins or sea lions in any zoo or sea-life centre around the world. A far cry from the Perspex tank, no bigger than a plunge pool, she was forced into as an eight-year-old.

Fake rocks were banked up towards the back and a wall of thick glass ran along the left-hand side of the room to another aquarium where you could clearly see dolphins swimming.

Whatever was in this pool was large and had access to water and to dry land. She wondered what was housed there. All she could see was an empty pool.

That was until a splash registered in the corner of her eye. *What was that? Was it a fin?*

Something had definitely broken the surface. The water had lapped against the sides, proving it was fast, and she had distinctly seen a glimpse of something grey with a black marking on it.

Isla was baffled and waited and waited for it to do it again. Nothing happened, but something was definitely in there and she had seen a small part of it, she was sure.

Not wanting to get caught before she had satisfied her curiosity, she quickly studied the door and its locking mechanism, mapping it in her mind's eye.

She decided to come back the next night and go in.

IRELAND, present day

Jay knocked on the door to the study at Ballygowan Castle. "Shh!" he whispered to the little ones at his feet.

"Come in," Dante's voice came through the door.

Jay slowly opened the door and poked his head inside. "I have some visitors for you."

Dante's face lit up. "Send them in," he said, in mock-seriousness.

Xavier and Alexia pushed in past Jay's legs. JJ was in his

arms. They ran into the room, then stopped in the middle and looked at each other, not sure what to do next. Then they looked back at Jay for reassurance.

Dante stood, overwhelmed for a second with emotion. He walked around his desk and went and stood directly in front of the two olive-skinned, dark, curly-haired little imitations of himself. The only difference was that they had eyes of emerald green.

He looked down on them from his great height, so they had to crane their necks up to look at him. "Hello," he said, still using his deep, official voice.

"Hello," they said in unison.

Alexia was swinging her dress and fidgeting with shyness.

"And who are you?" Dante said, desperately trying to keep the smile out of his voice.

Xavier, much more confident, immediately introduced them both, poking Alexia in the chest, who scowled at her brother. "Ow!"

"Do you know who I am?"

"You're the king," Xavier said, with pride.

"He's Daddy," Alexia said, getting ready to argue.

"He's king *and* daddy," Xavier said, with satisfaction.

Dante looked over at Jay with delight, a broad smile beaming.

Jay couldn't help but be moved at his oldest friend being presented with his little miniatures for the first time.

Dante crouched down so he was on a level with them. "I'm really happy to meet you two," he said, more softly.

The two children each reached out and put the palm of their hand onto one of his cheeks and gazed at him with a look of concentration.

Mystified, he looked over at Jay for an explanation.

"They're reading your thought patterns, you know, like

the Murrs do? … I think they have to touch skin till they get good at it."

JJ, who had been watching the meeting from Jay's arms the whole time, whimpered and struggled to get down and join his brother and sister.

Jay knelt to put him on the floor and JJ pushed between his siblings, smacking a little hand on Dante's mouth.

Dante couldn't help but laugh. "Hey, bruiser! You can tell whose this one is … he's already smacking me in the mouth," he said, looking over at Jay.

Jay laughed indulgently. "He's got more of a temper than me."

Dante nodded and smiled at the boy. "Is he reading me, too?"

"We don't know yet. He may just be copying the other two."

JJ squealed. "Daddy … Daddy," he said, pointing at Dante, then at Jay.

Both men laughed at the ludicrous situation.

"That's right," Dante said, grinning at him, pulling all three into a hug. "I think you have your answer there, Jay."

Dante motioned for Jay to sit on the sofa near him. "Where is she?" Dante asked, over the top of the kids' heads.

"Making arrangements with her mother to go to Murrtaine."

"She's not?" Dante said, wide-eyed.

Jay quickly shook his head. "No, I don't think so. She reckons JJ has to go underwater regularly to see his Murr doctors and to keep his underwater capabilities."

Dante visibly relaxed.

The children wandered off and quickly became distracted by knick-knacks in the room, which allowed Dante time to sit and talk to Jay.

"She said you can keep Xav and Alex with you while she's away if you want?" Jay said.

"Yes, of course … I would love to get to know them," Dante said, watching their little enquiring minds examine the things that interested them.

"What about your girlfriends?" Jay said, raising an eyebrow.

Dante laughed, but there was little mirth in it. "No, I've fu — got rid of them," he said, realizing quickly he couldn't curse in front of the children.

Jay smiled but was surprised.

"Nah … I sort of got bored, you know?"

Jay thought briefly about their last meeting. It must have had a greater effect on his friend than he thought. Dante's brief hint of vulnerability was quickly masked.

"How was she … you know … after?" He could no longer look Jay in the eye.

Jay sighed. "To tell you the truth … I was a bit hard on her."

Dante turned to him sharply, and he fixed him with a deep frown.

"I just told her a few home truths … I …" Jay rubbed the back of his neck. It was still a sore subject to him. *Fuck.*

Dante relaxed a little and just nodded, understanding perfectly. "Are you two okay now?"

"No, not really. I think that's the real reason she's going to her mother's."

"She has to pledge … I'll know what's going on with her then."

Jay nodded. He found that strangely comforting despite the obvious absurdity.

. . .

ISLA, two years previously

The following evening, Isla carried out her usual routine to the letter. Then, after lying in her cot for two hours, she set off to find out what was in that pool. All the training in the world couldn't stop her heart from pumping in anticipation as she made her way there.

When she reached the plate-glass door, she recalled the map of the lock mechanism she'd stored in her mind's eye, sent out a mental feeler and the lock buzzed and clicked open.

She stepped into the room and shut the door again quickly in case it triggered an alarm somewhere else. Briefly, it occurred to her that the surveillance camera in the enclosure looked frazzled already. A creature as important as she believed it was should have better security.

Isla proceeded slowly further into the room. The air felt surprisingly chilly. She was expecting the room to be balmy; she wasn't sure why, but it told her it was a cold-water creature.

While she pondered what it could be, she dragged her black T-shirt over her head and pulled down her black sweatpants and stepped out of them so she was left standing in a black one-piece swimsuit.

After scanning the area one last time, just in case, she padded to the edge of the pool. Kneeling down, she rested on her arms and leaned over, looking intently into the clear blue water. All she could hear was a gentle lapping.

A bang to the left made her jump. She lurched to her right in reflex, then realized it was a dolphin banging on the glass from the aquarium next door, having spotted her. "Go on, little one," she said, and motioned with her hand for him to move away. She was jittery enough.

Taking a deep, fortifying breath, she leaned over the side

of the pool again and breathed out. She shook her head and opened her eyes and looked once more into the clear water. But there was nothing in its depths because he was standing right behind her and he was huge.

CHAPTER 4

sla, two years previously
Fear needed time to register and he gave her none. Before she could turn round to face him, something like a sledgehammer slammed into her consciousness. She barely had time to put up her mental grills when she hit the water, with him landing on top of her.

He pulled her straight down with him, slamming into her brain, image after image, and blow after blow. It was blood, carnage, fear and hate, all vying for prominence and battering her mental barriers.

She opened her lungs, more from instinct than conscious thought, as she needed everything to defend the onslaught battering her mind.

Over and over, he battered her until she could see her grills fracture and eventually break down, so the full power of his mental pictures began to hit her mind like an old cine reel. Everything was a picture of death, destruction and slaughter; young girls being ripped limb from limb and men's hearts stabbed and throats bitten out. Each image came with a feeling that registered as fear, hate and sheer aggression.

All her life, she had been a trained soldier, continually sharpening her skills, and she could honestly say, even in times of extreme danger, she had never been beaten. But today, at this exact moment, without a shadow of a doubt, she had been thoroughly beaten and battered down.

Her arms and legs no longer flailed, and she felt herself being pulled along in the water by her hair. Every time she tried to gather her thoughts, he seemed to know, and another image bombarded her. Her shields were now completely gone. With the last slam, all she could do was retreat to the corner of her mind to her peaceful place. The one her sensei had taught her to keep, and she reminded herself of the serenity it always gave her.

The onslaught stopped.

She'd stopped moving and was sure she was at the bottom of the pool. Feeling under her with her hands, she felt soft seaweeds. She was exhausted but continued to think of warm thoughts of her early childhood in Japan as though they were her last memory.

Time passed and nothing else happened. She risked opening her eyes slightly and looked quickly around her and saw she had been brought to a clearly purpose-built under-water cave. It was only slightly illuminated, so she could see well. When her eyes rested on him, she scrambled back until her back grazed against the jagged rocks of the cave walls.

There, in front of her, was a manlike creature studying her quizzically. He had to be almost seven feet tall. He was smothered, from head to foot, in vivid black stripes overlaying his pale-grey skin. His black hair was long, almost to his waist and fanned out all around him. His obsidian black eyes were fixed on her curiously as if she were something he didn't understand.

Exhausted and resigned to being a prisoner and figuring if he was going to kill her, he would have done it by now, she relaxed and studied his black savage lines. They accentuated his high cheekbones and square jaw, and more ran from his shoulders, pointing inwards to his heart and skirted the ridges of his muscled stomach and disappeared around to his back. They zigzagged the length of his arms and legs. His dark eyes never left her.

She would have pondered on their obvious similarities if she didn't feel so utterly defenceless. Her head ached as his mental tentacles roamed her mind, and there wasn't a damn thing she could do about it.

TIA, present day

Dante came to the great hall and halted. Tia stood with her back to him, facing the fountain, wearing nothing but a green bikini. Golden skin; even more so after her prolonged stay in Barbados, newly grown hair, beautiful slim figure; despite having three kids, always sent any sane thought southward.

He shook his head and continued towards her, only stopping a few inches behind her.

"I'm going to meet with my mother, Dante," she said, before he spoke and without turning round.

He smiled while he picked up a lock of her hair and bent his head and kissed her shoulder as soft as a whisper. "Are you still running from me, Tia?" He stepped up close to her while speaking and gently put his arms around her waist, breathing in her scent at her neck. "Thank you for bringing them. They are the most perfect and beautiful gifts anyone has ever given me." He wanted to envelop her, knowing her avoidance was always because her resolve was weak.

Tia turned into him and hugged him back, burying her

face in his chest. His arms came around her and crushed her to him. He relished these times of surrender, knowing how dearly they cost her emotionally.

"I'm sorry, Dante. I should have brought them sooner … I just wanted to be normal with Jay, you know … a proper family."

"I know, babe. It's all okay… but you have to wake up now and get real. You'll never be normal."

When she looked up at him, all he wanted to do was kiss her, but he needed to make his point.

"I don't want any of this shit, Dante. I never have."

"Look, babe …" she was so distracting. "I would give you anything that was in my power to give, but your freedom? Well, it's not one of them."

She swallowed hard and looked away from him, fighting back her tears.

"You are not just Tia Storm, are you? … You are a royal Atlantean Siren. A queen, for fuck's sake, responsible for the survival of a whole nation."

She snapped her head to look at him angrily. "Well, excuse me if I don't rush to help a bunch of people I don't know or care about."

Dante knew she was thinking about her lousy childhood and he couldn't blame her for that. "But what about little JJ, Alexia and Xavier, eh? … Remember the tank in the lab? … You want that for them?" He knew he'd struck home when she flinched – a low blow.

"I don't know how to do it," she said in a broken voice.

"You just got to accept it … just let it go, Tia. Stop fighting."

"Fighting what?"

"Fighting everything … fighting me." His arms were rubbing up and down her back and he could feel her resolve weakening as it always did when he spent any time with her.

It was always just a matter of time; which was, of course, the reason she avoided him.

He spoke into her hair. "You can't keep running, Tia, please. Before I have to teach you a lesson – a brutal lesson. Far worse than a couple of silly girls."

More than belonging to the state, she had to learn she was his, whether she was living with Jay or not. That nothing was ever going to be black and white with the three of them, and he wasn't always the bad guy. She just had to accept how things had to be.

She looked up at him, squinting, trying to read what he meant. "What lesson?"

"Carry on the way you're going, and you'll find out." He sighed deeply. "And part of me looks forward to it." His body temperature already rising, he brushed his lips against hers, knowing she was angry with him.

She pushed her hands up between them, trying to push him away, but he wouldn't allow it. "No, Tia. You can't hide what you feel. Just stop this messing around." And he kissed her again, hard on the mouth, invading and owning. Then scooped her up before she could struggle and stepped over the wall of the fountain. Carrying her in his arms, fully clothed, he pulled her under the water with him.

Once the water had filled their lungs, Dante shrugged and kicked out of his clothes and swam with her along the coastal rocks of the castle and into an underwater lagoon. They came up out of the water into a large cave.

When Tia put her feet down and looked around her, she could see they were in a catacomb beneath the castle. Dante had had it made into a private bedchamber.

She turned around in wonder. The lagoon was lit from beneath, giving the water a subtle neon-green glow and was the only electric lighting in the cave. Candles were dotted in the natural alcoves in the walls. A large black wrought-iron four-poster bed draped in fine black gauze stood alone on the beach and the water lapped underneath it. She struggled to take it all in.

Dante was watching her intently for her opinion.

Wow ... an Atlantean's dream crib, she projected to him.

He laughed, thrilled she liked it, and pulled her to him again. *I've wanted to make love to you here ever since I finished it,* he said, holding her and looking deep into her eyes.

Love? She projected with an eyebrow up.

He looked wounded. *Love ... You know it's love.*

And she battled with herself as she always did, loving Jay. But Dante was her drug and she always fell off the wagon. Maybe he was right. Maybe she did love both of them.

They stood waist-high in the lagoon. She reached up and touched his cheek. *Am I doomed, Dante?* she projected sadly, but her eyes were already skating down his body. Taking in his tall, lean physique, his beautiful, devilish eyes and dark skin, his tattoos that called her and warned her at the same time.

He flashed her that smile that was the killer strike. *I'm afraid so,* he thought sympathetically, and slowly pushed her down beneath the water.

Tia sank slowly while he remained standing, watching her take him into her mouth below the surface in one long, greedy swallow. He wanted to savour the beautiful sight, but triumph and ecstasy forced him to throw his head back and his eyes to flutter closed. These times were so rare – too rare, when she gave herself over to total abandon with him, *and fuck this was good – so good.*

She worked him hard and built her rhythm to a demanding pace and he soon shouted his release through his hoarse throat. She took in every part of him, showing no mercy, absorbing everything, and he would give her all of him.

His face now flushed, his heart hammering, he sank beneath the surface with her. It was only the beginning of a long night.

By the time he joined Tia on the bottom of the lagoon, she was completely transformed and otherworldly. Her eyes were like huge luminous disks absorbing the light in order to see. He pushed her forcefully beneath him and came up level with her face.

Dante held her face between his hands and looked at her briefly before he covered her mouth with his. She knew what he wanted and began a steady stream of her life's essence into him.

Fuck ... Nothing could ever top this feeling, ever. There wasn't a drug on earth that could even come close. On one level, it was the pledge, the transferal of her power and the link between them, but on its deepest level it was her offering of herself – her whole spirit and everything she felt, binding the fabric of their very being.

Breathing the love they felt always led to sex and he penetrated her within moments, moving with her slowly. Her answer was to respond sensually. Arching her back to move with him. *Ah, babe.* His heart rushed and quadrupled its beat so he thought it would burst.

Tia continued to breathe for him until he thought he could take no more and climaxed over and over. His heart blossomed into the feeling of ultimate joy that truly knowing her to her life-source gave him.

Still locked to her mouth, kissing her gently, he floated down in the aftermath. A feeling of love blanketed him, and a wonderful cocooning warmth emanated from her, while the velvet water caressed them.

Dante kissed her reverently. *I knew you loved me ... now you can never deny it. I know the very soul of you.*

But she didn't deny it and looked at him for a long, quiet

moment into his eyes. *Let me know you, Dante ... like I can know no one else.*

He nodded solemnly, grateful that he alone was the one who held that privilege. Slanting his mouth over hers, he let himself flow into her. From the depth of his being, his spirit came pouring into her and they glowed from head to foot. With it came an arousal as if they'd never come together only minutes before, and he entered her again. Giving to her what she had given him seemed the most natural thing in the world and he wanted to give everything to this woman, till there was nothing left to give.

There was only one thing that haunted their time together and was like a dark shadow in the recesses of her mind – small but there nonetheless. Jay was a distant echo during their lovemaking. Determined not to ruin this special time between them, he simply made a mental note that her love for Jay was still real and strong but tainted with feelings of inadequacy, uncertainty, frustration and anger. She yearned for him, craved him, and despaired of him, but their physical bond was strong, albeit one-way.

It baffled him how she could feel so inadequate; she was so precious to him. Nevertheless, he stored the information, not sure what he would do with it. Unsure if it would be of any use, as they were all bound so tightly together.

Dante was grateful that Jay didn't have Atlantean abilities to complete his bond, because he knew how Jay felt about Tia, even if she didn't, and if she could share this with him ... he was sure he would lose her. And that, he was certain, he would never allow. *So help him God.*

Isla, two years previously
Darres was perplexed by this one. They'd tried everything to tame him; young men to befriend him, young women to

mate with him, scientists to study him, so he had learned, very early on, that when someone ventured into his domain to destroy them – utterly and completely.

Ultimately, he would drown them, but first, he forcibly entered their minds to learn of their intentions; their weak Human brains could never take it and they quickly died. But before they did, he learned that they always had ulterior motives. And so he remained alone.

Even after all this time, he had never learned a single word of the Humans' language. They never lived long enough and he never needed to. He only spoke in the language of his birth, in pictures and feelings. That was until now.

The first thing that astounded him about the woman he now studied was that she breathed the water as well as walked around like a Human. And when he forcefully entered her mind, she had mental barriers, weak though they were. He didn't take long to gain entry, but the fact that she had them was new.

However, what completely intrigued him was the beautiful picture she showed him, which came with feelings of serenity, love and peace; feelings that he hadn't seen or felt since he was a small boy.

Curiosity and loneliness were her motivations for coming here. He continued to probe her mind with interest at what he would find, and she no longer resisted him.

Darres inched forward carefully. He stopped when she seemed to gather herself to fight or protect herself, which was every time he tried to get nearer.

He felt frustrated, as he couldn't communicate with her. He wanted her to know he no longer sought to harm her. Quickly, he navigated to the language centre of her brain and absorbed the information there. It would take him some time to sift through it enough to organize his thoughts into patterns that she would understand. He decided that a little was better than nothing and started with a few rudimentary things.

NAME, he projected.

Her hands came up to her ears, her eyes squinted and he felt pain in that part of her brain he still occupied.

NAME, he tried again.

What? came back to him clearly but painfully. *Isla ... My name is Isla. You're hurting me. Who are you? What do you want with me?*

Darres didn't yet understand her thought patterns well enough to respond, but decided to impart his name to give her a clue; *DARRES ...*

Not so loud, she thought in pain again.

Darres, he thought with less force.

Her hands moved down away from her head.

He inched closer.

When she went to scramble away from him, he put out his hand in a gesture to stay still in the hope she would know he wouldn't hurt her.

He looked at her arms. He longed to touch her skin that was now covered in black markings, slimmer and more dainty but very like his own. He dared not hope, as they were the first he'd seen in a very long time.

She seemed to understand and he managed to get close enough to reach forward and gently take her hand. He brought it up to his face and examined it closely. With his forefinger, he traced the lines that went around her forearm and then slowly reached toward her face.

He halted, sensing she was still scared.

You must let me go back, she tried to make him understand. *They'll find me here and then there'll be trouble.*

Could he understand? She didn't think so if his expression was anything to go by. All she had made out so far was that he had asked her name.

Isla froze as he began to touch her, but he was gentle, and she slightly relaxed with him. He seemed fascinated with her markings. It was as though he had never seen them before.

She allowed herself a sneaky peek at him. His markings were a more vivid, extreme version of hers. The only other markings like hers she had ever seen were those on the monks, and theirs were so pale they were barely visible.

This male's power and size terrified her, and the fact that he'd so quickly taken complete control of her. She hated that.

He blanched as if she'd hit him.

God! Could he? Did he just feel what she felt?

It was quite possible, as she knew he still held a connection in her head.

Quickly, she tested her theory by conjuring up a picture of her sensei with all the feelings it evoked. She missed him so badly that she rarely allowed herself time to reminisce; it was just too painful.

The creature sat up straighter and cocked his head to the side like a dog listening to its master. *Yes, he had got it.* Somehow, she just knew it.

Then, in a flash, a picture came to her of a small boy with his forehead pressed against the forehead of an older man, striped like him, holding each other's arms and circling in the water. The feeling she was left with was that of great love, which dissipated with the vision.

She was left reeling. The boy was him, and the man was his father. She got it. He was answering her with an example of love for him. Fatherly love.

She racked her brains where to go with this next. She decided to go straight to the memory of when her sensei was murdered and relayed it in full motion like she had never been able to do all these years. Not since they had dragged his body away and she froze, showing no emotion at all.

Again, he moved his head at an angle. He was like a child, absorbing everything like a sponge. Then came his reply; the same boy caught in what looked like a fishing net, surrounded by Human scuba divers. They cut him free, but instead of releasing him, they took him prisoner, and the feeling of fear, anger, frustration and eventually helpless resignation washed over her like a torrent.

Wow, she got the whole thing. He couldn't have been more than five or six years old. *He must have been kept here all this time.* She nodded to show she understood. But she had to go back; they would both be in danger if she got caught there. She pointed upwards. *GO,* she tried to think as clearly as she could.

He seemed to hesitate. Then he scared her briefly when he came right up in her face and put his forehead on hers. After having seen his memory with his father, she guessed it was a greeting or a show of affection.

He stayed still with his eyes shut and his head on hers for a moment, and then retreated slightly. She bowed her head regally, like her sensei taught her.

Then he shocked her.

Come ... back ... Isla ...

It came clearly but haltingly to her. He was learning words amazingly fast.

Sorry ... I am, he continued. His eyes closed in pain.

He was saying he was sorry for hurting her. Despite feeling battered and bruised, both physically and mentally, she recognized something in this male; something that she needed to know more of. *I will come again.*

He pointed to the side of her neck. *What is?*

He was pointing to her implant. Absently, she put her

hand to it, unsure how he knew it was there. *Poison.* It was the only word she could think of to reply.

He pointed to his own neck. *Poison.*

She could see a slightly raised ridge of skin about an inch long and she knew he had one as well. She nodded. *I must go now.*

He took her by the hand as if he understood her perfectly and led her out of the man-made cave and back to the pool surface. There, they trod water facing each other for a moment, until he came close and put his forehead on hers again. *Go well,* he thought.

She felt quite touched by the innocence of the gesture and found herself battling tears, so unlike her, she could only put it down to the roller coaster of overwhelming events. She turned away from him and nimbly pulled herself out of the pool, expelling her lungs with a cough and wincing with the pain. With that, she felt his presence leave her mind.

For a moment, she couldn't drag her eyes from his, so dark, soulful and mysterious mere inches below the surface of the water. His language was childlike, but she was very aware that he was every inch the powerful male. Male what? She wasn't sure yet.

She took a last look at him, dragged her clothes back on over her wet body and hurriedly left the room.

CHAPTER 5

ia, present day

Tia and Dante had ended up on the bed. Jay had taken his leave hours before, knowing the pledging would have to take place before she went to Murrtaine. So this allowed her these few precious hours with the bane of her life.

They made love and breathed for each other often, Dante always treating their time together as if it were his last moments on earth and she loved him for that.

As she ran a finger over the artwork on his pectoral, he groaned, throwing her over onto her back again. *You know you would be happier with me, don't you?* he whispered in her mind.

He was right, after all, he'd read her emotions and probably knew how insecure she always was with Jay. She pushed him backwards so she could crawl up his body, licking him as she went.

Are we not going to sleep at all tonight? he thought, grinning.

There is plenty of time for sleep when I am in Murrtaine.

They were about to kiss when they were disturbed by a

louder-than-usual lapping of the water against the walls of the cave and both turned to face the lagoon.

Two female heads broke the surface and swam in closer until they could stand waist-high in the water. Tia recognized them immediately as the two nymphs she'd taken a swipe at back in New York.

Easy, Dante said, feeling her stiffen.

She looked at him to gauge whether he knew anything about this, but she could only see him worry about what she would do next.

I'm just going to speak with them, that's all.

He slowly let her go, but stood up, wrapping a sheet around his naked lower half so he could jump in at any moment.

Tia went to the water's edge, looked back at Dante, then waded in to meet them. She stopped only a few feet away.

Both girls bowed their heads reverently. "Forgive us," the redhead said, obviously having no trouble with speech after swimming. "We didn't mean to interrupt your highnesses, but the king dismissed us and we wanted to ask for another chance?"

"We fear we have displeased him," the other one said.

Tia took a breath and composed herself. She hadn't been sure what she would say to them until the last moment. If they had come in all cocky and shooting their mouth off, she would probably have sent them off like last time. But she looked back at Dante, shuffling his feet with nerves at the edge of the beach, draped in bedding. She couldn't help but smile.

She made up her mind. "You know who I am?" she croaked.

"Yes, your highness," they both said.

This pleased her. It meant Dante hadn't tried to sweep her

under the carpet. "I would ask that you continue to attend to the king's needs." Better the devils she knew.

The girls looked at each other, their eyes wide.

"But when I am here and with the king, you make yourself scarce, okay?"

They both nodded enthusiastically.

"You work for me, not the king. Is that understood?"

They nodded sagely. "What if the prince, Jay, requires us?" one asked.

"No! He is my Protector and mine alone. Is that clear?"

They both bowed and began to step backwards. "Thank you, your highness." Then they slowly sank beneath the water and disappeared.

Tia waded slowly, in deep thought, back to Dante. He held her by the tops of her arms and searched her face. Realizing that he wouldn't let it go until she told him what was said, she projected the whole conversation to him from her mind's eye.

She expected him to be pleased, but watched him frown as if he didn't understand something as he sat on the edge of the bed, trying to think.

"What is it, Dante? Did I do something wrong?"

He looked at her, hurt. "Is that an indication of the difference in your feelings for me and Jay?"

"No! No, that's not it at all, Dante." She touched his cheek gently. "No, I realize I've been selfish. You are the king, and I don't want you to be lonely when I can't be with you."

"And Jay?"

Jay's words, *I'm no saint*, had gone round and round in her head since he'd uttered them. She rarely knew how he felt about her and he never told her, so those words from his own mouth only proved all the more painful. Cut to the quick, she'd had to come to terms with the fact that Jay was admitting he was no more loyal than Dante, and he wasn't just talking about flirting with nymphs. So, the two of them just turning up like this was like a gift, one that she could use to affect Jay in the only way that would make a difference. He was usually far too cool to react to anything else.

She plonked herself down next to Dante on the bed. "Right, what I'm going to say to you, I want you to memorize and repeat it to Jay, word for word, got it?"

Dante looked at her with interest, wondering where she was going with it.

"I won't give Jay that freedom because I'm with him most of the time and he is my Protector."

Dante sighed and nodded.

Tia took a deep breath before she delivered the blow Dante was to carry to Jay. "And because he is not my equal, *you* … are my equal."

Dante's eyes opened wide with the implications of what she was saying to him. Whether or not he understood why she was saying them, she wasn't sure yet.

"That's going to go down well," he said, a slow grin creeping across his face. "You like living fucking dangerously."

"You will tell him?" She wanted to make sure that Dante delivered the message in the way it was intended.

"Hell, yes," he said, laughing, and pulled her into his arms.

This was what she loved about Dante; he never took anything for granted with her. No, if Jay was no saint, then he'd better bloody start saying his prayers.

Isla, two years previously

Isla spent a frustrating four days away on a mission with her handler. With him twenty-four/seven, it felt like a lifetime until she was alone long enough to venture back to Darres. The timing was terrible, as she didn't want him to think she had abandoned him, which was really illogical, as the guy had tried to kill her and outright bullied her into dishing up all the secrets of her mind.

Thankfully, alone in her room at last, she followed her usual routine, then slipped out and stood in front of the plate glass of Darres' enclosure. Clicking the lock, she was inside. Just as before, there was no sign of him. He probably hid so he could be sure of who had entered.

A horrible thought stung her. *What if they had moved him while she was away?*

Then, as soon as she had the thought, *Don't worry, little one, I am still here.*

She hitched a breath, shocked at the response to her thoughts; perfectly pitched words arranged so she understood. *Darres*, she thought, looking all around her.

Come into the water.

She quickly stripped, ran to the edge of the pool and dived in. Opening her lungs straightaway, she still couldn't see him. Then, just as before, she felt his presence behind her and turned slowly. *How did he do that?* There he was, as huge and as terrifying as the first time.

Before she had time to arrange her thoughts, he grabbed her arms and put his forehead on hers, closing his eyes and circling with her. A warm vibration flooded her. It wasn't unpleasant and she closed her eyes as well.

Little one ... I thought you would never return.

She had to get quicker at concentrating her thoughts. *I'm sorry... they sent me away. I had no choice.*

He pulled away from her and studied her face.

You've learned my language? she thought, incredulously, *in four days?*

Yes, he thought. *It took me a while to go through all the information and decipher it.*

She shook her head, amazed. He thought that was a long time?

Come ... come to my cave. We can talk there. He took her hand and swam with her to the place he had taken her to before.

As they swam, she became aware for the first time that he was totally naked; she assumed because no one could ever get near him. Although he was huge, he was perfectly formed, well-muscled and with not an ounce of fat on him. He had a handsome face and the darkest eyes she had ever seen.

They arrived in the cave and she launched into her questions; she had a list a mile long. *Who are you? What are you? Where did you come from?*

He held up a hand to stop her. *Slowly, little one, I am new to your language ... I am Darres, Prince of Murrtaine. Tell me about you.*

I am Isla ... Isla Snow. I know I am from a people who come from the sea, but that is all I know. I was brought up in Japan ... on land, she added.

He smiled. *The place in your mind's picture.*

She nodded and looked into his face; he really understood what it meant to her.

He picked up one of her arms and ran a finger over her newly emerged stripes. He shook his head in disbelief. *You are one of my people, I am sure, but you blend in with the Humans, so you are very rare. I heard stories of the Atlanteans as a small boy.*

Atlanteans, she repeated, more to herself. *You have been here all this time?*

He nodded. *And similar such places.*

To think I've been here too and knew nothing of you.

They remained quiet and thoughtful for a few moments.

You hurt me, she thought eventually.

I know and I'm sorry. There have been many before you; I thought you were another such as them.

What are you saying?

Humans sent to trick me, make a friend of me to use me, to mate with me ... his eyes averted from hers.

Heat flashed through her when she realized what he meant, and she fleetingly thought of Malleven.

Darres looked quizzically at her.

She remembered the images that Darres had smashed through her barriers with. *You killed them?*

Yes, everyone... until you.

How do you live or eat?

They put my food in through a hatch ... I take from their brains and learn. I go through their memories and experience them. It passes the time.

The ones you've killed?

Yes, and the ones who get close enough for me to scan. But I interact with no one.

She felt such an overwhelming feeling of sadness for him. She thought her existence was miserable. To have been so utterly alone all that time.

He interrupted her thoughts. *The man ... in your vision, was he your father?*

She shook her head. *No, my teacher. I never knew my father.* She hesitated, not wanting to say the part where she loved him. However, when she looked closely at Darres' face, she saw that he knew. She frowned. She could obviously keep no secrets from him now that he'd been inside her head and she wasn't sure she liked that.

Darres touched her arm lightly. *Isla, I will not forcibly enter your mind again, but your feelings are obvious to me; I cannot help it, you radiate them.*

She remembered her sensei's words to her, and thought how disappointed in her he would be.

Darres' face broke into the most beautiful smile, the first she'd seen. *Don't worry, Isla, your secret is safe with me.*

She couldn't help but grin back at him. He had a sense of humour. Why that should be a surprise, she didn't know. He was totally fascinating to her. Without bidding, her eyes skated over him, and she felt her temperature rise.

Who is the dark-skinned man?

Her eyes went wide when she knew he was referring to Malleven. Was he that obviously associated with her? *No one,* she hastily replied. *Just someone I don't like, that's all.* The last thing she wanted was for him to see how foolish she'd been with such a reprobate, and eager with it.

Darres watched her with a calculating look.

Before he could ask her any more embarrassing questions, she quickly gathered herself. *Listen, I have to go.*

He didn't protest, possibly reading her feelings yet again and knowing it was a sore subject. *Will you come again?* His eyebrows were drawn together in a wonderfully uncertain expression. Butterflies tickled her stomach. She went in closer to him and he pulled her to his forehead again. This time, when she broke away, she rested her lips chastely on his. It lasted only a few moments and both of their eyes remained on each other, but he didn't push her away.

She ended the kiss first. *I'll come as often as I can.*

She couldn't look at him any more, worried about what she would do next and betray the weird feelings he was bringing out in her. She turned away, swam out of the cave and left his pool.

TIA, Bluebell Hotel, London, present day

A couple of months had passed and Tia had remained in Murrtaine. Dante thought warmly of the last night they had spent together and smiled to himself as he walked up to the bar in the Bluebell Hotel. The place held good memories and was originally owned by his father. He'd signed it over to Jay when Dante had first married Tia. It was now Jay's base while he ran the successful Bonaci Corporation.

Jay dismissed the member of staff he was in the middle of talking to, clapped hands with Dante and pulled him into a tight embrace.

"Long time no see, brother," Dante said, perching on a barstool.

Jay ordered them their usual drinks: "Two JDs," then turned to face him. "How's the kids?"

"They're grand … little rascals though."

They were quiet for a few moments while they both sipped their drinks. Jay broke it first. "Any news?"

"Not much … little JJ is good. That's about it."

Jay sighed and shook his head.

"What?" Dante asked.

Jay rubbed his forehead. "Ah, doesn't matter."

"No … out with it."

"No, it's just … you know … how we left it. Then no word?"

Dante nodded and shifted uncomfortably. He hadn't had the heart to deliver the message Tia had asked him to relay when they were last together, knowing there was only one way it could go down.

Jay was studying him when he looked up from his drink. "You know something?"

"No I don't … it was just something…"

Jay started to become impatient. "Look, if you know something, then just say it."

Dante studied Jay's face for a moment. He knew the information would create a situation; he just wasn't sure how big. His friend was cool, but there were limits to everyone's temper, even his.

"Dante … come on," Jay prompted. His face was completely blank as if he was ready for what was coming.

"I'm just trying to get it straight … what she said."

"For fuck's sake!" Jay's eyebrows drew together in preparation.

"Okay!" He relayed Tia's words exactly as she'd told him to.

Jay didn't take his eyes from his as he said it.

"Then her last words were that I should tell you word for word." He watched his old friend for his reaction. "Technically, under Atlantean law, you are as good as her brother and my brother, having been adopted by both families, so it's bollocks really."

Jay smiled and nodded. Then rubbed his chin with his hand.

"You can see why I chickened out of telling you for this long?"

Jay just nodded, still not speaking.

"She has to come back soon," Dante continued. "She has to pledge again."

There was still no response from Jay. His quietness was always a worry. Dante kind of preferred it if he would rant and rave, but that wasn't his style. "You can't just leave her … you know that, right?

Jay shifted in his chair. "That's not what I'm thinking … I don't know … I mean, what do you do after a statement like that?"

Tia really knew what she was doing. To be looked down on, whether as a man or in general, would possibly be the only thing that could get a rise out of Jay. "I know what I'd do."

Jay turned his head to face his friend and sighed with weariness. "What?"

"Teach her a lesson she won't fucking forget." Dante grinned as he took a swig.

Jay laughed, but was showing interest even if it was just out of curiosity.

"No, it's true. I've already warned her. If she fucks off or refuses to do her duty again, I will punish her. So she knows." Dante finished his drink with a final gulp.

"Punish ... how did that go down?"

"Oh she don't know how yet, but she knows I will ... and she ain't gonna like it."

"Are you gonna tell me? I may even help you."

Dante laughed out loud. "That would be so fucking fucked-up, but it would certainly prove a point." *Yeah,* the two of them joining forces was the perfect punishment – well, part of it.

Dante ordered more drinks. "It's all to do with clipping her wings ..." He laid out his plan to Jay.

Jay took a deep breath and nodded. "Given the circumstances, I'd say that it's perfect."

Dante watched him closely while he clinked glasses with him, and although he had a face like thunder, he was taking it way too well.

CHAPTER 6

sla, two years previously

Isla visited Darres as often as she could. Usually after lights out when her guards took for granted that she was asleep. As long as she was in her cot in the morning, they didn't suspect a thing.

It grew into a routine where they would meet and join foreheads in the Murr way, then settle on the seaweeds in his cave and communicate. He would question her about the memories he'd seen when he had forced his way into her mind, and she would explain them as best she could and describe the places she had seen growing up. He was fascinated, but never went into her head after their first meeting.

Darres, in turn, would describe the wonders of Murrtaine, where he came from and promised to take her there one day when they escaped.

But we can never escape, Darres, Isla thought sadly. *Our implants ... they will kill us.*

I will find a way, he promised.

I'm not sure how long I can spend underwater either. Could we not go over land?

I am the strongest in the water. My bones are weak on land. We wouldn't get far. And I am slightly conspicuous, he added with a small smile.

She smiled back at him, allowing her eyes to rake over his body. He was huge and she wasn't sure whether his stripes disappeared as hers did when she was out of water. Plus, he was completely naked.

I'd better make sure I bring you some shorts.

He frowned. *Human clothes ... would they fit?*

She laughed. *We'll give it a go.* She got serious again. *Did you take the plans for the campus and the locks from my mind?*

He looked guilty, then he nodded.

Then if anything happens to me and I don't come here for some reason, you must get yourself out, okay? she said, touching his cheek gently.

I won't leave without you.

Listen, Darres. What they get me to do is risky. It is quite possible that I could be injured or killed or, worse still, captured.

He remained quiet while he thought about what she said.

It's hard to believe you tried to kill me only a couple of weeks ago, she thought, changing the subject.

Darres frowned. *Exactly how long is a week?*

Her heart broke for him in that moment. Of course, he had no real concept of time, having been locked up for so long and never having mixed with Humans. She thought carefully about how best to explain it. *A period of daylight and night together is one day. There are seven in a week and fifty-two weeks in a year.*

Darres nodded, getting it straight away. *Then I will wait for you for one year, and then I will go straight to the sea.*

Good. You are at the furthest point here and right next to the sea. She was relieved he wouldn't be left to rot. Somehow, she knew that the chances of them getting out together were slim.

Darres leaned forward and came close to her face. Instead of laying his forehead against hers, he touched her nose with his, then his cheek gently next to hers.

She held her breath. Heat flashed through her and a weight hit her chest, so heavy she thought her heart would burst. The only other time she had felt it was the brief time she had spent with Malleven, which seemed a distant memory now.

Darres pulled slightly away from her, studying her as if he was thinking on something. His body was still so close to hers, warm and needing to be touched. Tentatively, she sent out a mental feeler to his mind; she had never dared to do it before.

He slammed her down hard, his barriers as strong as a bank vault. His eyes narrowed as if he didn't trust her, but he didn't move away.

She tried to recoil away from him, hurt. *I'm sorry ... you see everything of me ... I just wanted to see something of you.*

What is it you want to know, he thought, more softly.

I wanted to experience what you felt and what you were thinking just then, that's all.

Okay.

It's okay?

He nodded. *I will allow it, but you will never break my barriers. They are too strong.* He studied her again as if deciding something. *I will teach you how to navigate an average mind, with little or no barriers... and to strengthen your own so that no one can ever breach them.*

As strong as yours? she thought, grinning at him.

I am not sure it is in my interest to do that.

They both laughed and embraced and when they pulled out of their hug, they stopped, their lips only inches apart. Something seemed to shift and the butterflies that inhabited her stomach became unbearable. The space between their mouths was diminishing until their lips brushed.

Isla found herself moving her mouth against his, and when he parted his lips slightly, Isla tentatively pushed her tongue into his mouth. He timidly circled her tongue with his and she didn't pull away.

He gently pushed her down into the seaweeds with his weight. Their bodies melded and moved together and she wound her arms and legs around him until they undulated as one. Her hands came upwards into his hair, where she pulled him tighter to her mouth, which was now alive with the taste of him.

Darres, I want to be naked with you.

He said nothing more, but pulled the straps down from her swimsuit, and she wriggled out of it. All the while, their kiss became more powerful and her heart rate built with an urgency she didn't understand. *I want more,* she moaned.

He released her mouth and kissed the column of her neck, down to her chest. Then he closed his mouth over the peak of her breast and kissed and circled its hard point with his tongue.

She arched her body up to his mouth, wanting him to take more. One of his large hands moved and held both of her arms behind her back, pushing her breasts up to peak further towards his face like an offering, while he worshipped them with his tongue, driving her wild.

His free hand travelled down her body and gently pushed between her thighs, which she opened for him without hesitation.

Darres ... I need.

His hand was gently stroking the inside of her thigh; higher and higher until he softly dragged his fingers along her hot, slick folds, investigating and making her mad with want.

She was writhing against him. Desperately, she tugged and drew him back up level with her face. Then she wriggled herself lower, opening her legs wide to position herself directly over his huge length. *I want this*, she moaned, and began to move against him while she bit into his shoulder and chest, urging him to help her.

I'll hurt you, he thought.

I want it, Darres ... I want you.

His large arms came around her slowly and locked her against him. There was no way she could free herself now. She was already partially impaled on him, but without leverage, he was so large she could go no further. But now he had clasped her to him, she clamped onto him with her arms and legs and he began to push and retract, push and retract, a little more each time.

More. She bit his chest and shoulder.

He leaned back to look into her eyes to gauge whether it was truly what she wanted. Then thrust into her completely.

Her mind stalled as she was swamped in pain.

He stilled.

Gradually, the pain and unbelievable sense of fullness gave way to absolute pleasure. Her heart was beating like a train and he seemed to sense the change in her and began to move again and she slowly moved with him. *Ah, Darres*, she moaned into his mind

His confidence appeared to grow and he built his pace in strength and ferocity and was soon pistoning into her. She was lost to all reason and locked her teeth onto the soft part of his shoulder and clutched him with her arms and legs for dear life.

Give me your mouth, he thought with his head next to her ear.

She released her teeth from his shoulder and looked up for his mouth, which quickly slanted over hers. He began to breathe a long breath, but it was not of air, but a torrent of his thoughts and feelings. Everything she had asked to know of him earlier. The strength and amount of it made her overwhelmed for a few seconds and she became delirious. An awe-inspiring feeling of love cloaked her and, before she knew what hit her, her womb clenched and she convulsed all over.

The heaving weight in her chest became unbearable in its need to come out, but at the last minute, she broke the seal of their lips and let the heat out into the surrounding water. Her sheath constricted around him and her nerve-endings exploded.

Darres, she thought. The feeling surprised her and dazed her all at once.

He plunged more deeply inside her, held her like he would crush her, and moaned into her mind. She knew he felt the same pleasure as her. *An orgasm,* she thought, remembering Malleven's words.

Their movements slowed and they relaxed and drifted in the blissful afterglow that followed.

Her satisfaction was only marred by her guilt that she hadn't shared herself in the selfless way that Darres had. She wasn't sure how she knew, but she was convinced that if she did that, he would know every part of her. Her sensei's words still reverberated: *never let them know what you love.*

She knew she should trust Darres, but she wasn't ready, not yet. He would have to be patient.

He didn't seem too disappointed in her though.

Isla ... I had no idea.

She looked up at his face as she was still pinned beneath his body. *About what?*

That it could be ... like that.

Me neither.

His brow furrowed as he studied her.

Had she thought of Malleven? I've never done that ... not completely.

He seemed to understand what she meant and kissed her on the mouth lovingly. *So I am your first?*

She nodded. *It was perfect.* But a stab of guilt hit her again when she thought of her holding something back from him. *But it wouldn't be for ever.*

They lay silent, entwined in the seaweeds of his cave, just feeling the warmth and the closeness of each other's bodies.

Darres must be the male her sensei spoke of; the one from the sea, surely?

DARRES CRADLED her in his arms. She already meant so much to him. He knew she had held back during their lovemaking, but trust would come with time, he was sure.

He guessed that sharing knowledge of each other was exclusive to his species and not the same as Humans at all. He had never come across it from the information he had gleaned from Human minds. Perhaps Isla knew nothing of it. She was preoccupied by something, though. Guilt was coming off her in waves.

The dark-skinned man came to mind. He was becoming a spectre. She hadn't mated with him, though; he was sure of that.

He would help her build up her mental defences, and then he would work on a way for them to escape. Then he would take her to Murrtaine and marry her. There, he would make her his completely.

The dark-skinned man she called Malleven would become something of the past.

TIA, present day

The communication reached Jay about a week later. During a harpoon-fishing trip with Dante's Murr cousin, Dax, Tia had somehow got separated from him and been trapped and caught in a fishing net. It was all the more disturbing as it was thought to belong to a scientific study vessel rather than a fishing boat and was believed to be out of the Florida Keys.

The Honourable Guard had been deployed to southern Florida immediately.

Jay closed his eyes. The implications could be catastrophic. There had been no communication with her, telepathically or otherwise. She had simply vanished off the face of the earth. But that didn't mean the worst, Jay reminded himself. She was tough and not big on responsibility to anyone. Even if she were okay, there was no guarantee she would let anyone know, least of all him.

He sighed. If that were the case, it looked as though the plan they'd cooked up was going to happen. *Fuck.*

ISLA, one year previously

Isla was led into a meeting room with Christophe. Ironically, it looked exactly the same as the one she'd been led into ten years earlier when her sensei was murdered, and even more so when she recognized one of the three men standing in front of her.

The greying, distinguished-looking gentleman was the Duke Ormond Delissi in the flesh. How many times had she wondered if he had known what had gone on after he had left the room? Then, with the following two shots, she guessed she had her answer when Christophe crumpled and fell at her feet. The difference this time was that she had formed no attachment to anyone in the room. Her emotions were stone cold.

The question plaguing her now was, why did they need to get rid of him? *Was she next?*

"Good day, Isla," the duke said, as if nothing had happened.

She bowed in a very Japanese way to make a point.

The subtle raise of his eyebrow told her he got it.

"You've grown into a very beautiful young woman, Isla."

She looked at him coldly without acknowledging the compliment.

He shrugged his head slightly. "It is time for you to meet your destiny and go back to the people you come from."

A glimmer of hope took root in the pit of her stomach when she thought of Japan, but it was immediately dashed.

"Today you will travel to Montana, and from there a member of the Florianna royal family will collect you. Your future husband will be identified and you will marry."

Her heart stopped. *No ... Darres.*

Delissi turned to one of the doctors standing with him. "Has the tracking device been removed?"

"Not yet, sir, it's a two-minute job."

"Get it done."

Isla's heart thumped. *A tracking device?* Inside, her emotions were rampaging. *If only she could get a message to Darres. She needed to tell him she had to go and that the implant wouldn't kill him.*

Isla stood with Delissi on the Tarmac at an airbase with the wind howling around them. The rain began to hit them in splatters. She had a plaster on her neck to cover up the minor wound where her implant had been removed. And she'd had to leave without getting a message to Darres for fear of alerting anyone to the fact that she knew of his existence.

Her feelings of desolation were only superseded by her

sensation of unease as she saw the plane that was due to collect her making its bumpy landing on the runway. Weighing up her options quickly and coming to the conclusion that there weren't any, she turned to Delissi. "Are you aware they have a male like me … back at the facility?"

Delissi turned to her, frowning, but didn't speak.

They keep him in a pool right out of the way, below the basement level. He's been there since he was a child."

She watched Delissi's face as his mind worked.

"Submerged continually?"

She nodded, but wondered what that had to do with anything?

"Leave it with me." And he completely changed the subject. "Now you have a destiny to meet."

Not quite believing her ears, she faced the plane again. It had come to a standstill, the door opened and Airstairs were joined to the side.

A tall, lone dark figure descended them and her unease deepened. Her heart began to sink into her stomach as he walked with panther-like steps towards her. She knew who it was; someone she never thought she'd ever see again.

"Malleven Mancini?" Delissi said.

CHAPTER 7

*D*arres had waited, got anxious, desperate, angry, then he mourned.

He was grateful he'd had the time to teach her to shield her thoughts. He went out of his mind when he dwelt on what could have happened to her. He'd taken to swimming laps of his pool to relieve the frustration and boredom. This particular day, a crackle sounding like a poor loudspeaker broke into his consciousness. A cold voice permeated the water. He stilled and circled his arms gently while he listened.

"Darres, I know you can hear me. I will make it as brief as I can."

Darres recognized the voice as the scientist who had been trying to study him for years, who resorted to drugging his pool water to knock him out when anything needed to be administered. He knew Darres would kill him on sight.

Deciding that he would listen to him no longer, Darres went to resume his swimming, but his next words made his blood run cold.

"Isla has gone, Darres. We used her to gain your confidence and the plan was a success. Now her mission has been accomplished, she has been sent onto her next assignment."

Darres was staggered. *No, it couldn't be? He would have read it in her intentions that first time he forced into her mind. He would have known.*

"Give yourself a break, Darres. Agree to work for us. What have you got to lose? Complete some underwater assignments. You can have as many women as you want. We'll see to that. Much more freedom ... think about it."

Darres remained still long after the transmission stopped. Then he slowly sank to the bottom of the pool. The turmoil in his mind had simmered down to a grim realization that she had been nothing more than a clever trick to tame him, and she had. *What was there to live for now?*

He screamed silently, on and on, until he was exhausted.

Escape, he decided, would be his purpose. Then he would find her. And when he did, he wasn't sure what he would do to her.

It took Darres a while to convince his captors that he had totally capitulated. He trained, took the women they offered and he made sure he didn't kill anyone. The weapons part of the process was the only thing he vaguely took any interest in. All he wanted was a mission at sea and a knife and then he'd be gone.

The wait was agonizing. It took several more months after Isla had gone before they were convinced he was ready. A practice exercise of placing a small explosive a couple of miles out at sea had been arranged. This was it. They gave him his instructions and he jumped in off the platform at the back of the boat full of monitors and study equipment.

His heart rejoiced as soon as he hit the cool water. Its

freshness, taste and temperature, that he'd long forgotten, came back to him and he frolicked like a young seal.

He put his mind back to the job at hand and reached his destination. He took out his hunting knife, put it to his neck and scored it open. He grit his teeth as he probed with his clumsy fingers to get a hold on the small piece of plastic. Fleetingly, he wondered where the poison was kept, but dismissed the thought immediately.

Darres pushed the implant into the wrapping of the small experimental explosive he'd been given, flicked the switch on the timer and placed it into a crevice on the seabed. Then he swam back towards shore as fast as he could. His powerful legs propelled him back to the shelter of the Florida Keys.

The boom behind him told him that the device had successfully detonated and his plan was working. He hoped his captors would think he'd been killed carrying out his orders.

In the meantime, he needed a place to rest where he could heal and keep out of the way of predators attracted to the blood that was streaming from his neck.

THE WATERS WERE warm and clear and the reef was a source of food, shelter and medicine to heal his neck before it festered. Darres had remembered a sea plant his mother had shown him many years ago that she'd used on his cuts and grazes.

He still had to be careful when it came to recognizing sea life and organisms that could hurt him. In the end, he relied on scanning the larger creature's minds to see if they were hungry and was careful not to rest or tread on anything small. It seemed to work.

He'd been there a few weeks when he ventured further out to sea. He felt a trawler go over the surface above him.

He didn't trust Humans and hid behind a large boulder. It was dragging a fishing net behind it. He couldn't believe his eyes and had to shake his head a few times to see if he was awake. Inside it was a blonde, striped girl, struggling like mad.

Isla!

Darres swam to it as fast as he could with no care whether he was seen or not. He took out his knife and began slashing the net, ripping and pulling, trying to get the girl out, but the rope was too strong.

Splashes above him told him that the boat had stopped and divers were jumping into the water.

Isla ... Isla. He kept on projecting to her.

When he opened a hole in the net just big enough to see her beautiful, ethereal face, he realized it wasn't her.

The divers came closer.

Who are you? he projected frantically.

She looked surprised, but not scared of him. She was so much like Isla; the same size and build, but her eyes were green and her skin was darker.

Go, she managed to project back to him. *There isn't time ... I'll be okay.*

The hole he'd made just wasn't big enough for her to swim through. He stared at her for a few moments longer, memorizing her face, and then he retreated, just in time, before the divers got there. Stunned, he watched while they took her away, just as they did to him when he was just five years old.

*T*ia, *Southern Florida University, present day*

It didn't take longer than a few moments for the two biologists to realize they had a real catch and decide to cover Tia up in towels to smuggle her on board the boat without her being noticed as weird. The story was that she'd been diving off her boat and it had drifted and she'd got into problems. No one seemed to suspect she was anything other than what they'd said, and Tia went along with it for self-preservation. She seemed to sense quickly that they weren't a danger to her and saw them as her best chance of escape.

They introduced themselves as Ben and Josh, spirited her away from the rest of the diving party, and took her back to the apartment they shared on campus. They needed to get her away from prying eyes and the obvious questions that would arise from her appearance.

It was difficult, first of all, as Tia couldn't speak and could hardly see, as her eyes were so dilated. Extended periods of time spent in water meant that they no longer returned to normal on their own. They assumed she was blind and mute when they first tried to question her. She thanked god she had her eye drops in her utility belt. Dante had got them from the Murrs. They restored her sight and helped them to look more Human when she was out of water. She stole a moment to pop a couple of drops in each eye as soon as she could.

The two men sat facing her, on the sofa opposite. Tia quickly gave them the onceover, taking in their beards, geeky glasses and weedy physiques and decided they weren't going to be any trouble. Besides, they soon made her a hot chocolate and a sandwich and made her feel welcome.

After an hour or so of them studying her, trying various languages, including sign, her voice came back. "So what's the deal? Am I your prisoner or something?"

They both looked at each other, amazed.

"What?" she said. "What did I say?"

"You speak," Ben said.

"You speak English," Josh said.

"You have a London accent," they both said together.

"South," Tia corrected.

They looked at each other again and laughed. "A water-breathing girl from south London," Ben clarified.

She laughed. "Oh yeah, when you say it like that." The two men's sense of humour delighted her.

"Do you mind staying a while and answering a few questions?" Josh asked.

Tia shrugged. "For a bit. I got to get back to the kids."

They laughed again. "You are so…." Then looked at each other.

"Normal." The other one finished for him.

Tia felt quickly at ease and they sat up well into the night chatting and she told them her life story as far as she knew it. There was loads of stuff she still wasn't sure about yet. It felt good speaking about her life for the first time with impartial people who wouldn't judge her for her failings and she felt there were many. They seemed such nice guys – good guys.

"So you are a princess?" Ben said in awe.

"Well, a queen, really, but I left him."

They seemed to find everything she said funny. It didn't seem that funny to her. Especially when she got to the part where Jay had been a complete dick in New York after Dante had walked in with his nymphs and she'd smacked one in the gob.

"Listen, Tia. Would you like to stay for a while? I mean, you don't have to, and we are by no means forcing you to. You can leave any time you like," Josh said.

She looked at them both, smiling at her while she made up her mind. They seemed like nice, ordinary blokes. Something she hadn't been around for a long time. "Well, it would be nice to get right away from it all … I suppose if I let them know…" Despite being away in Murrtaine a while, she really didn't want to face Jay yet. Suddenly, going to college seemed a really attractive idea.

"Oh, go on then."

"That's a yes?"

"Yeah, okay," she said with a soppy grin. *Why not? What's the worst that can happen?*

TIA HAD BEEN with Ben and Josh for a couple of days. When helicopters kept going overhead and circling out at sea looking for something, she explained that she was frightened of being caught. She had asked Ben about the helicopters and he said they came from the military facility nearby. The Murr who had tried to rescue her came to mind. The two biologists promised to keep her secret at all costs.

She'd called Sean, her personal Protector, and asked him to keep her location a secret. She told him she was okay and just wanted to stay for a little bit longer.

Dante was sending mental pushes to her constantly, which she was ignoring. He would only start ordering her to come home. She was also receiving them from her sister, Lacy and suspected that Dante was putting her up to it.

In the end, she decided to answer Lacy as the softer option.

What shall I tell him then, Tia? Lacy asked.

Tia really wanted to ask how Jay was, but was scared of the answer, knowing that Dante would have delivered her message by now.

Just tell Dante I'm okay. I've made friends with the blokes who caught me and they are hiding me so no one knows I'm here. I'm enjoying the peace, Lace. I'll let him know when I'm ready to come back – just a few more days.

Okay, Lacy said. *Be careful.*

Thanks, babe. Oh, to hell with it, Lacy ... How's Jay?

Oh, you know Jay ... I can never work him out.

Tia sighed. *Yeah, I know what you mean.* She felt her sister drift away.

TIA WAS HAVING a great time with her new friends. They introduced her around campus as an exchange student from England. It didn't take long for her to volunteer to DJ at a student bash when they were let down at the last minute. Ben and Josh were now enjoying a new celebrity status, as they were cool by association with Tia.

What she was enjoying most about being there was that Ben and Josh were so easy-going and allowed her the time and space to be an ordinary person.

The one thing she hadn't paid much mind to was that whenever she played her music, her Siren's power would pulse, driving any Human party-goers wild, but also making her extremely easy to locate by Dante, who could feel it through their mutual bond.

It had been a couple of weeks and they were enjoying a cosy night in, just chilling and listening to music. Tia was determined to ensure the two biologists knew the difference between their house, garage, drum 'n' bass and dubstep. It was a constant source of amusement to her that their record collection consisted of Simon and Garfunkel, The Beatles and Barbara Streisand. Not that she had anything against those artists, but where was their soul?

She was just explaining 'the one' as an essential component of funk when there was a loud knock on the door. They all looked at each other as it was a bit late for visitors, even by student standards.

Ben got up to answer it. Tia's heart stopped with trepidation and she felt like she should hold him back, but resisted.

She jumped out of her seat when Ben was thrown back from the door onto his back and Sean was there, standing over him with a fist poised and ready to punch him in the face.

"NO!" Tia shrieked. "Sean, stop!"

Sean squinted over at her. "Fuck, Tia, what's going on?"

"I told you, Sean, they're my friends."

Sean was perplexed and looked from Tia to Ben and back again. Then he yanked Ben back onto his feet with a strong grip on his shirt.

Sean's confusion quickly turned to anger. "You can't just go off like that, Tia."

"Bloody hell, Sean, I'm not a prisoner." *Shit, what was the bloody big deal?*

Sean's phone rang. He put it to his ear. "Yes, I'm with her. The situation is contained."

Tia swallowed. *Please say that's Cash, or the Guard, or anyone other than Jay.*

Josh stood up to protest.

"Sit the fuck down. You don't know what you're dealing with," Sean said, stabbing a finger towards him.

"Sean, please. I sort of told them who I am," Tia said sheepishly.

Sean rolled his eyes and deflated slightly. "You've just complicated things, Tia."

"What are you going to do?"

"We'll wait till Jay gets here."

Tia's heart sank. *Fuck!*

A split second later, Jay walked in, accompanied by two of the Honourable Guard; one was Keenan, her sister's husband. Ben and Josh shrank back and gulped at the size of them. Jay didn't look at her.

He walked straight to Sean and spoke quietly to him. Then he faced Ben, who was still standing next to Sean, afraid to move. "You have a kitchen or another room I could use to speak to Tia for a moment?" Jay asked politely.

"The kitchen is there," Ben said, pointing to a door leading off the living room.

Jay nodded in that direction for her to go, still not looking her in the eyes. She walked slowly, looking at everyone as she passed them. Keenan winked at her and she smiled back, grateful for his warmth.

She gulped as Jay closed the door behind them so they were alone. Then, eyes down, he backed her into the corner of the worktop without saying a word. She let out an involuntary yelp when he lifted her under her arms and sat her on the worktop. When she was on a level with him, he finally looked her in the eyes.

She was genuinely scared. Dante, she could deal with. He was like a caged animal when he lost his temper, but Jay? He just looked ominously into her eyes. *Shit.*

She wasn't sure whether he was going to kill her or kiss her. She hoped for the latter. He was standing in front of her, pissed off, dressed completely in black, looking totally fanciable. A slow grin crept across her face. She couldn't help it.

Jay snorted a laugh and had to turn and walk away from her as if he were getting a grip on his temper, or like a child who didn't want to be made to laugh when they wanted to keep having the hump. He turned back to her with his hands on his hips, shaking his head. "What is it in this situation, Tia, that you find funny?"

"You really want me to answer that?" she said, still grinning.

"Yes, I do," Jay said, still trying to fight a smile.

"I just realized that I fancy you when you're pissed off and being all macho."

A small laugh escaped him as he rubbed his eyes with his thumb and forefinger and summoned strength from somewhere. "Fucking hell, Tia," he said, shaking his head.

"What?"

"You know Dante will punish you after this?"

"Yeah, blah, blah, so he keeps saying. I'll just stay away longer then."

"I have to take you back. What about the kids?"

"I won't be gone long; just a bit longer," she pleaded.

"You don't get it, do you? You have no choice now."

She remained quiet. *How dare they.*

"What's the story with them two?" Jay demanded.

"They are my friends … they're marine biologists."

He shook his head as if she'd misunderstood. "Which one are you with? One of them … both of them?" His eyebrows were raised in question.

She blanched with a frown. Then she felt angry and hurt. "They're still breathing, so that's a good sign, eh? … When did you start thinking I was some sort of slag, Jay?" she said, swallowing back her disappointment. "I was with *you*, remember? It was you who made me take the kids to him. You! I was doing my best to avoid him, like I always try to. I fight this destiny–fate–duty crap all the time, and you don't help me … you never help me!" She ended up shrieking at him and then hated herself for weakening and bursting into tears. She buried her head in her hands.

Keenan poked his head around the door. "We need to go."

Jay nodded at him. "We'd better take those two with us. I'm not sure what Dante will want doing with them."

Keenan looked sympathetically at her and went out again.

"We have to go," Jay said quietly.

"I'm not going." Her eyes were red from crying and her nose was running. *Shit.*

"You can either walk out of here or I can carry you out; it's your choice." He went to walk towards her.

Tia batted his hands away from her and jumped down from the counter. "Get your hands off me." Never did she imagine the day when she couldn't bear Jay to touch her, and she pushed past him and into the living room, trying to get a rein on her anger.

When she looked up again, poor Ben and Josh were standing together with their hands handcuffed behind their back. She pleaded with her eyes at Keenan. "Please, Keenan, that's not necessary, is it?"

"I'm afraid so, Tia. It's orders."

She looked at her two friends and sobbed anew. "I'm so sorry I dragged you into this."

The other guard ushered them out of the door. They were tetchy so near to a military base. Government agencies were never far away to snatch Tia again – she was, after all, an important commodity.

sla, Milan, one year previously

Isla was forced to endure the whole journey from Montana to Milan with Malleven; she sat in silence and he laughed to himself and looked at his large purple ring periodically. She was convinced he was totally mad.

When they reached Milan, they transferred to a car and were chauffeured to Malleven's apartment in the expensive Viale Luigi Majno area. The chauffeur carried their small bags and put them down in the large marble hallway. It occurred to Isla that the sum total of her life was held in that small bag.

Malleven tipped the driver and he left immediately. Then Malleven closed the door and stalked towards her, stopping right in front of her without saying a word.

She looked into his midnight-blue eyes; she'd rehearsed what she would say to him if they finally met again, a million times. That he was a rat and a reprobate, that she loathed him for taking advantage of her, but most of all, the thing that still rankled was that he'd tried to wipe her mind so she would have no knowledge of what he'd done.

Anger flashed through her in an instant, and before she really knew what she was doing, she drew back lightning fast and punched him squarely in the mouth, causing him to stagger backwards. She stood, breathing hard, waiting for the backlash and shaking her stinging hand.

Malleven stood back up straight and blinked at her, took a fine white linen handkerchief from his expensive jacket pocket, dabbed his mouth, then looked at the blood.

She stood watching him and was dumbfounded when he smiled back at her. She readied her stance again. *Here it comes,* but all she felt was a mental push from him and she slammed down her barriers.

He cocked his head in interest and smiled again as if she'd surprised him. "You have learned much, Snowflake. Are you not going to tell me what that was for?" he said, dabbing his lip.

She rarely swore, but somehow nothing else would do. "For fucking with my mind."

He laughed a little and bowed his head slightly. "Perdona-mi." He grinned at her.

"Why are you laughing at me?" she asked, nonplussed.

He shook his head slightly, as if baffled by it himself. "Because you are indeed my perfect mate."

Tia, present day

By the time Tia reached Ballygowan Castle, she felt a mixture of anger and trepidation. Jay, Keenan and Sean rode down with her in the lift to the subterranean level in silence. The lift opened and Jay nudged her out of the doors, where she turned right on the marble dais and paused at the top of the staircase. She could see her mother, father and uncle were all standing with Dante below in the great hall, as they walked down the steps. The kids were there too and ran up to Tia and Jay excitedly when they caught sight of them.

"Hey!" Tia said, and cuddled and kissed them one by one.

A nanny Dante had employed came forward and whisked them off for milk and biscuits, allowing them to get down to business.

Tia stood back up and looked all around her. "What is this, a welcoming committee?"

Dante's face remained serious. "They are here to make this legal."

A deep feeling of foreboding crept over her. "A kangaroo court?"

Dante ignored her from the large, high-backed armchair he was sitting in, like a throne. "Let's meet our two friends here first, shall we?" Dante said, pointing at Ben and Josh, who were still handcuffed. Reeve pushed them towards him.

Tia went to rush forward, but was grabbed by Jay. "Fuck off," she spat, pulling away. She was pleased when she registered the shock on his face. She called over, "Leave them alone, Dante … they helped me."

Dante put up a hand. "Okay … I'm a fair man. Tell me your side of things; how you came to be holding my wife prisoner."

"They didn't! " Tia shouted out.

Dante held up his hand again to shut her up. "Speak," he said, turning his attention to the two biologists.

Ben related the story of how they had accidentally caught Tia in the net used on their study vessel, how they had become friends and so they had kept her secret.

Dante was looking over at Tia, tutting, shaking his head and really enjoying himself. "You are really foolish, Tia, putting people in danger like this. What am I to do with them now?" He threw up his hands in a dramatic gesture. "Humans that know too much, for fuck's sake …"

Tia despised him at that moment for enjoying toying with her friends and scaring them half to death. She tried a different tack and ran over to him and held onto his arm gently. "Please, Dante, sleep on it. Don't do anything rash."

He looked at her, his eyes smiling brightly. "And what would you give me to save them?" he said slyly. Then he laughed out loud.

She scowled at him.

"Aargh, I'll sleep on it … take them to the dungeons," which he found especially funny.

She looked daggers at him, which tickled him more. "For fuck's sake, Tia … Take them to the bedrooms prepared for them, but put the necessary security outside." He nodded to Reeve, who led them away.

Dante turned to her, no longer laughing. "Now for the serious business … I've asked your family to be present, Tia, because it has become apparent that you cannot be trusted with your freedom."

"Excuse me?" Tia could not believe what she was hearing. She looked at every person, one by one, for a hint that it was some kind of sick joke, but their faces remained stony and solemn. Her hand went to her mouth as she stifled a sob.

"If everyone agrees, in the interests of the crown, I am restricting Tia's freedom to the castle walls, and eventually outside if accompanied by myself or Jay."

This was like some kind of nightmare. "What about my Protectors?" she said, as a last hope.

"They have been dismissed."

"You have no right!" She rushed at Dante, but someone stopped her.

"I am the king. I have every right," Dante said firmly. He looked around at those assembled and they all nodded a single nod of agreement.

"Don't I get a say?" she pleaded.

Dante turned to face her again. "You don't."

"I'll run at the first opportunity and I'll make sure you never find me," she spat with as much venom as she could muster.

Dante ignored her and nodded at Keenan, who walked forward and handcuffed her wrists quickly.

She looked over her shoulder at Keenan and then back at Dante. "You are fucking joking," she said, stunned. "It's the twenty-first fucking century."

"Only in the Human world," Dante said quietly, looking as if he genuinely felt sorry for her. He looked over at Jay. "Is Rex here?"

Jay nodded.

"Tell him to set up in my study, can you?"

Jay nodded again and disappeared.

"What's going on … who's Rex?" Tia was really starting to panic now. Dante's sanity was always questionable at the best of times.

Dante had Keenan take her away while he thanked all her family.

WHEN THEY REACHED Dante's study, there was a high doctor's couch set up in front of the desk. Tia wasn't sure what was happening, but she was positive it wasn't good. It had all the feel of the times she'd been forced to go to the dentist as a kid.

She began to back up, but Keenan stopped her progress. "Easy," he said softly.

Just as she was thinking about making a run for it, Jay walked in with a large, muscular man covered from head to foot in tattoos – well, she assumed he was, as they poked out on all his visible flesh – including his neck and temples. *Shit.*

Her sense of foreboding was quickly bubbling up into severe anxiety. "If he comes near me, I'll kill him, I swear."

Dante nodded at Jay. "Get the kids."

Jay turned to walk out of the room.

"Fucking low blow," was all she could think to say … except: "I release you! Do you hear me, Jay Gardiner? I release you!" she screamed at the top of her lungs, barely holding it together.

The tattoo guy was getting nervous, she could tell. She knew he'd clocked her handcuffs moments before they were removed and he clearly didn't know what was going on. But, as usual, Dante could talk the hind legs off a donkey and after walking away with his arm around the guy's neck, speaking softly, the guy visibly relaxed and nodded.

Shit, she was fucked. What on earth would Dante do? She was convinced now that he was barking, raving mad.

The tattoo guy sat on a swivel stool on the other side of the couch.

"Get onto the couch quietly, Tia, and I won't bring the kids in," Dante said.

"You bastard!" she spat as she pulled herself up.

"Face down," Dante added.

She swallowed and complied slowly.

Dante quickly re-attached cuffs to her wrists, tied her ankles, put a strap across her thighs and lower back.

Tia could only watch as Rex set up his tattoo gun or needle thing – whatever it was called. She stretched her upper body round so she could give him a good, hard stare and tried to keep the trembling from her voice. "Touch me with that needle and you are dead … do you hear me?" she said, low and venomously.

Rex looked over at Dante, standing on the other side of her, "I'm not prepared to do this unless you knock her out.

This is more than anger, she is petrified – probably of needles."

Dante looked down at her body, a mass of trembling muscles. "Okay … I'll send someone in." And he left the room.

Isla, Milan, one year previously

"You aren't my mate," Isla said in a rare outburst of temper.

Malleven smiled as if she delighted him. "What makes you so sure … You have somebody in mind?"

She shook herself quickly; she was giving herself away with her stupidity. She must remember she was dealing with a clever male. "No, it's just that my mate wouldn't take advantage of a young girl and then try to wipe away her memory so she had no knowledge of it."

He continued to smile at her. "He would if he couldn't help himself with such a beauty and he didn't want her to get in trouble afterwards."

He was confusing her. She had to remember that he was trying to get around her any way he could.

"Come, Snowflake, let us have a drink together."

She followed him into a large, tasteful living room full of grand paintings and dark, polished furniture. He gestured for her to sit on a sumptuous sofa while he poured two drinks of a clear liquid, disappeared for a moment and returned with ice in them.

"I've never had alcohol," she said, taking the glass from his hand.

His gold watch glittered with diamonds, she noticed as he touched a finger along the back of her hand.

She felt a tingle and a mental push. He was trying to read her again. Slam, went her shields, firmly this time. *What did he want?*

He smiled but didn't refer to it and neither did she. "Drink, Snowflake. Now is the time to be wicked and try all the things that are bad and wrong and do everything you are not supposed to; in fact, I insist on it."

Heat flashed into her cheeks and shot to her womb. *Everything about him was so sexual.* The worst of it was that she knew he knew.

Malleven smiled and sat opposite her. "Drink," he prompted again, and knocked his back in a single gulp.

She sipped hers and shuddered.

He laughed. "Perhaps vodka isn't your tipple." He got up, went out of the room and returned a minute later with an open black bottle and two more glasses. "Try red wine, Snowflake. This might suit you better."

He walked to a telephone, dialled a number with elegant fingers and spoke in a beautiful language for a few moments.

She sipped her drink and had to admit that she liked the warm, fuzzy feeling it made in her stomach.

Malleven replaced the receiver and came back and sat opposite her again. "I have ordered some food."

"I can't eat …"

"Meat," he finished for her. "Neither do I. It is common for us." He sat back in his chair and studied her.

She felt uncomfortable under his scrutiny.

"Drink, Snowflake … it will make you relax. You are bound to feel strange." He paused. "Why don't you let me in? I can make you feel better," he said seductively.

Her eyes shot to his in fear. She wondered why it was so important to him. She shook her head vigorously. "No, thank you. Never again."

He looked at her, intrigued, as if she had given something else away. *She really needed to shut up.*

Malleven was quiet again when she said nothing further. "Is there nothing you wish to ask me?" he said, eventually.

She sipped her drink while she thought about that. " Okay … you said you'd come for me?"

"And I did."

She frowned. "After two years?"

"Snowflake, please understand that things had to be handled carefully. You had to be released with care, so you came to my family. I had to make a lot of preparations."

He looked into his drink as he spoke and she wondered what he wasn't saying, but her head was beginning to feel very fuzzy and her arms and legs heavy.

"Why don't you lie down, Snowflake, if you feel tired? Take off your shoes and lie back."

She looked to the side of her at the sofa full of cushions and it did look really inviting. She kicked off her shoes and put her feet up.

"Another drink?" Malleven said.

"No, thank you."

"Come, let us make a night of it."

A buzzer sounded. "Ah, the food." And he went out to the door, while she dreamily listened to the echoey noises in the hall and the deep, rumbly Italian voices and then the door closed. He returned and spread the food out over the low table in front of the sofa.

She lazily looked at it. "I'm sorry, Malleven, but I'm really not hungry."

Malleven didn't seem that perturbed. He reached for the bottle of red and held out the other hand to her. "Come, Snowflake, let me put you to bed."

CHAPTER 9

*M*alleven pulled her up to standing, then walked her slowly out into the hallway and through a door to a magnificent master bedroom. It had an enormous wooden bed and double doors leading onto a huge balcony. Even in her foggy state, she admired the silks and brocades – the sheer grandeur.

He led her over to the bed and began to undress her. It was a slow and methodical process. Nothing was hurried, as if he savoured every moment until she was completely naked.

He pulled back the silk sheets and pushed her down onto the bed, then lifted her feet to swing her round onto it. He covered her with the sheet and it was so delicate it tickled her sensitive skin like feathers.

Then he poured her another glass and placed it by the bed. "Drink, Snowflake. It will help you sleep." She leaned over, took the glass, had a few sips and lay back down.

His eyes never left her while he unbuttoned his shirt and placed it over the back of the chair. It occurred to her that she should be feeling nervous as he revealed his tattooed, beautifully formed body in front of her; after all, she didn't exactly know him. Instead, she wasn't fazed and continued to watch him stare at her confidently, determined not to like what she saw.

Malleven stalked to the other side of the bed and joined her. He faced her and leaned up on an elbow and began to trace his fingers along the delicate skin of her arm. Her eyelids flickered so sleepily; she could barely keep them open.

"Shh," he whispered when she went to say something.

"Do you know what you are, Snowflake?" he asked. "Did anyone ever tell you what you were meant to become?"

She moved her head slowly, from side to side. Speech just wasn't forthcoming any more. Now and then she felt him try and push into her head, but even this sleepy, she remembered Darres' training. He had warned her that they had tried to get at him in his sleep and so he had perfected his sleep shields to daytime strength, and he had imparted that knowledge to her. Today, she was glad of it, because she was absolutely sure now that she had been drugged, probably for the sole purpose of getting into her head. She wasn't sure yet why, but one thing she was certain of was that although Malleven was physically attractive to her, he was dangerous on a whole other level to anything she had come across before.

"Would you like me to tell you the story of where you are from, Snowflake?" he continued, running a finger over her cheek and down her neck, lulling, relaxing and tempting. She wanted to lift her head and say yes, but she felt powerless.

His voice purred on anyway. "Many years ago, our people came from a distant world called Atlas. It was a water world and everyone could breathe under water. They came to earth and built a city called Murrtaine and left a colony."

Her ears pricked up. *Darres' home. She must listen to this and learn. If only her head hadn't gone to pieces.*

"Soon, the inhabitants ventured on land and met and married Humans and the city of Atlantis was built. Both yours and my families descended from there."

"But our forefathers from Atlas returned and destroyed Atlantis for straying too far from its ideals and cut off Murrtaine for ever. However, they left a prophecy that when an Atlantean mated with a Murr and five daughters were born, they would be hidden in the world for the princes of the five families to search for and marry, and then a king would be crowned to reunite them all."

She managed to turn her head to the side to face him, although her voice wouldn't work.

He nodded. "Yes, Snowflake, you are one of these and I am a prince from one of the royal families." He was holding out his hand in front of his eyes, smiling and shaking his head as if he didn't believe it himself. "This ring is only purple when I am near you. It shows you are destined to be mine, Snowflake."

"Yours," she whispered sleepily.

"For ever, my sweet." And before she knew it, he had rolled on top of her.

He kissed her mouth gently at first. "Let me in, Snowflake," he projected from outside her barriers, although he was pushing again.

"No," she said, as firmly as she could. Instinctively, she knew that this was different to when Darres entered her mind. This was some kind of control he sought over her – a complete surrender – and would use any tactic to get it.

Malleven said no more but took her mouth fiercely. "You will not give me your mind?" he whispered between biting down her neck to her breasts. "Then you will give me your body."

She groaned as he nipped at her breasts painfully and pushed his hands roughly between her legs and felt the wetness already pooling there.

"Yes," he said. "Your body gives in to me even when you do not." Then he adeptly flipped her over onto her front, placed his cock hard against her core and plunged into her deeply. Relentless, with every thrust, he spoke words, not of love but of ownership. How she was his, how she would never escape him, how he would fuck her every day, whenever he wanted, however he wanted, and she would grow to love it, crave it even, till she would go mad without it.

Her traitorous body responded wildly to his treatment of her until she screamed with every thrust and the bed creaked and banged against the wall and he bit her back and neck savagely to mark her and punish her body until she shouted for help as her orgasm overwhelmed her to the point of unconsciousness.

Thankfully, blissful clouds enveloped her last thoughts before she slept. If her life before had been a miserable existence, then she had now descended into hell.

Tia, present day, Ballygowan Castle

Jay was leaning against the wall in the corridor outside the study with his eyes closed, listening to everything. He'd had no intention of getting the kids and hated that they'd used them to get her to comply, but the only way to leave her was to get himself released—and released without Dante suspecting he'd done it deliberately. To be a Siren's Protector was a lifelong job, unless the Siren released you. Plus, there was the question of the bond. *Fuck knows what could be done about that?* He would have to tread carefully.

In the beginning, when Christian Dubonnetti (Dante's father) had come to his office in New York and told him about the prophecy of the Darkly Begotten, he'd dismissed it as a load of shit, believing he was as mad as Dante always said he was. But when he got to thinking about everything in his life and the trouble he had caused Dante and his kingdom already, he had to start believing that it was true and the prophecy *was* fulfilled in him.

The ugly circumstances of how he came to be conceived hadn't surprised him, given the life his mother had led. No matter how he looked at it, even in moments of selfishness when he thought, *fuck it,* and decided to keep Tia for himself, it always came back to the two-way bond she and Dante shared because they were both Atlantean, and how they couldn't keep their hands off each other, no matter how much they tried and hated themselves for it. He was kidding himself if he ever thought it could be any different.

So it wasn't anything as honourable as saving the Atlantean monarchy, or his best friend's love, or even the respect of Tia, the only woman he had ever loved. The truth of it was, he could never be enough. Not fast enough, not strong enough, he could never be anywhere near what Dante could be. And the sickening thing was that, loving Dante like he did, he couldn't even hate him for that either. Didn't that just prove his soul was as black as Christian said? *Fuck, he had to get out of there before the whole fucking lot of them drove him mad.*

Dante walked out and interrupted his thoughts. He whispered to a guard, who left immediately.

"Listen, this has gone too far," Jay said as soon as Dante turned his attention to him. "She's fucking in bits in there."

"I know, mate, I'm not doing this as some stupid practical joke, you know … Tattoos are ownership and belonging for us … Fuck, Jay, you've got enough of them … Look, there are still three other Sirens unaccounted for out there. If someone gets them and spots Tia while she's out on her jollies, not doing what she's meant to, we're fucked … Do you get it?" Dante said, poking Jay in the chest.

Jay looked down at Dante's finger for him to stop making his point. His temper threatened to bubble up to the surface, but he tamped it down with cool logic. "So she has to have your coat of arms to show she belongs to you …" Jay said, schooling his features.

"Then at least they would know she's taken and by whom, and there ain't a lot they can do about that," Dante said.

Jay was grateful when the nanny came around the corner, stopped in front of Dante and bobbed a curtsy.

"She's in there, nurse, she's terrified."

The nurse nodded and entered the room. They could hear Tia screaming, then silence. The nurse rushed out of the room, curtsied again and almost ran away.

Next out was Keenan, who threw a bloody towel at Dante, who caught it. "Next time, do your own dirty work … The nurse ripped her arm trying to inject her."

Jay watched Dante's face harden as he walked slowly towards Keenan. He never took criticism well. "Just make sure you keep your own woman in line so I don't have to put my mark on her." *Ah, fuck!*

Keenan flew at Dante.

Jay jumped between them, feeling the impact of Keenan like a freight train. He hefted Keenan back. "Calm down, mate. Let's take it down, we're all stressed."

Keenan, who had grown close to Jay, looked at him with exasperation. "What are you sticking up for him for … he got you released … You sure that wasn't his plan?" Keenan said, disgusted, and pulled away from Jay's grip and marched away down the corridor.

Jay took a deep breath and looked at the ceiling. *He had to fucking get out of there.*

"It's true … she's done it," Dante said, quietly. "If you've ever wanted your freedom, then she gave it to you tonight. She may never give it again."

Jay continued to rest his head back against the wall. "You mean I have a choice?"

"Yes. She's released you. You could stay if you want, but if you choose to go, you still can't just walk away. I'd need to speak to the Murrs first … you are joined, remember?"

Jay nodded. To be bound to a Siren was at a genetic level. He had no idea how splitting up worked. "I don't know Dante, the kids, fuck … it's complicated." He couldn't even begin to think about the kids.

Dante touched him on the shoulder. "Sleep on it. Let me know in the morning."

"Fuck, Dante," Jay said, overwhelmed with the enormity of the decision, despite his need to go.

"What are friends for?" Dante said, looking at him out of the corner of his eye, watching him closely – too closely.

Jay began to pace up and down, pushing his hand through his hair while he thought. He looked back at Dante. *Was he suspicious already?* Jay knew that to have Tia to himself was what he wanted ultimately; still, he could never let Dante know why, otherwise he'd never let him escape – as perverse as that was. It was uncanny how in tune the two of them were, even before the bond that linked them through Tia.

"Look, mate, we are in the same boat."

Jay stopped pacing and frowned at him. "How do you work that out?"

"The only person she's going to hate more than you is me … and there is no divorce," Dante said with a hapless smile. "Come on, let's go back in."

Jay followed him back into the room. He had to keep telling himself that this was the right thing to do. *Wasn't it?*

. . .

Rex looked up, his baseball cap turned backwards, as they walked in. "You owe me big after this, you two. I could get locked up."

Jay's eyes went straight to Tia, sleeping peacefully. He frowned at the new bandage on the top of her arm, then anger swiftly followed as they'd removed her jeans. The tattoo was on the left-hand side of her behind, at the top of her thigh and would be visible in a bikini. *Fucking hell.*

It was a work of art, though. About the size of a saucer, the outline was almost complete. The Dubonnetti coat of arms, he knew so well, his was identical, except hers would have a crown over it.

"What colours do you want in the banner?" Rex asked.

"Pale blue and yellow – my colours," Dante said.

Jay looked down at the body he knew as well as his own. Could he really walk away? He wouldn't miss all the shit, that's for sure. But could he go through life never feeling her, holding her, loving her? He didn't have a choice, though, did he. Even if he wasn't what Christian said he was, there was no way she would ever let him get near her now. That made up his mind for him, and he walked towards the door.

"Where are you going?" Dante asked.

"I'm going to find Sebastian … I want to talk to him, find out all the implications."

Dante nodded thoughtfully. "Okay, man … I reckon we'll be a while yet."

Jay couldn't say anything else and left the room.

Jay knocked on the small sitting room door that was part of Sebastian's living quarters. Sebastian, Tia's father, was having coffee with his brother, Alfonzo. Both men were princes, elder statesmen and his benefactors, trusting him with running the whole family business.

He was glad he had them both together. He didn't want to say what he had to say twice.

"Ah, Jay, please sit." Sebastian gestured to a free armchair across the table from them.

Jay sat, then coughed uncomfortably and went straight to the point. "I wanted to speak to you before I come to a decision."

Sebastian nodded slowly.

"Tia released me tonight," he blurted.

The two men glanced across at each other, then nodded their heads, but it was Alfonzo, the family head, who spoke first. "Given her nature, it is not surprising to us."

Jay felt slightly deflated. He had expected a few questions at least.

"It was inevitable," Alfonzo said, smiling slightly.

Jay's eyes darted to his. *What did they know?*

"Since she and Dante were bound and married," Sebastian added, his knowing eyes resting on his.

Jay nodded and nervously rubbed his palms on his knees. "Do you know what I need to do ... you know, to be free so it doesn't harm her?"

The two men looked at each other. Alfonzo continued, "We would need to speak to Darl, Lord Advocate of Murrtaine. But I believe it is a case of medication, which needs to be taken daily for life. You are joined, you see."

Jay nodded. It made sense.

"We can request the necessary medication straight away. I am not sure how easy it is to come by. I don't know how long ago anything like this has happened; if ever?" Alfonzo said.

"Will she be okay?"

Sebastian smiled at him. "We know you love her, Jay. You have always done what is best for her. She will be fine eventually. And we want you to continue in your current professional capacity for the Bonaci family."

They had, as always, surprised him with their generosity. He stood, thanked them and shook both their hands. He wished he could shift this weight off his chest. For someone who had just secured his freedom, he felt more weighed down than ever.

Isla, *one year previously*

After a few days, Malleven took her to New York. It was like living in a nightmare; he was charming and sophisticated to the outside world and brutal behind closed doors. She was covered in bruises and in a constant haze from being drugged. She began to refuse to drink and when that didn't work, she refused to eat. She thought she was winning when he became infuriated with her, but all it did was heighten the stakes and make it an even more enjoyable game for him. However, on occasion, he would show her his vulnerable side, and then he would completely disorient her.

On the first morning in New York, Isla was awoken by Malleven tossing, turning and shouting in his sleep. His dream seemed more disturbing than ever. She lay watching him, indecisive as to whether to intervene or not, until her sense of compassion forced her to get a cooling cloth to dab his sweating brow and whisper calm words of comfort.

Gradually, his movements relaxed and he slowly opened his bloodshot eyes and became fully cognisant.

Isla yelped as he moved, quick as a flash, and snatched her to him, rambling loving words in Italian. She allowed it, lying stiffly in his arms until he put her away from him slightly and they faced each other on the pillows, both studying each other's faces.

God, what a complex, terrifying man. "Do you want to tell me about it?" she said, cautiously.

Malleven closed his eyes and she was shocked to see him

gather his strength before he spoke. She flinched when he picked up a single lock of her hair and pushed it away from her face. He seemed to be stalling, deciding whether or not to trust her.

"Do you always have the same dream?" she persisted, tentatively.

He nodded and swallowed hard. "Since I was a bambino."

"Tell me … perhaps I can help dispel it?"

"It is always the same thing … I am under the water … I am being held by an invisible force … it is impossible for me to move … I cannot breathe."

The fear in his eyes was a tangible thing, and for a second, his vulnerability evoked some instinct within her to comfort him and forget his cruelty to her. She pulled him to her. "It's okay," she whispered. "It's only a dream."

She wasn't sure who was more shocked at her demonstration of affection, him or her; they lay so still. Then, as if he'd recognised a chink in her armour, his fear soon gave way to a frenzied lust and a need to claim her more ferociously than ever before. His thrusts almost pushed her off the bed, and with his mouth next to her ear he reminded her in perfect rhythm: "You … are … mine … and … will … always … be … so … until … death … parts … us."

ONE DAY, she woke up feeling a little more like her old self and went into the kitchen for food. She sat on a high stool at the counter and took an apple from the fruit bowl. It felt like the safest thing. It wasn't long before Malleven sauntered in after her. Her heart sank. He went straight to the fridge and poured what looked like iced water and held it out to her.

"No, thank you," she said straight away, going back to her apple.

"Why won't you drink, Snowflake … it's only water?

"I'm not thirsty," she said quietly.

"Come, come now, I worry for you … what are you afraid of?" His face was all concern.

"What. You've. Fucking. Put. In. It," she said slowly, through gritted teeth.

He shook his head, smiling, and held out his hand, palm up, and on it was a white tablet. "Just take it then, Snowflake, and all this silliness will be over." His smile turned into a wide grin as if he were mocking her.

"Aargh!" she screamed at him and batted the outstretched hand away, knocking the tablet onto the floor. Pointless, but it felt good.

She went to rise from her seat to storm off, but found she couldn't move. She struggled and looked up into Malleven's laughing eyes with fear and hatred. *He was a demon.* How could she ever hope to beat a man like him?

Malleven cocked his head to the side and studied her, smiling indulgently. He had the look of someone capable of anything. "I will make a deal with you, Snowflake," he continued, "let me enter your mind, and I will not make you take the tablet?" He let his words sink in for a moment. "The choice is yours."

Isla clenched her fists and looked furiously into his oh-so-reasonable face, and her heart pounded. The choice was no choice, of course.

Then, just as he knew it would, her calm snapped and she flew at him, screaming like a banshee, raising her fists in a flash, ready to punch him. But he was ready for her. It was a ruse to give him the excuse and the excitement of overpowering her, which he did easily.

Her limbs froze and she felt herself fall like a felled tree. He caught her quickly and gently set her down on the cold marble floor. He crouched and lovingly pushed the tendrils of hair from her face.

Every fibre in her revolted and she wanted to spit but found she could move nothing. She knew what he would do. He prised his fingers into the corners of her mouth to force it open, then popped in the pill as if administering to a wayward child. "There," he said, clamping his hands over her mouth and jaw to make sure it didn't come back out.

Isla screamed and writhed inside, but all that came from her was a deep moan of utter despair. His hands didn't move until the pill had completely dissolved. Her moaning eventually ceased and tears streamed down her temples onto the floor. Dizziness and nausea then replaced her feelings of desolation as the drug began its journey around her system.

"Shh," Malleven said, as if to comfort her. "Let me in," he whispered, coaxingly. "I will make everything better for you … give yourself over to me …"

The tentacles of his mind tried to creep around her mental barriers and she thanked god for the umpteenth time for Darres' training. "No … Noo," she moaned.

Malleven's face hardened, then he conceded a nod as if he respected her strength. He picked her up and rocked her to and fro in his lap.

Calmed by drugs and the apathy of the trapped, she relaxed and her heart sank lower into despair. She knew now that he would never be satisfied until he had complete dominion over her, and to him that meant complete capitulation of her will.

AFTER A FEW NIGHTS in New York, his boyfriend turned up. *Yes, boyfriend!*

"Who the fuck is she?" Antonio screamed at the top of his lungs.

Isla adopted the stance she'd honed over years of showing absolutely no emotion; she just stood still, staring ahead of her until she was ordered by Malleven to sit. He then asked Antonio to stop shouting. Malleven took great pleasure in formally introducing them to each other. "Antonio … meet Isla Snow … or should I say Bonaci … my mate. Antonio, the king's brother, meet Isla.' Then he laughed loudly, finishing with, "I want the two of you to be friends."

"Friends!" Antonio shrieked.

Isla decided that she wouldn't mind an ally and chanced a glance at Antonio, then averted her eyes, while her heart thumped.

Her heart went out to Antonio as he clearly loved Malleven. He let out a tirade of what he'd been through with his father on Malleven's behalf and revealed his obvious hurt at seeing her with Malleven in nothing but their silk robes. Malleven showed no compassion and merely used his power to silence him. She daren't intervene; Malleven was too strong, too powerful and held all the cards.

Poor Antonio. Isla saw his face crumple from confusion to pain. "But…" was all he could manage to say, over and over.

"Look at your ring, Antonio," Malleven said, pointing.

Isla couldn't help but look too. She understood now the importance of the rings to the princes. It was proof of who she was. After that, the conversation got beyond her.

"Your experiments have concluded … you managed to make it work?" Antonio said.

"This ring has not been tampered with. It is pure." Then Malleven pointed at her, "She is indeed mine."

Isla looked at Antonio's face and watched the colour drain away as Malleven's words sank in. *What did it all mean?*

"So you can make a legitimate claim now?" Antonio stated.

Isla's mind was reeling. *What experiments? What claim was he trying to make?*

By the time her mind came back to the conversation, Antonio was explaining how his father had disowned him after he'd beaten him. That he had no need of him because he had the Darkly Begotten – whatever that was.

Then the darkness that came over Malleven made Isla take notice and Antonio fearful. "Do you have any idea what the Darkly Begotten is, Antonio?"

"My father says he will ruin Dante's reign from within, like a virus, going unnoticed until it's too late."

Isla's ears pricked at the mention of 'Dante'. She knew that he was the king and her sister's husband. Did Malleven intend to destroy him? She listened keenly whilst keeping her eyes down so as not to alert Malleven to her sudden interest.

"The Darkly Begotten can be wielded and guided to do its harbourer's bidding," Malleven was saying.

"Who is its harbourer?" Antonio said.

Isla knew it must be Malleven purely by the smug way he was describing it. The exact same way he sounded when he managed to outwit her.

"I will be the most powerful magician of all times," Malleven continued.

Isla jumped slightly when Malleven suddenly reached for her hand and pulled her to her feet, along with Antonio, and joined their hands. "I want the two of you to grow to love each other as you love me. With my mate," he continued, running a loving finger along Isla's jaw, " and her sisters ... I will be invincible."

Isla tried to remain unaffected by his words, but her brain stalled. Antonio continued to question him, but she didn't hear any more after that. The tone in Antonio's voice revealed he felt the same as she did. That Malleven was a raving sociopath intent on taking her sister's husband's crown, a fate worse than death. She shuddered at the thought that everyone would be at his mercy and she would never escape.

Isla couldn't even begin to fully understand what it all meant, but she would find out. She must find a way to stop him from drugging her so she can think clearly and plan.

Since being with Malleven, all she had wanted to do was die. Since she was eight years old, she had thought that if she could just escape the facility, she could find a way of getting back to Japan and be happy again. But how wrong could she have been?

Now she was filled with a steely resolve that she wanted to live. To find out who her sisters were and get to the family she had never known. She wanted to see if life could be good again. And, most of all, she wanted to find Darres and explain that she hadn't abandoned him. To do that, she must survive. No matter what.

TODAY WAS A SUNNY, hot day in New York. The freak heatwave was continuing, Malleven had said that morning. He ordered her and Antonio to become friends and went out on business. She had said she would if he let her sober up from the drugs. He had assessed her with a calculating look, then kissed her on the forehead, and with a "very well", disappeared. It was a small victory

Now she and Antonio sat opposite each other on sun loungers, both battered and bruised, neither willing to start a conversation.

He'd been subdued ever since he'd heard the news that she was Malleven's legitimate mate. He had stayed the night as he had nowhere else to go, which must have been awful for him, as Malleven bedded her as energetically and noisily as usual in the very next room.

Then Malleven had showered, leaving her in the heap

he'd used her in, and left the bedroom. Some moments later, she heard his voice rumbling through the wall and then the bed in Antonio's room squeaking energetically.

Her heart thumped as she listened to it. She wasn't hurt or upset; she was afraid for Antonio and what Malleven would have them doing next. *Was this Malleven's way? Or was he just showing both her and Antonio that he could do what he wanted with whomever he wanted?* She suspected the latter.

Then Malleven returned to their room, showered and got in bed as if nothing had happened. She pretended to be asleep till morning. Then, when she awoke, he pulled her closer so she lay with half her body over him and called out to Antonio, "Come join us, Antonio, don't be alone."

Her heart stopped.

"Fuck off, Malleven … I'm not your bitch!" Antonio shouted back.

She didn't move a muscle, but again Malleven surprised her.

He laughed loudly, tightened his grip on her and kissed her forehead. "You see what insubordination I have to put up with?" Then he snuggled with her and dozed a little longer while she lay awake in his arms.

CHAPTER 10

She studied Antonio while he sat lost in his own thoughts. He was very good-looking. Tall and blonde with light-grey eyes.

"I am no threat to you, you know?" she said eventually, careful not to rest her eyes too long on his battered face.

He turned to face her with a look of disgust. "No threat? … How can you possibly say that? You are his mate, legitimately proven by divining ring."

"I don't want him," she said simply.

Antonio barked a laugh. "No, of course not. It didn't sound like that either last night."

She understood how it must have sounded and remained quiet for a few moments. She wasn't sure how to phrase what she wanted to say. She would have loved to confide in him, but didn't know if she could trust him. *He was* so *Malleven's bitch.*

"Perhaps if we worked together, I could have some respite?" She hoped he got her drift.

He narrowed his eyes on her. "Like what?" he said flatly.

"While he's with you, he leaves me alone."

He still said nothing, but his brain clearly whirred.

"Why do you let him treat you like that?" she asked.

He relaxed back in the sun lounger, sulkily, as if he was annoyed at her.

"Malleven is not like anyone I've ever met."

She watched him fidget with discomfort, trying to find the words.

"He has no love in him," she responded.

He looked up quickly. "You're wrong!" Then he continued, more softly, "He's just very extreme in everything he does. When he loves, when he's angry, when he's passionate and possessive."

She tried not to show her confusion. There was no doubt that Antonio loved Malleven, but she failed to see any of those things as attributes, only ways to control and get his own way.

"He loves me as much as he could love anyone," Antonio said, vehemently.

He was probably right about that.

She changed the subject. "You know my family?"

It worked as she watched him visibly relax.

"Yes," he said and he lay back down into the cushions.

"Would you mind telling me about them?"

"Your mother is a Murr, very beautiful."

Murr. She had to be beautiful.

"I only met her once, at your sister's wedding celebration," Antonio continued.

"My sister?"

"Yes, Tia. She is my brother's..." and he seemed to check himself, then spoke more quietly in case they were overheard. "Half-brother's mate. Dante."

"And he is king?"

Antonio nodded.

So Malleven wants to take the crown from my sister's husband?"

He looked into her eyes intently. "Not just the crown but your sisters as well."

Isla watched his face for a moment. "And this is all right with you?"

He shrugged as if it didn't matter. "He needs all of you to be king and hold the crown."

She did a quick calculation. "So your brother needs all of us too?"

Antonio gave her a look as if she wasn't as stupid as she looked. "Don't let Malleven hear you say that."

Her lips curled into a rare smile at him. "You see … we could have each other's back?"

He sat up on his sun lounger, as if he were considering it as an option.

The thought had given her hope, though. If she could just get to her sister and her mate – he can't be worse than Malleven, surely. She'd have to find out as much as she could. "Why do they need us all?"

"For fuck's sake, girl! … you wanna get me killed?" He got up with a huff and stopped right next to her. "For your breath," and he walked back into the apartment.

Breath? She frowned. *Whatever that meant … she had to find out as much as she could.*

Just as she had plotted and planned for two years, mapping the facility, she would prepare. She had to be ready when an opportunity presented itself.

*T*IA, *present day*

When Tia awoke, she found herself lying on her side in Dante's bed in his subterranean bedchamber. She looked over her shoulder and there he was, sleeping soundly next to her.

She followed the dull ache down her body with her hand and flinched when she felt the dressing at the top of her thigh where it joined her hip. Sitting up, she peeled back the gauze and looked at it. *Bastards.* There, in black ink, was the Dubonnetti coat of arms stamped on her like a prize heifer.

Her head felt achy and groggy. She guessed it was the hangover from whatever they knocked her out with. She sat up slowly and held her forehead while she tried to remember the events of the night before. A pain so strong pierced her heart when she recalled that everyone she loved had been in on it – well, almost. Perhaps Cash had wanted no part in it, and Dante had dismissed Sean as soon as he'd brought her back.

Dante stirred. He reached across her in his sleep and rubbed her back. "Come lie with me," he mumbled.

It wasn't until she went to pull away from him in anger that she heard the jangle. She looked down at her ankle and couldn't believe her eyes. She was chained to the bedpost.

She crawled down the bed and shook it. "I thought I could go anywhere in the castle?" she said, her voice rising in anger.

Dante slowly opened his eyes. "Not when you are near water." His face remained impassive as he watched her.

"I want my own room," she spat.

He stared at her for a minute, so she didn't know if he'd woken up properly. "You brought this on yourself," he said, eventually.

She began shaking the chain manically again. "No, I didn't … I didn't ask for any of this… I've been forced to do everything." She stopped jangling the chain and sagged. "Marrying you was one of them," she said, her eyes half closed in contempt.

"We are all trapped," Dante said after a pause. "Well, except Jay."

She frowned, then remembered, and her face fell. *Oh my god.* In her temper, she'd released him. "Has he gone?"

"He hasn't decided yet … I have to find out what he needs to do. There is the matter of the physical connection."

"What's going to happen to the kids?" She couldn't believe everything had got so out of control.

"I will have custody of all three. Jay can see JJ whenever he wants."

She tried to hide her emotion, but it came bubbling up in her voice. "What about me?"

"With supervision."

"What? I'm unfit now?" The tears cascaded down her cheeks and she made no attempt to wipe them away.

Dante remained unmoved. "They are royal, Tia. Heirs. I can't risk you running with them."

"That's ridiculous. You're linked to me wherever I am. I can never get away from you," she spat.

Dante sat up and sighed. "That's just it, though, Tia, isn't it. You fuckin' block me out whenever you feel like ignoring me. What am I supposed to do if you decide to fuck off to the other side of the world on a fuckin whim?" he said, throwing his hands down and shaking his head.

She desperately needed to get away from him, as usual, he was stifling her. "Can you unlock me? I need to go to the bathroom, and then find my sister," she said, between sobs.

Dante rose from the bed and walked around it and produced a key. He unlocked the manacle and stood back up. "If you behave, you'll get more freedom … less if you don't."

She felt his eyes on her while she rubbed her ankle.

"Listen, Tia, you just refuse to accept how important you are."

He went to touch her foot and she snatched it away.

"Yeah, yeah, I know … the fucking kingdom." She slid off the bed and stamped off through the sand to the bathroom.

She wandered the underground corridors of the castle, hiccupping sobs, running over and over everything in her mind.

The one thing she had always clung to and held at all costs was her love for Jay. Determined never to give it up despite all the pressures against it, she resisted the absolute bond with Dante, threatening to swallow up her soul and every ounce of her individuality. But what was she to do now, when the object of her obsession, Jay, had turned against her and thrown her away as if she didn't matter at all. *Fucking hell. What could she do now?*

It felt like she'd been wandering for hours when she came to the door to the bedroom she knew her sister and Keenan used.

She knocked gently. She had no idea what the time was.

A quiet female voice called out.

Tia opened the door and stood on the threshold in just her vest top and knickers. She stood and looked at the bed where her sister and the big body of Keenan lay, who was just registering who she was. "Can I come in with you? They won't give me my own room," she said in a small voice.

Lacy said something quietly to Keenan, who shifted over. Lacy opened her side of the bedcoverings and Tia slid under the sheet with them. Keenan's arm went over Lacy and Lacy's went over her.

A last hiccup escaped her as she relaxed into the warmth. "Thank you," she said, more grateful than they'd ever know.

LATER THAT MORNING, Keenan stood showered and dressed. He couldn't help smiling to himself, looking over at the two girls asleep, intertwined in *his* bed. "Payback's a bitch," he muttered to himself.

No wonder Tia was always in trouble. She always had an uncanny knack for always doing the wrong thing. And getting into his bed, however harmless, was one of them. Dante would hit the roof and didn't that just make his day?

Keenan did genuinely feel sorry for her. He'd seen, first-hand, how hard she'd tried to make a go of it with Jay. But Dante always demanded to see her, and Jay, being his best friend, put the kibosh on it time and time again. *Fuck*, no wonder she needed to run away at times, any sane person would.

There was a loud knock on the door, interrupting his train of thought. He threw it wide open so Dante could see the whole room. "I was expecting you."

Dante looked at the bed and then at Keenan. "You have anything to do with this?"

Keenan held up his hands in surrender. "She wanted to be with her sister ... and, to be honest, I can't blame her. She was the only person who didn't sell her down the river last night."

Dante gave him a black look, turned on his heel and stormed off.

ISLA, New York, a couple of months previously

Over the months that passed, Isla and Antonio fell into an uneasy truce; neither fully convinced the other could be trusted. Isla started to relax in the knowledge that at least Antonio had begun to believe her when she said she didn't love Malleven, even if he couldn't fathom how that was possible.

Malleven would come and go, sometimes for long periods at a time, leaving them alone together. At first, he would lay traps; weird, magical barriers using her blood so he would know if she left the apartment. She wasn't sure how it worked or even if it was a bluff, but he needn't have bothered as she never ventured out.

It had crossed her mind to run, of course it had, but she had no friends, nowhere to go and, more importantly, no money or passport. So she waited and built trust until she was ready to find a way to reach her sisters and, ultimately, Darres.

She watched TV constantly, learning about the outside world of which she knew so little. She sneakily asked questions to garner snippets of information, like where her sister lived in the world in relation to them. The answer was usually Ireland, but sometimes Antonio would say she was in Murrtaine.

Her heart jumped. How lucky her sister was to go there. That meant that she might be able to go there too one day and stay underwater that long. Darres would be there, she was sure of it.

She asked Antonio where Murrtaine was, and was disappointed to learn that hardly any Atlanteans knew of its location and absolutely no Humans. It was all knowledge she stored away.

Try as she might, Malleven still didn't fully trust her. Every time she asked why, he would answer that 'she never let him in her head'. And that 'true mates shared everything', and studied her with shrewd eyes. She had to be so careful not to give herself away. She racked her brains to find a way to win him round; to get him to think she loved him without giving him access to her mind. That, she instinctively knew, would reveal how she truly felt for him, which was why he wanted it so much. No, she had to think of another way to make him relax his guard with her.

Then, one morning without warning, Malleven

announced they were to pack as they were moving to Italy that day. His business in America was concluded, and just like that, her life changed again.

AFTER A LONG FLIGHT, they were chauffeured to a large Florianna residence in the countryside just outside Milan. A majestic shingle driveway swept them up to the large white-washed building with an ornate veranda at every window. The white a perfect canvas to show off the well-appointed Cypress and Olive trees, and beautifully contrasted pink and red Rhododendron flowers.

The magnificent residences were nothing more than gilded cages to Isla, and she made no comment as they went inside. The interior was as magnificent as all the other places Malleven had taken her to. Tasteful and expensive; wall-to-wall dark wood and beautiful brocade soft furnishings.

Malleven had sent word ahead for his cousin and close friend Cesaré to join them. Malleven apparently had something of the utmost importance to show him. Cesaré replied immediately that he would meet them there the next day.

Antonio flopped down onto a large, sumptuous sofa and watched Malleven prowl up and down while his brain worked. Isla sat perched on the edge of a seat, watching the pair of them. The atmosphere was charged.

"What are you up to?" Antonio asked, eventually.

Malleven stopped and pointed at Antonio. "Now it begins … do you understand?"

He was talking about something she knew nothing about.

Antonio's mood changed instantly and he slowly sat up, wary of Malleven's unpredictability.

"Tomorrow night I will be working in my laboratory. No one is to disturb me."

"Okay," Antonio said, looking up at him.

It was as though she wasn't there.

"Tomorrow Cesaré arrives. I will take him out. When we come back, he will be very drunk. Then, the following day, I will introduce him to Isla ... he will be the first of my family to know she is here."

"I don't get it?" Antonio said.

Neither did she. It was as though he were talking in riddles.

Malleven looked briefly across at Isla, then back at Antonio. "Not yet." Then he appeared to snap out of his serious mood. "Come ... get dressed. We'll go out – the three of us."

THE THREE OF them sat at a small table in a bustling bistro in the picturesque town square. The evening was warm, the atmosphere was vibrant and the food was rustic but delicious. Malleven and Antonio ate and chatted.

Butterflies tickled Isla's stomach; somehow, she knew that she had reached a momentous moment in her life. She picked at her food. Many locals knew Malleven and some even knew Antonio, and both gabbled away in fluent Italian. She had discovered that most Atlanteans spoke it. It didn't matter as it gave her the opportunity to people-watch.

It was then that a pretty, curvaceous Italian woman sidled up to their table and flung her arms around both Antonio and Malleven, completely ignoring her. Then she promptly sat on Malleven's lap and kissed him in an overfamiliar way.

Malleven kissed her and mumbled some affectionate-sounding words, but it wasn't until he flashed his deep-blue eyes at Isla that it gave her the idea. It was obvious that he was looking to see her reaction.

In a split second, she seized her chance and threw a full glass of wine over the pair of them. She rose quickly from her chair, cutlery crashing, and ran off into the crowd.

She didn't have a clue where she was going. She just ran, quickly enough to look in a temper, but not fast enough to lose them. She counted. It took no more than thirty seconds for Malleven to catch up with her and lift her off the ground. Antonio went to swiftly hail a taxi. All the while Malleven carried her, Antonio attempted to talk him down. "Easy, Malleven ... She's just a girl ... Calm down."

"Shut up, Antonio," Malleven said as he threw her in and got into the seat next to her. Antonio got into the front seat next to the driver. "Please, Malleven," Antonio said nervously, looking at the driver.

Malleven said nothing but held her hand tightly all the way back to the villa, as if he thought she would jump out of a moving car. Then he manhandled her out, leaving Antonio to pay, and shoved her in through the front door.

As soon as they were in the house, a powerful force lifted her off the ground and his hand gripped her around her throat. She was choking. All she could do was relax into his grip and hang there.

Antonio hurried in behind them. "Malleven, please." Antonio pleaded.

Finally, Malleven spoke. "She drew attention to us in the middle of fucking town ... no one must know my true connection to her," he hissed, looking into her eyes like the devil himself. All the while, he was attempting to breach her barriers.

"She was just jealous, Malleven. You were humiliating her at the table," Antonio reasoned, touching him gently on the arm.

Malleven looked sideways at Antonio, then squinted at her while he thought about what Antonio had said. Then he released her, to flop to the ground and roughly pushed her towards the bedroom. "Leave us, Antonio," he said over his shoulder. "You have nothing to fear."

CHAPTER 11

Malleven pushed Isla onto her back on the bed and was on top of her in a second. He gripped her jaw tightly with his hand and searched her face. "The girl made you angry?"

She gave a small nod, but her eyes screwed up in pain at the tightness of his grip.

Malleven squinted again. "But I can fuck Antonio and that is okay?" he said, shaking his head. He relaxed his grip slightly to allow her to talk.

"Antonio and I have grown accustomed to each other … like a brother … we look out for each other," she said, truthfully.

Malleven remained still, then his eyes appeared to soften slightly as if he was pleased with her. "You are my mate, Snowflake," he said tenderly. "There can be no other female for me now." His eyes looked soulful and he kissed her lovingly and deeply.

Briefly, she had to ask herself if she had not shot herself in the foot, but it was too late now and she would have to see it through. So she brought her arms around him and kissed him shamelessly back.

He growled his approval and ripped the shoulder down from her dress and kissed her flesh. "Tonight, Snowflake, I will make love to you for the first time." He began to worship and treat her body as she would have expected a lover to behave, softly, reverently, lavishing it with attention, drawing out every sensation and driving her wild with the skill of a practised lover.

For just a short while, she could forget all the misery he'd heaped on her and gave herself over to the physical pleasure that he somehow had a talent for. When she became over-heated, he left her to go to his dresser and brought back a clear liquid, which he gave her to drink after taking a few sips himself.

Then, instead of forcing his body on her, he entered her slowly and built gradually, taking her on a carnal journey with him, steadily increasing in pace and strength. "Let me in at last, Snowflake?" he whispered in her ear.

"I can't … I'm sorry, Malleven. I'm damaged. I am unable."

He slowed while he searched her eyes and, satisfied with her explanation, he nodded. "Okay, it will come in time." Then he rolled with her onto his back. It was a huge concession, as he was giving her the dominant position.

Malleven sat forward with her so that he could nip at her breasts and pull the hard peaks into his mouth while he moved with her and ground her into his hips. Then, sensing she was close, he lay back and pushed a thumb between their bodies and circled her engorged bud. He whispered words in Italian that totally did it for her. She cried out with the strength of her climax. Perversely, the most mind-blowing orgasm of her life was achieved while riding the man she wanted to escape from at all costs. He lit her up like no one else.

She collapsed against him and he lay with her held against his chest while they both breathed hard. Then, as if he mirrored her exact same thoughts, "You turn me on like no other woman, Snowflake," he said, kissing her head.

"What is happening tomorrow, Malleven? I'm scared."

"Tomorrow I begin to take the kingdom."

Her heart stopped. "How does that involve me?"

Malleven was silent, then he phrased the words he wanted to say carefully. "When you meet Cesarè tomorrow, his ring will go purple for you."

"But I thought? ..." She sat up so she could look into the face that was such a contradiction, perfect lines and yet dangerous, beautiful in the darkness. There was simply no one else quite like him.

"You are mine, never forget it. But I cannot turn up at Dante's court with you. If they didn't kill me on sight, they certainly wouldn't let me near your sisters, which are essential to my plans."

She ran a finger along his high cheekbone. This was the most he'd ever confided in her and she wanted him to continue.

"This last year, I've been working on a way of affecting the outcome of the divining ring's power to detect a compatible mate." He smiled at the memory. "You see, I had no idea that the fates would favour me and give me you to make a legitimate claim ... and unfortunately by then certain plays had already been made."

"I don't understand?" she said, confused.

"Tomorrow, I will see to it that Cesarè's ring will go purple for you," he said, stroking back her hair from her forehead while he looked into her eyes. "He will present you to the king as his ... you must work for me there, Snowflake."

The extent of his plans was dawning on her. She was to

be his undercover agent. She waited for him to continue, not daring to breathe.

"You will be pledged and married to the king,"

She shook her head to protest.

"Shh … I know … but it is necessary. Don't worry, I will guide you and soon you will deliver your two sisters to me. I will be searching for the two sisters yet to be found, and with my legitimate claim through you, and your sisters' pledge, the crown will have to pass to me."

Isla lay her head back down on Malleven's chest and he pulled her tight to him, kissing her hair again. "Sleep, Snowflake. It is a big day tomorrow."

Her heart was hammering in her chest. She prayed he wouldn't feel it. "Won't I have to … you know … sleep with Cesaré, to convince him?" she asked, carefully. She had to make sure of the rules of the game.

Malleven snuggled down and kissed her again sleepily. "You will do this for me," he said as he slowly dropped off to sleep.

Isla was wide awake. Cesaré was going to be her ticket out of there.

Tia, present day

The time had come for Lacy and Tia to pledge to Dante again. They would both get into the water just outside the huge panoramic window below sea level at Ballygowan Castle. During the ceremony, they must both breathe their life force into the king for him to absorb their power, and he must breathe into them to complete the link, so he had a complete psychic bond with the Sirens. This had to be completed every few months in order for none of them to get sick.

Lacy waited with Tia next to the large fountain gateway

to the sea and felt terrified. Tia was ready to go into the water, but was too quiet, too still.

Lacy had got used to seeing her sister drunk and disinterested these days, but today was more than that. She remembered she'd shown her these pills once. Dante's brother, Antonio, had given them to her a while back when she was at Cash's ranch. They were used to reduce Murr tendencies when they wanted to go on land. Something just told Lacy that it would be today she used them. It was one of her hunches that she just couldn't ignore.

She knew Tia didn't want to renew her pledge to the king. She seemed to have turned her great love for Dante into something hatred didn't even cover. It was worse than that – an apathy that Lacy had never seen in her sister before and they'd grown pretty close. Today, she believed Tia had taken the tablets to make the exchange of essence impossible.

Lacy looked over at Dante, who looked nervous and unsettled as well. She was relieved he had taken the precaution of having Naomi, their mother, there just in case, so he must sense something as well.

Keenan came over to her. He was jittery as well, but for a different reason. He hated that she had to share the intimate process of breathing with Dante, but he was always there, no matter what it cost him emotionally. "Be in and out as quick as you can," he whispered, while he hugged her to him.

She revelled in his body warmth as she stood only in her swimsuit. "I want to wait for Tia today, Keenan … I'm worried."

Keenan followed her line of vision towards Tia, standing, staring into space, lost and alone. "I've never seen anyone look so empty," he said, shaking his head.

At that moment, the three children came running in, probably at Dante's instigation. They ran up to Tia's legs, pulling at her arms and tugging to be picked up. She crouched down to their level and hugged them, closing her eyes as if savouring the contact.

Lacy could see the tears streaming down her face. She put her hand to her mouth. "Keenan," she blurted.

He turned back to her, "What is it?"

"Tia's done something stupid … I just know it."

"Like what, Lacy? I can't stop this without something concrete."

"She's got these pills … God, she's going to hate me. What if I'm wrong?"

"What pills?" Keenan demanded, holding her by the shoulders.

"They are pills that Antonio gave her ages ago. She said the Murrs take them to get rid of their characteristics when they want to go on land."

"Fuck!" Keenan looked around while he rubbed the back of his neck, shifting from foot to foot, not knowing the best thing to do.

"I might be wrong, but look at her?"

He took a deep breath and nodded. "Ah, fuck, I'd better tell him."

"She'll hate us," Lacy said, watching Keenan walk towards Dante, and she fought back her tears.

"If she dies, we are all fucked, Lace," he said. He strode over and pulled Dante to the side. Lacy observed the worried look that appeared on Dante's face.

Then Tia must have clocked the conversation and guessed what was happening, as before anyone could get near her, she had hopped over the fountain wall and disappeared under the water.

Dante ran, flat-out, to the fountain and called Lacy and Naomi to help him. Lacy leapt over the wall and followed. As soon as they reached the sea, they quickly opened their lungs to the water.

It wasn't long before they came to Tia's body, suspended in the water, unmoving, no bubbles – nothing. Naomi took charge and asked Dante to breathe for her so they could get her back to the castle. Lacy helped hold her steady while Dante got a seal with his lips and began to breathe slowly as they swam back.

The journey seemed to take forever until eventually they passed Tia's limp body over the side of the fountain to the waiting arms of Keenan and Reeve. They laid her out on the floor and Dante got to work with CPR. It wasn't long before Tia began to cough and splutter and moan. "Leave me alone," she rasped, batting away every hand as they tried to help or touch her.

Dante ignored her feeble attempts to hit him. "Call a doctor," he called over his shoulder as he carried her towards the bedrooms.

"Human or Murr?" Keenan shouted back, holding his arms out.

"Murr."

"Come on," Keenan said to Lacy, cuddling her as they walked. The transmitter was in the study.

Dante had rummaged through Tia's stuff and then the bin and found the empty strip of pills. He rushed with it to the study where Keenan was talking to the doctor through the special brainwave converter linked with Murrtaine.

Dante placed his hand directly on a panel so it could read his thoughts without the need for speech. He projected to the Murr at the other end a picture of what the pills looked like and the symbols on the packet.

A metallic voice spoke the words that the Murr would attend the castle, and as with all overdoses, the best thing to do was to make her sick. He wasn't unduly worried about her physical well-being but more for her mental stability. Dante had already received the message in pictures and headed back to the bedroom where Tia had been taken.

When he arrived, the nurse was already there with a large bowl, tending to Tia while she threw up. "Thank you," he said, exhausted, and slumped down onto the bed to wait for the process to be over while he rubbed Tia's back.

Eventually, the nurse laid Tia back against the pillows. "She'll be all right now, I think. Let her rest, sir, but don't let her sleep for a while," she said.

When they were alone, Dante moved higher up the bed and held Tia's hand. Her eyes were puffy and red and almost closed as they rested on Dante. She was a shadow of the person he knew and loved.

She patted his hand feebly. "I'm still here for you to torment."

Dante felt tears streaming down his cheeks and rubbed them away with his fingers. "You win."

"What do I win, Dante?" she whispered. "What is there left I could possibly want?"

"Your freedom?"

A tear trickled down her face and she smiled. "Where would I go, eh?"

Dante had known she'd been depressed, but he'd never in a million years realized she'd got so bad.

Jay had warned him that she sank low at times. The last time had been when she'd left Dante after their marriage. It struck him that this was just like then, except this time she'd split up with Jay. The thought pierced his heart. "I thought you might want to spend a few months with your biologist friends in Antarctica?"

Her eyes opened wider with surprise. "I thought you'd … you know … got rid of them?"

"Fuck's sake, Tia, No … I set them up with funding in return for their silence."

She looked relieved and nodded, then visibly relaxed. "Thank you. Maybe when I'm not so tired." Her eyelids fluttered and she began to drift off.

"Stay with me," he said, shaking her. "You have to stay awake for a while."

She opened her eyes again, but he could tell it was a struggle.

"Talk to me?"

"What about?"

He could barely hear her and her eyes rolled again. "Anything – why you're so unhappy … make me understand?"

A tiny mirthless laugh escaped her, then she frowned as if searching her thoughts.

"What are you thinking?" he prompted, tapping her hand to make sure she stayed awake.

She looked at him for a few moments. "This life for Sirens, Dante, is so wrong."

"I know."

"No, hear me … you place us in shit lives in the Human world, then when we come to find out who we really are, we are not equipped to deal with it. Bloody hell, we're not even prepared for life, let alone the destiny and duty we are supposed to fulfil." Sobs began to wrack her tiny body and her hands flew to her eyes. "I'm a shit queen and a shit mother," she wailed.

Dante drew her up and against him. "Shh … no, you're not, babe … you're not."

He held her until her crying died down to a shudder every now and then. "You are right about the traditions, though," he said, picking up her hand and kissing it. "What would you do different?"

Her eyes moved away from him while she thought about it. "You can't leave them with their mother?"

He shook his head. "It's not safe for them all in the same

place. The families could steal them all, governments, any crackpot loony tune."

"So that's why they're hidden?"

He nodded again.

"What about letting each family have one ... you know, like Keenan had, so they could grow up together?"

"It's a nice idea. But it's the Orb. What if destiny dictates that they all go to the same family?"

"What, the rings?"

He nodded.

"Can you tell when they are young?"

"I think so."

"Then you could take them to each family one by one, you know ... till you find the right one."

"I think it's a good idea, unless they all belonged to the same family, which is rare. It could work, as long as everyone behaved themselves and didn't try to steal each other's. I'll bring it up with the council when it is formed." It briefly occurred to him that if the books were correct and they were in the last days, there wouldn't be any more generations of Sirens anyway, because Atlas would return. That wasn't important right now. She was talking to him and opening up, and that meant everything.

"You will?"

He kissed her hand again. "You would have preferred to have been brought up with me?" he said, amused but doubtful.

She smiled at him, for the first time in ages. "You would have got on my nerves, but I think it would have been marginally better."

He laughed out loud – partly in relief. Humour was a step in the right direction, even if it was at his expense. "I do love you, Tia. I want you to know that."

She smiled weakly. "I know ... I bear the scars to prove it."

CHAPTER 12

*I*sla, *Milan, a couple of months previously*

Malleven embraced and kissed his cousin when he arrived at lunchtime the next day and wasted no time whisking him out straight away. It was important that Antonio hid Isla until the big reveal and essential that Malleven got Cesaré drunk so he could swap his ring to work on and return it before he knew it had gone.

Malleven took Cesaré into Milan's Navigli District. It was a place they had frequented many times together.

"What's with all the cloak and dagger, Malleven?" Cesaré asked when they walked into a crowded bar.

Malleven smiled at his cousin. How blasé he was about everything. Easy for someone who had everything land in their lap without having to work for it. "I have a surprise for you, Cousin. But first, I wanted to spend some time with you. It has been too long."

Cesaré clapped him on the back and ordered two drinks. Then his eyes strayed to a leggy blonde coming out of the ladies' room to the right of the bar. He grinned at Malleven.

He hadn't changed. "No, Ches, just us tonight."

Cesaré cocked his head to the side. "You are starting to worry me now."

"Drink!" Malleven ordered. "Time enough for girls."

Cesaré did as he asked and downed his drink in one.

"Keep them coming," Malleven said to the barman.

They passed the next couple of hours chatting about old times, escapades at college and the laughs they'd had training with their serious uncle.

Malleven studied Cesaré. By now, he was half cut. He briefly considered him all over Isla as he'd seen a hundred times with girls in the past. The guy was good-looking in a grungy, surfy dude type of way. Would she respond to Cesaré as she did to him?

He dismissed the thoughts as weak. He'd soon reclaim her after and she would submit to him totally – mind, body and soul. "So what are you doing with yourself lately, Ches?" Malleven asked.

"Searching as everyone is."

"You think she will turn up in your bedroom as one of your conquests?"

Cesaré laughed easily. "Good point. No … I've been to Australia. Brisbane, then across to Perth. Then I went to California."

"All the surfing hotspots, I see … such a bore for you?" Malleven said, glancing at him sideways.

Cesaré laughed again. "She might be a surfer."

Malleven raised his eyebrows and took a swig of his drink. "You don't think she might have been kept from swimming?"

Cesaré shrugged. "Ah well, the search has been interesting."

Malleven poured another drink for each of them from an

expensive bottle he'd just ordered, careful not to let on that Cesaré was doing most of the drinking. "Have you ever thought that you might actually find one, Ches? What will you do then? Will you carry on as you are?" His whole plan rested on Cesaré unwittingly playing his part, and that meant taking it seriously.

Cesaré thought for a moment, then shook his head. "The chances of me finding one, and her being for our family, and being mine, must be several million to one."

"But if you did?" Malleven persisted.

Cesaré sighed. "Well then, I guess I'd have to grow up."

Malleven smiled. "Let's drink to growing up then," and he lifted his glass.

"To growing up," Cesaré repeated.

As soon as Malleven stumbled through the door late that night, supporting a very drunk Cesaré, he called for Antonio to help him get him to bed. Taking no chances, he popped a powder in some water and insisted that Cesaré drink it to ward off a hangover.

"You're a great friend, Malleven," Cesaré slurred, and gulped it down.

He was out cold in seconds.

Malleven removed Cesaré's divining ring from the middle finger of his left hand.

"What if he wakes?" Antonio whispered.

"He'll be out till morning ... Where is Isla?

"Asleep."

"Good. I must take a blood sample, then no one must disturb me, is that clear?"

Antonio nodded.

Malleven breezed into the room he shared with Isla. She

stirred as soon as he entered, as if he had disturbed the air currents. "Malleven?"

"Shh!" he said. "Give me your arm?"

She did as he asked. He produced a syringe, tied a band tightly above her elbow, smacked her vein and drew several small vials of blood.

She lay still, with hooded eyes, watching him work. When the job was done, he bent and kissed her properly. "As soon as it is finished, I will return," and he left her in darkness.

Isla took great care with her appearance that day. Cesaré had to be pleased with her. She decided on a tailored dress that Malleven had chosen for her in a delicate peach that made her skin look creamy and flawless. She left her blonde curls cascading, applied a little mascara and defined her lips just enough to make her look natural but rosy. All would make her clear-water blue eyes stand out.

Eventually, Malleven came for her. He paused in the doorway and let his eyes linger over her. "Good," he said. "I couldn't have chosen better myself."

She blushed and he pulled her to him, but it wasn't a hug of lovers but one of ownership, and he rubbed his thumb over the peak of her breast through her dress, making it stiffen.

He put his mouth to her ear. "If I had the time, I would fuck you before you went to him."

She was careful not to look into his eyes for fear he would do just that; her traitorous body already wept.

"Come … let me introduce you to your new mate."

Isla was pleasantly surprised when her eyes finally rested on Cesaré Florianna, third son of the main branch of the royal Florianna family. He was standing in the cool court-yard in low-slung jeans and a baggy white cotton shirt left loose.

His hair was long to his shoulders, light brown, curly and singed by the sun. His face was unshaven and his eyes were the most gorgeous shade of violet, but above all, he had a kind face, one made for laughter and not cruelty.

Cesaré turned to her as soon as she appeared in the courtyard. "Fuck, what a vision!" Then he put his hand to his mouth and asked for a pardon.

He looked at Antonio, who smiled back at him.

"May I introduce Miss Isla Snow?" Malleven said.

Cesaré walked forward immediately, picked up her hand and kissed it. "Enchanted," he said. He stepped back and took her in from the floor up, approving and nodding to Malleven.

Before Malleven spoke, he glanced at Cesaré's hand. "Look at your ring, Cesaré!"

Malleven held up his own ring and turned it around. Isla could see that his was now turquoise, where once it was purple. Cesaré was transfixed by his own, which was now the colour of ripe blueberries.

Cesaré looked stunned. He looked at Malleven, unable to speak, then back at his ring, at Isla, then he walked away and sat down. "My god. I don't believe it." Then he gabbled some-thing extremely fast in Italian. "How did you know?" he said to Malleven.

"I didn't," Malleven lied. "Isla came into my possession and I thought I would show her to you before she went to the family ... now *you* can present her."

Cesaré walked over and hugged Malleven to him, then rested his eyes on Isla. "I still can't believe it." He let go of Malleven, then came over to her, picked up her hand and stared earnestly into her eyes. They were honest eyes. "I promise to do my best to be worthy of you."

At that moment, she could think of nothing to say; she felt the lowest of the low. She just bent her head demurely as she'd seen the Japanese women do in her childhood. "And I you," she replied.

Cesaré seemed delighted with her and laughed aloud. He lifted her up under the arms and swung her round and round, clearly full of joy for the future.

*T*IA, *The Bluebell Hotel, London, present day*

Dante walked into The Bluebell a week later. "Hey!" he said to Jay, embracing him.

Jay clapped his back and ordered their usual drinks. "How's things … are you staying here?"

Dante shook his head. "Things have been bad and, no, we're not staying here."

Jay was quiet for a moment, watching him. "Tia is with you?"

"Yes, but she won't come here. I'm only here to stop over before we fly to Chile."

Jay nodded as if he wasn't surprised, but his eyebrows drew together, requesting further info.

"I gave in," Dante said with a sigh. "I'm taking her to be with her scientist friends in Antarctica."

Jay nodded again. "She's been that bad then?"

"Fuck, Jay, like you wouldn't believe. She's drunk most of the time or asleep. She's taken to sleeping with Lacy in Keenan's fucking bed."

Jay bit his lip to camouflage a smile.

"Fuck off, Jay, it's not funny."

Jay dropped the humour when he realized Dante was being deadly serious.

"Last week," he continued with difficulty. "She tried to kill herself … she's still not right," he said, looking up and shaking his head.

Jay cursed under his breath. "What did she do?"

"She had these pills that Antonio had given her at Cash's, right before she was taken."

Jay frowned. "What were they?"

"Some Murr suppressant tablet. Basically ridding her of all her Murr traits. She took the whole lot, then went into the water and almost drowned … Wait till I get my fucking hands on Antonio." Dante's fists clenched while his blood boiled just at the thought.

"Is she okay … physically, I mean?"

Jay was searching his face for an answer. It made him pause for a beat. "Sort of … she has almost no power, though. I got into the water with her just before we came here. She could barely support herself, like she had nothing in her to give, as if she were dead inside."

Dante studied Jay, rattling the ice cubes and staring into his drink. "Have you been taking your meds, Jay?"

"Yes, every day … why?"

"Oh, I dunno … I just hoped … I thought maybe she was like this because of the bond … you know, like pining or something." He watched Jay for a few more moments. "Listen, Jay, will you go see her?" Dante hedged.

"Ah fucking hell, Dante, that's not a good idea for all kinds of reasons."

"I know it's a big ask, I wouldn't, only I thought you were always her voice of reason … I'm scared, Jay." He knew he was grasping at straws, but frankly, he was running out of answers. He wondered where Jay was getting his strength from, he truly did. It *must* be the meds. He just couldn't understand it otherwise.

Jay narrowed his eyes at him as if searching his face for a

hidden agenda, and he had to admit there usually was. "If she loses her power there is no worth in her four other sisters, Jay. It has to be five. Everything depends on it … no more fucking kingdom for anyone."

"And if she can't complete her end of the bond with me, she may even die." There, he'd said it. The real truth of it; behind the tattoo, the imprisonment, every fucking thing he did where that woman was concerned. Because if she wasn't on the earth, if he lost her totally, he'd go into a tailspin that not even Jay could get him out of.

Jay sighed deeply and closed his eyes as if he were drawing on every reserve of strength. "Look, I can't promise anything. Fuck, she hates my guts now. I don't know what good it will do … All right … where are you staying?"

JAY LET himself into the best room at The Caspian; thanks to the key card that Dante had given him. The room was almost in darkness, except for a small vanity light left on a mirror over the dressing table. He walked in slowly and quietly, not wanting to startle her and not sure what he would find. His heart beat wildly, for what he didn't know. Maybe it was because he hadn't seen her for a while. Who was he kidding? The gaping great hole in his chest hurt like his heart had been wrenched out with a crowbar. Jay swallowed, got a grip and walked into the main room.

He came up to the side of the king-size bed in the centre and saw her tiny form. She was lying on her back with her head on the pillow. Her brows were pulled together, frowning even in her sleep. *God,* she looked as though she were lying in state. He fought the urge to touch her. A sheet and a blanket covered her, right up to her chin. She rarely slept with anything on her. Everything about the scene seemed wrong somehow. "Tia," he whispered. Nothing.

Jay took a deep breath, *Fuck it,* and he began unbuttoning his shirt. It was an impulse he couldn't explain, no, not an impulse, a weakness. Jay Gardiner absolutely never did weak. *He was free at last, for fuck's sake. Why on earth would he put himself in the path of the bus again?*

But when he stopped undressing and thought of waking her up or, worse still, just walking out the way he came in, it seemed impossible to contemplate. So he resumed shedding his clothes and slid under the bedclothes with her.

Jay came up next to her, reached a hand out over her abdomen and touched her gently. She moved towards him instinctively, as if she starved for his touch, but she felt cold – really cold.

Tia turned on her side and pushed herself right up against him. He felt her take in a deep breath at his neck, breathing him in.

"Jay, where have you been?" she whispered.

Heart hammering, he looked down at her. She was still asleep and probably dreaming. He'd only got in the bed to hold her and be close for some insane reason, but as she moved up against him, moaning and murmuring, his need for her seared through him as strong as it ever was. *What were those fucking meds actually doing?*

Testing her, he gently rubbed his hand all over her back and tentatively kissed her face in tiny nips until he got to her mouth, where he hovered, breathing. He brushed her lips with his a couple of times.

"Jay … are you back now?" she said so quietly he almost didn't hear her.

He ran his tongue over her lips as if in answer and she opened them slightly and he pushed his way in – invading, demanding, owning. He groaned on a curse.

She placed her arms around his back, dug in her nails and scratched him hard. When he felt her need in the sting, there was no holding back then. Jay rolled with her onto her back and pushed her arms above her head and held them at the wrists.

Jay gloried in the feel of her skin next to his, but then froze. Gone was the scorching body heat. She was as cold as she'd been at his first touch. Here he was, moving on her like he would any Human girl.

Jay leaned up on his arms and looked down on her, still frowning, sleeping face. He slowly let go of her arms. She didn't move and lay in exactly the same pose. He glanced up at her wrists. They looked dark, *were they bruised?* He touched them gently with his fingers and found them to be wet. Touching his fingers to his mouth, he tasted the wetness – blood.

He went to shake her awake and demand she explain what the fuck she'd been doing when the taste hit his tongue; or rather, the buzz hit his brain like a line of pure coke. *Fuck! What was going on?*

His heart rate jacked to a hundred and fifty. He found himself breathing hard. After a minute, it felt like his heart had stabilized, so he licked his fingers again to test it. *Whoa,* up he went again. Jay found himself grinding his pelvis into her. She responded with a groan and reached for his face with those wrists; those bloody wrists that lured him.

As she touched his cheek, he turned into the hand and kissed the palm and then lower and lower to her wrist, where he tentatively licked with the barest of touches with his tongue.

Tia moaned and pushed up with her hips, as if asking for more. He licked her again, this time longer and harder, catching any escaping rivulets that had travelled down her arm. Her other arm came up and he did the same. It was driving him wild, like having a line of coke with a Sambuca chaser, and then doing it again straight after.

Eventually, he lost all restraint and put his open mouth along the superficial cuts and just drew hard. Tia was writhing in pleasure.

Fuck, this was so wrong on so many levels, but it was the most erotic thing he'd ever done in his whole life, and always with this woman. She ensnared him.

Jay shuffled his legs between hers to widen them. She was naked; that much hadn't changed. He nudged at her while he let go of one of her arms and latched onto the other, licking with the tip of his tongue over the wound, mimicking how he kissed her intimately. She widened her legs in response. Something snapped in him and he pushed into her as hard and as far as he could in a single thrust.

She gasped.

Jay growled into her wrist. Everything felt so animalistic. He was completely out of control and so unlike himself, as if something took him over and he thrust into her in a punishing rhythm.

When he'd drained as much as he could from either wrist, he pinned them above her head again and drove her harder until he bent and bit her neck with his release. The pain seemed to drive her with him. The more he bit, the harder she came, rippling her inner muscles again and again.

He sagged on top of her. *Fuck, that was amazing.* His breathing began to return to normal and his mind cleared of the red mist that had descended. His cheek rested next to hers. She breathed against him as if she'd been running.

She turned her face to put her lips near his and sucked his lower lip into her mouth and bit it – not too hard, as if testing its consistency. She let it go. "That's really you, isn't it ..." Said as a statement, not a question.

He nodded his head slightly so she could feel him.

Before he had a chance to register what she was doing, she moved from under him and pushed him off with one hard shove. Then she pounced on him, straddling his hips and pinning his own arms either side of his head.

Jay just looked up at her, allowing her to dominate him while he studied the features of her face. Confusion was the overriding expression on it, turmoil, then pain, following shortly after.

"Jay, what are you doing here … I thought you were trying to break the bond?"

"I am … you wanna tell me why you did that to your wrists?"

She frowned, then scowled at him. "You don't get to ask me questions like that anymore, Jay."

"You didn't get hot," he said flatly.

"Didn't Dante tell you? I don't have my powers any more. So I'm useless to him. I'm just like a regular Human girl now. No breathing for anyone …" She frowned again. "You still didn't tell me why you're here?"

Jay didn't answer for a moment. *Had she really done it believing she would make herself useless to the pair of them?* It was more than the breathing thing for him, and she knew it. He loved her differences, the things that made her, her. Alien. *Had she done it in spite?* "Dante asked me to come and see you, and I wanted to see if you were okay?" he said in a low and even voice.

"So this is a pity fuck then, is it?"

"Tia … I came because I care about you … I don't know what came over me? I saw the blood … then it was all over," he said, honestly.

She let his arms go as if he'd reminded her and she looked at her wrists. He put his arms down and rubbed them over her thighs, straddling his body, and watched her face.

The cuts themselves were superficial and would heal so they could barely be noticed, but he knew the pain was on the inside, somewhere buried deep, and she needed to let it out. It wasn't the first time he'd seen it in someone.

"I've done it ever since I was young," she said absently. "It makes me feel better."

"I can help you if you like?" Jay said quietly. "You know … deal with your responsibilities, being a queen and a mother."

She stared at him in disbelief. "You're not my Protector anymore, Jay."

"I know, and I don't want to be … not your subordinate, or your servant. But I will be your friend if you want one?" He knew it was madness. The idea was to get as far away from her and Dante as was humanly possible, but try as he might, some fucker always dragged him back in.

He'd spent so much effort trying to stay away from her that it wasn't until that moment in close proximity, that everything became clear to him; exactly what he wanted. "I intend to carry on with my meds."

Tia went quiet for a beat, then narrowed her eyes. "Why didn't you ask me to release you if you weren't happy? Why did you have to be so cruel?"

Jay closed his eyes and sighed. How could he tell her that he was the fucking Atlantean version of the Anti-Christ, that he would have destroyed Dante if he'd stayed with her? Taking the king's wife, whatever the extenuating circumstances, made Dante look weak and vulnerable to be overthrown, and he couldn't do that to him. "I didn't fully understand it until the opportunity presented itself," he said, tightening his cloak of composure around himself. "I would never have used the kids against you."

"But you did, didn't you, to get me to do what you wanted. Everyone I loved turned against me that night. I was branded, imprisoned against my will, and custody of my children taken away from me."

Said like that, he had to admit it sounded bad. "What was he supposed to do, Tia?"

"You didn't have to help him … I can't believe the way you stick up for him."

He sat up, lifted her off him and got up and began dressing. "You weren't being a mother, though, were you?" He watched the words fly and hit her in the heart like a pickaxe.

Tia crawled back under the covers as if she'd only just become aware of her nakedness. "I didn't exactly choose it, Jay. I was captured in the beginning."

Jay continued to dress. He could tell she felt guilty about staying away longer than she should, so he didn't labour the point.

"Will you see JJ often?" she said, quietly.

"Yes, of course … all three of them." When he'd dressed, he sat down on the edge of the bed. "I meant what I said, Tia. I want to be there for you, but not like before. It's not me; I can't do it like that. You're married to Dante with a two-way bond; something I can only guess at. I feel half the pull you do – I'm on medication for fuck's sake and look what happens. How can I blame you for always weakening for each other?"

Jay didn't want her to try and convince him any differently to save his feelings. So he didn't elaborate on the fact that Dante could share more with her, give her more emotionally, and protect her more than he ever could. And that was the clincher, wasn't it? When push came to shove, he was just a Human. So it wouldn't matter what she said or did, he could never allow himself to be wide open and be with her on the level she needed.

"But I don't have to hang around for it. I need my freedom," he said hoarsely, standing up and sliding his arms into his expensive leather jacket. "If it's any consolation to you at all, you've ruined me for other women."

He bent down so his lips were no more than an inch from hers. "You have to find a way to be a queen and yourself, Tia … I know you don't believe it, but a lot of people love you," and he kissed her chastely on the lips.

Her hopeless eyes followed him as he straightened up. "I never wanted to be a queen."

Jay didn't answer – he had nothing left. Instead, he walked out while he could.

CHAPTER 13

Isla, Italy, a couple of months previously

Isla was to leave with Cesaré immediately. Malleven advised him to waste no time in introducing her to the family so they could decide the best course of action regarding the kingdom. From that moment, Malleven made no eye contact with her. She felt strangely cast off. *Weird.*

He spoke to Cesaré privately for about thirty minutes while she packed her few possessions. It crossed her mind how many times she'd done it before. Each time her life had changed beyond recognition afterwards.

After no time at all, she was ready to go. Malleven kissed her on the forehead like some parental guardian and told her to be well. It was all she could do not to show her amazement.

Next, she hugged Antonio. She felt real emotion when she said goodbye to him. Even though he saw her as a rival, he had been a companion and advisor to her these past months.

After farewells were made, she got into Cesaré's dust-covered red sports car. She noticed it had a little horse on the bonnet. Cesaré gabbled something fast in Italian, then after a couple of ciaos, he hopped in, started the engine and they sped away.

Isla felt exhilarated and not just because of the speed of the car. Her mind was whirling. She had actually got away. But she mustn't get ahead of herself. She could have swapped one master for another, after all, that was the routine since she'd lost her beloved sensei. The question was, how demanding would this one be?

She stole a glance sideways at him. His skin was light but tanned. He was good-looking in a 'not taken too much trouble' kind of way.

Cesaré took his blue eyes off the road and caught her studying him. He smiled. He had great teeth, too.

Realizing she'd been caught, she faced front again sharply.

"Don't be scared of me, baby … my cousin explained you haven't been around men that much?"

She looked back at him and had to school her features to remain blank. *Could it be that Malleven had actually told him she was a virgin?*

She gave a slight nod. So that was the card she would play for as long as possible. He obviously was unaware she had been with Malleven for months.

"There is supposed to be some crazy attraction between us, so I hear …" he said, grinning.

She spoke for the first time. "My life was very regimented at the facility."

He nodded. "Yeah, so I understand … Look, I know you don't know me at all, and I'm not the most … how do you say? … Upright of citizens, but you? … Well, you change everything for me, okay? I've never had a purpose before."

"You need a purpose?" she asked, genuinely interested.

"Don't you?"

She stared at him and a picture of Darres flashed into her mind. *Yes, she did.*

"Before today ... my life consisted of women and surf, with a little study squashed in between ... Now, I'll make it my life's work to be ... better," he said, and looked out of his side window as if he had become embarrassed.

She was touched by how nice he seemed and like no one else she'd met so far. "Do you fight?" she found herself asking.

He turned his face to her again and frowned.

"Spar ..." she said.

He smiled in recognition. "Why yes. I'm a little rusty, though. I've neglected it of late."

"Maybe we can train together?" she said, allowing a trace of a smile to play on her lips.

"Yes," he said softly, watching her mouth. "A good place to start." Then he laughed loudly, as if a thought had just occurred to him. "I thought the fighting came after the honeymoon."

She smiled, not really getting the joke.

"Hey ... I can show you some Florianna tricks. We are known as the family of powers, you know?" he said, in a mysterious voice.

She smiled again at his playfulness.

"That's it, babe. You don't smile much, do you?"

She looked at the winding road ahead. *I haven't had much reason to as yet.*

*T*IA, *present day*

Dante was brooding over his drink at the bar when Jay returned. Jay sat on the stool next to him without saying a word. Dante ordered two drinks, then looked at Jay intently, waiting for him to speak.

Jay downed his drink in one. "Shall we go out? I feel like getting on it tonight."

Dante raised his eyebrows but agreed. He decided that Jay's peculiar mood shouldn't be prodded at this stage. "Let's go then." And went to get off his stool.

"I need a quick shower and change before we go."

"I'll come up with you," Dante said, frowning, his hackles rising with Jay's troubling, hostile attitude.

"Whatever," Jay replied, already walking away.

The two of them went up in the lift and went into Jay's room on the top floor. Dante went straight to the armchair in the corner, sat in silence and watched Jay pull a clean shirt from his wardrobe. "You gonna tell me what happened?" he said, eventually.

Jay began taking off his shirt. "Well, you're right about her hating us both," Jay said. He flung his dirty shirt on the bed and went to walk towards his bathroom.

"Well, one of us, evidently," Dante said, his temper building quietly, slowly standing up.

Jay turned, his head weary and hung low. "Are we starting something, Dante?"

"Have you seen your back?"

Jay backed up to his full-length mirror and blushed when he saw the deep-red scores on each side of his back, across his shoulder blades.

He looked red-faced over at Dante and almost laughed. "She was asleep when I got there."

Dante walked over to his old friend and stood no further than a foot away from him, his fists clenching and unclenching. "So you fucked her …" he said flatly.

Jay's face hardened and he closed the gap so they were nose to nose. "What can I say? What do you expect when you leave her unattended?"

Dante laughed in a humourless blast, recognizing the

echo of his own words once said to Jay. Then any humour left him suddenly. "I sent you there to help her."

Jay sighed, taking a step back and leaning his weight on one leg. "Look, if we are gonna start," he said, moving his hand to and fro between them, "then let me ask you this first: did you know she self-harmed?"

Dante's face creased in disbelief. "What are you talking about?"

"She cuts herself … she'd done it just before I got there."

Dante stood down from his confrontational stance, the wind gone out of him, and sat back down in the armchair. He leaned forward, pushing his fingers through his hair. "How long has she been doing that?" *How could he have missed it?*

"Since she was a child, I think." Jay sat opposite him now; the stuffing had been knocked out of him.

"She has no power?" Dante asked.

Jay shook his head. "She didn't even overheat when we …" And he trailed off.

"Fuck, that's bad." Dante pinched the bridge of his nose and tried to think. "I don't know what to do?" Dante said, throwing his hands down.

"For what it's worth, I think her loss of power is psychological," Jay said.

Dante shrugged, not convinced.

"There is still power in her blood."

Dante looked up sharply. "How would you know unless you? …"

Jay nodded. "I couldn't help myself, I tasted it by mistake. But then it fucking possessed me like a demon. It was supercharged or something. It blew my mind."

"Oh fuck, Jay." Dante stood and began pacing. "You must never do that again, okay?"

"Okay, but I don't understand … you have vampires, don't you?"

"Yes, but they only do the necessary ... between mates as it's against the law ... And you've blown the effectiveness of your meds," Dante said, as the thought occurred to him. "It's like giving an alcoholic a drink, for fuck's sake, Jay."

"Don't worry, it won't happen again ... I intend to continue them. Nothing's changed."

Dante just stared at him as if what he said just didn't compute. The fact that Jay could make love to the woman he loved and then walk away again.

"I offered to be her friend rather than her Protector," Jay said, interrupting his thought process.

"Did she go for that?"

Jay shrugged. "I don't know, I left it with her ... but one thing I realized, Dant, we've got to stop fucking with her head. No more stupid games between us," he said, moving his hand between them again.

Dante nodded, convinced it was the right thing to do.

"And where is Cash and Sean?" Jay said.

Dante rubbed his forehead. "I stopped them seeing her. I can do that when she's with me."

"Let her have them, they are good guys."

Dante nodded. "Shall I still let her go to Antarctica?"

"I would say yes. Tell her it's time to get her act together, and when she's ready to come back, things will be different."

Dante nodded with a new resolve, glad to have a plan. "I will."

"You know she thinks we only want her for the breathing thing?" Jay added.

Dante frowned. *Surely not.* Then shook his head as the words sank in. He stood and motioned for Jay to do the same. He pulled him into a hug. Dante breathed into his friend's shoulder while he thought on what he'd learned. The faint smell of Tia was all over him, but he hugged him hard and smacked his back. "We'll do it, won't we? Somehow, Brother?"

Jay nodded into his shoulder.

When they pulled apart, they both had tears in their eyes.

Isla, Italy, a couple of months previously

It took an hour and a half for Cesaré to drive north to yet another Florianna villa situated on Lake Como. They drove through the black iron electric gates and onto the shingle drive that swept up to the spectacular sand colour building covered in vines and balconies. Pink and red flowers dotted the shrubs in the borders and trees offered precious shade.

The car followed the path that swept around a beautiful classical fountain strategically placed in front of the huge wooden double doors, where Cesaré slowed the car to a standstill. "Here we are," he said quietly, smiling.

Isla looked into his smiling eyes. *Could anybody's face be more different to Malleven's?*

"How long will we be here?" she said, to break the awkward silence more than anything.

"Chill out, babe. We'll stay here and get to know each other for a couple of weeks," and he touched her chin. "It'll give me time to notify all my family. They'll all want to meet you." He held up his ring. "They'll want to see for themselves … then we'll work out what to do from there."

"What's to work out … Aren't I going to the king?" It came out of her mouth a little too quickly.

He turned in his chair more to face her, "We have to decide as a family how we play it, Isla. We are every bit as powerful as the Dubonnettis."

She frowned. "Play what?"

"Whether we choose to back the king or not."

Her heart was beating wildly. It had never occurred to her

that there was a chance she wouldn't be going to Ireland ... did it Malleven? *What if he came and retrieved her if she didn't?*

She swallowed hard.

"Come, let's go in," Cesaré said, opening the car door.

Isla got out, stony-faced. How sick she was of never being in control of a single thing in her life

ISLA WAS grateful when Cesaré showed her to her own room. She put her clothes away in her wardrobe and changed into her swimming costume and robe. Cesaré said they had a pool there. It had been a long time since she'd swum and she found she missed it more and more. Darres popped into her head again for a second. She sighed, dismissed the thought and left her room to join Cesaré downstairs.

He was in the kitchen and smiled as soon as he saw her. He fixed them both drinks in his easy, relaxed way. "Are you going to show me some of your moves then?"

"What, now?"

"Why not?"

"Where?"

"Follow me. There's space out by the pool."

Isla walked behind him as he led the way outside. His lean, tanned body was naked except for worn cut-off jeans. He was covered in the now-familiar Atlantean tattoos. She recognized the Florianna crest; Malleven had one identical.

They walked over to a patio on the other side of the large, inviting rectangular pool.

"Here will do," Cesaré said, and kicked off his flip-flops.

She dragged her eyes away from the water, took off her robe and did the same. "Do you have a style?"

"Nope ... a bit of everything ... I'm kind of a lover, not a fighter," he said, with a large grin. He put up his fists in an exaggerated pose of a boxer. "What training have you had?"

"Erm … Shotokan karate, hand to hand, knives, swords, firearms," she replied, matter-of-factly.

He frowned and put his guard down for a second, then put them back up. "Go easy on me, okay?"

She nodded once, then moved so fast he didn't see her flip and quickly unzip his fly. She landed back into her ready stance.

"What? he said, holding his arms out.

She nodded at his crotch area with one eyebrow up.

He looked down and saw what she'd done, laughed and pulled the zipper back up. "You're fast, I'll give you that, but you only had to ask, baby."

The smile dropped from her face. She wasn't used to playful sexual banter. She simply didn't know how to react to it.

"My turn," he said, his grin turning even more mischievous, if that were possible.

Having no clue what he would do next, she readied her stance again. She watched him glance around the garden, looking for inspiration. Then she saw they rested on a lemon tree growing nearby.

He grinned wider. Then, quick as a flash, three lemons came hurtling towards her at once. She only just batted them away in time; she was so surprised by him. "That's not fair."

"Florianna tricks," he reminded her, laughing.

It took her back to the skills her sensei possessed, and with a grim realization she finally understood how Malleven always managed to get the better of her. "Can you show me how?"

"Of course," he said, walking towards her in his easy gait. "It's just a matter of visualization and concentration." He circled her as he spoke until he was standing directly behind her and bending his head down to look over her shoulder. "Look at the small flower pot over there … Imagine it lifting."

He gently lifted her arm with his so it was pointing towards the pot. "Until you become well practised, centre your energy along your arm, through your finger, to the base of the pot."

Cesaré held her arm and she was acutely aware of the contact. He was very distracting, breathing next to her ear. She shook herself out of it and focused again on the pot and concentrated hard.

Nothing happened at first. Then the pot wobbled a bit. The effort was enormous. She strained; sweat beaded on her brow until the pot fell over.

"Well done," Cesaré said, laughing next to her cheek. He went to bring his arms around to hug her and she adeptly side-stepped away from him. She couldn't go down that slippery slope. If she ended up kissing him, her life would get even more complicated and her conscience was pricking her enough where he was concerned.

Cesaré stood with his hands on his hips and shook his head as if he'd been punched. Then smiled slyly at her. "You know you make me want you more when you play hard to get?"

She turned her head to him. That wasn't what she was going for at all.

"Still, I like a challenge," he added.

She sagged. It seemed her life was complicated already. It was going to be harder than she thought keeping him at arm's length.

The sunny days passed quickly for Isla, despite the waiting. Cesaré was a very easy person to be around, always kind and friendly.

Each morning she woke, swam and trained with him. He helped her practise her telekinesis and she was getting much better at it. Soon, she was levitating a lemon two inches from the ground and holding it for a count of ten.

In the afternoons, she would rest, then Cesaré would take her out shopping or walking or just to a pleasant alfresco café. Life with Cesaré was a welcome respite for a while.

Today, they had decided to stay in the pool, as it was just too hot. It gave Isla the opportunity to study Cesaré's stripes. They followed a very different pattern to hers and were a lighter colour grey.

Cesaré caught her eyes on him. "You like them?" he said quietly, swimming up closer.

"They are different to mine."

"Yes. You are from a different family. You are Bonaci."

She longed to ask so much, but was frightened of slipping up. She ventured a little. "And Malleven … is he the same as you? He is so dark."

"Yes, but his genes are a little more diluted than mine. His mother was Florianna and his father was a common Atlantean from Southern India."

She absorbed the information like a sponge. She'd had little interaction with Malleven other than the physical. "Can you breathe the water?" she asked.

Cesaré shook his head and sank low in the water, coming even closer. "I'm hoping you will initiate me."

Her eyes went wide; she didn't like the sound of that.

He turned away from her. "Forget it. I have said too much." Then he laughed, turning back to her. "And you'll be lucky to get Malleven in the water. He hates it."

This surprised her, but when she thought back, there were no pools in his homes, and knowing his love of fine things, he was bound to have one. Even so, she couldn't imagine anything bothering Malleven. "Really?" she said.

"Yeah. Between you and me, I think it scares him."

Isla remembered the nightmares Malleven had repeatedly. Always underwater and always where he couldn't breathe. He must have been drowning.

ALMOST TWO WEEKS HAD PASSED. Unfortunately, she was really beginning to like Cesaré. He was a hopeless womanizer and she caught his eyes straying several times. He would simply pull his eyes back to her with a polite "Scusi", like a naughty boy and make her smile. It didn't feel like she was a prisoner at all.

Although as time went on, whenever she started to relax, she would remember that she must get to Ireland to find Darres and, more importantly, get there to work for Malleven, otherwise he was going to come to this oasis and drag her back. The thought alone made her shudder.

Cesaré broke through her brooding. "Come, let's take a nap," he said, leading her up out of the pool and wrapping a towel around her. "Too much sun isn't good for your beautiful pale skin." She reluctantly followed him up the grand staircase to bed.

CHAPTER 14

*I*sla's heart was in her mouth when Cesaré took her to her room. He didn't go back to his own but told her to change into something dry, and she found him lying on her bed with just a towel around his waist when she came out of the bathroom.

She stopped short when she saw him resting on an elbow, waiting for her. He patted the bed next to him. "Let's take a nap together today, Isla," he said.

Taking small steps, she slowly went over to the bed. She pulled her T-shirt down over her knickers and crept onto the bed a little way off from him.

"Come nearer, baby … I won't hurt you … I promise."

Isla moved over a little bit. He did the same and made up the difference so he was close enough to look down on her face. He studied her for a bit. "Did somebody hurt you, baby?" he said.

A lump rose in her throat and she barely held it down with her overwhelming need to cry. She just nodded.

"I would never hurt you, okay?"

She nodded again.

Cesaré leaned down, put his lips on hers and kissed her gently, closed-mouthed. He hovered to let her get used to him there.

Her heart bled at the tenderness of it. She squeezed her eyes shut, not able to look at him or think too deeply about what he was doing.

"Look at me, baby," he was saying.

She opened her eyes.

"It's just a kiss." He kissed her again, but this time he ran his tongue along the seam of her lips. He was so gentle and coaxing. "Open for me," he whispered.

Isla did as he asked and his tongue ventured tentatively into her mouth. He touched and swirled it with hers. He murmured and deepened the kiss and rolled his body onto hers.

Her hands moved up the smooth skin of his back and threaded into his hair. She pulled him to her and began to kiss him hungrily.

Cesaré murmured Italian words under his breath and kissed and bit down the column of her neck. While his mouth explored, she found she was panting. *My god, what was she doing?*

If she slept with him now it wouldn't alter the fact that she was helping his friend and cousin to trick him into taking the kingdom for him. And here she was, kissing him and gaining his trust and acting like a prostitute.

Carefully she pulled her hands down to her chest and pushed them between their bodies. She screamed, "Get off me!" and pushed with all her strength. He rolled off without hesitation. She jumped up and stood sobbing. Her emotions were so near the surface they just overflowed.

"I'm sorry, Isla, truly I am. I thought you were ready."

The look of misery on his face and kind words only made her feel worse at being the cause and she cried harder.

He got up slowly off the bed and went to the door, where he paused. "I won't touch you again unless you want me to. I'm sorry." With a face torn in anguish and confusion, he left the room.

Isla threw herself face down on the bed and cried her miserable heart out. *How much more could she take.*

TIA, London, present day

Tia was in the bath when Dante got back to their hotel room. He took one look at the bed and ordered housekeeping to come and change the sheets.

Dante was sitting on the newly made bed in the dimly lit room when Tia came out of the bathroom, all pink from a *hot* bath with no stripes on her body at all. In his hands were the bandages and ointment he'd taken from Jay's.

He wasted no time. "Show me your wrists."

Tia went to him and did as she was told without complaint. He examined them, hating that he'd never noticed the scarring before. Guess that was why she'd made a fashion accessory out of her sweatbands. He shook his head bitterly. There were about six to eight superficial cuts on each wrist, surrounded by bruising. Gently, he rubbed the ointment over them and bandaged each wrist in the crisp white linen, then finished them with a small knot.

Every now and again, he glanced up at her face, watching him quietly. "Come and lie down. I want to talk to you," he said, pulling her onto the bed with him.

He shed his clothes down to his boxers and she dropped her towel. They lay facing each other with their head on a pillow.

"I'm sorry," she said eventually. "I was asleep."

Dante put a finger to her lips. "Shh ... I know ... he's a slippery bastard."

"He told you?" she said, in dismay.

"We talked … I want me and you to talk … I want you to feel you can talk to me, Tia."

"About what? …"

"You know, I could do with someone to talk to as well sometimes?" he said.

"You have Jay, don't you?" she said.

"We're not as close as we were," he said, with a sigh.

She swallowed and dipped her eyes.

"It's not your fault," he said and he lifted her chin to look at him again. "I'm not strong like Jay you know?"

She frowned. "Yes you are … in a lot of ways," she added.

"You've been cutting since you were a child?" he said, holding her arm up gently so as not to hurt it.

She nodded.

"I used to self-destruct with drink and drugs as soon as I was old enough to get hold of them. And that was easy in my family … you see, we're more alike than you think … Did you get beaten?" he asked.

She nodded. "Usually for getting caught underwater in the bath, or singing along to a pop song."

Dante felt his eyes misting over and he blinked the moisture away. What a miserable life she'd had. "I used to get beaten by my father. Now it all makes sense. He probably had an idea I wasn't his."

"My brothers would tell me to cry so he would stop quicker, but the only control I had was to infuriate him by not letting him break me … and then I'd escape the shit by getting out of it as often as possible, which lowered his opinion of me even more.

"Then, when I was about seven or eight, he brought Jay home. I picked on him something unmerciful, initially out of jealousy, because my dad loved him. But Jay was always a shrewd kid and he soon cottoned on to my dad's treatment of me and he never once grassed me up for being unbeliev-ably cruel to him.

Dante laughed to himself. "And when he stood up to me after weeks of putting up with me, and beat ten barrels of shit out of me, I started to warm to him."

Tia smiled at that.

"Then I remember one day we went into the village to get some sweets at the local shop, and a group of local lads all started picking on him because he was English and making fun of his accent and the fucker offered them all out."

Tia giggled. He knew she could just imagine Jay doing something like that, all red and fierce. "What did he say?" she said, her eyes glistening.

Dante did his best Jay impression. "'Come on then, you Irish fuckers,' he shouted at them. I was stood there amazed with me mouth open, 'I'll have the fucking lot of ya' he went on … and he kicked and punched spinning like a whirling dervish."

"What did you do?" Tia asked, her eyes shining.

"Me, well, I watched in amazement for a bit till some big kid got a lucky shot in and split Jay's lip, so I waded in to help him. There was two of us against six, and we pasted 'em …"

Dante was lost in his memory for a moment, then focused back on Tia. "I remember, when they ran off threatening to tell the garda, me and Jay just stood there out of breath, looking at each other. Swollen eyes, split lips and cut knuck-les, but we knew at that moment that we had an understand-ing." Dante sighed and shook his head. "And we've had it ever since." He blinked his tears away and saw that Tia had them as well.

He wiped hers away with his fingers and placed one next to her temple, tapping it gently. "Can I speak to you in here?"

She hadn't let him do that in ages, blocking him every time he'd tried.

She nodded. "I don't want to shag though," she said, as if the thought just occurred to her.

Dante laughed out loud. "You are so classy when it comes to sex, Tia. That's what I love about you … you're like a bloke."

She laughed with him. "Okay. As long as you remember." Then she closed her eyes and waited.

A second later, Dante walked into her mind's eye space. It was always a black expanse with a large bed in the middle of it, lit from above. He looked so tribal in his fully transformed state, completely naked and stripy.

He came and sat on the bed with her and pointed down at her arms. "That's a good sign."

She glanced down at herself and saw she looked as Atlantean as he did. "I'm stripy … that means?"

"That means that if your mind still sees you like that, then maybe Jay was right."

"Right about what?"

"That your problem isn't physical."

"He thinks I'm a fruitcake," she said, wounded.

Dante laughed. "We're all fruitcakes, babe." He pulled her down to lie with him on the mind's eye bed, which strangely had leopard-print sheets on it. He gathered her to him so her head was on his chest and a leg over his. "Does this mean you've got a thing for leopard print?" he said, pointing down at the bed.

"I don't know," she said, laughing. "Weird though, isn't it?"

They were quiet for a while.

"So why did you want to come in here?" she said, sheepishly, still waiting for the recriminations for sleeping with Jay.

"I wanted to see your skin, and I wanted to see if you'd let me."

"Oh," she said, nodding, relieved.

They were quiet again.

"Jay said I need to find a way to be a queen and myself," she said, eventually.

"He's right, but only you can work that one out."

"Will you help me though, Dante ... be a good queen, I mean?" she said, looking up into his face. The only thing that had ever come easy to her in her life before was DJing. In fact, even being a mother filled her with self-doubt.

He looked down at her with something like adoration. "I'd love to ... anything."

She nestled into him again. Dante always made her feel so safe and secure. Something she never questioned was his love for her.

"It's not going to be easy, though, Tia, I'm bound to make mistakes. It's kinda like the blind leading the blind, ya know?" he said, glancing down at her through half-closed eyelids.

Gazing back at him, her heart thawed a little more. Underneath the surface, he really didn't recognize the hard-working, competent king he was becoming. *Tinged with madness.* "You've done really well so far." And she meant it. "Well, except branding my arse."

Dante laughed. "I *was* sorry about that, but it wasn't all about stopping you running, you know?"

She sat up to look at him more squarely. "What was it then?"

"It's about letting everyone know you're mine."

Her heart sank a little. *Yeah, property of the state.*

Dante frowned as if she wasn't getting it at all. "Look, I wanted you to feel what I feel when I see it on you, so I had one done for you as well. But it might not? " He was twisting his hip around so they could both see.

Strangely, when she looked down at the left-hand side of the top of his thigh, it was the only one of his many tattoos that came through to be seen in her mind's eye. "Wow, what is it?" She recognized her name amongst the black swirls and arcs, but that was about it.

"It is the Bonaci crest. There's your name and I put my name with yours. And see the three crowns underneath?"

"The kids!" she squealed. "Even little JJ."

"Of course little JJ, I see him as the same as the other two."

She reached up and kissed him hard on the lips. "Thank you for that. I love that you love him like that."

Dante held her fast when she went to pull away. "It's not hard. He's Jay's mini-me, after all," he said softly.

She smiled and their eyes locked for a long moment.

"So you don't mind yours so much if I've got one?" he whispered.

"No, I don't," she said, actually quite surprised at herself, never having been a tattoo person.

"When I get back from my trip, I'll try to be better … I'll try to make your life easier … But it doesn't mean you can take the piss," she added.

He squeezed her to him. "Thanks, babe … but don't change too much, part of me enjoys fighting with you."

She grinned, "I'll do my best." She knew that was the truth. Despite his growing serious side, the mischievous one was never far below the surface.

As if proving her point, he looked down at her through half-closed eyes. "You sure you don't fancy a shag?"

She punched him playfully, causing him to double over. They rolled around laughing and play-fighting like children until they were in a tangle with the sheet, out of breath.

Dante's face got serious for a moment. "Come to me to talk in future, Tia, okay … No matter what it is?"

"Thank you," she said, nodding. She felt as though she had learned a new side to Dante tonight.

Instead of kicking off because she'd had sex with Jay,

albeit unwittingly, he'd come to her when she was at her lowest and asked for nothing for himself. He even shared some of his own secrets and worries with her, and that was the most precious thing he'd ever given her. She felt he'd become a true friend tonight instead of just a lover.

Weirdly, Jay had made himself the opposite, and she never thought she'd say that. Despite protesting he wanted to be her friend, tonight Jay had turned himself into a fuck-buddy.

She studied Dante's stripy face next to her and traced a finger along the savage lines under his cheekbone and thought she would never have predicted this outcome.

Slowly, they drifted out of her mind and into their conscious bodies. She looked down at herself, neatly lying in Dante's lap, so he was spooning her, with his arms linked around her waist.

She lifted the sheet to check and saw their matching tattoos.

"Do you like it now?" he asked, sounding sleepy.

"It's growing on me."

He nuzzled into her shoulder and neck. "I know something else that's growing on you."

ISLA, Italy, five weeks previously

The Florianna elders had been arriving throughout the day. When they were all assembled in the library, Isla had been presented proudly by Cesaré. Never had she felt so nervous in her life before. Despite feeling degraded like a slave at the market, so much depended on their accepting her.

She watched with her heart in her mouth as they all mumbled words of wonder and appreciation and looked down at their left hands at their turquoise rings. Cesaré's father nudged him to hold his hand up high so all assembled could see that his was the deep purple required to be a Siren's mate. Then, just like that, she was led from the room.

When they reached the large hallway, Cesaré picked up both her hands. "I have to go back in alone, Isla."

She frowned up at him. "Aren't I permitted to know what's going to happen to me?"

"Of course," Cesaré said, smiling kindly. "I'll tell you as soon as it is decided." And with that, he left her and went back into the room.

Isla was left standing there, gobsmacked. To think that room of strangers held her future in their hands.

The door hadn't fully clicked shut. Looking to either side of her, she crept over to the door. Putting her ear to the gap, she could just about make out the deep Italian voices, but her heart sank when she realized the whole conversation had switched to Italian and she understood very little.

Just before she went to turn away, something – a sixth sense made her freeze to the spot. The hairs on the back of her neck began to rise and tingle. Beads of perspiration appeared on her brow. Someone was standing directly behind her.

CHAPTER 15

"Have they decided anything yet, Snowflake?" Malleven's voice purred so close to her ear. "Alas I am quite late for proceedings."

She shook her head.

"Turn around," he ordered.

She turned slowly with her eyes still downcast.

Without a word, he grabbed her roughly by the arm and pulled her with him along the hallway, through a small door to the servants' staircase and shut the door behind them.

He shoved her forcefully against the wall and pinned her there with his larger body. "Has he taken you yet?" he whispered, with his mouth millimetres from hers.

She shook her head, unable to speak to him.

"Answer me, woman," he said, grabbing her coarsely between the legs and making her gasp.

"No, he hasn't touched me," she blurted. "Malleven, someone will see."

"Yes…" he said, grinding his hips into her and biting her earlobe. "Delightfully dangerous, isn't it?" And he spun her round and slammed her face against the wall.

All she could do was gasp as he lifted her skirt and pulled her panties out of the way, unzipped his own fly and plunged deeply into her.

Malleven stilled. "Shh," he said at her ear. "You must hold in your cries, Snowflake." Then he proceeded to pump into her mercilessly and repeatedly. Harder and harder while she panted and he moaned. One hand held her hips in a vice-like grip and the other roughly held one of her breasts.

It took little more than five minutes before his skilled fingers found its way and circled her engorged bud and her climax reared up on her and consumed her, causing her to fall back into him in complete surrender. He laughed exultantly when her body milked him and he bit her shoulder hard and ground himself into her when his own release overtook him.

Malleven stood still for just a few moments, composing himself, and zipped his trousers back up. Then he turned her to face him, pulled her skirt back down and arranged her blouse for her. "There … a virgin again," he said, smiling.

Sickened, she finally brought her desolate eyes up to meet his. "I can't hold him off for much longer," she said flatly, in the hope it would wound him.

His mouth quirked at the corners slightly as if he knew the words were said in spite. "Then you will have to fuck him, won't you." he said, kissing her roughly, then whispering at her ear, "I will enjoy reclaiming you." Then he pushed her towards the servants' stairs and smacked her behind. "Go. Use the servant's staircase. You can get to your room at the other side of the house."

She turned back to look at him, bewildered.

"Go!" he ordered.

She scurried up the stairs, barely containing her tears. *Would she never escape him?* Her own body's constant surrender to him was its own profound misery.

She stopped abruptly on the last stair, almost bumping into the maid, Petra, standing there.

"Pardon!" Petra said, and bobbed a curtsey.

Isla couldn't speak but quickly skirted her and ran back to her room.

WHEN MALLEVEN APPEARED AGAIN from the small doorway into the hall, Cesaré had just come out of the library and caught him with a hand on his shoulder.

"Where have you been, you old dog?" Cesaré joked, with a look of mock suspicion on his face.

Malleven never missed a beat and just straightened his tie. "Your maid pounced as soon as I arrived … I couldn't disappoint, Cousin," he said, with a faint smile.

Cesaré laughed in his easy way and nodded on a sigh. "Ah yes, I have neglected her of late!" "Come, let us get a drink … I'll bring you up to speed," and he put his arm around Malleven's shoulders and steered him to the gardens.

They settled with their cool drinks beneath a natural canopy of canes and vines, which made a perfect shady spot.

Malleven sipped his drink as cool as ever, watching Cesaré with interest and waiting for him to speak.

"What has been decided?" Malleven asked, eventually.

"We will watch and wait … see how the new king conducts himself."

Malleven conceded a nod. "They are considering making their own bid?" Nothing he hadn't thought of already. Either way, he intended to stay in the shadows until the eleventh hour.

"His Siren is still causing him major problems; living with his best friend and brother, then taking herself off to one place after another. She has far too much freedom."

Malleven raised an eyebrow. He'd enjoy bringing that one to heel. "What of the sister?"

"She seems happily mated and pledges willingly to the king."

Malleven nodded thoughtfully. "So the elders wait for stability?" It was understandable. They wouldn't just hand over something as precious as their Siren to an incompetent king. And they wouldn't make their own bid without sufficient evidence of his incompetence.

"I won't let her go to a man who can't keep his own house in order," Cesaré echoed.

Malleven imperceptibly blanched at Cesaré's thinking that Isla was his to give or keep at will. Still, his cousin's seriousness surprised him. "My cousin has finally grown up," he said, with a hint of a smile.

Cesaré grinned. "Had to happen sometime."

The two of them remained quiet for a few moments. Malleven itched to know the state of affairs in the bedroom between Cesaré and Isla. He chose his words carefully. "You are happy, Ches … with your beautiful Siren … is she all she was promised to be?" Malleven prodded mischievously, thinking of his body pounding into her soft, lush wetness at the bottom of the stairs only a few minutes before.

Cesaré's face got serious and he shook his head. "She means much to me, Malleven, but I am yet to touch her."

Malleven frowned in mock concern. "But I thought the attraction between a Siren and her mate was impossible to resist?"

Cesaré sighed. "I am unsure what has happened to her before she came to me, but she is not ready yet." Then he visibly shook himself out of his doldrums. "Never fear, Cousin, it is only a matter of time … she has simply made herself a more desirable challenge."

Malleven smiled broadly and held up his glass in salute. "Let us drink to that … to bedding your Siren."

Cesaré laughed, saluted back and knocked back his drink in one gulp.

Dante and Tia travelled on the royal Dubonnetti plane, the long distance to Punta Arenas, Chile, asleep most of the way. The only time they woke was to eat, drink and for bathroom breaks. Dante spent the whole journey in the secret space of Tia's mind's eye.

They discovered that the earphones they shared, playing music Tia had previously mixed, could be heard while they slept in their suspended state, giving them a soundtrack to their frolicking and conversations.

"Why can't you be with me always so we can be happy like this?" Dante asked, trailing his finger along the stripe on her cheek as they reclined naked on the leopard-print sheets.

She stared into his eyes earnestly. "I feel happy like this because you are letting me go."

He nodded and pulled her tighter into his body. "I know, babe, but me and the kids can't help missing you."

It was a blow straight to her heart; one he didn't mean, but the children were a constant source of guilt to her. All mothers felt guilt one way or another, but for her, it was because she was never good enough. She just didn't feel equipped. The fact that they were now looked after and cosseted by nurses and nannies only seemed to compound it.

As precious as her children were to her, to be any use to them at all, she had to get her head straight. About being an Atlantean, a queen and a mother, her fucked-up feelings for Jay, who no longer wanted her, as well as never being able to call her life her own ever again. A life she'd fought so hard to win, from her miserable childhood, to her short spell in prison for killing Dannyl, her first Protector, who'd abused his position in what felt like a lifetime ago. Everything had turned to shit and become so messed-up that she didn't know what was up any more. The only way she could sort out the mess in her head was to get right away; only it had become a pattern. This time had to be the last.

Tia felt bad about leaving Dante, too. She knew he was quiet, thinking the journey would soon be over and he would have to leave her for two, maybe three months, possibly never regaining this closeness between them.

Eventually, their time was up and they awoke when the stewardess gently shook them on landing, and they organized themselves, ready to face real life. It had been a blessing spending the journey in their private intimacy, but they knew they couldn't stay there forever.

"What is Lacy's mind's eye space like?" she asked, as the thought occurred to her.

"You'd have to ask Keenan. I never go in. I just project thoughts … apart from the time you were with me and we were searching for her memories."

She nodded, remembering the occasion. She didn't know why that knowledge pleased her so much, but it did.

It was time to leave the comfort of the private jet and transfer to the plane, which would fly them to McMurdo Sound, and change again to Anvers Island, to the little research station, remote and safe enough for Dante to leave her there.

The journey was exhausting, but eventually they walked down the steps of the tiny plane to the icy wind whipping their faces. Four anorak-swaddled men waited a few feet away as they stepped down. Tia was so excited to be there.

Josh and Ben were the first to step forward and greet her. She flung her arms around their necks; tears scalded her face in the cold as she kissed them both fiercely, never expecting to see either of them again.

They both shook Dante's hand. "Nice to see you again, Your Highness," Josh said.

Dante nodded. "And you."

Tia could tell all he was thinking was to get into the warm; cold-water creature though he was, he wasn't used to this cold.

Tia's eyes drifted over to the two other men, smacking their arms around themselves and shuffling their feet to keep warm. They both grinned back at her through the fur of the hoods of their parkas.

Tia screamed in recognition when she realized who they were and threw herself at them. Cash and Sean enveloped her in a three-way hug.

"For fuck's sake, do that indoors," Dante cut in, wanting to speed things along so he could get warm.

DANTE AND TIA were shown into the main entrance at Palmers and relaxed into the immediate warmth as the door closed behind them.

"Is there somewhere private we can talk before I leave?" Dante asked Ben and Josh.

"Of course. This way." They showed them through some double doors and down a corridor to a meeting room. "Your other friends have arrived already, sir. Your instructions for their comfort have been followed," Ben said.

Tia looked at Dante, intrigued.

"Good," was all he said. "Perhaps you could settle Tia into where she is going to be staying?" Dante said to Cash and Sean.

"Sure," Cash said, guessing Dante didn't want Tia privy to what was being said and led her off in the direction of the bed dorms. Their guardsmen trooped off to the canteen.

When Dante walked into the meeting room, Vionne was already sitting there with two Murr companions. Vionne was the eldest son of the Borge family and a prince of Murrtaine. Dante had requested that he meet them there, as a Murr outpost existed not far from Antarctica, and would act as a perfect point of contact in case Tia had any kind of emergency while she was there.

Vionne had agreed, as it was a good opportunity to visit his outpost and also build on his diplomatic ties with the new king, his cousin.

Vionne stood and greeted Dante in the Murr way of mind projection, having no vocal cords. He then introduced him to the two Murrs with him, permanently stationed at Murrla – the outpost nearby.

Dante was surprised to learn that one of them – Axyl – was Vionne's brother. He would have liked to ask why he didn't mind being stuck all the way out here, but as usual, Vionne read him perfectly and answered the question: *Axyl is a twin. We lost our brother many years ago, when he was just a small lad. He prefers it here.*

Forgive me. Have you all been treated well? Dante asked, kicking himself for his straying thoughts.

Vionne smiled, *Yes, very well, thank you.*

Dante knew that Murrs could not stand well when they first came out of long periods of time in the water. Their legs extended and their bones became flexible for swimming efficiently. When they came out of water they needed an hour or two for their legs to compact and set into shape before they could put much weight on them. Ben and Josh had also seen to it that some extra-large clothes were made available to them, as their own were specifically designed for the water and would draw too much attention to them.

Dante joined them, sitting at the table and Josh brought steaming cups of coffee for each of them. Ben broke the silence, "Josh and I wanted to thank you, Your Highness, for your generous donation to enable us to continue our research here."

"You know it comes at a price?" Dante said, his face hard. "And repercussions should the queen's safety be compromised in any way?"

They both nodded nervously. "Everyone has been told she is a student of ours."

Vionne projected something to Dante, to which he smiled and nodded. "My cousin has just reminded me of what a livewire my wife can be. You need to be watchful, she doesn't give herself away."

"We will watch her carefully," both men said.

Vionne passed Dante a small box.

The two biologists watched with curiosity.

Dante opened it, revealing six vials of the clear Elixir liquid. "These are a precautionary measure."

Ben and Josh looked at each other and back at Dante in confusion.

"You must drink one of these now, then again in five days, then repeat."

Ben reached over and pulled the box to his side of the table. "Can we ask what it's for?"

Dante shuffled in his seat, not quite knowing how to put it. He looked at Vionne for support. Then just launched into it: "If Tia were to get too close to either of you, she may decide she wants a more physical bond with you ... Fuck! She could kill you, okay?" *There it was; he'd put it out there.*

Both men blushed, getting his meaning, which pleased him slightly. At least that proved that getting closer to her wasn't uppermost on their minds. "Good," Dante concluded, rapping his knuckles on the table. "Any questions?"

The two biologists looked at each other, then Josh spoke up. "Are we permitted to study Tia, purely in a scientific capacity, of course?"

"As long as you understand that nothing could be published."

They looked at each other uncomfortably again. "And your cousin?"

I can fucking hear you know, Vionne projected, glaring at the two men.

Both men felt their temples, with wide eyes, at what just happened. "Amazing," they said.

"Look, it's up to Vionne," Dante said. "But I'll tell you this much, my cousins here are from the purest race of Atlanteans. We call them Murr, after where they're from. They have been left unchanged for ten thousand years – since the time we came here."

Ben and Josh took out notebooks and scribbled away madly.

Tia is half Atlantean and half Murr – very rare."

"Atlantean?" Josh asked, his pen poised for a moment.

"Descendants of Atlantis. I am royal Atlantean. I didn't start out with the underwater capabilities of my Murr cousins, but my blood is still very pure. There is a little Human DNA mixed in over the millennia." Dante didn't elaborate on how he now possessed those capabilities through his bond with Tia. That was another story for another day.

"The last category is common Atlantean. Sean and Cash fall into this. They have Atlantean genes of varying purity. Some still have Atlantean traditions as Sean and Cash do, others aren't even aware of the blood they carry." Dante left it at that.

The two scientists looked captivated by his explanation. "We will guard her with our lives," Ben said.

"Good," Dante said, rising from his seat and touching Vionne lightly on the shoulder as he did so. *I'd like a few moments alone with Tia before I leave*, he projected.

There was a gentle knock at the door, as he knew she had approached. "Come in, Tia," he said, looking directly at the two scientists.

They stood immediately when Tia walked in, blinking, amazed at what they'd just witnessed.

Five minutes, Dante projected to Vionne and Axyl as they walked out.

Vionne stopped and hugged Tia briefly before he left.

Ben and Josh quickly sensed they wanted to say goodbye and left Dante and Tia alone.

"So … this is it, babe … you sure I can't tempt you to come back with me?" Dante said, pulling her towards him, linking his arms behind her. She locked hers around his neck. "It's not too late, you know."

She nestled her hands into the fur on the hood of his coat and shook her head and smiled. She pulled him down to meet her mouth with his and kissed him sensually and slowly.

"Okay, that's a no then." He was quiet for a few moments, not quite sure how to phrase his next question. *Ah hell.* "When you come back … will you come back to me and live with me and the kids?" He closed his eyes, feeling vulnerable with the need in his question.

She rubbed the pad of her thumb over his cheek and looked lovingly into his eyes. "I don't want to promise, Dante, but the way I feel about you right now, I will."

He hugged her tightly, lifting her off the ground, realizing that was as close to a promise Tia could ever give. "That's good," and he closed his eyes tightly while he crushed her to him.

When he pulled away and put her down, he put a finger

to her temple. "Work stuff out, okay? Get better while you are here."

"You mean my power?" she said, swallowing and looking away.

He pulled her face back to look at him. "Yes, but also you. Things got a bit mixed-up for a while."

She smiled up at him. "Yes they did, didn't they." She looked down nervously. "What if my power going is something to do with releasing Jay? What if his medicine is doing something?"

Dante looked over her head while he thought about it. "No … surely it couldn't." He looked back down at her, "You want him back?"

"No, Dante, please. That's not it. It's just that we all assumed it was to do with the tablets *I* took, but it was all at around the same time … you know?"

He nodded. "Leave it with me. I'll discuss it with Vionne and the Murr doctors." He brought his forehead down to rest on Tia's as if gathering himself together.

"What is it, Dante?"

He shook his head as if dismissing his negative thinking. "No … it's nothing. I just thought we had a way out of our ties, the three of us." He sighed. "I got this feeling in my gut that it's never going away."

She hugged *him* tight this time. "Don't, Dante … we'll deal with it, okay? We love each other … we'll work it out."

He clung to her for a few more moments, then put her away from him. "I have to go now," he said, wiping his eyes with his fingers quickly. Then he gathered himself up and became all business again. "Vionne is waiting to fly to McMurdo Sound with me. We've got stuff to discuss."

He let go of her hands and walked towards the door.

"Dante?" Tia called.

He turned and looked at her with sad eyes.

"Tell the kids I love them every day?"

He nodded. "Of course." He went to turn again.

"And Dante?"

He stilled again.

"If you could go back in time and not have met me, would you?"

He blinked and looked over, surprised at her, as if she should have known the answer. "If I could go back in time, Tia, I would have put you with me from birth." And with those parting words, he turned back and walked out the door, closing it quietly.

Tia was left staring at it, her heart pounding.

Isla, present day

Cesaré had given Isla all the space she needed since the debacle of his last attempt to kiss her. She had done her duty and met all the elders of the Florianna and allowed herself to be tested as a water breather in line with Atlantean tradition, so there was no doubt she was a Siren.

Nevertheless, doubts lingered. Not about her authenticity, of that he was sure, but of whether she was his. Hopes of gradually gaining her trust were slowly evaporating. She avoided him as much as possible.

He was many things, and most of them bad, but he wasn't stupid. He'd read the books, he'd asked around and the fact remained that they should be all over each other. A mystical attraction should have completely ensnared them by now. And while he thought she was gorgeous and the challenge was driving him crazy, his eye was still prone to wander.

Petra, the maid, was batting her eyes at him all the time, not fully understanding why he never came to her any more. Well, there was only so much rejection a man could take, especially one with his reputation and appetites.

Isla was now taking her afternoon nap, so he took the opportunity to creep into the study and pick up the phone.

"Malleven?"

"Ches … How are you … Isla is okay?" Malleven's voice purred.

"I'm fine … yes, she's fine." Cesaré went quiet. Now that he had Malleven on the line, he felt so stupid. How could he say what he meant?

"Ches, you are beginning to concern me … spit it out."

Cesaré bit down his embarrassment and just launched into it. "She has been with me weeks, Malleven, and I don't seem to be able … we haven't …"

There was a pause for a beat. "Ches, I told you she's had a hard time of it, didn't I?"

"Yes, yes you did, but … I don't know, we should, you know … be all over each other?"

Malleven paused on the line again.

"Malleven, are you still there?"

"Yes, I was just thinking … Ches, she just needs time."

"I'm thinking about asking my father to have my ring checked."

Malleven laughed. "And how do you propose to do that? He would never let you relinquish her anyway. And, Ches … most princes would saw their own arm off for a purple ring."

Cesaré sighed. He was right, of course. "I just don't know what to do?"

"Look, don't do anything hasty. After all, if news got out that the famous Florianna playboy was not even able to attract his own most compatible mate, you'd never live it down," Malleven laughed.

Cesaré was forced to laugh with him, even though he felt wretched. "I know … my life would be over."

"I tell you what," Malleven said. "I can get to you in a few days. I'll use my contacts and see if I can bring you a virgin divining ring to put your mind at rest, and maybe I can have a little talk with Isla while I'm there?"

Cesaré was sceptical. "I'm not sure what good it will do, but thank you."

"I understand, but we did spark up a small friendship in the short time I knew her."

"Okay," Cesaré said, his heart lightening with hope. "I don't know what to say, Malleven … I owe you one."

"That you do, Cousin. That you do."

CHAPTER 16

$\mathcal{J}$ay moved slowly underneath her and she moaned in response.

"Hey, baby ..."

Jay turned his head to the side where the second girl held out her wrist for him to sniff a line of coke.

He leaned over and vacuumed it up noisily, making sure it hit the highest point in his nose. As it reached his brain and the power surged into his heart, he was hit with a reminder of Tia breathing for him, so strong it felt as if he'd been speared through.

Growling, he flipped the girl riding him onto her back, pushed her legs up by her ears and pounded her till she screamed her climax. He finished on an empty release – a mix of drink and drugs, as well as his state of mind, was not conducive to him letting go and so he flopped on top of her.

He allowed himself a few moments for his heart to slow down and his breathing to ease and rolled off the girl and onto his back. The third girl came and sat by his head and pushed the hair off his hot forehead.

"Thanks, girls ... that's just what I needed."

The second girl lay down to his left, while the first girl he'd just banged lay purring to his right. "We hardly ever see you anymore," she complained.

He slapped her thigh playfully. "We certainly made up for it tonight," he said, his eyes barely open.

The girls giggled. "You just give us a call anytime, okay?" the third girl said.

Jay pulled her face down from her sitting position and kissed her on the lips. He was fond of these girls. They'd been friends a long time and he liked to look out for them when he could.

The door of his suite banged loudly, audible even over the loud dance music playing.

They all looked in the direction of the door, then at Jay for what they should do.

"Just ignore them," Jay said, eventually, too lazy to get up and make up bullshit.

The knocking persisted.

Jay looked over at the leggy blonde. "Open it and get rid of them, Kat. There's a babe."

She rose from the edge of the bed in nothing but a thong and walked to the small hallway to open the door and threw it open wide.

"Fucking hell," Dante said, blinking. He knew there was a party going on, but wasn't expecting that eye-opener. "Hello, Kat ... Long time no see ... I assume he's in?"

"He told me to get rid of whoever it was."

"That's anyone except me, darlin'," and with that Dante neatly pushed past her and into the hall.

He strolled into Jay's bedroom and made a beeline for the loud music and turned it down to a tinny hiss. His eyes roamed the room and decided it looked like a scene from *Trainspotting*. "Fuck, Jay. You've had yourself quite a party."

Finally, his eyes rested on Jay lying in the bed with the

two other girls, both naked, his head on the stomach of one and the other spooning his tattooed back.

"You're not going to lecture me, are you, Dant?" Jay said on a groan with eyes like slits.

Dante breathed a sigh and held both hands up, "Me? Never."

"Why don't you reacquaint yourself with Kat? There's a new bath in there," Jay said, lifting a heavy arm and pointing in the direction of the bathroom as if Dante didn't know where it was.

"Nah, you're all right, man." Dante looked apologetically at Kat, not wanting to offend her. "I'm just here to talk to Jay."

Jay lay back onto the pillows and put his forearm over his eyes as if he didn't like the sound of what was coming. Then pulled it down and looked at the ceiling. "Can you get me a scotch, Dant? I want to take the edge off before my headfuck takes hold."

Dante knew first-hand what that was like. Years of drug-taking gave him a headfuck like you wouldn't believe. He moved to the sideboard and poured two scotches. He bet Jay's were the worst, the place his head was obviously at – *fuck*, he'd never seen him so wasted.

Jay sat up and took the scotch with just a thin sheet covering his bottom half. "Sorry, girls, I'm gonna have to kick you out," he said, taking a large gulp.

Dante watched as the girls scampered around looking for their clothes, dressing and generally getting their shit together.

"Kat?" Jay called.

She walked over to him seductively and kissed him on the lips.

Dante watched Jay take out a bundle of cash from his trouser pocket on the floor next to the bed, roll it up discreetly and push it into her hand. Nothing he hadn't seen before, his boy was a sucker for a working girl.

"Thanks, baby," Kat said, straightening up.

"No worries … don't forget, if you need anything, give me a shout. You too, girls," he said slightly louder to the others.

"Thanks, Jay. Take care of yourself," they said, and all three trooped out of the room, leaving Jay and Dante alone.

After a minute, Dante couldn't help himself. "What's this … reverting to type?"

Jay tilted his glass at him in sarcastic response.

"You don't have to look after every two-bit whore you know, Jay."

"Don't call 'em that, Dante. Not to me anyway."

Dante held up his hands in submission. "Sorry … Sorry. Fuck! I didn't know it was still a sore point with you, mate? Your mind's fucking gone, Jay … gone." Dante shook his head slowly.

"Shut the fuck up, Dant. Just say what you came to say. I've got the headache from hell steaming up on me, so you got about five minutes."

Dante stared at him. Even when they were youngsters, wild and screwing everything with a pulse, he'd never seen Jay so reckless and out of control. It shocked him. "Are you too wasted to hear me, Jay?" he had to ask.

"Just fucking say it."

"Okay," Dante sighed. "I've been talking to the Murr Doctors about the meds and what seems to be happening with you and Tia."

Even the mere mention of her name was a noticeable blow to Jay. He visibly recoiled.

"I still don't know how they're supposed to work?" Jay said, squinting and having to lie back into the pillows.

Dante walked over and topped up his glass. "Do you want me to explain it as they told me?"

"Go for it," Jay said, lifting his glass.

Dante perched on the edge of the sideboard. "Okay, basically, when a Siren breathes her essence or spirit into you, it enters the body and binds itself to the fabric of your DNA." He paused, making sure Jay was with him.

Jay nodded. "Go on."

"As soon as it happens, as you know, you are bound for life. But it needs constant feeding or topping up, otherwise it gets weaker and weaker, leaving both parties with symptoms of withdrawal. That's why you can't just leave her without her releasing you, otherwise you both get sick."

"Even me?"

Dante nodded, "Yeah, especially you." He knew Jay was referring to the fact that he only had a one-way bond with Tia, as he was Human. "It is your DNA she has bound herself with."

"How does she get sick then if I can't breathe for her?"

It was a reasonable question, and one that confused the hell out of Dante. "As far as I can tell, it's like she's given a part of herself to you, one that she needs to continue for life, otherwise her spirit grieves. Something must feed back to her even though you don't breathe for her."

Jay's head appeared to be sinking lower, along with his mood. "So how'd they work ... I still don't know?"

"The meds are supposed to work by mimicking the topping up as if she's breathed for you and tricking your body so you can both separate and not get sick."

"So what ... why are you telling me this?" Jay said, his eyelids opening and closing slowly.

"It ain't working, mate."

Jay put his face in his hands. "Argh, you're not trying to drag me into the shit again, Dante, are you? ... I thought you wanted her with you?"

"Of course I fucking do," Dante said, exasperated with

him. "Look, when you wanted out, and she released you, I thought hoo fucking ray … at last. But she has no power, Jay, still. Not only do *I* need it, but it ain't safe for her. She's defenceless."

Jay's face creased in pain at the thought of going back.

"You're not in control either, are you, Jay?"

"What you talking about?" Jay said, straightening up, offended.

"You are reckless, Jay. Look around you."

Jay sneered at him.

"You took three known working girls up to *your* room, in your own fucking hotel. If you got raided, if Alfonzo found out, you'd be out of Bonaci Corps before your arse knew it. Reckless, Jay, and not like you at all." He knew he'd hit home when Jay didn't say anything clever back, just absorbed the words.

"So what do they say has gone wrong?" Jay asked, worn out.

"I don't fully understand it myself. Something about the pills she took trapping her Murr abilities and spirit at the same time. That means your meds can't reach her spirit to feed back to her. So, you're both in a kind of grieving process, or something. I don't think they know, to be honest. It's been so long since the drug has been needed, they don't even know if they've got the recipe right."

"So the upshot of it is I've got to come back?" Jay said, getting up and lurching towards the bathroom. "I've got to be sick," he said, holding up a finger for Dante to hold on a moment.

Dante sat and smiled as he heard Jay hurl down the loo a few times, then flush. Then he watched as he came out, found some boxers, put them on, and flopped down onto the edge of the bed.

"How the fuck's it gonna work?" he groaned, and looked up at Dante with sorry-looking bloodshot eyes.

Dante got serious with his old friend. "Let me be clear, Jay. I want her with me."

Jay put his hands up in defence and slumped backwards onto the bed. "No worries from me. Just tell me what you want me to do? …" He trailed off.

Dante stood and wandered over to his wasted friend. "We've got to make it work, okay, Jay? … the three of us."

"Mmm," was all he got in response, as Jay lay comatose.

"Where are your meds, Jay?" Dante said, shaking him.

Jay just turned onto his side, murmuring.

"Fuck!" Dante said to himself, looking around the room that looked like a bomb had hit it.

He wandered into the bathroom and opened the cabinet. There on a shelf was the bottle he recognized. With a deep sigh, he undid the lid, tipped the contents into the toilet and flushed them away.

He watched the water swirl, taking the tablets with it; churning and washing them away, his dream of a reunion with Tia taken with them. Because with Jay back, as unjust and frustrating as it was, he knew he'd be relegated to second place.

TIA HAD FALLEN into an easy routine with her friends and Protectors in Antarctica. She appreciated the sacrifices they'd all made for her and got weepy when she contemplated it over a chilled-out glass of scotch in the evenings. She knew Cash had his busy ranch to run and Sean had Sarah – his wife and their baby, Ronnie.

Their response was telling her off for being such a girl, filling up her glass and informing her that they wouldn't have missed the trip for the world. It bothered her that Sean was away from his family, though.

Ben and Josh had been in biology heaven, having Tia to study and the Murrs, who visited discreetly from time to time, and promised her that everything was absolutely worth it.

This alleviated her guilt a little and she certainly needed the time away. Things had got a bit out of control for a while, so she didn't allow herself to think about Jay too deeply. The fact was that despite the last time she'd seen him, he had wanted out, and no amount of ranting and raving on her part was going to change that one iota.

No, she had to make the most of the here and now, as she had been in Antarctica for around eight weeks already. The trip was inevitably coming to an end with winter creeping up on them. The twenty-four hours of daylight were beginning to be tinged with twilight that was getting longer and longer each day. The music had to be faced sometime.

She'd got up early that day, promising Ben that she would go out with him and help collect his readings from the instruments he'd got dotted about on the glacier a little way off from the station.

They both finished their toast and coffee and donned their thick parkas, thermal mittens and walking boots and set off on the Skidoo – easier for the short journeys than the large Spryte vehicle. Cash and Sean preferred to stay warm in the gym and Josh had his head over a microscope studying algae samples he'd collected over the last few days.

Tia and Ben passed a pleasant hour stopping off at the various stations he'd erected over their time there. She wrote down the figures on a clipboard while he called them out.

A loud boom made the ice shake beneath them, sending the delicate equipment haywire. Ben frowned up at Tia from his crouch position. There it went again.

"Fireworks?" Tia said.

"I doubt it … Daylight twenty-three hours a day?… Come on," Ben said, standing up and leading the way back to the Skidoo.

Then a plane shot over their heads so suddenly that it made them both duck. They looked at each other, baffled.

"A jet?" Ben said, unable to hide his concern, which made Tia's heart thump in fear.

Several more bangs clapped in the distance like the sound of a thunderstorm breaking.

"Quickly," Ben said, speeding up. "I don't like this."

They began to grab their tools and instruments and throw them back into the bag.

"Quick, Ben, the plane's coming back." Tia's alarm bells were ringing and they were vulnerable out on the glacier.

"Wait!" Ben said, stopping suddenly. "I've left something," he said, turning and jogging back the way they'd come to the last meter they'd read.

"No, leave it!" Tia found herself shrieking.

The plane whooshed over their heads again and the boom belted the ice they were standing on. Tia screamed and covered her ears with her hands. Ben disappeared from sight.

It was a living nightmare. Explosions, flashes and tremors seemed to be all around them. Tia leapt off the Skidoo to run to the last place she had seen Ben.

She skidded to her knees when she realized what she first thought was a rock protruding from the ice was, in fact, Ben's head and shoulders, with only his arms preventing him from disappearing completely into the huge schism which had opened in the ice.

"Ben!" she screamed and tried to pull him from under his shoulders, but he was too heavy and his yelp of pain told her that his body was wedged in tight in the hole.

His head lolled to the side. "It's no use, Tia. I can't feel my legs … the ice is moving." A shrill, inhuman scream escaped him.

Tia brought her hands up to her mouth in utter despair. He was being crushed before her eyes.

Engines came roaring up. Cash and Sean jumped off their Skidoos while they were still moving and ran to where Tia was kneeling. Tears stung her face in the cold.

Gentle hands touched her shoulders. "Tia," Cash spoke softly.

She scrambled around and clutched him to her and sobbed. "Get him out, Cash … oh, get him out."

"Take a look, Sean," Cash said, over her head.

Tia took her face from Cash's chest to follow Sean's movements. He talked to Ben and tried to get a good look into the ice fissure. He knelt back up and shook his head back at Cash.

"Get him out, Sean," Tia shrieked.

"Ah fuck, Tia," Sean said, with a pained expression. "The ice has crushed the lower half of his body … Out here … he won't last five minutes."

Tia flew at Sean like a lunatic, pummelling his chest. "Get him out … Get him out, Sean."

Sean just absorbed the battering and looked hopelessly at Cash. Cash pulled her back into his arms. "We must get you out of here, Tia," he said, softly next to her ear.

"No," she wailed.

"Tia?" Ben's voice called. "Please, Tia," He wavered and panted with the effort.

She scrambled onto the ground to get near him. "We're gonna get you out, Ben. Don't worry," she said, wiping her eyes on the back of her arm.

"Tia, stop." Ben's voice hitched in pain. "Sean … Cash," he called in a strangled whisper.

The two men bent down to his eyeline. His face was ashen and sweat beaded from the exertion and agony.

"What's happened at the station?"

"It's gone," Sean said.

Ben drifted in and out of consciousness and stared at him for a few moments as if trying to remember something; "Josh?"

Cash shook his head. "It was hit with several missiles … we were away from the main building, in the gym. We got out just in time."

Ben closed his eyes. Whether from pain from his injuries or his loss, it wasn't clear; probably both.

"Who did it?" Tia said, desperately, then sagged. *Stupid question.* Anyone and everyone was after her.

Sean answered, "We couldn't tell … No markings on the planes. It's my guess they were out of Chile." He let the words sink in for no more than a minute. "Listen, Tia, they'll be back on foot soon, looking for survivors. We've got to get you out of here."

"No!" She fell on Ben, clutching what she could of him. "I won't leave him behind."

"Tia," Ben said softly, his voice getting fainter with fatigue. "You must go. It's really important that they don't get you."

She was crying unashamedly now. Sobbing her heart out. She barely noticed the party of Murrs approaching them, straight from the direction of the sea. They were still dressed in their glistening, body-hugging clothes; their bleak black eyes and vivid stripes against their grey skin a stark contrast to the blue-tinted white all around them.

Walking slowly and uncomfortably, not because of the cold but because of the pain in their legs, suspending their weight out of water before their limbs could set rigid. They looked like aliens out of a *Star Trek* episode.

They came up to the group huddled around Ben. Sean and Cash nodded a greeting. They'd alerted them with a beacon Dante had given them in the form of a button on a watch.

Cash turned back to Tia, who was watching the quiet men blankly. Still not willing to let go of Ben. "You must go with them, Tia," he said firmly.

"I'm not leaving Ben alone," she said, flatly.

One of the Murrs crouched down from his great height so he could look into her face.

She stared into his eyes, mesmerized for a moment. "I know you," she said, absently.

He cocked his head at an angle. *I was here when you came. I am Axyl, Vionne's brother.*

"No, before," she said, totally hypnotized by his eyes, so black they looked like deep space.

He appeared to ignore her, probably thinking she was irrational. *I have a small marine craft a few metres offshore. We can take you to safety*, he projected to her in a soft yet authoritative voice.

Her face went to crease again. "Ben," she said, and more tears spilled over her cheeks, reddened now with wind scald.

Your friend is dying, he said in the same soft tone, so matter-of-fact, showing no emotion at all. *His spirit is slowly leaving him while we speak*, he continued. *You can feel it.*

She knew he spoke the truth, her sobs renewed and she held onto Ben tighter. "No one should die alone." Her eyes remained glued to the fathomless pools of Axyl's eyes, strange and otherworldly.

You are a Soul Breather, Tia.

She nodded, missing his point. "I know. All this … it's my fault."

"Come on, Tia," Cash said, putting a consoling hand on her shoulder.

You can breathe for him and then carry him away with you, should you so wish. Axyl continued to look into her face questioningly.

His words sank into her slowly. He smiled when he knew she had begun to understand what he meant. "Will he stay with me?" she whispered.

For ever reverberated through her mind. *His spirit will join yours ... Never alone ...*

She swallowed hard. She totally got what he was driving at. Being a Siren, she had the gift of giving her spirit to those she loved, but what separated her from every other Murr and the side to her she had never explored was that she had the grave responsibility of being able to take a spirit away. More than that, she could take another soul to the very point of death and keep it with her always.

Tia nodded, pulled out of Cash's sheltering arm and faced Ben again. She was beset with doubts. *With her powers so stunted, would it work?* Then she closed her eyes for a moment to centre her energy.

When she opened them again, Ben's face was grey and he was drifting into unconsciousness. She took off her gloves with her teeth and placed her palms flat against his cheeks. With her face wet with tears and her nose running, she made sure he looked deeply into her eyes.

"You look like shit," he said.

She hiccupped a laugh. " I love you, Ben."

"Ah fuck ... am I gonna need that potion, cos I left it in my back pocket?" he said breathily.

She laughed again and edged closer.

Ben went quiet, sensing that this was it. As if he knew what was coming and was bracing himself for it.

She leaned forward and tenderly put her lips to his. All the men standing around averted their eyes, somehow knowing this was a private, sacred moment.

"Open a little," she whispered.

He kissed her gently and opened his mouth. She gently began a slow stream of her breath into him. A long and achingly loving blow down into the heart of him. As if she were blowing a soothing breeze on something that was hurting. Her heart bled that it was so weak and meagre.

Despite its lack of strength, Ben's eyes rolled up into his head and he groaned while his skin glowed orange, then yellow. Before he lost consciousness in the euphoria, she whispered, "You'll never be alone." Then she reversed her breath to inhale, praying that her lack of power would make it possible.

Her question was quickly answered with a macabre feeling of elation as his life force began to enter her. The bright light gradually drained from his face, his eyes slowly closed and his face greyed until the tiniest light remained on his lips, which switched off swiftly like a light bulb.

Tia slumped with a shaky feeling of dizziness from her heart surging as her body became swamped with him and she waited for the whirl inside her to settle. Thankfully, it was only an outward-bound problem she had with her power.

Giving her no time to dwell on it further, Axyl went to lift her. *We must go now, Tia,* he projected. *They are coming ... Your friends must get a head start.*

She roused herself from her stupor. "Cash ... Sean?"

They cannot make the journey with us, Axyl said. *They would die.*

"I'm not leaving them," she shrieked suddenly, angry that he would suggest such a thing.

"Tia," Sean reprimanded sternly. "We can go overland to McMurdo. We'll be fine, but we need to get going, okay? ... We'll get on the next plane. Go!"

She looked at Cash, bewildered. There was only so much heartbreak she could take in a day.

"Come on, gal," he said, kindly. "We need to get going."

She swallowed and snapped herself out of it. She was putting them in danger by wasting time. They needed the head start before the soldiers came. "Okay, she said directly to Axyl.

They stood up and she hugged both Cash and Sean quickly and watched as they got back on their Skidoos and rode off across the ice sheet in the direction of McMurdo Sound.

Axyl held her by the arm and steered her towards the icy sea. Fear overwhelmed her for a second. Could she still breathe underwater with so little power? How could she possibly make the long journey home?

CHAPTER 17

sla, present day

Isla had been crapping bricks all morning. Cesaré had dropped the M bomb at breakfast in passing, saying he was expecting Malleven later that day. Her mind and her heart were going a mile a minute. The sex in the servants' stairwell had played through her head a thousand times and flashed into her mind again now.

Malleven seemed to get off on the danger of getting caught, and when he got near her, despite her dislike and distrust of his character, her body submitted to him and gave her away like the hussy she was. So she knew he could take her any time, any place, anywhere, just like he said he could the first night he'd had sex with her, and she couldn't do a damn thing about it.

The thought of killing him had crossed her mind many times, but unfortunately, she needed him and Cesaré to get her to the king's court. Without them, she had no idea how she would get there.

She lay on her bed with a cooling cloth over her brow, pretending to have a bad headache, but with the knock at the door, her heart sank and her hackles rose and she knew straight away who it was. "Come in," she said quietly.

Malleven came in after thanking the maid for showing him the way. He stood in the centre of the room, looking at her for quite a few moments. His face was unreadable.

Her heart beat wildly. Whatever he wanted it wasn't good and her body was already melting into a pool of want, her womb clenched, and she closed her eyes.

"What is this shit, Isla?" he said eventually, low and menacing.

"What shit?" came out in a small, scared voice.

He spread his arms wide dramatically. "All this ... avoiding Cesaré. He has asked for his fucking ring to be checked."

Her eyes flashed up to his.

Malleven nodded slowly. "That's right ... I had to bring a new ring with me to put his mind at rest ... Why are you fucking everything up for me, Isla?"

"I'm not ... I mean ... I don't mean to ... I mean, I do like him."

Malleven seemed to soften a little, walked over to the bed, and sat on the edge, staring down at her. "Why don't you fuck him, Isla ... I've given you my permission?" His eyes were half closed as if he were secretly pleased with her and she found her eyes straying to his mouth.

What she really wanted to say was she didn't need his fucking permission. It was that she actually liked Cesaré and couldn't bear to string him along and use him, and that not being physical with him made it seem not quite so bad as making him fall for her completely. Of course, she knew Malleven assumed that she was so into him she just couldn't get near anyone else. *Well, let him choke on his own ego*, and she glanced at his perfect mouth again. "I only seem to be able to do that with you," came out instead in a husky whisper.

Malleven pulled the sheet from the top half of her to reveal the thin chemise covering her naked body. Slowly, he pulled the thin string strap from her shoulder, exposing her beautiful, plump, pert breast, hardening and straining for his touch.

Malleven bent his head and licked across the top of her hardened nipple whilst not taking his eyes from hers. "You love me, Snowflake?" he murmured.

She had begun to understand that he used her name when he was reprimanding her and the pet name when he was being affectionate. She nodded almost imperceptibly.

Before she could grasp what he was doing, his hand reached down into her silk panties and his fingers pushed into her wetness.

She gasped.

"You want me here, Snowflake?"

She nodded and moaned.

"Only I can make you feel like this because you are mine."

His face was arrogant while he circled her bud with his finger to prove his point.

She pushed her head back into the pillow and from side to side in blissful agony.

"I don't have the time to fuck you … do you want me to make you come?"

"Yes … oh yes," she gasped, and pleaded with her eyes.

He ripped the gusset out of her panties with his strong hand and bent his head and plunged his tongue deep into her folds.

She cried out.

"Shh," he scolded and laughed into his kiss.

Then he replaced his tongue with his fingers. "Do you see how you are in my power, Snowflake?"

"Yes," she groaned.

"So if you have to fuck Cesaré, it is no threat to me … do you understand?"

She stopped thrashing, blinked and looked into Malleven's eyes as what he said filtered through to her. His total delusion where she was concerned astounded her. "You want me to?" she asked, her face a mask of outrage.

"You must." He circled her bud, bringing her so close. "Do you want to come, Snowflake?" He took her bud into his lips, driving her wild.

"Yes, please, Malleven."

He released her momentarily. "And you will fuck Cesaré?" he said, teasing and pausing again. Bringing her to the brink over and over and not allowing her the blessed release her body craved. "It is cruel if you do not," he continued. Goading, pausing, playing and teasing, he tortured her.

"Malleven, please …"

He laughed, pleased with her. "Say the words."

"What?"

"Say. The. Words," he enunciated.

"I will fuck him."

"Who?"

"I will fuck Cesaré."

"Good. And you will make sure he doesn't doubt you." He plunged his fingers deeply and drew her bud into his mouth and worked her to abandon, while she rocked and pushed herself against his mouth; groaning her well-needed release.

A few moments later and Malleven left her in a panting heap of disarray and went to find Cesaré, who was waiting by the pool. "I must leave now, Cesaré … before I forget … here." He reached into his trouser pocket and pulled out a deep-blue velvet bag and passed it to Cesaré. "Your replacement ring, but I don't think you will need it."

Cesaré's eyebrows went up with surprise. "I wish I shared your optimism.

"I have spoken to her. She promises she will make more of an effort from now on, and she told me to apologize to you."

Cesaré frowned. "Really?"

"Use that Florianna charm quickly … You will be approaching the king soon."

Cesaré nodded ruefully. "Yes. He seems to be getting his house in order and becoming someone who could actually lead us."

Inwardly, Malleven balked at Cesaré's naivety. Outwardly, he smiled. "Stars willing, Cousin." And with a departing "Ciao", Malleven left him.

EVERYONE SAT around in the armchairs of the great hall at Ballygowan Castle, killing time with Dante. A game of cards was going on with swearing and coins clinking onto the table while they waited.

Several guards, Keenan, Lacy and even Jay were there, but Dante wasn't playing. He was pacing up and down. Tia was due back any time now and he couldn't concentrate on anything else. He was furious, convinced it was the Americans who had attacked Palmers, where Tia had been staying.

They'd lost their bargaining chip in the third Siren. And now he was sure they had changed strategy and become determined to eliminate a Siren. That would remove the imminent threat of a return of their ancestors and kinsmen from the planet of Atlas. Promised to return, legend says, when all the Sirens were accounted for.

Overall, a feeling of apprehension hung in the air. Tia had survived another threat to her life. Although no one was airing the words, everyone knew that Jay was back, and there would definitely be trouble. Dante wanted Tia home safe and he was in no mood to share this time.

Dante knew Jay was watching him closely. He also knew that although Jay was playing with the others, he was as anxious to see Tia safe as he was; he was just better at hiding it. *Fucking Mr Cool.* Yep, since he'd flushed away Jay's tablets, he'd noticed Jay getting back to his old self again. He should be happy about it, but he wasn't.

"She won't come any quicker with your pacing," Jay said.

Keenan grinned.

Dante stopped and turned, ready to say something smart back, when he stopped. He felt it. She was near – definitely.

"What?" Jay asked, knowing immediately that something was up.

Dante didn't answer; his mind was about a quarter of a mile away. He ran toward the fountain, stripped off to his boxers, hopped over the wall and disappeared into the hole that took him into the tunnel and out to sea.

Dante swam about a hundred yards from the castle to where the rocks gave way to the sandy seabed. There, buzzing, a few feet from the ocean floor, was the small marine bug that had travelled the thousands of miles with Tia inside in a suspended sleep.

He marvelled at the beauty of the technology in front of him. The craft was a greeny-blue jelly-like oval, with lights pulsing through it like a blown-up version of a microscopic organism, just like he'd studied at school.

Dante came up alongside it, wondering where the doorway was, when Axyl came through a flexible hatch in the bottom like the neck of a balloon. Dante went to him and touched his shoulder.

Axyl projected a picture of Tia peacefully sleeping inside. Her sleep was artificially induced to make the journey safer for her with her lack of power. Dante squeezed his shoulder by way of thanks. The most serious of the Borge brothers had come through for him and he would never forget it. Tia was passed down through the hole in the floor to Axyl's arms, still fast asleep. He carried her to Dante. *She is fine,* he projected. *Just take her inside and breathe for her. She will expel her lungs and she will wake.*

Dante nodded. He pointed back at the castle and flashed a picture of food and a feeling of comfort to Axyl, and then a picture of his private chamber. Axyl understood then that he needed a private reunion. There was no way he was letting Jay near her yet. However Axyl was a loner, unlike his brothers and made his excuses. *I will go to see my family in Murrtaine and rest there. It has been a long time since I have seen them.*

Dante thanked him again and promised him he owed him and took Tia from his arms. Then he swam with her to his subterranean bedchamber, savouring and holding her to him like the precious creature she was.

They broke the surface of his lagoon and he stood with her, waist-deep in the water. He gazed down at her face, still sleeping peacefully, and wished he could keep her to himself for ever.

She had the faintest stripes – a slight improvement, but the length of time she'd been in the water, she should look like a Murr right now. He was just thankful that she had just enough of her abilities to still breathe underwater, otherwise … he shuddered at the thought of what could have happened.

Here goes. He bent his head over her and pushed his tongue between her lips and began to breathe gently. It wasn't difficult to summon his spirit; it bubbled up in him with his emotion and spilled into her.

She glowed red, then orange, and then a white light travelled down to the centre of her chest. He kept going until she jolted, coughed and spat water. He tilted her more upright and held her to him with her face over his shoulder.

Dante knew when she started breathing when he felt her smelling his scent deeply at the crook of his neck. He closed his eyes and groaned at the sensuality of it. *Hello, babe,* he projected.

Her arms slowly went around his neck and she clutched him fiercely. He crushed her to him. *Fuck, I've missed you.*

Tia pushed herself back slightly so she could look into his face with her huge ruined eyes.

God, he loved this woman.

She pulled him to her and kissed him as if she couldn't quite believe he was real.

When they pulled apart after a few minutes, Dante projected, *Can you breathe for me, babe, so I know how you feel?*

A look of worry crossed her brow, but she nodded. He put his lips to hers and waited. A light tingle played across them. It was small, but it was there nonetheless – a warmth.

Dante broke away and looked at her when he felt a small shift in her emotion. She looked like she would cry. *Hey, don't worry … I've got rid of his meds. It's just a matter of time … okay?*

She swallowed hard and nodded.

It worried him that not enough of her essence had gone into him to complete the bond and so she was unable to project her thoughts to him. He couldn't let his terror of the implications of that show and frighten her right now.

Come on. He picked her up and carried her towards the bed. He went to put her down gently, but she stood up and led him back to the shallow water and he let her, not sure what she wanted.

When they were ankle-deep in the water, she turned to face him. "Love me," she croaked, simply.

No further words were needed, and he pushed her over and tumbled with her into the water. They locked lips and rolled over and over. He shredded the Murr garment she was wearing in seconds and whipped off his shorts. Skin contact was the only foreplay needed and he plunged deeply into her waiting, wanting body.

Dante moved within her deeply, stoking her, biting and sucking her neck and shoulders to prove it was real. The here and now was what they both needed: to love, to feel, even if it hurt. She scratched him in response and he delighted in the pain, sharp and sweet, tangible and physical.

When he felt her getting cold, he breathed for her, warming her from the inside, and drove into her when she came, over and over. She thrived on his rough handling of her and wrung everything out of him, hungry for his touch. Dante breathed for her throughout their love, till his heart would burst and they were utterly sated.

Kissing her thoroughly, slowly, adoringly, he picked her up, carried her out of the water to his bed. There, he grabbed a towel, conscious of her new body temperature now that she was out of her suspended sleep and his breath was wearing off.

Dante lay with her on the bed, partially on top of her to warm her but not too much to squash her. He pushed her wet hair away from her face whilst staring down into her eyes.

Are you home now? he asked, eventually.

Her eyes welled up with tears and she nodded.

Hey. He didn't want to push her before she was ready to tell him what happened at Antarctica. *Are you all right ... did anyone hurt you?* he thought, anger suddenly just beneath the surface.

Tears escaped the corners of her eyes when she tried to speak. Without her mental bond, she couldn't project what she wanted to say. Instead, she ended up just mouthing the words: *I love you so much.* Dante crushed her lips to his.

Eventually, he leaned back up away from her. *Are you hungry ... do you want anything?*

She shook her head. "Sleep," she whispered. "With me…"

Of course, he thought, his brow furrowed in concern. He arranged the bed for her comfort and drew her to him and made sure she was covered in the black silk sheets.

Tia fell asleep first, and as he drifted off, he felt the nearest he'd ever come to heaven.

THE NEXT MORNING, the kids came rushing up to Tia in the kitchen, ecstatic to see her. She kissed and hugged them all repeatedly. Dante watched on dotingly until their excitement died down and he had to bring up the subject he'd been dreading. "Will you see Jay today?"

"Can I have today with the kids, Dante? I'll face him tomorrow."

A feeling of relief surged through him like you wouldn't believe. "Of course … I'll tell him to stay away today."

After breakfast, Tia took the kids into the great hall to the corner where her record decks were set up. "Today I'm going to turn you all into DJs."

"Yeah!" they all shouted. Even JJ was jumping up and down with glee. Although she was sure he didn't know what a DJ was.

Tia set them up in turn to have a go, popping the earphones on and finding two records with an easy beat to mix together and coordinate. There was much giggling and delight as they discovered what it was all about and they jumped up and down and clapped their hands. "Can I have a go," they said repeatedly. Each of them began to nod their heads to the beat, copying their mother.

Dante stood just out of sight, watching like the indulgent

father. Jay went to go through the hall to the lifts, paused when he saw Dante, and stopped to see what he was looking at.

Dante glanced to his left and saw a micro expression of emotion sweep across his friend's face and then disappear as quickly as it came.

"She's good with them."

"You sound surprised, Jay. Of course, she's good with them," Dante said, studying him closely. "She's their mother." This was the first time Jay had clapped eyes on her in months. It had to affect him. He had to hand it to him, though; apart from the first flicker of emotion, his face remained cast-iron. That suited him just fine and he turned back to watch them.

They stood side by side, watching, both not helping the smile on their faces.

"Don't put the earphones on both ears, Xav, you won't hear two beats if you do that," Tia explained.

"Oh," Xav said, punching the air and shouting, "Having it large!"

Dante and Jay both burst out laughing.

Eventually, Jay put a hand on Dante's back. "I'll be back tomorrow to face her."

Dante turned and embraced his friend, then watched him walk off to the lift.

He sighed, hating that his friend was hurting. Nothing could be done. *It's me or him ... whatever.* He turned to watch the children again.

THE DAY JAY was dreading came. He had to face Tia sometime. Dante had said they could use the library as a meeting place.

He waited nervously, then walked to the sideboard and

poured himself a scotch to steady his nerves. He scolded himself for being such a pussy.

There was a knock on the door and he called out for Tia to come in.

She walked in, looking as nervous as him, and he thought she looked a bit pale. He dismissed the thought when he remembered she'd spent weeks in the Antarctic – not exactly balmy.

She stood awkwardly in the centre of the room.

"Want a drink?" he said to break the silence, knocking the one he had back and pouring another straight away.

"Okay," she said, quietly.

He passed her the glass and saw she was physically shaking. He tutted. "Look, I don't want to be here either, Tia."

She nodded, looking into her glass. "Can't we just get it over with and go?"

Jay laughed.

Her eyes snapped up to his.

"It's not that simple."

"Why not?"

Jay made sure that when he walked towards her, he stood uncomfortably close, in her personal space. "It's about releasing our emotions, Tia. Then I think your power will be free."

She looked anywhere but into his eyes. "How about hate … that's an emotion?" she said.

Jay barked a laugh. "That's a start," he said, studying the face he knew so well. She knew so little about men. She held them in her power so effortlessly, but didn't understand them at all. *God,* an unscrupulous man could play her so easily, it was shocking. 'Snakes and snails and puppy dog tails,' he remembered his mother saying when he was a small boy. 'That's what little boys are made of, Jay.' *Yep, never a truer word. Fuck it!* "Look, nothing's going to happen here, Tia. We should go out, have a drink and let our hair down."

Her eyes widened in shock.

"Not here though … on my turf," he continued. "Grab your coat. We're going to London."

He wasted no time and whisked her off to the airport while Dante was busy, onto the Bonaci jet and over to London. They were out and in a bar by 7 p.m.

The minute they set foot into the West End, Jay came into his own, and out emerged the social butterfly he was comfortable being.

TIA TAGGED ALONG WITH JAY, bar after bar, club after club and almost drink for drink. She was quite drunk. She knew he'd had the odd livener as well; she'd seen enough of it in her time. She didn't know why it surprised her, but it did. Another thing she didn't know about him.

Everywhere they went, most people knew him, especially the ladies. She wasn't sure whether he was deliberately being a prick to make a point that he was single or whether he genuinely couldn't help it. She supposed Dante would be as well known if he were here. After all, they'd been inseparable for years. But one thing she did know was that if Dante had been there, he'd never have taken his eyes off her for a second. She missed him then, and his warm blanket of love.

The last club they came to was The Kats Wiska's. That was the final straw. Several girls draped themselves all over him while he stood at the bar. One passed him her number, which Tia saw him put in his pocket. Another was whispering in his ear. Most of the girls weren't strangers, that was obvious. *Fuck,* she wanted to go.

She'd been in nightclubs her whole adult life, but never had she felt so alien. Perhaps because she had been in the most isolated place on earth for weeks, or perhaps it was just the company.

She stood all on her own with her back to the black painted wall, telling any male clubber to fuck off, should any dickhead try to approach her.

FROM THE BAR, Jay was still aware of her. He saw her fucking off any chancer who had the guts to come near her. *Fuck*, she was such a contradiction.

Jay excused himself from the girls he knew and sauntered over to Tia. "You seem pissed off?" he said, passing her a drink.

"I'm not really in the mood, Jay. I might go."

"You've got the hump with me talking to the girls who work here?"

She looked at him scathingly. "I get it, Jay, okay? They are your nymphs … you don't need to spell it out. I learned that lesson in New York, remember?"

Jay raised his eyebrows, surprised she was so astute. Then he narrowed his eyes. "You have your friends too, Tia," he said.

She balked. "Yes, *friends*, Jay … I have only slept with two men in my whole life. So, yes, I am thick and naive. But I have friends – close friends – and I lost two this week. One died in my arms." Her voice quavered and her eyes filled with tears. "I had to take his essence into me so he didn't die alone. I will carry his soul with me till the day I die. And Cash and Sean are still missing. So sorry if I don't fully understand your set-up, Jay, but frankly, I'm too tired to give a damn. So I'm going to go, okay?" She pushed past him and up the stairs to the street.

Jay joined her a second later and put his jacket around her shoulders. He hailed a cab and got in after her. He was about to say The Bluebell, but when he saw how ruined she looked, he said the airport instead. No point in drawing this out.

Jay sat and studied her and watched a tear roll down her cheek. He wanted to touch her and take the tear away, but felt unworthy. *Fuck*, he underestimated her. He always made the same mistake of assuming she was like any other Human girl.

He knew she loved her friends. It was a deep love, even though it wasn't physical. She was such a pure spirit. He always tainted her with his corrupt mind and the women he'd been around all his life. Darkly Begotten reverberated in the recesses of his mind. *Fuck.*

She had ended the life of a man she loved and absorbed his spirit into her, and now had that memory with her for ever. He couldn't begin to think how painful that was. He didn't know what he'd been thinking tonight. He guessed he hadn't thought much at all. "I'm sorry," he said, simply.

"Sorry for my loss, or sorry for being such a prick all night?"

"Both."

A sob escaped her. "Thank you," she said, eventually.

"I guess I'm not what you thought I was," he said, quietly.

She looked over at him with soulful eyes, "I didn't think you were anything, Jay. I just enjoyed being with you and loved you." She said it sadly, as if it were as natural as breathing and, devastatingly, in the past tense.

He looked away and out of the window at the brightly lit shops drifting by. That was it in a nutshell, wasn't it? She just took people for what they were at that moment. Not from their past, or reputation or where they came from. She was a rare spirit and he'd crapped on her from a great height. *Fuck.*

Tonight, he hadn't needed to take her to those kinds of places. If he'd wanted to, he could've used his charm offensive and swept her off her feet and, who knows, possibly freed her power. But the truth of it was, he didn't want her getting into him all over again. It just couldn't happen like that anymore. The idea was to free her power and that was it. So he guessed that was his fucked-up reasoning for dragging her around, to give her a nice big eyeful of the shallow fuck he really was. "You are with Dante now and happy?" he asked, looking back at her, dreading and conversely praying for a yes.

She nodded but looked down at her hands. "I'm only here for his sake."

Jay chuffed a mirthless laugh. That was so typical. Dante would be jealous because she'd spent time with him, and she was only doing it for Dante. The poor cow couldn't win whatever she did. "I'm glad you are happy with him, Tia."

"Really?"

"Yeah, really." And he meant it. His best friend had really grown up in the last few months, and he knew that all he ever wanted was Tia and to be a good king. He was happy that Dante was getting his wish, especially as it couldn't be him. "We've got to get your power back, though, Tia." So much rested on it. Dante needed her power to be a successful, strong king with all her sisters. She'd already fuelled many of his new abilities.

But more importantly, she had to be able to complete the bond with Dante and him, so they all didn't get sick and die, and to have the essential link that would help to keep her safe.

She nodded and sighed. "What can we do?"

"I know it sort of backfired tonight, but I did genuinely think that if we could spend some time together, something might happen."

"It didn't happen when you got in bed with me?" she reminded him.

He nodded, conceding. "But I was still on the meds then."

She swallowed hard. "I don't know how to open up to you any more, Jay."

"I know," he smiled wanly. "We'll have to get to know each other again." *Fuck knows how he would keep his hands off her.*

She took a deep breath and nodded.

"And I've got to stop underestimating you."

She smiled genuinely then.

CHAPTER 18

*I*sla waited a few days before Cesaré paid her any attention. She guessed he had to muster up the courage. There, hanging in her room, he'd left a beautiful dress in an antique-rose colour, along with a note:

To my beautiful mate.
Be ready at 8, I will collect you for dinner.
Ces x

Her heart pounded as she read it. It was like a love letter. *My god, what was she doing to such a lovely man?* She looked straight ahead of her and, for a split second, contemplated running away. She figured anything was preferable to this evil witch Malleven was turning her into.

But needs must. She had no choice in the end, and so she bathed and dressed, ready for him to collect her.

When he came, he looked and smelled delicious. He'd had a rare shave and wore a pink shirt over his trademark low-slung jeans. His perfect blue eyes twinkled.

She let him lead her to the gardens, now cooling down

after the heat of the day, giving way to a spectacular sunset. There, on a beautiful patio, overlooking the view of the lake and village below, was a small table and two chairs, laden with food left prepared for them.

She wiped a small tear from the corner of her eye.

"What is it, Isla?" His face was all concern.

She shook the melancholy away. "Nothing, it's perfect."

He pulled her chair out for her and sat opposite. She didn't meet his eyes but gazed out over the hillside and felt the most wretched person alive. "No one in my life has been this kind to me, Cesaré, and I don't deserve it."

He picked up her hand and kissed it. "You do deserve it, Isla. You must give yourself permission to allow me."

Isla looked into his solemn eyes and could have wept at the goodness she saw there. "I am not what you think I am, Cesaré."

"Nonsense," he said, frowning. "Let us talk of pleasurable things and perhaps I can make you smile?"

She swallowed the lump in her throat and smiled for him. *If only Cesaré could have been her mate, and she had never met Darres, how simple her life could have been.*

She looked back at the house and realized for the first time that all the staff had been dismissed for the evening. The food had been prepared beforehand, all to give them privacy. *God, tonight was the night. If ever there was going to be one.*

Cesaré clicked a remote control and jazz music began to play, sultry Billy Holiday. "Will you dance with me, Isla?" He stood and held out a hand, but his face was stricken with an adorable insecurity that she would turn him down.

"I don't know how," she said, with regret.

He cocked his head at an angle and frowned. "You never learned?"

"I've never danced."

He looked at her for a long moment. "What a terrible life you have led," he said, sadly. He snapped his fingers. "Come … it's not hard. I would be honoured to be your first dance partner."

She fought the urge to run from the table, crying at the irony in his kind words, and stood instead. He led her to a space a little way away from the table and pulled her in close with one hand, and with the other, he held the hollow of her back.

It felt gentle and caring, and for a moment, she relaxed and allowed herself to sway gently with him.

"You are a natural," he whispered, next to her ear.

She smiled up at him. "Thank you."

Cesaré pulled her tighter to him so her lower half was against him and their legs touched as they moved. "You don't feel scared of me anymore?" he said, next to her ear again.

Isla snuggled into his shoulder and just shook her head.

He drew her in, tighter still and put both his arms behind her back so she had to put her arms around his neck. They continued to sway and move their feet slowly to the music. He pulled away from her slightly and stared into her eyes. Then he bent down and brushed her lips with his; the barest touch, and pulled back, searching her eyes again.

He was gauging her reaction to him. She moved her hands up to his cheeks and brushed them with her thumbs and guided him down to her mouth again. They continued to move to the music.

This time, she kissed him. It was gentle and closed-mouthed. He remained passive and allowed her to explore him without pushing her. She tentatively licked the seam of his lips and he opened his slightly.

Isla ventured inside his mouth with her tongue and he met her gently with his, coaxing, caressing and stroking. He let her explore the kiss for herself, following her lead, never rushing, going totally at her pace. It felt like the kiss lasted a lifetime, but was over all too quickly.

Cesaré eventually pulled away and smiled. "Let us eat," he said.

She nodded. And he led her back to the table. A wonderful evening followed – talking, drinking wine, and sharing funny stories from his youth. He spoke of his love of surfing. She could listen to his lovely accent in his deep voice rumbling all evening.

"What about you, Isla … what do you love?"

Like a stab to the heart, the words came to mind: *Never let them know what you love...*

She must have been miles away.

"Isla … Isla?" Cesaré was saying now, all concern.

"I'm sorry," she said, coming back to the present. "I was remembering something someone once said to me a long time ago."

Cesaré studied her for a long while, in the way she was getting used to. "You don't have to tell me if you don't want to." He was smiling, and reached for a strawberry and offered it to her to bite.

"Japan!" she blurted.

He seemed taken aback and frowned.

"My home … that's what I love." She looked away from him to hide her embarrassment at her outburst.

She knew he was watching her, but he didn't question her further. He seemed to know she had revealed a major thing to him and felt vulnerable.

A little more of her died inside at the thought of what she had to do to him.

"Spend the night with me, Isla?" Cesaré said, his voice broken, husky with emotion.

Their eyes locked together. Cesaré's face was serious, like a little boy with no game or guile.

"Okay," she whispered.

A cautious smile crept over him and he relaxed. He stood, grabbing a bottle of champagne with one hand and, reaching down to her with the other, he pulled her up to stand.

They walked hand in hand back to the house.

It felt like a walk of shame and lasted an eternity. They had only reached the third or fourth step on the grand staircase when a commotion erupted behind them.

They stopped and turned. Her heart, already pounding, sped up if that were possible. Several people had bustled in through the dark wood front doors, gabbling Italian at rapid speed.

"Ah shit," she heard Cesaré mutter.

"What ... who is it?" she said, frowning up at him, then recognized one was his father.

He didn't answer as he was already walking back down the staircase. "Mama, Papa ... Sandro ... what are you doing here?"

The woman clutched him to her and kissed him, then studied his face closely in the way she guessed a mother does when she hasn't seen her offspring in a long while. She pinched his face and kissed him again and released him just as quickly to approach Isla. "Ah ... the beautiful Bonaci," she sighed, and hugged her too. "I am Elena ... Cesaré's mother."

Cesaré quickly came and put his arm around Isla and introduced her.

"Where are the servants, dear?" his mother said loudly. "We have bags outside."

"I can help you, Mother ... I dismissed them for the evening ... it's late," Cesaré said, glancing at Isla with a brief look of regret. The plan for the rest of the night was ruined.

Isla couldn't help feeling that if a god existed and was

watching from heaven, then he'd helped her tonight. She gave a small smile back, which she was sure that Cesaré took as her being as disappointed as he was.

Cesaré's brother started bringing in their heavy bags. "Are you staying a while?" Cesaré said.

"Tomorrow we leave for Ireland, Cesaré. It is time we speak with the king," Cesaré's father said.

Isla daren't breathe. *Could what she'd waited for have come at last?*

"What about Isla? She is not ready to face him," Cesaré said, looking between his father and mother.

"That is why I'm here," his mother said, smiling. "I thought it would be nice to get to know my new daughter while you make the necessary arrangements."

Oh no... that was the last thing she wanted. The thought of being left alone with Cesaré's mother terrified her. *What if she saw through her?* She'd heard of a mother's intuition.

It suddenly occurred to her that she had never spent any time with females in her whole life. Apart from scientists and doctors, she had never interacted with women at all. She swallowed hard.

Cesaré's family began to disperse and take some of their belongings up to their rooms. It finally left her and Cesaré alone. He approached her and held her by the shoulders. His eyes smouldered. "It seems we were not meant to be together tonight."

He didn't know how truly prophetic his words were.

She smiled at him sadly at the disappointment on his face, but she couldn't help feeling she'd had a reprieve.

DANTE FELT a mixture of joy and disappointment when Jay and Tia returned. He'd prepared himself for the inevitability of Tia falling back into Jay's arms.

When she stomped past him and went straight to bed, and he was forced to ask Jay if it went okay, his heart thumped when Jay replied that nothing had happened as they were now strangers.

The realization that Tia was now closer to him and cooler towards Jay was a bolt from the blue, quickly followed by the sinking thought: no power, no kingdom, and, much more basely, that he needed to feel her spirit inside him desperately.

Dante let the dust settle and for Tia's hangover to pass, allowing her to chill out for a couple of days. Then Jay came to inform him that he was returning to London.

"We'll come with you," Dante said on the spur of the moment.

"Really?" Jay said, surprised.

"You were right about getting out with Tia and letting your hair down, except this time I'm coming."

"What, the three of us?" Jay said, his face showing a rare mixture of doubt and apprehension.

"We'll have a craic, why not?"

Jay shrugged, still not convinced. "Okay," he said, shaking his head.

"The three of us, though, Jay. No fucking off with other people ... for one night it's just us."

Jay sighed. "Why not ..."

Dante nodded once. It was decided. He didn't know why Jay was so hesitant. He had nothing to lose.

THEY ALL ARRIVED at The Bluebell later that night. Tia was quiet, but Dante was sure he'd win her around. He pulled her to him when they arrived in their room next to Jay's and kissed her.

Tia looked up into his eyes. "Why are you doing this … apart from the obvious, I mean?"

"You've got to stop thinking tonight," Dante said, gently circling her temples with his thumbs. "Your cogs won't stop turning … let go and just have a nice time."

"Is that your expertise?" she said, smiling.

"Yes … hedonism and underwater sex."

She laughed easily and he squeezed her to him.

"Let's go," he said.

Two Santalini guardsmen joined them and followed along unobtrusively. Dante had long resigned himself to the fact that being royal meant always having them around.

He made sure they went to all the cooler nightspots, with a good ambience and chilled music; not the dives that Jay had dragged Tia to a couple of nights before. He knew exactly the places she would appreciate.

He made them all drink shots, told anecdotes from their youth and got them all dancing. Jay loosened up until they even linked arms, the three of them, as they walked in the street to the next club.

Both he and Jay excused themselves when girls came over; which was often, as they were well known, but Dante had no urge to mingle with any of them. He even introduced Tia as his wife a couple of times and enjoyed the shock on the girls' faces. They really spent the whole evening in their own little world.

After about the third bar and the second club, they were all flagging. Tia was pissed enough to jump onto a podium with one of the club dancers and cavort suggestively. Dante looked at Jay, who read his mind and they both laughed.

TIA WATCHED her men from the podium as she danced. She felt warm and fuzzy as she watched them and it wasn't just because of the drink. They were laughing together and she witnessed their bond up close. She felt privileged to see it and would have loved to know them as children.

Her gyrating was only halted when she watched a pock-marked, wiry man go up to Dante and push him, provoking him to fight. Dante held his arms up, not wanting any trouble.

She slid down off her podium and made her way nearer through the crowd. The sudden alertness and presence of the guards made her worry and hurry towards them.

As she got there, one of the guards barred her way. "Stay back," he said, but he was watching the situation and not looking at her at all, ready to jump in should he be needed.

"Come on then, rich boy," she heard the troublemaker say.

Then everything happened so fast.

A flash of silver and he whipped out a knife. Dante jumped backwards, fast, in reflex, out of slashing distance. Then, before anyone else reacted, Jay grabbed the bloke's wrist, twisting it and breaking it while he freed the knife, and had it at the man's throat in seconds.

By then, the club bouncers were homing in on the trouble and came over to Dante. He touched Jay on the back to get him to stand down and let the man go.

"You're lucky you're in public," Jay whispered through gritted teeth. He pushed the guy roughly and stood up, not breaking eye contact. Eventually, he gave the bouncer the knife. Another yanked the man to his feet and the pair bundled him out of the place through a back entrance.

Tia had just started breathing again when the manager came over. He shook Dante and Jay's hands. He obviously knew them and said he recognized the interloper as a known troublemaker.

However, the incident had sobered them all up.

"Come on," Dante said, putting his arm around both hers and Jay's shoulders. "Let's go back."

They were quiet and subdued in the cab on the way back to The Bluebell. Dante broke the silence. "Where did you get that handy with a knife?"

"Keenan," Jay answered flatly, with no further explanation.

Dante nodded, obviously not needing one. Then he grinned, "Are you going for membership of the fucking Santalini as well now?"

"Fuck off," was Jay's reply, but he couldn't stop a grin creeping across his face.

Just like that, Dante had lightened the mood. She loved him for that.

When they arrived at The Bluebell, they piled into Jay's room. He'd promised them a chilled bottle of bubbly to bring their mood back up. He popped the cork and gave each of them a glass.

Tia quickly shucked her jacket and jeans to get more comfortable, and sat cross-legged on the foot of Jay's bed.

"Are you hot, Tia?" Dante asked, with an amorous look on his face, leaning with his back against the headboard.

"No ... just wanted to get comfortable."

Jay sat in the same position next to Dante and looked over at him with narrowed eyes. "Don't get any ideas ... I'm not fucking three-waying it."

Her face must have been a picture as Dante looked at her and laughed while he took a roll-up out of his pocket. "Is that a joint?" she asked.

"Fuck, I haven't smoked in ages," Jay said.

"Ah, keep your hair on, folks. It's just one ... it'll give us a giggle, is all." Dante lit it, took a long, hard toke and leaned back against the headboard. Then, passing the joint to Jay, he slowly exhaled, not taking his eyes from hers.

She studied them, both a little worse for wear but devastatingly hot, the pair of them. "Have you ever … you know, three-wayed it before?" She just had to ask.

The two of them looked at each other and laughed. "Yes," they said, both together, as they looked back at her.

"A few times," Jay added.

"Sometimes more than three," Dante added.

Her eyes must have widened with each comment as they both laughed at her. "What about homosexual experiences … I mean … have you, two?" she said, turning the tables back on them.

They both looked at her with screwed-up faces of disgust. As if she dared to even think such a thing.

"Fuck, no," Jay said, affronted. "He's not my type."

Dante was finding Jay's discomfort highly amusing. "We can't guarantee every girl we thought was female was though," Dante said, breaking into fits of laughter between words.

Jay ended up joining in and Tia laughed with them. It was hysterical. "You were just a pair of naughty boys," she said, in pain.

They tried to straighten up and stop giggling. "That we were, Tia," Dante managed to say eventually. Another fit of giggles caused Dante to cry in pain. "For fuck sake, Tia, blow in your man's face, will you. I'm in pain here." They all fell about laughing again.

The situation of why they were there, mixed with the drink and the smoke, had reduced them to gibbering wrecks of laughter and the realization of it made them laugh all the more. Tia felt helpless with laughter, too.

Eventually, she moved up the bed and motioned for Jay to shimmy down so he could lie flat on his back. She crept up between Dante and Jay and reached down to slowly cover Jay's lips with hers.

They were now completely silent except for London Grammar playing hauntingly in the background. Dante was watching closely, creating added pressure. She crouched over Jay and slowly lowered her head until her lips were just a centimetre away. His face remained deadpan – just. But just as she went to blow, the corners of his mouth twitched and a giggle blasted from her mouth instead of her essence, making her collapse in a fit of laughter on top of Jay. Dante joined in helplessly.

"Fuck," Tia said, trying to straighten the muscles in her face. "Do it again.'"

Again, she approached tentatively, but was forced to abort her mission when she felt the bed shake with the shudders of Dante's laughter, despite him trying to hold it in. Three more attempts and she concluded it was hopeless. Each time she was nearly there, all three of them dissolved into giggles.

"Give me a blow-back, Tia?" Dante said. "Imagine that, Jay, smoke mixed with Siren breath."

Tia guessed there was no point in continuing and turned the spliff around in her mouth so the lit end was inside. She leaned in to Dante's face, cupped her hands and focused the stream into Dante's pursed lips.

There was a tingle in her chest, nothing more. The essence that left her was a tiny glow, and not much to speak of at all.

Dante kept his eyes closed with the pleasure of the concoction and rested back against the headboard. "Fuck. It's like a bong, Jay," he said, exhaling loudly.

Tia looked at them all in varying positions of disarray. "Did it ever occur to you that us three are running a nation?"

They all laughed haltingly as they visualized the absurd idea.

"What are you saying?" Dante said. "That's fucking treason, Tia. I could have you locked up for that." He tried to hold a straight face.

"Oh, not again," Tia whined, and they all collapsed with laughter.

Jay sobered himself. "Give him the joint," he said, motioning his thumb in Dante's direction.

Tia obeyed and frowned at him.

"Try again," Jay said.

As she went to move closer towards him, he flipped her onto her back and under him quicker than her brain could track. He suspended himself over her, staring into her heavy-lidded eyes.

"That's my cue to go," Dante said, getting himself up and off the bed with great effort.

Tia sensed him leave and wanted to grab onto him, but instead, her eyes never left Jay's.

JAY WAITED LONG ENOUGH for his door to click shut and Dante to be far enough away not to hear and then sprang off her. The sudden action shocked her. His eyes stayed on her menacingly while he walked to the bathroom, disappeared, and she heard the hiss of the shower being switched on.

She swallowed hard. The mood had grown suddenly serious. "I don't need the shower any more, Jay," she said quietly when he came back out.

"You will," he said, and reached a hand down to pull her to her feet.

She padded lazily behind him to the bathroom. He turned on her immediately and pulled her vest top over her head. He appeared to gaze at her appreciatively while she stood in just her underwear. Without a word, he pulled his own T-shirt over his head and then stepped out of his jeans.

He reached his hand under the spray to test the temperature. "We'll start with the water warm and turn it down when we need to, okay?"

She nodded, sceptical that it would be needed.

"Get in," he ordered.

She did as she was told. There was something so sexual about the way he was all business. Her traitorous body couldn't help but respond. However, she felt firmly with Dante now and Jay had left her in the cruellest way; and yet Dante had pushed them together in the hope it would release her power. It was enough to send her crazy.

Next off were his boxer shorts and he stepped in insolently close to her. That innate defiant confidence he had about him with anything sexual, quaked her knees as it always did. She closed her eyes to calm her wildly beating heart. "Do you love me, Jay?" she asked, her eyes flashing open.

He sagged, closing his eyes momentarily, as if she'd ruined the moment. He shook his head sadly while he gathered his thoughts. "It's hard for me to love … I told you a long time ago. That I wouldn't allow myself to feel for you like that."

She swallowed the lump in her throat that kept on rising. "Do you like me then … I mean, as a person?"

Jay drew back slightly with his brows drawn together. "Of course I like you. You are one of my favourite people."

She took a deep breath. "Because I love you, Jay, but I don't think I like you very much."

He raised his eyebrows in surprise at that. "But you like Dante, though?" he said with his head on an angle, slightly mystified.

"Dante is honest." She paused while she thought. "Crazy, but honest … but you … you're not honest with yourself, or me."

The air was knocked out of her as he pushed her roughly

against the shower wall. Her eyes were wide with fright, looking up at him.

"I can live with that," he whispered, lowering his mouth next to hers. "It's probably safer that you think that way."

Before she could analyse too deeply what he'd said, he picked her up like he always had and put his mouth on hers roughly, harsh and demanding.

Her shock instantly dissolved like she was born ready for him. She devoured him hungrily, pulling his hair between her fingers, scratching his shoulders and pulling herself higher so she could be lowered onto him. Nothing about it was loving and nothing was gentle. It was all about want and need, anger and passion. She worked herself onto him to the hilt and she combusted. Heat flamed from her toes so strong, she didn't know if she had climaxed immediately.

Jay paused momentarily, looked into her face and then turned down the dial. He growled into her ear as he resumed pumping. "You're back."

She cried out when he bit the soft part of her shoulder. What was locked down broke out. Everything became free; her ability to feel, her love, her spirit, the very root of who she was, exploded around him.

CHAPTER 19

Just for a little while, Jay put to the back of his mind the logic that told him he was toxic and that he should never touch her and must get the fuck away from *her*, Dante and everyone that meant something. Instead he turned her and braced her to the wall and pounded into her for all he was worth. He couldn't remember ever wanting to bury himself so deeply. He wanted to be so close he could lose himself. It was something primeval, something animal. This woman was his.

His climax built strongly. Higher and higher, he'd never felt this intensely for another living soul. He slowed instinctively, knowing it was time. He moved his lips gradually while her head was turned sideways against the wall, from her ear to her cheek, then slowly to her mouth. His breathing was ragged with his exertion and anticipation. "Now, babe," he whispered.

He adjusted his rhythm to move in and out of her, deliberately goading her slowly. She responded to him by finding his lips and licking them. He parted his slightly and sucked her tongue into him where he circled it with his own.

When he needed to control the kiss, he plunged his tongue into her mouth as he penetrated her deeply, making her gasp loudly. It was coming, he could tell. She'd become more still; she gripped his tongue with her teeth so he could no longer move it. He matched her by reducing his movements, waiting for her. It had been so long. He knew it would be strong.

Then suddenly, like a saucepan boiling over, it cascaded into him. A great torrent of her spirit held down, repressed, now freed. He gasped as it flooded into him, so powerful that he went limp for a second and fell against her.

Jay caught himself quickly and strengthened the seal on their lips, allowing nothing to escape. He was determined to absorb all of her, not knowing if it would ever happen again. The flow went on for so long that his consciousness was erratic, but he didn't care. His life was wretched without her and if he had to go, he was sure this was the method he'd want to take.

The feeling was ecstasy. He lost count of the number of times he came. It had all blurred into an eternal orgasm that went on and on while they stayed rooted to the spot.

Eventually, the stream petered out and his muscles vibrated on a contented hum. The heat in him raged and his heart jumped and palpitated while he tried to catch his breath. Slowly, he released his grip on her upper body but still rested against her, breathing hard.

Jay became aware of how quiet she was when his heart began to return to normal and he opened his eyes. He couldn't help smiling when he saw she was hooped from head to foot in her beautiful black stripes. "Comic book girl," he said, hugging her. "Thank you," he murmured, next to her ear. *Fuck, he'd missed this.* The wonderful feeling of love and belonging she had selflessly given free of charge, regardless of the emotional cost to her.

Still, she didn't speak. He reluctantly pushed apart from her, wrapped a towel around his waist and passed one to her, which she took and wrapped around herself. They walked back into the bedroom and he flopped down onto the bed with his forearm over his eyes. He could feel he was burning up – he was raging hot. He'd had much more of her than was usual.

Jay couldn't resist peering under his arm to take a peek at her and watched as she sat in the furthest corner of the room in an armchair. *Guilt, fuck.* He felt shit enough as it was.

That was how she must have always felt when she was with him before and had to spend time with Dante. He covered his eyes with his arm again, not able to bear to look at her. "Are you okay?" he asked quietly. Speaking was an effort.

"I'll live," she said, eventually. "I'm sorry, I couldn't control it like I always do."

"I could tell."

A light tapping on the door stopped her reply.

"Come in, Dant," Jay said more loudly.

Tia was sitting with her forehead in her hand, quietly weeping, still flushed from their lovemaking, stripes plastering her whole body, when Dante walked into the room. "It worked then," he said quietly, all remnants of humour gone.

He walked past Jay and passed him a vial of clear liquid that Jay knew straight away was Elixir. Dante had known what would happen and had come prepared. *Shit.*

Jay removed his arm from his eyes and took it from him. "Thanks, man." He took a brief glance at his old friend, whose eyes were bloodshot from drink and smoke. The understanding of how Dante had felt while he'd been alone, knowing what was going on, passed between them. "You'd better take her," Jay said, hating himself.

Dante looked over at her and nodded. "Are you coming

with me, or are you staying?" he said, softly, like he had no idea of her response.

She buried her head in her hands and sobbed into them.

"Take her," Jay said, more forcefully, not able to bear listening to her any more.

Dante walked over to her and crouched down. He whispered something into her ear and she nodded. When he picked her up, she buried her face into his chest. "Later, man," he said to Jay as he walked out.

Jay just put up his hand.

WHEN THEY REACHED their room down the hall, Tia was still crying. Gently, he sat her on the edge of the bed and asked her to look at him. In the end, he pulled her hands away from her face.

"Hey, why are you crying?" he asked, crouching down to her eyeline.

She looked into his eyes but didn't answer.

"Don't feel bad ... I'm just relieved you came back to me after super stud." He said it with a smile, but it wasn't far from the truth. Somehow, he had always known that Jay was the key to freeing her power. Not only did Jay's bond need replenishing as his own did, though not as often, but the exchange of breath was always a connection of emotion and, in their case, cut off suddenly. It stood to reason that it could only be the two of them that could bring it back – a necessary evil.

His soothing words just made her wail.

"Listen ... Tia. Please. I don't want you to feel bad... Tia!" he repeated, till he got her attention. "I made you do it. I brought you here and I made you ... It was necessary, okay?"

As his words seeped in, she gradually stopped crying. He knelt on the floor, between her knees, cuddling her and rocking her to and fro. "Do you want me to run you a cool bath so you can sleep in it?" he asked.

She hiccupped and agreed. "Have you ever slept under-water?" she said, hiccupping again.

He shook his head, "No, never."

"Do you want to try it with me?"

He nodded, then got up and walked to the bathroom and started running the water into the large oblong plunge bath about three feet deep.

When it was almost full, they both lowered themselves in so just their heads were out of the water. They sank back to wet their hair and gazed at each other. She had stopped crying, but her eyes were red, a mixture of alcohol and tears. "I want to give you something tonight, Dante ... something new."

Dante's heart thumped. *What was there possibly left for her to give?* He waited for her to explain.

"When I breathe for you, you must breathe straight back. Do you understand?"

He agreed with a frown, not really understanding what was new, but he trusted her and allowed her to lead him.

"I am feeling very strong, you must tell me if it is too much?"

"Okay," he said, softly, and came towards her. He wanted her badly, not able to feel her essence in so long; there was no way he was going to refuse.

She stared into his eyes for a long moment, then submerged and he followed. He allowed her to dominate him and push him to the bottom of the bath, where she lay on top of him and let the water into her lungs. He followed her lead.

Tia didn't wait and locked her lips on his, blowing a steady stream straight into him. He wanted to float in the sensation of sheer pleasure. *Now, Dante,* she projected. He roused himself and reciprocated. He tried to keep his breaths even, but his heart was skipping all over the place.

As soon as he finished, she replied with more, and he repeated, until they were breathing on a continuous loop, as if they were each other's oxygen supply.

First of all, it overwhelmed Dante and he thought he would have to stop her; the feeling was so acute. Instead, he worked through the rushes and palpitations until he swam in the euphoria. In the end, he had it so together that he could walk into Tia's mind's eye.

When he walked in, he found her standing waiting for him. "What is this?" he asked in wonder.

"I think it's the next step."

He walked right up to her until he gazed down into her beautiful striped face. "The next step to what?"

"I'm not sure … but I think it's the next step to togetherness … watch." And she turned her back to his chest and took a step backwards. "It feels necessary, Dante."

Gradually, the light around the black expanse got brighter till it was so bright it blinded him. Tia lifted up his arms with her own underneath them and he was startled to see their stripes begin to move and appear to blend together. Their arms liquefied into one. She took a step back into him, and the light went white.

ISLA SPENT AN UNEASY NIGHT, even though she was alone. Cesaré had left early with his father; she'd heard them go. That left her in the house alone with Elena, Cesaré's mother.

Isla lay in bed as long as she could, but was forced to get up when Petra, the maid, knocked to tell her that Elena would be taking her breakfast outside and expected her to join her shortly.

With a deep feeling of foreboding, Isla showered and

dressed in a casual sundress and sunglasses. It was in the vain hope that she could hide behind the dark shades. This was indeed her greatest test to date.

Her heart was in her mouth and she felt sick as she approached the composed, ram-rod straight woman, who sat reading the paper on the shaded patio next to the pool. Her eyes strayed to it with longing. If only she could disappear into its depths and stay hidden. It was a feeling that was becoming overwhelming these days.

"Good morning," Isla said timidly, forcing her eyes back to Cesaré's mother.

Elena looked up from her paper, smiled, and indicated to the chair opposite for her to sit.

Isla took the seat and sat quietly.

"Do you take tea or coffee first thing?" Elena said.

"Oh, I don't mind … anything."

"It's not a test, Isla. I'm merely trying to get to know you."

"Tea," Isla asserted more forcefully. However, she was beginning to think that a test was exactly what this meeting was.

She watched Elena pour the tea from a pretty china pot. She was beautiful, Isla decided, but her face was all hard lines, like one of the classic models she'd seen in the magazines she'd been allowed to read. With her hair blonde severely scraped back from her face and lips painted red, she was a picture of no-nonsense efficiency.

Elena pushed the filled cup and saucer in front of her and told her to help herself to the array of pastries. Then she sat back and watched Isla butter a slice of toast. "Are you wary of me, Isla?" she said, smiling.

"Of course," Isla answered honestly. "You are the most important person for me to please."

Elena's face got serious. "Wrong, Isla … Cesaré is the most important person for you to please." She sat back in her chair, having made her point. "Please him and you please me."

Isla's face blasted red. She'd just made her first blunder with this woman. She had to be careful what she said, otherwise she would see right through her. Elena was formidable.

Then she went straight for the jugular. "I understand it was Malleven who first found you?"

Isla clinked her knife loudly as it slipped from her fingers and hit one of the delicate china plates. She blushed again.

Elena cocked her head to the side, waiting.

"Yes, he did," Isla said, eventually. *Get a grip*, she chided herself. This woman was walking all over her.

Elena changed tack. "You were held by the authorities?"

Relieved, Isla nodded. "Since I was a child."

Elena frowned as if she were sceptical. "What on earth did they do with you all that time?"

Isla felt a rare flood of anger, always having such a lid on her emotions most of the time. *Did she think she had been at some kiddy camp all these years? No, she'd done messing with this woman and she didn't even know her yet.* "I was an assassin ... I killed people ... lots of them. I was trained, assigned, and I did my job ... well." Isla finished her words unequivocally.

Elena acknowledged her with a small bob of the head. "Honesty ... Now we get somewhere."

Isla could have screamed in frustration. The woman was infuriating. She tried to calm herself down. Perhaps that was her intention: to get her to slip up and lower her guard. She gathered herself. "What will happen ... when Cesaré gets back, I mean?" she said, resting her hands in her lap.

"Providing they reach an agreement with the Dubonnetti king, we will all go to court ... More tea?" she said, smiling sweetly. "You have no qualms about killing?"

Isla just stared at her in amazement. *What was she supposed to say to that?* "Like who?" she said, exasperated.

Elena cocked her head to the side again. "Cesaré."

"Cesaré'?" Isla balked, gobsmacked. Why on earth would I want to do that? I like Cesaré"

"Only like?"

Isla narrowed her eyes slightly, knowing she'd fallen into the little trap Elena had set for her. "What do you expect me to say, Elena?" Isla said, drained. "We barely know each other."

"Give me your hand," Elena commanded.

"What?" Isla said, bewildered.

"Give me your hand," Elena repeated.

Isla slowly did as she was asked. As soon as it was close enough, Elena grasped it; slapped something into the centre of her palm, closed her hands tightly around and held it closed in a fist.

Isla squirmed slightly when she felt sharp edges digging into her skin.

"Hold still," Elena said.

"What are you doing?"

"Do you have any knowledge of your true purpose and power within the Atlantean nation?" Elena asked, her eyes boring into hers.

Isla frowned and tried to pull out of her grip, but Elena held her fast. "What? No … I know I must go to the king …"

"What of Cesaré?" Elena sniped.

"I don't understand … I have to marry the king."

Elena narrowed her eyes while she roughly released her grip on Isla's hand. "Open it," Elena commanded.

Isla slowly opened her palm. There, dug and pitted into her skin were what looked like glass or diamonds, except not all of them were bright; some were a dull grey colour of varying shades, as if charred by fire.

Before Isla could ask what they were, Elena pulled her fingers down flat so she could see the stones clearly. Isla, mildly annoyed, looked her in the eye, waiting for an explanation.

"Spirit crystals," Elena smirked. "The men are not the only ones with powerful stones."

Isla immediately thought of the divining rings all the princes wore and shifted in her seat with unease. Then Malleven's interference with Cesaré's. "What do these show?" she asked.

"Spirit crystals absorb dark energy from the soul and therefore reflect exactly what is there," Elena said, as a matter of fact. "The brighter the crystals, the purer the spirit."

Isla looked into her hand again. Her heart plummeted and she closed her eyes for a moment, as if exposed as the fraud she was. Some were bright – a few, but a lot were dark – some almost blackened.

Then Elena seemed to snap herself out of her present mood, smiled brightly and let go of her fingers. "Never fear, dear, no one has yet had completely brilliant stones. We all have a little of the darkness in us."

And just like that, the meeting was over.

Elena signalled for the maid, Petra, who was hovering in the doorway, to come and collect the plates and Isla used the opportunity to excuse herself. She scurried off as quickly as she could without actually running; the urge to do so was almost overwhelming.

Her chest felt tight and she clutched her throat. *Please, god, get me out of here ... let me get to my family.*

ELENA WATCHED the girl disappear like a frightened rabbit, then turned her attention to the maid. "Sit, Petra."

Petra obeyed and sat in the chair Isla had just vacated.

Elena sighed, "I fear what you suspected is true."

"It is, Madame, I know it is ... I rang you as soon as I saw

…" Petra trailed off before she put into words the graphic sight she had witnessed a couple of weeks before.

"And you think she loves Malleven?" She had nothing against Malleven; in fact, she liked the boy. She thought him hard-working and studious, making the most of his opportunities. She was no fool; she knew he was a rogue, but what healthy red-blooded boy wasn't?

Petra widened her eyes as if she wouldn't go that far as to assume it was anything resembling love. "They were getting very close in the servants' stairwell, madame…" She was letting Elena join the dots.

"While Cesaré was in the house?"

"He was in the meeting with the elders, madame."

Elena was quiet, absorbing the information. She narrowed her eyes at the girl. "Why do you tell me these things … you know Cesaré can never be for you?"

Petra dabbed the corner of her eye with a napkin dramatically. "I have known Cesaré since I was a little girl, madame. It is true I love him, but I am content to just be there should he need me."

Elena nodded, satisfied with Petra's answer and her acceptance that her position was nothing more than a plaything. Her mind came back to the pressing, troubling thoughts. "I fear I believe you … and yet the ring doesn't lie." She shook her head, not knowing what to make of the whole situation.

"We will continue as if we know nothing. You will come with me to Ireland. I will request you as my personal maid. You will be useful there."

Petra's eyes shone with her new importance. "I swear, madame, I will be of the utmost use."

"I have heard rumours of her sister, the king's mate. He continually has trouble with her, always turning to his own friend." Petra offered.

Elena shrugged. "It may be they are fickle in character, but ..." she trailed off in thought.

"Madame?"

"I fear it is something much more disturbing."

THE SCREAM WAS piercing and permeated the corridor down to Jay's room. It was about 2.30 p.m. and Jay had only just showered and dressed following his heavy night and subsequent hangover.

He walked briskly towards the loud rapping on his door and snatched it open, in no mood for aggravation today. He froze, surprised. "Maria ... what is it?"

"Mr Gardiner ... come quickly," the maid said in her thick Italian accent.

Jay followed her, but he already had a sneaking feeling that she was taking him next door, to Dante and Tia's room.

The two Santalini guards were still stationed outside and could not understand what the fuss was about.

Jay threw them a "what the fuck?" look, to which they both shrugged. "She went in to clean the room," Reeve explained. "It's empty."

"What's wrong, Maria?" Jay said, trying to get some sense out of the shaking, hysterical woman.

"In the bath, Mr Gardiner ... I don't know what it is ... maybe an animal?"

Jay began to suspect what she may have seen. He asked one of the guards to take her down and get her a nice cup of tea. He promised her he would sort it out, till in the end she reluctantly agreed.

Jay cautiously let himself into Dante and Tia's room using Maria's universal key card. Nothing seemed out of place. The bed hadn't even been slept in.

Slowly, he made his way to the bathroom, hoping he

knew what he would find. He pushed the door so it opened wide. Steam was rising from the filled bath. *Shit, that can't be right.*

He walked to the edge and peered down.

There, in the hot bath, were Dante and Tia, fully transformed, joined at the mouth in a tight embrace and glowing all over. They were radiating so much heat that they had heated the water in the bath dangerously.

"Trey?" he called to the remaining guard.

Trey appeared quickly.

"Help me," Jay said, trying to reach down into the water to heave Dante out.

Trey went to the other side and between them they managed to prize Dante out of Tia's arms and away from her mouth. They pulled him up over the side and out of the bath, sitting him on a chaise lounge. Jay patted his back until his lungs emptied and he coughed and appeared to come back to life. When he could support himself, they went back and did the same with Tia.

Jay quickly got towels for them both and draped them around their shoulders. Between them, he and Trey managed to move them to the bed in the bedroom, where they sat on the edge, still not appearing to be properly awake.

Dante looked spaced out and not with it at all. Tia was clinging to him, completely disoriented.

Jay looked at Dante's face and his eyes were weird. They were flickering from their usual slate grey to green and then going clear, like silver or water, and then they flickered green again.

Their stripes were heavy and black. Jay had never seen his friend look so alien before. It disturbed him. "Dante … Dante, man … Speak to me?"

Still nothing. Jay tried a different tack. "Tia!" And he went to shake her.

Dante's hand came at him lightning fast and grabbed his wrist. *Don't do that, Jay.* Jay heard in his head, except it sounded strange, as if Dante and Tia had spoken in unison.

"It's okay, Dante, it's only me. You needed to get out. You were overheating … the fucking maid found you."

Dante continued to look at him strangely, with his weird eyes rapidly changing, not seeing. *Leave us, Jay. I will meet you later. A couple of hours is all I need.* The strange double voice filtered through to Jay's head again.

Jay looked over at Trey and Reeve, who'd now joined them. They looked quizzically back. He straightened up. "We'll leave 'em to it. I'll check on them in a bit … stay outside though … let no one else in."

The guards nodded and turned. Jay followed them out, glancing back over his shoulder, concerned for his friend.

JAY LEFT it about an hour before he could stand it no longer and went back to the room to check on them. "Has anyone come out yet?" he asked the guards, still outside the door.

They shook their heads. "No, they've been really quiet," Reeve said.

Fuck. Jay paced in front of the door a few times, unsure what to do. "I'm going to check on them again. You two stay here."

He knocked quietly. When he got no answer, he used his key card and let himself in. He stood in the small hallway before he reached the bedroom and listened.

Nothing.

Jay cautiously walked into the bedroom. *Shit,* the bed still hadn't been slept in. He hoped they hadn't gone back to what they were doing when he found them. He walked around the bed and stopped when he heard a splash, then a murmur. It was coming from the bath.

Jay inched closer. The door was open, so he had a clear view.

At that point, he should have just turned around and gone back out the way he came, but he became rooted to the spot. He couldn't take his eyes off the bath.

Dante was leaning back against the soft padding that ran around the edge and he was still covered in stripes. His arms were out, holding onto the sides to steady himself, and Tia was facing him, kissing him hard and moving on him. Then she grazed her teeth down his neck and slowly disappeared below the surface of the water.

Dante threw his head back and moaned, then slid down under the water as well. Then there was nothing, just the water lapping over the sides now and then.

Again, Jay knew he should have turned away, but an absolute fascination just kept him there. This is what she was with Dante that she could never be with him. It gutted and compelled him equally.

Then Dante burst up out of the water like a marine animal, bringing Tia with him and they both took a breath. He pushed her to the furthest side and turned with her so his back was to Jay, then he began to move slowly and rhythmically against her from behind.

Jay watched all the tattoos and stripes on Dante's back move hypnotically with his muscles. Murmurs and sighs of pleasure echoed in the room. His glutes contracted and released as he pushed in and out so very slowly. Tia then straightened and turned and Dante lifted her onto the side facing him and he resumed his slow, sensual strokes until they gradually slid back into the water together and were submerged again.

Jay blinked. He realized he was sweating and breathing hard just watching, *fuck*. He'd never witnessed anything so erotic or so repellent in his life. He wasn't sure who he found more fascinating to watch or who he hated more for what they were doing.

Their heads emerged slowly out of the water and they both spat the water from their mouths. *Are you okay, Jay?* Dante projected, turning around to face him.

Fuck ... busted. Of course, he must have known he'd been there the whole time.

Tia, obviously embarrassed, crept behind the shelter of Dante's much larger body.

As if he wouldn't know she was there.

"I came to see if you were okay?" he found himself saying lamely.

I'll meet you in the bar in an hour when my voice comes back.

Jay just said, "Fine," and he turned and walked out.

Dante strolled into the bar, early evening, having shaved, showered, and changed, fresh as a daisy, as if nothing had happened. Jay had been brooding over his drink. The bar was still quiet.

He ordered Dante's usual when he saw him approach, but remained quiet while Dante pulled up a stool and sat down next to him.

"You not going to say anything to me, Jay?"

Jay faced him with his face blank. "I don't know what to say, mate … except maybe, sorry. I shouldn't have watched you, but fuck … I couldn't help it," Jay said, still not quite believing it himself.

"You've got a problem, though … I know you," Dante said, continuing to look at Jay, waiting for him to cut the bullshit.

Jay faced him irritably. "I've never seen you look like that. So … so."

"Alien?" Dante finished for him.

"She's changing you, Dant, more and more."

Dante shook his head. "No, Jay. It's what I've always been. You've just refused to see it … All our lives we've been in your world … don't you remember, all the girls … all the screwing? You were like the Terminator."

Jay stood up and went to turn away, then thought better of it. "You had your fair share."

Dante narrowed his eyes. "Come on, Jay, I was slaughtered and most of the time I couldn't even finish. I just didn't know no different. I went along for the craic. But you know … deep down … I knew it was all wrong, that something was missing. Now we are in my world … and it's like fucking coming home."

Jay breathed a sigh and nodded. He understood, of course he did. He gave a mirthless laugh. "I don't know which one of you I hate more for fucking the other one."

Dante threw his head back and laughed heartily, then put his arm around his friend's shoulders. "I gave you more than a fighting chance with her and you left her, remember?"

Jay smiled and nodded. He was right, of course. "I just don't seem to be able to get involved in anything more than a physical relationship with a woman."

Dante raised his eyebrows. "You're lying, Jay."

Jay looked at Dante with impatience and then just gave in. "Tia told me she loved me but didn't like me very much last night." He stared into his drink again.

Dante grinned. "Oh yeah?"

"She said I'm not honest … but you are; crazy but honest?" Jay said, looking at his friend cynically.

Dante laughed, eyebrows up, showing his total agreement. "In a nutshell, my man … The trouble with you, Jay, is you associate love and sex with your mother … you need a fucking shrink!" Dante laughed into his drink.

Jay was really insulted. "Fuck off … no way." He narrowed his eyes. "Well, if that's right, and I'm lying about my feelings for Tia, how does that work, then?"

"I dunno," Dante shrugged. "Maybe because she's not

Human, and so it's okay to like her … fuck knows … I'm no shrink."

Jay tutted and mulled over his drink while he thought about what he said.

"I think you're upset because the only two people you've ever cared about were fucking, is all."

Jay looked up to argue and then changed his mind. There was truth in that. "What was going on today then?" he said, changing the subject. "You looked so spaced out, I was worried about you."

Dante smiled and leaned on the bar as if he was experiencing a sweet memory. "When we left you she was upset, so I ran her a bath to sleep in. She asked me to join her and she showed me something."

Jay squinted his eyes, not sure he really wanted to know.

Dante continued. "It was mind-blowing, Jay. You know the feeling when she breathes for you?"

Jay nodded.

"Imagine that in a continuous loop, breathing for each other for several hours."

Jay straightened. "Fuck," was all he could say. His bond with Tia was only one-sided as he was Human, and he had only experienced it for a few seconds each time and that blew his mind. He shook his head.

"It was like a possession, like becoming one person."

"So you know everything?" Jay said, cautiously.

Dante knew why he asked that question. "Yes, but we agreed to leave our memories … for now."

"Why?" Jay said, needing to hear the words.

"You … we thought we shouldn't know everything about you."

Jay breathed out with relief.

"Have you ever wanted to know what an orgasm is like for a woman?" Dante said, grinning.

"Fuck yeah."

"Well I know, and it's good." Dante smiled and nodded sagely.

Jay laughed at his friend. "Really? Fuck … you bastard."

They went quiet for a minute after that revelation.

"I'm sorry, Dante."

"For what?"

"I don't seem to be able to keep my hands off her and she's yours now." He shook his head. "And you're married, for fuck's sake."

"Look," Dante said, becoming serious again. "I said the same thing to Tia last night. I pushed you two together. It was necessary, and it worked, okay? Neither of you wanted to do it. It's fucked-up … I know it is. But I pushed you both into it." Dante pulled Jay into a hug. "Don't sweat it, man. Okay?" Dante said, quietly in his ear. "But remember, I have access, if I want, to her memories." He pulled away and winked at him.

"Fuck," Jay said. "I'd better stop slagging you off."

Dante laughed. "And I'm fucking powerful now, Jay. More than ever before."

Dante and Tia travelled back to Ireland on the royal Dubonnetti jet and left Jay in London. Jay had agreed to keep his distance from Tia as much as possible, only seeing her when necessary. That was to see JJ and for her to breathe for him every so often to replenish the bond. They'd given up on the meds for a while until the Murrs could perfect them.

Dante was relieved, as although Jay was off his meds, because he was Human, his bond didn't need renewing as often as his own with Tia, being two-way. This gave Dante the space to concentrate on his family for the first time. He could have Tia all to himself and for them to interact together as a real family. It was the happiest he'd ever been.

He'd left the Americans sweating after the attack on Tia in Antarctica. They didn't know what his next move would be. Dante wanted them to learn their lesson – that they needed him onside if they were to be kept in the loop with Atlantean goings on and the progress of the last days and possible return from Atlas. So he had recalled his real father, the ambassador – Duke Ormond Delissi – as a clear message of a breakdown in communications. Let them shit themselves. He'd meet with the president when enough time had elapsed and it suited him.

He'd also heard rumours through his Murr contacts of a sighting of a Siren on the west coast of the US. Spies were being sent out all over. The possibility of a fourth Siren was exciting, but he'd have to box clever. His adversaries would be nervous. His power was growing every day as it was. With the fourth Siren, his position would be pretty much assured.

That brought his attention back to the third Siren, still not exactly in his possession yet. He knew the Florianna had her somewhere, but she had gone to ground and no one had seen or heard from her in months. That was a worry as it could suggest that they intended to keep her for their own bid for the crown. If that were the case, then the race was on for the remaining two Sirens.

He hoped that good sense would win through and they would join forces with him and see the sense in stability before Atlas returned.

So when he received the communication on his return to Ballygowan Castle, for an audience with him from Prince Cesaré Florianna, it filled him with hope that an affiliation was still on the cards. However, always in the back of his mind was the knowledge that it had been his enemy Malleven Mancini who had obtained her, and he happened to be a close cousin and friend of Cesaré's. He had also been behind Lacy's abduction. He still didn't know what his game was or how much Cesaré knew, if anything. He told himself that Cesaré's wanting to see him was still a positive move and he waited for his arrival with anticipation. *Fuck, he was growing to love this king shit.*

CESARÉ WAS the third son of the mystical family of Florianna. During the scandals surrounding Dante's ascension to the throne, the family had remained quiet and watchful, observing whatever way the Fates fell concerning the stability of Dante's new kingdom.

It had been no secret that prior to him being king, Dante was a drunken playboy. Then, no sooner had he found his Siren and become king, he'd been deposed by his own father and brothers, and his Siren wife split her time between him and his best friend. However, of late, his Siren, Tia Storm, appeared to be living happily with him and their three children, even if one of them wasn't his own.

Cesaré felt he couldn't exactly cast the first stone, with his own playboy reputation, and the fact that he and Isla hadn't exactly consummated their relationship yet.

When he'd confided in Malleven, he had urged him to waste no time in approaching the king, especially as she wasn't bonded, leaving herself and the Florianna house vulnerable until she did. So Cesaré had contacted his father and asked him to make the necessary contact with Prince Alfonzo Bonaci–Isla's uncle–to make the necessary arrangements for an audience with the king. It had been bloody sod's law that his mother and father would turn up right when he was about to finally get it on with the Siren in question. He decided it would be prudent to go ahead with the audience.

· · ·

THE KING WAS WAITING, seated in the great hall of Ballygowan Castle with both Alfonzo and Sebastian Bonaci. Cesaré approached with his father and elder brother, Sandro.

Cesaré was in awe of the room. It was huge, black and dominated by a massive window to the sea. Lit like a large aquarium, the window faced an ornate fountain in the centre where he'd been told a tunnel led to the sea underneath. The rest of the room was sumptuously furnished with an array of soft cushions, leather seating and ornate tables, giving the whole place a gothic feel.

Dante stood when they approached and shook all their hands warmly. Cesaré had met him a few times years before, and usually on the club circuit if he ever ventured onto Dante's stomping ground in London.

They both asked after each other's health and Dante asked them to sit. There was a moment of awkward silence that followed, where both princes assessed each other and waited for the other to speak first. It was Cesaré who broke the silence. "You know why we are here?"

Dante remained silent for a beat. "I hope."

Then Cesaré thought, *fuck it,* and launched in. "Forgive us for the delay, your highness, but we, as a family, wanted to observe from the sidelines, to see certain outcomes, to be sure you were a worthy king to offer our support."

Dante smiled. "Support … you mean, to offer your Siren's pledge to me?" he said, getting straight to the point.

Cesaré stared at Dante and he recognized in their silent exchange a mutual respect, in that they both had come a long way from their misspent youths. "If your highness is in agreement, I should like for you to meet her, and perhaps we can go from there?"

"She is not with you today?" Dante said, his eyes straying to Cesaré's father.

Cesaré steered the king's attention back to him, letting

him know he was very much his family's spokesman now. "We thought it expedient to come alone for this meeting."

Dante grinned. "She is with your family in Italy?" he asked.

Cesaré inclined his head.

"I was thinking of taking my family for a holiday to our residence in the Lakes. Perhaps you could call on us there. Tia would love to meet another of her sisters." Dante said, still appearing amused. "As would her father and uncle," he added, gesturing to either side of him to Alfonzo and Sebastian.

"How is she?" Sebastian asked.

Cesaré sympathized with the kindly looking man who had made the supreme sacrifice of giving up his daughters for the state. "She is well … but her time with the American authorities has left its mark on her," Cesaré said, cautiously.

Dante frowned and Sebastian looked desolate.

Cesaré continued, "I am yet to know the full extent of her ordeal, but I know she was trained as a government agent and had very little interaction or affection with other people. It has left her …" he was forced to pause with his emotion, "empty … your highness."

Dante studied him for a few moments, his mind working through the implications of what he was hearing. Cesaré didn't want to divulge his failing with her yet. He still felt there was time to rectify that.

Thankfully, Dante didn't press him further. "Very well," Dante said, brightening. "I will arrange to move us all to Lake Como in a few days. "Please call on us there. You will be welcome, Cesaré."

Cesaré and his delegation stood and bowed, recognizing the conclusion of the meeting. This was it. It was going to be make-or-break time for Isla, because she would have to bond with the king, and that meant getting up close and personal.

He just hoped she could cope with it because if she couldn't, he wasn't sure what would happen.

Now things were hotting up with Cesaré finally going to meet with the king, Malleven travelled through the night to his temple in Syria. A special meeting with his high priest had been arranged.

The next part of his plan could go either way. Ideally, Isla would pledge to the king, then, when Cesaré was bound to her, Malleven would bond with her and have a link to them all. But if something went wrong, he needed a backup plan, and that was what brought him to his brotherhood head-quarters this night.

He entered the huge sandstone room, bathed in a warm light from lanterns placed in alcoves around the edge. Nasr was seated on a throne on a raised platform in his full magi regalia of satin black robes.

Malleven knelt in front of him and waited to be blessed before he could stand up. Nasr made sure enough time elapsed to put him in his place.

"Up," Nasr said, and Malleven rose and kissed his ring. "Why are you here, Malleven … it is not the time for us to commune as brothers?"

"I come to seek your assistance with a matter of the utmost importance, High One," Malleven said, and waited.

"Continue," Nasr said.

"The Fates have decided that I should be chosen as mate to one of our highly prized Royal Sirens."

Nasr smiled. He was Human, but well-versed in the customs and prophecy of the Atlantean race. They had often worked together with the Magi over the millennia. "For that, you would need to be tested before you could claim her, would you not?"

Malleven bowed his head. "That is correct, High One."

Nasr sighed and shook his head. "They would kill you on sight, Malleven. It is no secret that you stole and imprisoned the Santalini prince's Siren." Nasr laughed. "And I know you well enough to know that you wouldn't go in through the front door when to arrive as a thief in the night would bring much greater dividends."

Malleven bowed his head again. He knew better than to contradict Nasr; he had an uncanny knack for seeing through untruths. "It could be that I have no other option than to go in through the front door," Malleven said, slowly raising his eyes to convey his meaning. "I would show strength if I arrived with my brotherhood," he said, averting his gaze again.

It was a game, one that rankled, having to be subservient to a Human such as Nasr. But he was powerful and the fact was that if his plans with Cesaré and Isla went off course, then he couldn't claim Isla without the magi behind him.

The Florianna would be devastated if they lost their seat in government in Cesaré and would see Malleven as a weak option because of his low birth, even if his ring was purple. However, the Florianna revered magic and all had heard of the magi and his connection with it, so if the magi stood with him, then the Florianna just might get behind him, and his dreams of being revered as a fully fledged Florianna prince would come true.

Nasr considered what Malleven had put before him for an agonizing few minutes until he squinted. "It is a risk for the brotherhood to openly stand with you."

"But one that would bring rich rewards, High One," Malleven said, bowing his head.

Nasr watched him for a moment with narrowed eyes. "How so, Malleven Mancini, who grew up with not a pot to piss in from his own family." The priest laughed.

Malleven let the slight pass and bit down, vowing he would have his day with the buffoon. "You are aware of the legend of the Darkly Begotten?" Malleven said, raising his eyes arrogantly.

Nasr's mirth disappeared and he narrowed his eyes on him again. "You know of its whereabouts?"

"I do, High One."

"And it is in your keeping?"

"I have it safely hidden."

"And what do you propose to offer the brotherhood to stand by your side?" Nasr said craftily, knowing full well that anyone would be reluctant to let go of such a prized possession.

"I would harness it and give the reins to the highest of all magi," Malleven said, bowing low, with his nose almost to the floor.

Nasr studied Malleven while he came to a decision. "You know the price should you betray your brotherhood, Malleven?" Nasr said, low and deliberate.

It had rarely happened, fear of it was so great, but Malleven had heard the legends where the spirits were summoned from the gates of hell to consume the traitor. That was after long and arduous torture.

Malleven wasn't overly concerned. He was too clever for that. "Loyalty is the quality I carry closest to my heart, High One," he purred, bowing his head again.

Nasr straightened in his throne. "Rise, my son. The magi will be your right hand to stand with you against your enemies and guard you when you sleep."

THE EXCITEMENT of meeting another of her sisters helped Tia push Jay to the back of her mind. She busied herself over the next two days packing and building up the kids' anticipation to a fever pitch.

It was evening and the kids were in bed and she snuggled into the sofa with Dante in the great hall, enjoying the chance to chat, laugh and lounge about which they had so little time for usually. He made her laugh, as always, with his roguish sense of humour and she felt content and easy with him, like the true couple they now were. "Why don't we go to bed?" she whispered, seductively.

Dante looked sideways at her through half-closed eyes, tempted to pounce, she could tell. "Soon," he said, as if she tested his patience. "First, I have to see Axyl; he will be here any moment."

She extracted herself from Dante's arms to sit up. "The Murr from Antarctica?" A pang of heartbreak hit her when she remembered her lost friends Ben and Josh, and there was still no word from Cash and Sean. She'd successfully put it all to the back of her mind.

Dante sensed her unhappiness and held her at arm's length to search her face. "Don't worry, babe, he just wants to say a farewell before he goes back to Murrla. He's been in Murrtaine since he brought you back."

A gentle lapping of the water in the fountain turned their heads just as Axyl and two of his lieutenants came up out of the fountain to rest on the wall, their overlong legs resting on the floor. Their feet shrank before their eyes and their leg bones solidified.

Dante pulled Tia up to stand with him and greet his guests. He called to two guards walking through to the lifts to help him move Axyl and his friends to more comfy seats nearby.

When they were all settled, Axyl looked at them both and grinned. *I can tell by your similar thought patterns that you now have a complete connection.*

Both Tia and Dante nodded and looked at each other in wonder at his astuteness.

And you can both hear me at the same time because of it, Axyl added, nodding. *We as Murrs bond with our females, but we can only guess at the pleasure and the strength of the complete connection.*

"Can I get you anything?" Dante asked, momentarily forgetting his job as host.

Axyl put up a hand. *No thanks. It is just a flying visit before we make the long journey back.*

"Thank you, Axyl … for what you did," Tia said, solemnly.

Axyl turned his strange black eyes on her. *It was my pleasure to help our queen out of trouble.*

Dante laughed aloud. "It won't be after about the twentieth time, she's always getting herself into fuckin' trouble, Axyl. The time before that, she managed to get herself caught in fishing nets off Florida."

The Murrs grinned silently. Having no vocal cords meant their laughter was strange and took some getting used to, but they took human-like facial expressions to convey they had recognized the humour in Dante's words.

"That's it!" Tia blurted.

All eyes suddenly went to her.

"What, babe?" Dante asked.

"It was you!" she said, pointing at Axyl.

Axyl frowned and looked to either side of him at his two lieutenants as if she'd lost her mind.

"Tia," Dante said, cautiously. "What are you talking about?"

She turned to face Dante and grasped both his hands to make sure she had his undivided attention. "When I got caught in the nets … before the divers got to me, a Murr … Him!" she said, pointing at Axyl. "He tried to get me out … I was so shocked I looked at him for a good few minutes. I got a good look at him. Then, because we were gawping at each other, wasting time, the divers got there and I told him to go before they caught him. I told him I'd be okay."

Dante looked over to Axyl to see if he could shed any light on what Tia was saying.

Axyl just shook his head. *Not me ... before this trip, I hadn't left Murrla for a year.*

Tia looked at him and frowned with confusion. "But it was you, I'm sure it was. Your hair was long though. ... I remember now ... you must have cut it."

Axyl's expression fell and he got serious. His lieutenants followed his lead and looked to him for direction. *I can assure you, it wasn't me. I haven't been out of Murrla in a year. My lieu-tenants can vouch for me.*

Tia pulled away from Dante. "I don't understand?"

Can you tell me exactly where you saw the Murr? Axyl said, his face deadly serious now. *Could you find the place again?*

Dante sat up. "What are you thinking, Axyl? She's made a genuine mistake, that's all. She meant no offence."

Axyl put up a hand to quell Dante's concerns. *I take no offence. And I believe she thinks she saw me there. But ...* And he faltered and shook his head as if to get his thoughts together. *I dare not hope ... but perhaps ... it could have been my brother.*

"Your twin that you lost?" Dante said, frowning.

Axyl looked as if he were in shock. *He disappeared when we were five. We never found a trace ... that is, until now.*

CHAPTER 21

As frustrating as it was, there was no going to Italy now. Instead, Dante and Tia made the journey to Florida by private jet to join the Murr search party organized to meet them just south of the Florida Keys.

After speaking to them the previous night, Axyl had gone straight back to Murrtaine to get the exact spot Tia had been captured from his brother Dax, who'd been fishing with her that day. Then he was to head a party and travel to meet them by marine-bug.

Dante and Tia were speeding along in their blacked-out SUV, driven and filled with Santalini guardsmen, to their rendezvous with their chartered yacht, primed and ready to go to the coordinates given to them. When they got there, they were to dive straight into the sea and swim downwards to Axyl and his brothers.

"I'm sorry, Dante," Tia said from the back seat of the SUV they shared.

He squeezed the hand he was holding. "Whatever for, babe?

"For delaying your meeting with my sister … I know how important she is to you."

He leaned over and kissed her. "We'll meet her soon enough. I think it's grand what you are doing to help Axyl … great PR, you know," he said, grinning.

She playfully hit him.

"Besides, I wouldn't want to miss the look on your face when you see your surprise."

Her eyes went wide. With Dante, it could literally be anything. "I suppose you're not going to tell me?"

"Nope, you'll see soon."

The car pulled into a parking space and two of their guard got out to check the yacht was safe and ready for them. They were given the all clear and walked briskly along the jetty, flanked by more guards. No chances were being taken with either of them any more.

The skipper greeted them and helped Tia onto the boat and told her to go towards the back, where refreshments were waiting for them. Dante followed.

When she arrived at the canopy-covered area with plush leather seating, she stopped dead, not believing her eyes at the two men sitting waiting for her. They were grinning at her, leaning back with sunglasses on, with a cold beer in hand, looking like a pair of Colombian drug dealers. Her mouth dropped open and she burst into tears.

They both stood and motioned for her to come to them.

"Come here, gal," Cash said.

Sean messed up her hair and then both men crushed her in a hug.

Dante walked over, smiling like the Cheshire cat, and took both their hands. "Thank you … for what you both did. I won't forget it."

Tia refused to let either of them go when they tried to talk.

"Everything went okay getting you out then?" Dante said.

"Yeah, Keenan and his men really came through."

"Let them sit down, Tia," Dante scolded.

She did, but made sure she sat between them, holding both their hands.

"When we got to McMurdo, the place was swarming," Sean said.

"We couldn't chance making ourselves known, so we had to hide out." Cash added. "The place had way too many personnel ... we figured they had been drafted in to search the surrounding area."

"Then Keenan turns up with his little squad on an army plane, radioed us when he was coming in, and we jumped on board and were away before any questions were asked ... So thanks for that," Sean said.

"You sent Keenan?" Tia said, looking at Dante tenderly. "You did that for me?"

"Nah ... I did it for me, Tia. You'd have made me life a fuckin' nightmare till you saw the pair of 'em again," he said, nodding at Cash and Sean and giving her his wide grin.

She grinned back, shaking her head. She should have known he would never want to see her miserable.

They all fell into easy conversation, the engines fired up, and they chugged out to sea to the point where Cash and Sean would have to wait on board along with the guards and Dante and Tia would disappear into the depths together.

THE MARINE-BUG PURRED near the ocean floor. The Murrs were waiting for Tia and Dante. When they arrived, Vionne, Dax, Caan and Axyl were all there, along with several other soldier-looking Murrs vaguely familiar to them.

The area they were covering was between the reef to

their right and some rocks to their left, which sheltered their bug from the tides moving it away while they searched.

Dante touched hands with them all in greeting and touched Axyl on the shoulder to let him know they wished him luck and knew how much finding his lost twin meant to him.

Tia had told them roughly where she was when the trawler had come over and they all fanned out a few feet apart, swimming near the ocean floor.

Axyl went some way ahead and now and then he would stop and send out a mental signature picture so strong, Tia would have to hold her temples. *What's he doing?* she projected to Dante.

He pulled her to him when he noticed how painful she was finding the mental blast. He guessed he was okay because he was so powerful now. *He is sending out a mental call, so Murrs can picture it in their minds from a long way off,* he explained.

Axyl kept it up for quite a while with no result. He turned and swam back towards the rest of them. *Maybe he's moved on?* he projected, shaking his head, looking bitterly disappointed.

Maybe he doesn't recognize your signature as a man, Axyl? He may be wary if he doesn't know who we are, Vionne reasoned. *Try calling him like you did when you were small.*

Axyl paused for a moment while he collected his memories, then swam back to his position at the head of the search party and tried again.

Tia grabbed her head when he started, *Fuck!* she thought to Dante. *It's so loud.*

Even Dante felt it that time. It wasn't a noise as such, but broadcast powerfully in a wave which could be sensed.

Then, as they began to swim between another crop of rocks, something swam at them, lightning fast. It was so fast that Tia's eyes couldn't track it at first and thought it was a large fish, but then it barrelled into Axyl, using its velocity to tumble him over and over in the water.

Tia saw the stripes, heavy and black, becoming merged with Axyl's with their speed; it was another Murr without doubt. He was larger and more powerful than any she had seen. His hair was long and tangled all around them.

She looked over at Dante for reassurance, who looked as uncertain as she was, and didn't know whether to swim forward to intervene or not.

Stop, Dante, Vionne's mental voice echoed.

Dante and Tia looked at him as he seemed to laugh and throw back his head in joy. They looked at Dax and Caan, whose faces were beaming as well.

Axyl and the other Murr were now twirling round and round with their foreheads together.

Are they fighting? Dante asked, concerned that no one was doing anything.

Vionne shook his head, smiling. *No.* He touched both his brothers to accompany him closer to where Axyl and the other one were now shamelessly embracing and slowing down their acrobatics, until they stopped to face each other, both clearly weeping.

Vionne went to him next and hugged him, then Dax and Caan were introduced, probably as they were younger and he wouldn't remember them.

Dante and Tia stayed back on the sidelines, not wanting to intrude on the touching family reunion. They couldn't help but be affected by the obvious love and joy between them and clung together.

Then Axyl appeared to communicate something to the stranger and pointed to Tia. He swam powerfully over to her and stopped only when he invaded her personal space and towered over her. He studied her with the deepest, blackest eyes she'd ever seen. He was unsettling but very handsome.

Dante drew her closer to him, making sure he claimed her in front of the stranger, obviously not liking the guy's lack of boundaries.

Vionne laid a hand on Dante's arm. *It's okay, Dante. He won't hurt her.* Then went on to introduce Dante to Darres as their king.

Darres turned his haunting gaze to him for a few moments, but switched back to Tia quickly. *Thank you ...* He projected eventually, as if searching for the words ... *Little one ... for finding my family.*

After being initially intimidated by him, she slowly smiled when she realized he wasn't going to hurt her and wasn't that great at Human language yet. She touched Dante's arm to use his strength to project back, *Told you I'd be okay,* she projected, grinning.

Darres smiled cautiously back, *but I didn't help you ... I took too long ... thought you were someone else,* he explained.

No worries, she said. *No point in us both getting caught.*

Axyl touched Darres on the shoulder, interrupting them. *Come, Brother. Let us take you home ... there are many who will want to see you.*

Darres paused for a moment, seeming reluctant to go, as if there was more he wanted to ask. Then he allowed his brother to lead him away in the direction of their marine-bug to take him home to Murrtaine. The place he hadn't seen since he was a child.

Tia turned her face into Dante's chest and he closed his arms around her. He knew through their bond that she was emotional and needed a good cry. She seemed to absorb others' emotions and took them on as her own.

After a while, when the marine-bug had purred into the

distance, he kissed the top of her head. *Come on, soppy. Let's get back to the boat. Have you forgotten you have your own reunion with your sister to get to?*

Tia's heart jumped when she remembered how right Dante was, another sister to get to know. She loved Lacy already. She hoped she loved this one as much.

They swam to the surface holding hands. *I wonder who he thought I was?* she projected. *There are not that many people who look like me.*

DANTE WAS LYING face down on the daybed with his chin on his folded arms, surveying the patio of his palatial villa on Lake Como. Life didn't get much better than this.

His three children were running around the edge of the pool, shooting each other with water pistols and falling in off the side dramatically when they got shot. Keenan and Lacy had just turned up and were sitting with him in the shade, waiting for Cesaré to bring with him the third sister.

Jay had joined them as well, as he had been with Keenan when the summons went out and it was a good opportunity for him to see JJ.

It had pricked Dante slightly, the amount of time Jay seemed to be spending with Keenan these days, but he shelved his reaction, deciding to analyse it later.

Lastly, his eyes rested on Tia, playing table tennis under a canvas canopy on the far side of the pool with Cash and Sean, who she hadn't left alone since they had turned up again. He suspected she was keeping as far away from Jay as possible, which was amusing him. The pair were always in such denial of their feelings toward each other when it was so obvious, even if he didn't have the bond and knew Jay better than he knew himself.

Dante grinned, watching Jay's eyes stray surreptitiously behind his chic, expensive sunglasses in her direction and rest on her as long as he dared. But, as always, he sat cool as ever, impeccably dressed, like a model from Abercrombie & Fitch.

Dante had no such reservations. He was of the opinion that people should take him as they found him and simply wore over-long navy-blue swimming shorts with nothing on his top half except his many tattoos and his Ray-Bans holding back his long, black, curly hair.

Yeah, life was good, and it was about to get even better, because once he had the third Siren, his crown was as good as secured. The game would get more complicated, but apart from his family, it was what he lived for.

THANKFULLY, Cesaré had put his foot down when his mother wanted to accompany them to their first meeting with the king. He'd explained to her that the king had specifically stressed it was an informal get-together, and that if everything went well, there was plenty of time for official introductions later. Today was all about reuniting the sisters.

When his mother had argued that he needed a strong delegation to represent the Florianna, he'd become exasperated with her, saying he approved wholeheartedly that the king loved his wife and family above any ambition. His mother had tutted and stomped off, obviously used to getting her way.

Isla secretly rejoiced. Her dealings with Elena were still frosty and she was positive that she didn't think Isla was good enough for her precious son. Cesaré had said it was a normal reaction of mothers to prospective daughters-in-law. Isla had to take his word for it, but wasn't convinced.

At last, it was going to be her time. Her heart skipped. This was it, finally, the first step to her going home. She had managed to avoid consummating her relationship with Cesaré by the skin of her teeth and was thankful for it. The times ahead were going to be tricky enough.

Just as her spirits began to soar, a phone call from Malleven brought her mood crashing back down around her ankles. He still managed to ruin everything, even from a distance. Despite what she thought of everyone she met today, he was going to use her to destroy them, particularly the king and her sister.

She closed her eyes. She had to be strong. It wasn't as if she had any choice.

Cesaré's father refused to let them go alone and the compromise reached was that they had to take his brothers, David and Sandro, with them in case of foul play.

God, what did he think would happen? Wasn't there enough foul play under his own roof?

At last, they were driven the short distance around the lake and up the hillside gravel drive to the beautiful Roman-style villa, home of the Dubonnettis.

Its perfect gardens of red and pink flowers, interwoven with stone balconies and surrounded by shady trees, just beckoned her in. It was breathtaking. She had to remind herself to school her features to give nothing of herself away, just as her sensei had told her all those years before.

A maid showed them in through the house to the large patio and pool area at the back. She halted at the idyllic scene before her, taking it all in, before anyone knew she was there. If ever she had imagined happiness within a family, then this was it.

There was a cluster of beautiful people lounging and chatting in the shade, drinking long, cool drinks, adorable children squealing and laughing as they dove into the pool like water babies, and another group playing ping pong and laughing when a shot got smashed and missed.

"Are you ready?" Cesaré whispered in her ear.

She smiled weakly up at him, "As I'll ever be."

DANTE SPRANG to his feet and ordered more chairs when he saw the guest of honour had arrived. Hands were shaken and drinks ordered and everyone became seated.

Ethereal was the word that sprang to his mind when he saw her. He was stunned by the image of her. Shrouded from the sun in chocolate chiffon, what little skin that could be seen was alabaster white. He quickly switched to Italian, expressing his admiration of her to Cesaré, who nodded, accepting the compliment.

"Would you mind taking off your glasses, Isla?" Dante asked. "I want to see the resemblance, that is all."

Isla looked over at Cesaré, who nodded and she slipped the glasses from her eyes and squinted in the light.

The colour surprised him, the palest blue, like lagoon water, but the pupils were over-large and the irises looked ruined in a similar way to Tia's. "Is she?"

"No," Cesaré answered. "Her sight isn't great, but she has developed her other senses so you would never know."

"But you can see more comfortably in the dark or under-water?" Dante said, speaking directly to her now.

She nodded a strange, slow nod and her face remained expressionless.

"Tia's are the same; they became worse the longer she spent underwater." Her eyes went to him then, as if she were lapping up the information. "I managed to get something that helps while she is out of water. Remind me to give you some before you leave."

Cesaré thanked him. Isla just blinked. "Isla spent extensive amounts of time underwater before she came to us," Cesaré explained.

"I can imagine," Dante said kindly. "Let me call Tia." He called and waved to the three at the table tennis table.

They jogged over. Tia stopped in front of Isla. "Her eyes … they're fucked like mine." Then quickly put her hand over her mouth. "Oops."

Isla beamed a smile, transforming her previously inexpressive face.

Cesaré laughed. "Well done, Tia … Do you realize how long it took me to get her to smile? I think that emotion was new to her, having been held most of her life by the US government. She had little interaction with anyone."

"Was it you in the tank at the airbase?" Tia asked.

Isla looked at Cesaré, who answered, "Milestorm?"

"I was there … just a short time, though. Dante and Jay rescued me," Tia explained, then looked around her when the men all started to cough. She rolled her eyes. "Okay, so did Keenan, Cash and Sean."

"Yes, she was released and came into my care shortly after," Cesaré said.

"That was a year ago…" Dante couldn't help saying.

"I beg your pardon, your highness, but it has only been a few weeks."

Dante frowned; he knew exactly when she was released because his real father, the Duke Ormond Delissi had facilitated it, much to Dante's annoyance at the time. "You dealt with the ambassador yourself?"

"No, my cousin, Malleven had first contact with him."

Then everything went a bit haywire. Isla dropped like a stone and Keenan went to stand and approach. *Sit the fuck back down*, Dante quickly projected behind him to Keenan as he bent to help the prostrate girl.

Dante glanced briefly at Lacy's desolate face. He knew

what that name meant for her, drugged and held captive by Malleven for a year. Ripped away from her life mate, brainwashed and used for her blood, leaving a huge hole in her memory, he had a lot to answer for. However, no one would tip his hand before he was ready. *Trust me, okay? I need to know how innocent Cesaré is.*

CHAPTER 22

Isla slowly revived and allowed Dante and Cesaré to lift her back into her chair, and Keenan sat back down, smouldering with fury. "Are you okay, Isla?" Dante said.

She nodded.

"Probably the heat." Cesaré offered.

Tia was frowning as if she didn't know what to make of it. "Fuck, her whole life in that shithole."

Dante offered her a sugary drink, which seemed to revive her a little more, and glowered at Tia while he sat back down. "Tell me, Cesaré, would you and Isla like to accompany us back to Ireland when we return so you can get to know us?"

"Your highness is most kind."

Just then, a commotion broke out under the gazebo. Everyone looked over, just as Xavier jumped on JJ, screaming and punching him in the head with all his might.

Dante and Jay jumped up at the same moment and ran over, each picking up their respective sons. They walked over to the group, carrying them. Dante shook Xavier slightly and turned him in his arms to face him. He was still crying and in a dreadful temper. JJ was silently rubbing his cheek and his mouth.

"How dare you hit your brother like that, Xav … Spar by all means, but learn to curb your temper," Dante said forcefully.

"He doesn't fight fair," Xav wailed anew. "I couldn't …" he sobbed mid-sentence, "Do anything."

Isla was looking through her sunglasses intently at JJ. He fascinated her for some reason. "Ask the little one to repeat what he did?" she said, shocking everyone with her impromptu intervention.

Dante frowned, then decided to go with it, and passed Xav to Tia. He held his arms towards Jay for him to give him JJ.

Jay passed him over reluctantly.

"Let's see … JJ," he said, bending down to JJ's eye level. "Can you show me the move you did on Xav that got him so angry?"

JJ kept shaking his head and looking back at Jay to save him, so Dante began to pretend to spar with him, tapping his cheeks with his fingers, then his tummy and the top of his head to rile him up to retaliate.

Then, without warning, JJ lunged at Dante's face and he only just caught his little fist in time, mere inches from his cheek. Dante blinked and whistled.

"What?" Jay said.

Isla smiled.

Dante looked up, astonished. "The little sod froze my arms and blinded me for a second to get his shot in." He fuzzed JJ's hair up. "I'm too big and powerful for you, Sonny Jim." He knelt down to his level again. "You'll have enemies aplenty, JJ, when you get older to use that on, but not your brother, okay?"

The little boy nodded and looked up at Jay for reassurance.

"Sparring is for fun and practice with your brother," Dante continued. "Never lose your temper."

"You and Daddy do," JJ said, whilst chewing his finger.

Jay smiled. "He has a point."

Dante's eyebrows rose, asking his old friend how the hell JJ knew that? Then he grumbled, "Do as I say, not as I do. I'm the king." His face was serious as he stood back up.

Then he went over and took Xavier from Tia's arms to comfort him. "I don't know how he did that?" he said to Isla, by way of some kind of apology.

"We all have varying levels of psychic ability; it's just a matter of training and focus." She looked over at JJ, "The little one is advanced for his age … May I?" she said, holding out her arms to Xavier.

Dante passed him to her and watched intently.

She appeared to study him. "Look into my eyes?" she said to the boy, and fixed him with a stare for a few moments.

Dante looked nervously over at Cesaré, who put up a steadying arm. "Don't worry, I'm sure she is just assessing him to see what psychic ability he has."

Dante was aware of Murr abilities to scan someone's brain; he was perfecting the art himself, and hoped she was being gentle with his son, as it could be quite unpleasant. It was disconcerting because Xav was sitting so still and was clearly enthralled by her.

Eventually, Isla blinked and passed him back to Dante.

"Well?" he asked.

"He definitely has the ability, but no mental blocks at all."

"What does that mean?"

"I was able to look anywhere in his mind. With training, he should be able to stop me or anyone else from having access at all … the little one has it already," she said, smiling over at JJ, then Jay. "I already tried and he shut me down immediately … he is an enigma."

Tia scowled at her, but Dante ignored it and hugged little Xav to him, tight. "You still mustn't lose your temper, right?" he said softly.

Xav nodded, then wriggled to get down with Alexia. Dante slowly slipped him down to his feet. "Can you help him … build mental blocks?" he asked Isla.

She looked over at Cesaré.

"If we spend some time in Ireland, I don't see why not," Cesaré said, smiling.

Dante clapped him on the back. "Let's have another drink," he said, and the skirmish was forgotten.

TIA SAT BACK DOWN with everyone else in the shade and new drinks were ordered, but she didn't take her eyes off Isla for a second. She made her feel uneasy and she couldn't put her finger on it. *What do you think?* she projected to Lacy, sitting a little way off from her.

Lacy looked back. *She seems okay, why?*

I dunno ... I don't trust her. Tia said, glancing over at the pale girl.

Give her a chance, Tia ... she's hardly gonna spill her guts to complete strangers.

Tia shrugged. *Suppose ... have you noticed how she keeps on looking at Jay?*

Lacy grinned.

Keenan noticed they were in cahoots and narrowed his eyes on them.

"What?" Lacy said to him with all innocence.

Tia deflected. "Do you have a power to do with music?" she asked Isla.

Isla looked over at her, showing no expression at all. "I had no access to music," she answered flatly.

"Perhaps you could explain your power to Isla; it may help her answer your question," Cesaré said.

Tia nodded. "Okay … I'm a DJ, they say I control Humans with my music … I don't know I'm doing it, though. Lacy's a dancer."

Isla remained silent. The silence stretched on for so long that everyone thought she either hadn't heard or wasn't going to answer. Then, out of nowhere, "I was trained to fight in time to a metronome?" she said, looking blankly at Tia to see if that was good enough.

Everyone was quiet, staring at her, not knowing how to comment on that.

Then, eventually, Dante broke the silence. "Perhaps Isla should be training Tia?"

"I'd like to see that fight!" Keenan said, grinning.

Lacy glared at him.

Tia shrugged, non-committal.

Isla smiled her enigmatic smile and inclined her head.

"Tell me, Isla, what other senses do you use to your advantage?" Dante asked.

After a beat, she turned her blank gaze on Jay. "I can tell you have ingested Atlantean blood and that you are Human."

Jay shifted uncomfortably in his seat and frowned, casting a furtive look Tia's way.

Cesaré sat forward quickly. "You must be mistaken, Isla. That is strictly forbidden under Atlantean law… Except for the Santalini," and he inclined his head towards Keenan.

Isla looked mortified. "Apologies," she said to Jay. "I must be mistaken."

Surely she couldn't still smell my blood, Tia thought. *That was ages ago. Unless?* … Her mind stalled. *Had he been sucking on someone else?*

The realization that Jay could have someone hit her like a thunderbolt. Her cheeks blazed and she tried to tamp her feelings down before anyone guessed. She looked over to Dante's knowing gaze. He'd sussed her feelings, *fuck.* Or, he had come to the same conclusion. Her heart sank.

Dante gave her a slight smile of reassurance. He never wanted to see her hurt, she knew. But he was a realist and a male and would expect Jay to have someone. *But a fucking Atlantean?* she wanted to scream.

Sit still and chill, Dante's mental voice came over to her.

He was always so bloody perceptive; he knew she was about to flounce off. She glanced over at Jay. *Shit,* he'd been watching her the whole time. You didn't need a two-way bond to watch the rainbow of emotions that had just crossed her face. *What are you looking at?* she sniped at him, knowing he could hear through the bond but not reply. He smiled his infuriating small smile and faced the conversation, which had now moved on.

Tia looked down at her fingers. She was with Dante now. Jay was in the past. He had left her and made no pretence at wanting anything more than friendship.

DANTE LED Cesaré off for a gentle stroll around the gardens. "What are your immediate plans?" Dante asked.

"Back to my house in Milan and then, if it suits you, in a few days, make a formal trip to Ireland to present Isla properly."

"Why don't you extend your stay in the Lakes and return to Ireland with us. Now I have you both here, I'm loath to let you go,' Dante said, smiling at Cesaré.

Cesaré laughed. "Ah, honesty in politics … refreshing. Your highness is most kind."

Dante stopped and faced him. "Look, Cesaré, you came

here to check us out, which you have done. You brought your Siren here, so it's safe to say you have made up your mind. Let's not beat around the bush. Until she is bonded, she is in constant danger."

They resumed walking. Cesaré nodded. "You speak the truth, of course. But you have to know that Isla is no ordinary girl. She is untouched and naive to a lot in the world."

Dante looked at Cesaré, puzzled. *How on earth had he kept his hands off her?* "All the more reason for her to pledge to me without delay. Then you must bond her to you quickly before someone takes her from you."

"So it is true … you are building a council?"

"Yes … I want princes such as you."

Cesaré looked him in the eye as if assessing him for flattery. Then continued to walk. "Very well … when were you thinking?"

"Tonight?"

"Tonight … what of officials … witnesses?"

"There will be enough witnesses; we can do it officially in Ireland. The important thing is to get it done fast."

Cesaré saw the sense in what he was saying. "Okay, I will prepare her as much as I can."

Dante touched his arm. "It's not her that needs to prepare."

WHEN DANTE HAD WANDERED off with Cesaré, the rest of the men left the girls and went to the other side of the patio to play table tennis.

Keenan kissed the top of Lacy's head. "I'll leave you three to get to know each other."

Lacy pulled him down to kiss him properly on the mouth.

Isla watched the whole thing, transfixed on such a loving

gesture. She caught herself before she was noticed staring too much and faced front again.

The three of them sat in awkward silence. It seemed to stretch on for minutes. It began to be embarrassing.

"Don't you want to ask us anything?" Lacy asked. "We don't mind."

Grateful for the prompt, Isla turned to her on her right. "Is he your mate … his ring and everything?"

Lacy smiled at her. "Yes. We're bonded and married. We've been together since we were kids," she said, happily.

Isla sighed. "You are lucky."

The conversation appeared to dry up again.

"You don't have the monopoly on shit lives, you know," Tia said, scowling.

Isla faced her on her left. "I beg your pardon. I didn't mean to offend anyone."

Tia cut across her; "You may have had it crap … in an institution and all that, but neither of us was hunky dory. I was brought up fostered with strangers, and Lacy and Keenan were in a children's home. Then some bastard came along and took her memory, so she didn't even know Keenan any more. So don't expect us to spill any tears … And it was one of your lot," she said, as an afterthought.

"My lot?" Isla said, desperate to dig herself out of the ever-deepening hole she was finding herself in.

"What Tia means is, she's not blaming you or anything, but the bloke who took me and erased my memories was a member of the Florianna; a man named Malleven," Lacy said, more kindly.

Isla concentrated on every muscle in her face so that she didn't so much as twitch while she calmed herself down at the mere mention of that name. She continued to look at Tia long after she had finished speaking. "I'm sorry, I could see the love, that's all."

"Go easy, Tia … we know you didn't mean anything by it. Don't you love Cesaré then?" Lacy asked.

"Oh, I've only known him a short while."

Tia was looking at her, assessing her again. Isla was dying to creep into her mind, but suspected she would be busted quickly.

"That's unusual?" Tia said.

"What's unusual?" Isla said. *Could she have slipped up again already? She was mad to think she could fool these people.*

Tia just shrugged. "Oh, nothing much, it's just the pull … you know, between mates. It's unusual to resist it."

Briefly, Isla thought of her physical reaction to Malleven. That piece of information explained a lot. *Poor Cesaré, I wonder if he thinks the same thing.*

"So your eyes?" Tia said, changing the subject. "They don't work that great?"

Isla shook her head, dubious about opening her mouth any more.

"Mine neither. Do you wanna try some of my drops?"

Isla blinked, flummoxed by the turnaround in conversation. "Okay."

Tia fumbled in her cloth bag, slung carelessly over the back of her chair, and pulled out a small bottle. "Tip your head back." She stood over her with the bottle poised upside-down.

Isla did as she was told.

Tia warned her it would sting and to keep her eyes shut for a bit, then popped a few drops in each eye. When enough time had elapsed, Tia told her to open her eyes.

Isla slowly opened them and blinked rapidly. *My god, everything was so vivid and clear.* She could see detail, colour and textures. Isla put her hands to her mouth to stop a sob. "Thank you," she gasped.

Lacy laughed. "You're welcome … your eyes are so beautiful. Show her in your mirror, Tia."

Tia shoved her compact into her face, which Isla grabbed before it smacked into her. She marvelled at her small pupils, almost Human-looking eyes.

She gazed at her sisters in turn and marvelled at their lovely faces, at their differences and their similarities.

"Now you can see better, you can keep those headlights off Jay, while you're at it."

"Tia!" Lacy said, shocked. "She's only joking."

"No I'm not."

"But I thought …" Isla was about to say she thought she was with Dante, the king, when Lacy cut in.

"It's complicated. Don't try to work it out. All you need to know is that both Dante and Jay are bound to Tia."

So much for schooling her emotions and being unobtrusive; she'd done nothing but put her foot in it since she'd been there. No wonder Tia was so prickly towards her. "I'm sorry, Tia. He just fascinates me. His aura is so dark," she explained in all honesty.

Tia just stared back at her and she thought she was off the hook until she blurted, "What's with all the blood bollocks then?"

Oh god. "Oh, I don't know … I was mistaken … I just thought he smelled of it, that's all."

Tia shrugged. "That skill could be handy. I might get you to tell me if he smells like that again."

"I can teach you to do it yourself, if you want?"

Tia was studying her shrewdly again. "So do you know what you're in for … with Dante?" she said.

"The pledge thing?"

"Do you know what's involved?" Tia persisted.

"Not really," Isla said, shaking her head.

"We're not allowed to help you," Lacy said, with regret.

"We can tell her it will be in the water," Tia said.

"Really?" Isla said, with longing. "I've spent so little time in water since I've been away from the Americans. I find myself aching to be in it … completely, you know?"

Tia nodded knowingly, as if she knew exactly what she meant.

"That's understandable if you were in it a lot before," Lacy said.

"I sleep in water sometimes," Tia said.

"That must be wonderful. I find myself wanting that more and more."

"Yeah, especially in the sea," Tia agreed.

"My god, yes. To swim in the sea." She almost shivered with the yearning.

Tia's eyes darted behind her, making her turn to see what she was looking at. Cesaré had come back into view.

The little reunion was over and she wasn't sorry; it had been exhausting.

Cesaré went over to his brothers and spoke to them in a huddle. Then Dante ran back through the trees out of sight.

CHAPTER 23

*D*ante guided Cesaré back to the others as the sun was beginning to set and a warm orange glow bathed the patio. Dante assessed his guests and noticed Jay was missing. His eyes scanned around the gardens and he just saw the back of his white shirt disappearing through the shrubs to the gardeners' entrance. He excused himself and jogged to catch him up.

"Hey, Jay … wait up?"

Jay stopped but didn't turn. He looked down at the ground with his hands resting on his hips.

"You were going without telling me?" Dante said, stopping short, frowning.

Jay turned around with his usual unreadable expression. "I'll be back later … needed to get away for a bit."

"You okay?" Dante asked, his face cautious.

Jay walked over and motioned for him to hug him and Dante didn't hesitate. As they embraced, Dante sniffed the skin at the crook of his neck.

Jay pulled away fast. "Stay the fuck out of my head, Dant!"

Dante laughed and put his hands up in surrender. "Okay …okay … I can see where JJ gets his strong mind."

Jay turned without answering and began to walk towards the gate again.

"She's right," Dante called after him.

Jay turned but continued to walk backwards. "'Bout what?"

"You smell of blood, Jay."

Jay stopped again as if his patience had finally gone. "Look, we're good, okay … I'm good. I'd tell you anything you needed to know, just like I always have."

"Don't force my hand, Jay …" Dante said, with disappointment.

Jay just opened the gate and disappeared.

WHEN DANTE WALKED BACK into view again, Tia intercepted him. Lacy noticed and joined them. Isla was dying to know what they all thought of her.

She sneakily looked all around her and made sure everyone was occupied. They were either playing table tennis or in conversation. Then she closed her eyes and concentrated. She cast her mind back to her village in Japan. The sights and the smells, the feelings and the noises, and how her sensei had taught her to differentiate them all using her spirit.

Slowly, she separated the layers of the sounds around her – a plane going overhead, birds, a child's giggle, and deep male laughter. She separated them, identified them, until she isolated Dante's single voice. He was speaking in hushed tones to Tia.

"He'll be back, Tia. He's just gone to get some time to himself."

A pause.

"What's been decided … with her, I mean?"

"It's gonna be tonight."

"That's quick … what's the hurry?"

"We decided not to let the grass grow. Cesaré says she's a bit green … untouched, he reckons … what?" Dante's voice said.

"I'm not sure … I just don't think that can be right?"

"What do you mean, Tia … spit it out."

"I think she might be pregnant."

Silence.

Isla's heart was hammering in her ears. She held her throat. She must hear the remainder of the conversation.

"No, I'm not certain … it's just the way she was talking."

"Well, I know something's not right," Dante answered. "I didn't want to burst Cesaré's bubble, but Malleven's had her for months. He has no idea."

"Malleven?" Lacy's alarmed voice echoed. "She didn't so much as flinch when we were telling her about what happened to me."

"I don't trust her," Tia said.

"Give her a chance, Tia. She may have her reasons for keeping quiet. Doesn't mean she's in with him," Dante said.

A tendril of hope entered Isla's heart when she heard Dante's compassionate words.

"What do you feel, Lacy?" Dante asked, as if Lacy had some sort of gift of foresight.

"Well, I get an overall good feeling from her. I can't tell specifics yet, but I feel us all coming together eventually. Sorry, I can't give you more than that."

They stopped speaking and Isla opened her eyes to see Dante walking towards her. Cesaré seemed to notice she was alone at the same moment.

They were both coming over to her.

Oh my god, please don't say anything, Dante. Please don't turn me away.

DANTE AND CESARÉ converged on her together, intensifying her feelings of anxiety. If Dante exposed her now, everything could be lost and she could be cast out or, worse still, sentenced to a lifetime with Malleven.

"Okay, Isla … Was Tia gentle with you?" Dante said with a grin, conveying that he doubted it very much.

She couldn't help but start to like him. "Yes, thank you," she answered carefully.

"Listen, I just want to bring you up to speed with a few things, then you and Ches can go off and do your own thing for a couple of hours," he said, winking at her. "Me and Ches have had a chat, and if it's okay with you, we thought it'd be a good idea for you to pledge straight away tonight … we can do the whole official thing later?"

Relieved, it still puzzled her why he was willing to continue as if nothing had happened, but she nodded anyway. "Okay."

Dante looked at Cesaré. "Can you give us a minute … I just want to go through a few things with Isla before tonight?"

Cesaré stood without hesitation. "I'll just go over and tell my brothers to go on ahead."

"Grand," Dante replied, his eyes already on her.

Would he say something now that he had her on her own?

"Your eyes … the drops work, don't they?"

"Yes … I can see properly, for the first time in ages … it's wonderful."

"Your eyes are beautiful … you are beautiful," Dante said in all seriousness.

His words threw her off balance for a second. She

blushed. He was studying her, but he didn't try to breach her barriers. She was grateful.

Still, he seemed to read her mind. "I don't want you to feel nervous, I want you to feel you can trust me." He beamed a smile, making an already attractive face a knock-out. "After today, we will be bound, that'll make us family."

She allowed a small smile to play on her lips, but she was still waiting for the inevitable questions.

"Are you bound to anyone already, Isla … it is important that I know?"

She shook her head vigorously. "I don't think so."

He laughed easily. "Don't worry, Isla, you'd know, believe me." He remained quiet, studying her for a bit. As if he were calculating something.

"Look, I can't help you too much, but your pledge … it must be given freely and willingly. I can tell you that the bond is a kind of knowledge of the person; a psychic communication, if you like."

Isla was enraptured by his description of it, and more than a little fearful. "You won't get in my head?" Because although she dreaded the bond for what Malleven planned to use it for, her deep-seated terror came from someone's absolute knowledge of her. *Never let them know what you love …* It was as good as cutting her wide open as far as she was concerned – complete vulnerability.

Dante paused for a beat as if he knew. "No, Isla. Not if you don't want me to. It's more like a knowledge of how someone feels; a sense."

She relaxed a little.

"Has someone forced themselves on you, Isla?" Dante said in a gentle voice.

Isla looked him dead in the eye and fought to keep the blush out of her cheeks.

"Because a psychic violation can be far worse than the physical kind."

God, she didn't want to answer. She was sure he was assuming it was Malleven, but still, it was as though he could see right through her.

"You have to trust someone sometime," he said, with a smile. "It may as well be me, we will be married?"

She couldn't help smiling at him. He was so mischievous.

"Don't worry, all I expect from you is the pledge."

"What's so important about it?" she asked, feeling a little braver.

"You know all the families are royal?"

She nodded.

"Well, all the men are princes. Take Cesaré, for instance; he is as royally bred as me. Had he found you first, he would have been king."

"So you just met your mate first."

Dante smiled. "That's it. But to keep the crown I must grow in power before someone steals it from me, and keep all the families sweet into the bargain … a virtually impossible task."

"And you do that with us?"

"During the bonding process, your power passes to me."

She let what he said sink in, having no idea what power source he was talking about. Probably another way she was a fraud.

He smiled apologetically. "The other thing I want you to be aware of is that if you bond with me, or anyone, come to that, it is physical."

She frowned.

"It needs to be replenished regularly; otherwise, we can get sick, but particularly you, as I have your sisters as well."

"For life?" she asked in a small voice.

Dante nodded. "But the good part is that you can bind to

a man of your choice after that. He will be your real husband. I'm assuming that would be Cesaré?"

She gave a weak smile and hoped he believed her.

He was studying her intently. Then he smacked his hands on his thighs and got up. "Grand! Ches … come take your woman. We'll see you both later." He turned his attention to her again, picked up her hand and kissed it. "Later, Isla Snow." His eyes stayed with hers.

Then he straightened, laughed and shook Cesaré's hand.

Isla could see by the warmth in the handshake that both men had a mutual respect for one another. That told her more than anything else. She already knew Cesaré was a good man, and if he trusted Dante, then maybe she could, too.

DANTE HADN'T PRESSED the issue of bonding too much with Isla; he knew once he had completed the process with her, he would know if she'd bonded with anyone else anyway. He'd spoken to her more to get a feel of her character, and to warn her what to expect tonight, as he had done with all the sisters, well, as much as was allowed. As far as Isla being pregnant was concerned, he would hold back on that for now. After all, it was just a hunch of Tia's and he didn't want to open that can of worms unless it was absolutely necessary and the evidence irrefutable.

It was pitch dark by 9.30. Dante was sitting at the table on the patio, waiting with Cesaré, Tia and Isla. Cesaré had managed to come back without his brothers when they saw that nothing apart from getting to know each other was going on. The nanny had been asked to put the children to bed early, which wasn't difficult after a full day of sun, play and fresh air.

Jay arrived with Keenan and Lacy. It was necessary for all

three Sirens to pledge at the same time and Keenan and Jay could keep Cesaré company through the difficult process. Thankfully, there was no viewing room in this pool, so Cesaré's feelings would be spared to a degree, not having to watch. Although that time would come, the initial pledging, the one that counted, would have already been done.

Dante stood. "Come, let's get this out of the way." He held his hand out for Tia to take. He sensed she was more nervous this time and hoped it was just because Isla was an unknown quantity, and not that she was feeling insecure about her bonding with him.

The girls all had their swimming costumes on under their clothes, and had quickly stripped and followed Tia and Dante into the shallow end of the pool.

The pool was beautiful and lit, so it shone a neon-blue-green and got very deep very quickly. The four of them submerged and took the water into their lungs. Dante was initially watchful of Isla, but soon relaxed in the knowledge that she was totally comfortable breathing the water.

Lacy ... you will go first, then Isla, then Tia last, Dante projected and pointed so Isla understood. He wanted to reassure Tia because she had to watch the whole thing, and it would be hard on her. Always at the back of his mind was the memory of when he had first lost her, when sea witches had pretended to be her sisters and had jumped him in the water. Tia had been heartbroken and left him.

First, Dante beckoned Lacy towards him with his hands. She swam up close, placed her hands onto his shoulders, slanted her mouth over his and breathed the gentle, steady flow of her essence into him. He smiled. His face glowed, then his chest and he took a moment leaning away from her while he absorbed the sensation. Then he pulled her back to him and returned the process.

Lacy went limp for a few seconds in his arms while the

blast hit her. He grinned and waggled her chin to bring her back to him. She shook her head and smiled up at him, giving him the thumbs up. *Thank you, wife number two. You'd better hurry back to Keenan before he comes looking for you and kills me.*

She grinned, put up her hand and waved to Tia and Isla, then she swam to the shallow end of the pool and got out.

Dante swam over to Tia and touched her cheek lovingly. *It'll be over soon.* She nodded and he swam over to Isla, who was watching them intently.

So as not to startle her, he beckoned her to him. She approached a little at a time until she was a couple of feet away. He leaned forward and pulled her to him and put his hands on her shoulders to steady her. He touched his fingers to her lips and then his own to let her know what he wanted.

As Dante could breathe for himself underwater now, he was not in danger from Isla; it would be Cesaré who would be tested. His gills had never been opened, and for that, he needed a Siren to accept him and breathe for him.

Dante pulled her slowly to his mouth. Her eyes were wide with fear. His lips gently parted next to hers and he waited, but there was no response.

Isla didn't seem to be getting the idea of what she was meant to do. Dante slanted his mouth over hers and tried a kiss, slightly opening his mouth. He willed her to get it soon, as he could sense Tia's growing agitation.

Dante pushed his tongue slightly into her mouth. She pulled back, shocked, staring up at him. He waited, unapologetic. She closed the distance again and put her mouth on his and he did it again.

This time, she didn't pull away but gently stroked his tongue with her own, and her eyes fluttered closed.

Shit, it was quickly looking like a full-on kiss here and he started to get impatient. In a snap decision, he decided to bend the rules and puffed a small blast of his essence into the back of her throat to put her back into line. It hit her like a jolt of electricity.

She sprang away from him, her eyes like saucers, but now he could communicate with her, *Don't be frightened, Isla. It was merely a demonstration ... now we will be able to communicate, okay?*

She nodded cautiously and came forward again.

ISLA DIDN'T LET on that she was fully capable of telepathic speech. She had practised it with the monks as a child, and spoke to Darres using it the whole time. She played along.

Dante pulled her to him, more roughly. He resumed putting his mouth on her and kissed her slightly again. Everything about this experience reminded her of Darres. *Oh, god, could she go through with this?*

She remembered the wonderful feeling that Darres had shared with her and she understood for the first time it had been the bond that Dante had been talking about. But instead of completing it and breathing into Darres, she had expelled it into the water around them.

Go with it, Isla. Dante projected, bringing her back to the present. *The light will grow and will come up and pass into me. That is the bond ... don't be afraid.*

Dante was being very patient with her, she knew, and he tried again. Now he was kissing her, a full and passionate kiss. Very quickly, she felt a tingling sensation in her chest. Her mind was in turmoil. Whatever was inside her was building in its strength and ferocity, but she instinctively knew if she let it loose, everything would be out of her control and she just couldn't bear to do that.

Instead of breathing into him, which everything inside her was crying out to do, she wrapped her legs around his hips and gripped him tightly to her body. She entwined her fingers in his hair and at the point where everything spilled over, she pulled away from his mouth and a light flashed all around them. *No!*

Fuck, Isla, what are you doing? You've gotta trust me. All the while Dante was speaking inside her head, his arms were holding her tight and he continued to kiss her neck to get back to her mouth.

CHAPTER 24

*F*uck, *this one was hot,* and there was no way she was untouched. If she had no carnal knowledge then she had some pretty fucking strong instincts. *Maybe Tia was right?*

It would have been the easiest thing in the world to move his shorts down slightly and relieve this girl's need – wherever it sprang from, *Fuck, he was like any other red-blooded male,* but this scenario was all kinds of wrong and all too familiar.

No, babe, you have to stop, he said, trying to extricate himself from the tangle of her arms and legs. *You must save that for your man.*

She groaned and gave in, going still in his arms. *I can't.*

Dante went still too for a moment and moved her chin with his hand so he could look into her face. *You spoke to me?*

Yes, she said, her eyes waiting for a backlash.

You can already speak telepathically ... someone has already initiated you ... you're bound?

No, please, that's not it. I've been able to do it since I was a child.

He looked into her huge, dark eyes, so fearful. *Listen, Isla. I don't know what you've been through. I can only guess at it. But I am the one person who will ask the least from you.*

She stared at him and swallowed hard. *What is it you want?*

Only your pledge. If you can find it in you to trust me, I promise you I will help you ... I mean it. He was holding her firmly by the sides of her face, speaking in her mind but conveying the strength behind his words with his eyes.

You will know everything, she said, hopelessly.

I will feel your feelings, then in time ... maybe you can fill in the blanks. He felt desperately sorry for her and pulled her close and hugged her. All three of the Sirens he'd met so far had had the most horrendous lives, but this one ... he couldn't help but think she'd had it the worst of all.

Okay ... Her small voice filtered through to him.

He pulled back to look into her face again. *Okay?*

I'll do it.

I promise it will be okay.

She nodded.

Just do it like you did before, except this time, I need to absorb it, okay?

She nodded again. *You need to know something first.*

He waited, dreading what she would say.

Somebody bonded with me ... but I never did it back.

He pulled her back into his body as if to hug her, but it was more to give himself time to think. *Shit, someone's bonded with her already. Was it that fucker, Malleven?* Quickly his mind whirred. *No, it couldn't be him because he was uninitiated. Lacy hadn't bonded with anyone when he had her. Had he found any of the other Sirens? That was possible but unlikely, as he would have heard something and Malleven would never have relinquished Isla.* So if Isla didn't do it first, that meant he could only be from one family – The Borge. A Murr had already claimed her as his own.

Dante didn't allow himself to dwell. It was time to push home his advantage and he looked into her eyes again. *You love this one?*

She took a moment to answer.

It's important, Isla.

Yes, she said, closing her eyes. *I've never told a soul.*

Dante could feel her shaking. She was a quivering wreck. There was no point in dragging this out further. He'd have to worry about Cesaré later. He pulled her up to his mouth and covered hers again. *Think of him then, Isla. Think totally of him.*

Dante began to kiss her tenderly at first, then he parted her lips with his tongue and kissed her deeply.

It didn't take long. The light hit his chest like a ball rebounding off a wall and completely winded him for a second. He had to concentrate on not breaking the seal of their lips. He allowed all of it to enter him, somehow knowing that he needed to learn as much as he could from this Siren. She was as important for her knowledge as she was for her power.

When the flow petered to nothing, he held her for a few moments and floated in the afterglow. *Fuck, she was strong.* He kissed her cheek. *Thank you for your pledge, Isla. But most of all, thank you for the trust you are putting in me.*

ISLA LOOKED into Dante's eyes and saw genuine feeling there.

Now it is my turn and then the bond is complete.

Isla nodded. She felt fearful but strangely liberated, too. Apart from her sensei, Dante was the first person she had trusted in her life.

Dante closed the gap between their mouths again. There were no tongues this time. That had obviously been his way to get her to summon her power.

Before her mind could question anything further, she felt

the warmth prickle on her lips, over her tongue, down her throat, till it hit her heart. Then it ignited.

When she opened her eyes again, and she was sure it was a few minutes later, Dante was smiling down into her face and she was lying across his arms, feeling a warm, fuzzy glow. She could stay there for ever, feeling so cocooned and wanted, not a care in the world.

Welcome back, wife.

She smiled up at him. *That's it?*

That's it ... I told you it's a piece of cake.

If she could have sighed with contentment under water, she would have done so.

Dante laughed as if he knew.

Did he know?

He nodded, grinning. Then he looked around him as if he had just remembered something. *Ah, shit.* He looked back down at her with regret. *I would love to spend some time talking to you, Isla, but we must get out. I have a wayward wife to sort out.*

Isla remembered then that Tia had been waiting in the wings for her turn. Dante let her go and she looked around.

Tia had gone.

WHEN THE BITCH had clamped her legs around Dante's waist like some sort of octopus and snogged the face off him, Tia had seen enough. She had been there before and she wasn't waiting to be humiliated a second time. She swam up to the shallow end and got out of the pool.

What's the matter? Lacy projected from Keenan's lap.

Ask the asshole, she replied, bobbing her head back in the direction of the pool.

She barely registered Cesaré's worried expression and glared at Jay to dare say one word. In fact, she was sure if he had, her veneer would have cracked and she would have bawled like a baby.

Tia stomped past their table, disappeared into the house and ran straight up to her room.

IT WAS QUITE a few more minutes and, just as the rest of them were starting to feel a bit concerned, Dante and Isla's heads broke the surface of the water and waded out.

Dante led her over to where Cesaré was sitting, put her hand in his and made sure his hand made contact with Cesaré's, so he could project speech to him. Cesaré was yet to bond with Isla, so it was the only way he could speak to him. *Don't worry, Cesaré, all went well.*

Cesaré's eyes strayed to the house as if he weren't convinced.

As my true wife, it's hard on Tia. But the pledge is complete. He smiled at Isla and switched to her mind alone. *You must bind someone to you quickly, Isla,* and he cast a furtive glance back at Cesaré. *We'll find the time to talk, though, okay?*

She nodded. *Thank you.*

Thank you, Isla.

Dante nodded at everyone, looked at the house and strode off to find his high-maintenance wife.

WHEN HE WALKED through the bedroom door, Tia flung clothes at his face, picked up her case and threw it on the bed, then began hurling clothes into it. Shoes were landing and bouncing back out again and over to the other side of the bed.

Stop this, Dante projected, trying to grab her arms to stop all the throwing. *This is not going to happen again. I won't allow it.*

Fuck off, shit head. It already has.

Dante yanked her to him and gripped her arms to her sides in a hug that she couldn't escape from.

Tia struggled like a mad thing, crying and raging about how she had to put up with him fucking all her sisters. The fact that Jay was still on her mind only served to compound the problem and the total feelings of betrayal.

"Shh," he repeated over and over, using his strength to quell her struggles. He put his mouth in her hair. "Shh," he said, to gradually calm her. *It was nothing, Tia ... I promise you.*

I've got eyes, Dante. I saw what was happening.

Dante lost a little patience with her then. *Look, I'm like any other male ... the process is arousing, I won't lie ... she is a beautiful young virgin.*

"Pah!" Tia blasted. *Yeah, right. She looked really virginal from where I was standing.*

Dante conceded a nod. No point in denying that. *Whatever ... she was grinding on me, of course I wanted to, but I didn't, okay? That's what counts ... I didn't, babe, because of you,* he projected more gently.

And you want to keep poor Cesaré onside! She pulled herself out of his arms, pushed past him and resumed throwing things into her case.

True to form, the patience in Dante snapped and he began to push her out of the room. *Go back to the pool, Tia. We haven't finished.*

If you think I'm getting back in there with you, then you can fuck off!

He continued to use his greater weight to push her along the landing and down the steps. Turning her and shoving every time she fought him and tried to get past to go back the other way. *I've had years of you and Jay,* Dante flung at her now, his own temper rising.

He's not there any more, and she's my fucking sister ... I have to put up with you being with four of them ... fucking four! she screamed in his head.

By now, they had reached the back door and he shoved her out onto the patio where the others were still sitting. She knew he would bank on her not causing a scene in front of everybody. *Well, he could think again.* She switched to real speech even though it was painful, and shrieked at him, "Fuck off, Dante!" It came out a loud, husky croak, and she fought with him tooth and nail to scramble back inside the house.

Shut the fuck up, Tia. You'll wake the kids. He continued to push her nearer the edge of the pool.

Cesaré looked really worried and began to stand, Jay had already stood. "Everything all right?" Jay asked.

Dante put up a hand. *It's fine, mate.* Then he decided he'd made enough explanations for one day and bent over, picked Tia up, and threw her as far into the pool as possible. Then he executed a perfect dive after her.

Tia swam back to the side as fast as she could and tried to scramble out. She saw Lacy put her hand to her mouth to stifle a giggle. Then a hand on her ankle dragged her beneath the water and out of everyone's hearing and sight. *Fuck off, Dante ... leave me alone.*

He wasn't listening and pulled her to the deepest and furthest point of the pool, which went into a little underwater cave. He pushed her onto the pool floor, pinned her with his body and held her head with his hands. His face, fierce and tribal, dared her to escape and her struggles slowed to a halt when she registered their futility.

Dante waited a few moments, then smoothed the tendrils of her hair from her forehead. *Tia, calm down. Let me project to you the whole experience, and then you'll know how I felt. I've got nothing to hide from you. You were right about her, okay.*

She relaxed a bit with the information, but then she stiffened again and tried to struggle. *Get the fuck off me, I'd rather eat razor blades than feel you all hot and bothered over her.*

Ah, come on, Tia. I'm a bloke for fuck's sake. He closed the gap between them and put his mouth on hers, nipping her. *Let me in, babe, please. Let me show you, then you'll know everything.*

Begrudgingly, she parted her lips, barely millimetres, but he pushed his way in, powerfully devouring and claiming. Before she could come to her senses, he blew a jet of his essence like a flood, strong and direct to her heart. And while she gasped and gulped him down, he projected the series of mental pictures, along with the feelings he'd felt at the time from the instant he'd first beckoned Isla to him.

It all happened in a split second. As if on super-fast playback and before his essence exploded in her chest and she could make no sense of what he was conveying to her.

His timing was perfect. The series of pictures halted as fast as they began, her head rolled backwards and she went limp as the joy exploded all over her body.

When he saw the elation on her face, he kissed her hard, yanked her swimsuit out of the way, and pushed into her. Before long, her costume was nowhere to be found.

Tia knew he was taking advantage of her stunned state, but his relentless rhythm soon drove her wild and took over, and her arms and legs snaked around him to hold him to her and give him some necessary leverage. He pistonned into her like a demon possessed.

Love with Dante was always passionate and demonstrative; a total possession until she was completely compliant to do with what he wanted, and tonight she felt it in him stronger than ever. Maybe it was to do with Isla, but possibly and more likely, it was to do with Jay, and how he was still able to hurt her and Dante could always feel it as if he did it to him.

Let me in your mind's eye? he whispered.

I hate you, she said, biting his ear and then his neck and forcing him to roll over so she was on top and straddling him.

Taking no chances, he pulled her body down tight to him. *Merge with me*, he whispered.

She shook her head and tried to pin him down.

Dante threw her off easily and grabbed her, pushing into her again and again, building to a pounding pace. He bent down, bit her neck hard and crushed her arms to her sides so she felt completely dominated. *Let me in*, he ordered.

He covered her mouth with his and blew his essence into her again. It felt overwhelmingly strong with the power of the three sisters.

I love you, babe, only you ... let me in.

Gradually, he beat down all of her defences, arguments and protests, until all that existed were the two of them, and he walked confidently into her mind's eye.

She was sitting with her knees up to her chin on her leopard-skin-covered bed, sulking and miserable.

There were no further discussions or preamble. He simply walked up to her, pushed her backwards and lay straight on top of her. Holding her chin, he blew straight into her psychic mouth while he thrust into her psychic body and moved in gentle rolling motion, so life mimicked mental representation, and the union was complete, and the light came over them. Their bodies drifted into each other's and the lines were smudged, crossed and moved until there was nothing left except a blinding light of love, understanding and peace.

IT WAS the pink light of dawn that greeted them when Dante led her out of the pool the next morning.

They walked past the gazebo, hand in hand, then she slowed. Dante left her to go ahead into the house, saying he needed food.

It was Jay, asleep in the hammock with JJ in his arms that had halted her. Naked and dripping with pool water, she tiptoed over to them and gently touched little JJ's hair. How peaceful and angelic they both looked. A cherub in the arms of a Greek god, she mused.

Her eyes raked over every inch of Jay's face. How rested he looked, and how little she'd seen him like that. She couldn't resist tracing a finger across his smooth, trouble-free brow, gently pushing back the wisps of his sun-kissed hair and brushing that sensual mouth so capable of such mind-blowing things.

His eyes flashed open.

She stepped back sharply and ran towards the house.

JAY STIRRED. He had woken from a wonderful dream. Tia had stood over him naked and beckoned him into the water. It was a dream that repeated most nights. He would always go to follow, but woke up too soon.

He sighed and then became aware of where he was and that JJ slept soundly in his arms. It was where he'd been since he'd woken up in the night looking for Tia. He shook his head awake and sat up. "Come on, mate, let's get you to bed." He guessed it must be around five in the morning.

When he stood up and arranged JJ over his shoulder, he saw small wet footprints slowly drying in the early morning sun, leading from his hammock into the house.

CHAPTER 25

*D*ante was in great spirits the following evening after having a wonderfully restful, lazy day with Tia and the children. He now had three Sirens pledged to him and his position felt the most secure it had ever been, both with the crown and in his relationship with Tia.

Jay was secretive and sloping off, a good sign. Keenan and the Santalini were aligned to him and, providing he could iron out a few wrinkles for Isla, Cesaré would soon be too.

There were still big questions to be answered, like what Malleven was up to, and who the mystery Murr was that Isla was in love with? His sympathy was undoubtedly with Cesaré, being Isla's true mate. He would help that relationship along all he could, although Cesaré's success with the ladies was world famous, so surely Isla couldn't hold out forever. Once she had tasted love with her mate, no one would stand much chance over time. No, life was good.

Tonight he had organized a dinner and invited Keenan, Lacy and Jay with Isla and Cesaré as the guests of honour as a good chance for them all to get to know each other. Their lives were now all tied together, so it was a good idea to become friends, especially as he hoped to go back to Ireland the next day. The official presentation of Isla needed to happen ASAP.

Cash had gone back to the States to attend to some business on his ranch, but Sean was still there. Dante needed to find out how he was getting along with his wife Sarah, too. He seemed to spend as little time as possible with her since he'd found out she'd been partly responsible for Tia's abduction by the American authorities last year. He'd ordered him to make sure she joined them in Ireland, so he was forced to spend some time with her. Besides, he didn't mind Tia's Protectors being in love with her, but he preferred it if they were hitched or, at the very least, attached to someone else.

The guests had arrived and their dinner would shortly be served on a long table on the terrace overlooking the pool. The kids sat for as long as their attention spans would allow, which was around ten minutes. Then they were charging about, shooting each other and playing hide and seek.

Tia was quiet. Dante was aware that there was an atmosphere between her and Jay. It had existed before, but had now become noticeable since Isla's comment about Jay's blood habit. And he was becoming sure Jay had one, as he could smell it on him again today. He would look into who it was, because while part of him rejoiced at Jay moving on, another part of him was fearful that he would have to act on the Anti-Blood Law if Jay made it too blatant.

Tia was also casting sly looks Isla's way. He knew Tia, and she was biding her time with her. He chuckled when he thought about how she would get her own back. He looked at Cesaré, then back at Tia and smiled at her, which she caught and smiled back. *Yeah, that was it.* It would end up a catfight, or she would snog the face off Cesaré. Whatever happened, sparks would fly. He'd better tip Sean off to keep a closer eye on things.

. . .

TIA'S EYES kept straying to Jay. She knew what Isla had been talking about now. He definitely smelled funny and, judging by the small plaster just below his collar line, whoever he was shagging needed to eat more because they'd been chewing on his neck.

She glanced at Dante, who was in conversation with Cesaré, talking about Isla's expertise in martial arts.

"She could train me?" Tia piped up, making the table go quiet. "What? If she's that good, why not?"

Cesaré smiled at her. "I'm sure Isla would love to."

Isla just gave a slow nod, *Oh yeah, can't wait*, she projected to Tia alone.

Tia narrowed her eyes. "Why doesn't she show us what she's got now?"

Dante looked at her and sighed with a "wait till I get you on your own" look, which she gave a fake grin back to. "Why not ... she's amongst family?"

"What do you think?" he said across the table to Isla.

"Do you have a metronome?" she asked Dante.

Tia cut in, "No, but I got a good beat." She grinned, went into the house and put on a rap track with a thumping break beat and turned it up.

The men all sat up, interested. Things were just about to liven up.

Isla walked down the stone steps of the terrace around the pool to the large gazebo where the ping-pong table had been the day before. Now it was a nice, clear space with some soft matting, a small table laden with drinks, sweets and cutlery for later.

She kicked off her shoes and slipped out of her skirt, leaving just her sleeveless black top and black briefs, emphasizing her long, pale legs. Cesaré rose and followed her, carrying several dinner knives in his hand.

Dante looked at Jay, who returned the look, then they all turned to watch.

Quickly, she picked her rhythm and began to move, ducking and weaving, punching, kicking and swerving in faultless timing in a super-fast Kata, executed with ease and perfect grace.

The men all looked at each other, recognizing a super-trained soldier when they saw one.

Cesaré laid out the knives on the table, closed his eyes, concentrated and levitated them all into the air, raising his hands while he did it. Then he turned all the blades to face Isla, still working her Kata, not even appearing to watch him.

The spectators shifted in their seats, nervously deducing what was coming next. Cesaré launched all the knives at Isla at once. She jumped extraordinarily high, kicking her leg around in an arc while she went upwards and batted each of the knives away in one go. They all fell to the ground and the table erupted in claps and cheers.

Tia's face was closed, but even she had to acknowledge a great trick when she saw it and clapped along with the others.

"Does anyone fancy their chances?" Cesaré called over.

All the men shook their heads and mumbled that they couldn't possibly fight a woman.

"I promise I won't let her hurt you," Cesaré said, laughing.

They all laughed, but mainly out of embarrassment at being called cowards.

Dante kicked Sean, who was sitting opposite Tia. "You, Sean. I command it."

"Ah fuck," he said, blushing, rising from his chair slowly and dragging his feet over to Isla.

"Dante!" Tia scolded.

"It's only a bit of fun, Tia. Chill."

Sean walked over to Isla and stopped about three feet away from her with his hands on his hips. She turned and walked away from him.

Before anyone was ready, she turned, cartwheeled and flew through the air, grabbing his head with her hands while she twisted and clamped her thighs around his neck. Then, using her forward momentum and body weight, she threw him to the floor, thankfully covered in soft matting for his hard landing.

Everyone clapped and cheered.

Sean got up, brushed himself down and returned to the table, a little red-faced in defeat.

"You've been done by a girl, mate," Keenan ribbed.

Lacy smacked him in the chest. "Shut up, Keenan."

"See how you can do then," Sean said. "She's lightning fast."

Dante laughed when Keenan rose to his full menacing height, and slowly walked over to her so she could get the full six feet five measure of him. He stood casually, resting on one leg, while Isla stood ready in a fighting stance with her fists up.

This time, she dropped to the floor, then faster than anyone could track, she opened her palm and a knife flew from the table to it. Then she back-flipped away from him, landing on her feet some distance away.

No one said a word. No one was sure what had just happened.

Keenan turned to face everyone with his arms outstretched. "What was that?"

Then everyone stared and murmured.

"What?" Keenan asked, perplexed.

"Your face," Dante called over to him. "Fuck, she's good."

Keenan walked back over to the table and felt his cheek.

When he pulled his hand away, blood was there. "What the fuck she do?"

"She cut you and flipped away in about two seconds," Jay said, raising his eyebrows.

Isla and Cesaré had joined the table again.

"Anyone else before Isla sits back down … Jay?"

Jay exhaled, shaking his head.

"It would not be fair me fighting a Human," Isla said.

"Oooh," echoed around the table simultaneously.

Dante grinned and watched Jay's reaction.

"Don't you worry, babe, you just do your stuff," Jay said, in his best patronising voice, while he rose from the table.

Everyone was thrilled with the prospect and cheered.

Tia was glad to see Isla had wound Jay up. The thing Jay hated most in the world was his manliness brought into question. She sat forward to watch this.

Jay walked over to the edge of the mats, not making eye contact with Isla. Then, before she could ready her stance for her next bout, Jay produced a small penknife from his pocket, kicked the supporting pole and cut the string to the gazebo. He deftly stepped back while the whole thing came collapsing down on top of Isla. All she could do was thrash around under the heavy canvas.

The table erupted in laughter.

Jay turned, took a bow and returned to the table without even breaking a sweat.

And that's why she loved him. Tia's eyes never moved from him as he quietly sat back down at the table.

Cesaré, who couldn't help seeing the funny side himself, was busy trying to pull Isla out from under the canvas. When he succeeded, she stood somewhat dishevelled with her hair in all directions and the whole table collapsed in laughter again. It was the funniest thing they'd seen in a very long time.

She retrieved her clothes and Cesaré led her back up the steps to the table where she stopped behind Jay. The table fell silent again, not sure if she could take the joke. "A worthy opponent," she said quietly with a small smile, and bowed in a very Japanese way to acknowledge his win. "I look forward to a rematch."

Jay just turned and smiled at her, non-committal, saying nothing further.

"Oooh!" the table all chorused again.

Dante laughed loudly. "That I want to see," he said, delighted.

Not if I can help it, Tia thought. *There was no fucking way she was getting her claws into him.*

ON THEIR LAST night in Italy, Cesaré and Isla went back to the Florianna villa to pack and get ready for their trip to Ireland, where Isla would pledge officially and be presented to the whole Atlantean world as the awaited third Siren and wife to Dante Dubonnetti.

Cesaré had watched Isla closely since she'd gone into the water with Dante and the domestic it had caused between him and his mate. She seemed subdued.

He carried her bag to her room, then pulled her to him and kissed the top of her head. "Did everything go well for you in the water, Isla?" He was itching to find out how she had reacted to being in close proximity to Dante.

She just nodded her head next to his chest.

He was hoping she would elaborate, but didn't want to push her. "Good … I've just got to let my family know what's going on, okay? Then I'll come and say good night."

"Okay," she said, letting him go.

He frowned and reluctantly left her to her packing.

Cesaré had called his mother, father and brothers to the

large study to announce that Isla was already bound to the king, and that they would all be setting off in the morning to attend the official presentation.

"When will *you* be bound?" his mother asked loudly.

Cesaré turned to her and saw concern mixed with anger in her eyes. He smiled weakly, "I hope it will be soon after, Mother," but the reality was that he had misgivings. He knew it was a ceremony where Isla could accept or reject him, and rejection for an uninitiated prince meant death by drowning. He pushed the thought to the back of his mind as the reasoning of a coward.

But the fact remained that Isla liking him didn't make him feel any great confidence, as they still hadn't slept together. He was starting to think that she just didn't look at him in that way, which was perplexing as a true mate. He inadvertently played with his divining ring.

Once the news had sunk in, the study began to empty so they could all make their preparations and pack. Cesaré swivelled round on his leather chair and stared out of the bank of windows behind him overlooking the lake.

The door clicked, but he ignored it.

A hand touched his hair, which made him jump. He turned his head to the side sharply and looked into the dark eyes of Petra.

He relaxed a little. She was easy company and had been his friend and plaything since she'd been an advanced-for-her-years teenager, and he would push her into the broom cupboard and touch her when her stern mother wasn't looking.

She walked to the front of his chair until she faced him, and without a word, hoisted up her skirt, put her leg over, straddled him across his lap and put her hands on either side of his face. "Cesaré, you look like you have the weight of the world on your shoulders, and are not the carefree lover you should be?" she said, moving forward and nipping his lips with hers, then moving to nuzzle and kiss his neck. All the while gyrating her hips against him, creating friction through his jeans.

His resolve was weak in his current mood and he gave himself over to the sensation and affection. It had been a long time for him – weeks – since he'd been with a woman.

She was undoing his shirt buttons and kissing down his chest to the top button of his jeans. It was erotic, something he shouldn't be doing, but that only served to heat him and turn him on even more. This girl knew what buttons to press. He was acutely aware that if she sprung him free of his jeans, it would be less than a minute before she was bent over the desk, screaming his name and to hell with the consequences.

"Ah, shit!" he cursed, and grabbed her by the shoulders and pulled her back up to his eye level.

"What?" she said, with disappointment, eyes bleary with lust and lips already red and swollen from kissing.

He couldn't speak; he was still debating whether to throw caution to the wind. She closed the distance between them and kissed him again, thrusting her tongue into his mouth to mimic what she wanted.

For a second, he gave in, but caught himself again. "Stop, Petra," he said, breathing hard. She ignored him. "Stop!"

"What is it?" she said, petulantly.

"I can't do this any more," he said, more softly.

"What, never?" she said, not understanding. "You are saving yourself for the pallid bitch?"

"Ah, no, Petra, don't be like that."

"She can't give you what you need … you know that." She renewed her efforts to wear down his resolve.

Cesaré laughed. "Stop, Petra … I mean it."

She pushed apart from him and glared at him in the eyes.

He hated that he had to hurt her feelings, and pushed a wayward black curl that had escaped her tightly pinned back hair. "Besides, it seems you have moved on to Malleven, the last time he was here?" he teased, with his eyebrows up in a question.

He was shocked when Petra's face transformed into fury. "Me?"

Cesaré frowned. "Yes, you ... he told me ... it doesn't matter," he said, trying to placate her. Surprised at her reaction, he rubbed a tear away from her cheek.

She recoiled, got off his lap and smoothed down the wrinkles from her conservative black dress. Then she looked him dead in the eyes. "I have never been like that with Malleven, Cesaré. Try asking your untouchable Madonna. The last time I saw Malleven, he was fucking her senseless at the bottom of the back staircase," and she went to storm off.

Cesaré grabbed her arm roughly as she went to pass him. "What did you say?" He wasn't sure he'd heard right.

"You heard me, Cesaré. I won't spell it out for you again," she said, and ran to the door.

"You're lying!" he shouted, dismissing her with a wave of his hand before she had time to disappear.

She looked back over her shoulder with her eyes full of tears. " No, I'm not the one lying to you, Cesaré. Ask your mother."

She slammed the door behind her and left him stunned.

He stared ahead of him, then strode to the bedroom his mother and father shared. Thankfully, when he barged in unceremoniously, his father was in the shower.

"Cesaré?" his mother yelped in shock at his intrusion.

"What is this about Isla and Malleven?"

Elena appeared to deflate and sank slowly to sit on the edge of the bed. "Petra told you?"

"Told me what, Mother ... is it true?"

He walked over to her, knelt on one knee, held her by the shoulders and looked into her eyes. She brushed his hair away from his waiting face with a hand like you would a small child you had to deliver bad news to. Then she swallowed as if she'd come to a decision. "You must go to Ireland and bind her to you regardless … You must secure your place on the council for the family. Do you understand, Cesaré?" Her voice wobbled with emotion.

Cesaré stared at the tears spilling down her cheeks long after she had finished speaking. She was effectively saying that it made no difference what Isla had done.

Blinking, gritting his teeth, he exhaled loudly. Then he stood up and walked back towards the door. "What of Malleven … something like this doesn't just go away?"

His mother seemed to gather herself and sat up straighter. "You mean, step aside for a bastard lowborn prince? She's your mate, Cesaré … Yours!" his mother ended, shouting.

Cesaré brought his left hand up to his face and studied his ring. *The ring didn't lie*. He nodded. "Very well." Then he stormed out of the room and spent a sleepless night running over his options over and over again.

Isla waited for Cesaré to come and say goodnight, but he didn't come. Eventually, she turned off her lamp and slept fitfully.

CHAPTER 26

The Murrs were the first to arrive at Ballygowan Castle on the day of the official presentation of Isla. Dante made sure he was in the great hall to greet them when Vionne and Axyl's heads came up out of the fountain.

They didn't come straight into the room, but sat on the fountain wall long enough for their legs to strengthen to be able to stand. Servants hovered nearby and passed towels to them. Dante shook their hands warmly and was mildly relieved at Axyl's twin's absence.

Dante still found it hard to believe that Axyl and the one they'd found were twins. They looked similar enough, but Axyl was reserved and cultured and the other seemed more like a barely tamed wild animal.

"I'm glad you could make it, Axyl. I thought you might have already gone back to Murrla?"

Soon, he replied.

"How is your brother?"

He is well, thank you. But there is much for him to get used to. And he is still not very good with people.

"I understand. Perhaps he can accompany you another time?"

Perhaps, Axyl said.

Dante could see that he found that occasion difficult to imagine. "Your rooms have been made ready for you, and suitable clothes are waiting."

When their bones had strengthened enough, the two Murrs stood and hobbled along the corridors to rest until they could walk properly and move amongst the other guests.

As SOON AS Cesaré and Isla had settled in, Dante called them to the great hall to go through last-minute arrangements and what to expect during the presentation that evening.

When they approached, Dante was immediately struck by the difference in Cesaré's demeanour. *What's the matter with Cesaré?* Dante projected to Isla. *Have you argued?*

No, Isla replied. *He has barely spoken since we arrived.*

Dante read Isla's emotions and they were way off the scale. The girl was petrified. He needed to get to the bottom of this fast. With so many people bound and linked through him, he couldn't afford anything to be left to chance. *Do you want me to speak with him, Isla?*

Yes, please, she thought. *I don't know what I did wrong.*

He was about to tell her it was probably nothing when he noticed Vionne and Axyl, now fully rested, walking into the hall and coming over to them. *Leave us now, Isla. I'll talk to him.*

Then he wasn't sure what exactly happened. He stood, ready to greet the Murrs. Isla walked past them in the direction of the bedchamber corridor, then dropped like a stone.

. . .

Dante saw to it that Isla was carried to her bedroom and settled into bed. He assumed she was just overwrought. He told Cesaré to come back and speak with him as soon as Isla was okay to leave alone.

Dante stopped in front of Vionne and Axyl, who were both concerned about Isla.

"I'm not sure what happened then … She seemed fine when I dismissed her," Dante said.

Axyl frowned and glanced over at his brother, who nodded.

"What is it?" Dante asked.

The girl … when she passed us … she looked at me before she fainted, Axyl projected.

Dante frowned. "I don't understand."

Go on, Axyl, Vionne prompted.

She reached out to my mind in the way of us Murrs … and called me Darres.

Dante still wasn't getting his drift.

Darres is my twin, Dante. She knew his neural pathways. She assumed I was him … I'm sorry, I had no idea who she was. She attempted to breach my barriers. I had to close her down.

It was only after she fainted that I recognised the significance.

Dante touched Axyl on the shoulder. "Don't worry, Axyl. I wasn't going to say anything yet, but I happen to know that Isla had a relationship with a Murr."

Axyl looked over at Vionne, amazed.

Dante didn't want to reveal too much to the Murrs yet. He needed to speak to Cesaré first. "Do you think you could get your brother to come after all? Perhaps you could tell him about Isla and what happened?"

Very well, I will contact him, Axyl said. *But with Darres, I can't promise anything.*

. . .

WHEN DANTE CAME ACROSS CESARÉ, he was staring out at the sea through the large window in the great hall. "Ches?" he called.

Cesaré turned around, but his expression was grim. "Dante," he said, in acknowledgement. "How is she?"

Dante nodded. "She's had a shock, that's all. It seems that she knows Axyl's brother. They may have met during her captivity with the Americans. She saw Axyl and that was it."

Cesaré nodded and sighed with relief.

"What's up, Ches … you are not acting like the husband-to-be I've been expecting?"

Cesaré swore in Italian under his breath and faced back to the window. "I don't know how to begin to tell you."

Fuck, Isla was complicated. The issues surrounding her were piling up and needed to be sorted. And although she was already bound to him, and that could never be altered, who she bound to *her* as her chosen mate was of the utmost importance. And now she had three possible suitors: Malleven, Cesaré and now Darres Borge. *Shit, this was one hell of a mess.*

"That she's been with your cousin, Malleven?"

Cesaré turned to him sharply. "You know … she told you?"

"No. She was released from the airbase in Montana a year ago into Malleven's care. I know this because the Duke Delissi organized it. Then she appeared to go to ground until you came forward with her."

"So you knew something was wrong?" Cesaré said, narrowing his eyes.

"Yes. When you said she'd been with you weeks, I knew something was amiss."

Cesaré put his head in his hands. "The maid … at home … she said that Isla and Malleven are … you know. I just can't make any sense of it. He brought her to me first. Why bring her to me if he loved her … he prefers males, for god's sake?"

Dante didn't know Malleven, but he was sceptical that he was even capable of the kind of love Cesaré was talking about. "Look, Cesaré, in the short time I've known you, I've come to like and respect you, and I can't think of a worthier prince to sit on my council. Does it matter, really?" Dante said, pointing at Cesaré's ring.

Cesaré nodded in appreciation of the compliment Dante paid him. "But it feels wrong, Dante. I've seen you with Tia and Keenan with Lacy. That's how it should be … it doesn't feel right."

Dante studied Cesaré for a few moments, then came to a quick decision and laid it on the line for him. "Look, you need to know, Ches … Malleven was behind Tia's handover to the Americans last year. We think he did it to get his hands on Isla. We also know that he was responsible for Lacy's abduction and kept her for almost a year."

Cesaré frowned and went to walk away from Dante. "No! I can't believe that. No. He is many things, but not that."

"Lacy was brainwashed, Cesaré. She has no memory of anything during and prior to that year."

"What on earth would he do that for, and then give her back? … it doesn't make sense," Cesaré said angrily.

"He didn't give her back. Keenan found her. But it was for blood, Cesaré. He was taking Lacy's blood. You are Florianna … Can you think of anything, anything at all, that he may have needed Siren blood for?"

Cesaré looked up for inspiration and thought about it while he absently played with the divining ring on his left hand.

Dante watched him ruminate for quite a few minutes. "Think, Cesaré. If he didn't want Lacy as a mate, what else could he have needed her for … her blood?"

"All I keep thinking is, the only thing Malleven ever worked hard at or appeared to care about was his experiments and skill at alchemy."

Their eyes both dropped to Cesaré's ring at exactly the same time.

"No … he couldn't?" Cesaré said.

"It works by blood?"

"But a male's."

Dante nodded and conceded he was right.

Cesaré narrowed his eyes. "But when I said I wanted my ring checked weeks ago, it was he who told me not to. And it was he who brought me a replacement … but why, why would he do it?"

"There is no time to work it out."

"What are you thinking?"

"I will tell Axyl a virgin ring is needed … urgently," Dante said.

ISLA LAY EXHAUSTED, propped up on a mountain of pillows in her room. The nurse had taken her vitals; after living in a lab for most of her life, the procedure was all too familiar.

She listlessly turned her head towards the door when she heard the click of it opening. An older-looking gentleman and a tall, willowy woman entered. Her eyes rested on them without speaking. She simply couldn't be bothered.

The man spoke first. "Hello, Daughter," he said, smiling broadly. "I am your father, Sebastian, and this is your mother, Naomi. We heard you had taken ill and so we had to come and meet you and make sure you were comfortable."

Isla blinked. What did they expect her to say? She studied them. Her father looked oldish; he was probably in his late fifties. The woman – her mother – was striking, but not exactly beautiful. *Murr.*

Hello, child, Naomi said, straight to her mind.

Isla's eyes widened. Telepathic communication wasn't new to her; Darres and her monks did it all the time. It was just weird hearing her mother for the first time.

The woman took a step nearer the bed and picked up her hand. A warm vibration shot up her arm like an electric current. Isla snatched back her hand. "What are you doing?" she said in alarm.

I am feeling your emotions, child, and offering my love to soothe you.

It was true, a wave of calm came over her, but it wasn't asked for and she didn't trust her not to take something.

Naomi stepped back and nodded demurely as if she understood. *Did she know?*

Isla became impatient. She didn't know them. They probably meant well. But the only love she had known from her early childhood had been from her monks and her beloved sensei. And, quite frankly, she had never given her parents much more than a passing thought, always assuming she'd been orphaned. Growing up in the lab meant her understanding of the concept of 'normal family life' was fairly tenuous, at best.

The woman bowed her head as if she understood yet again. It was unnerving. Her father put a supportive arm around her and looked concerned, first towards Naomi, then Isla.

We understand how you must feel, child, Naomi said. *But we had to come and see you to let you know that we love you, and have always loved you ... and that we are here for you now and always.*

Naomi seemed to become distressed by Isla's lack of response and Sebastian took her in his arms. Isla watched, still dispassionately. She felt exhausted and couldn't muster up the wherewithal to question or even accuse them. Quite honestly, their getting upset because she wasn't doing cart-wheels at meeting them was the least of her worries.

"Your mother is upset because you are so unhappy," Sebastian said. "We will leave you now, Airla. If there is anything you want to ask us … anything you need to know, we will be here for you."

Isla was sobered. "Thank you," she said, in a weak croak. But she could never imagine a day when that would happen.

Sebastian smiled kindly and nodded as if his work was done, dabbed Naomi's eyes with his handkerchief and led her from the room.

Hell! She felt worse than ever.

DANTE EXCUSED the nurse in Isla's room and went and sat on her bed.

"I'm sorry, Dante … I don't know what happened. "I've never done that before."

Dante didn't want to frighten Isla with the prospect of her being pregnant, especially as he wasn't sure of that yet, but he did need some proper answers out of her. "Did you already know Axyl, Isla?"

She shook her head and kept her eyes downcast.

"He said you called him Darres," Dante persisted.

Her eyes came up to look at his and she blinked. "I won't let you in my mind no matter what you do," she said, vehemently.

Dante raised his eyebrows at her strong response and smiled. "What, force myself on you … not my style, babe … I'm just talking, is all," and he put his hands up in a "don't shoot" pose. "It's just weird because Axyl had a twin brother," he said, watching her face. Not a flicker. "He got lost to him at around five years old?" Dante persisted, still no response.

"Who he found again recently, with Tia's help. Off the coast of Florida." *Bingo.*

Dilation of her pupils, flare of her nostrils, flush in the cheeks, a major response. "Don't you want to know how he is … your Murr?" Dante said, slowly smiling.

Isla sagged and exhaled loudly as if caught out and found guilty as charged.

"Axyl has contacted Murrtaine for him to come here," Dante said.

Isla's eyes went wide with fright, which surprised Dante. "What's the matter, don't you want to see him?" He'd assumed that this was the one she loved.

"I don't want him to get hurt," she said, anxiously.

Dante was a little confused, but played along as if he knew nothing. "Who would hurt him, Isla … Cesaré … because he's your mate?"

Tears brimmed and ran down Isla's cheeks and she shook her head. "No, not Cesaré."

"Who then, Isla?"

She shook her head again. "I can't."

Dante went to stand. "I can't help you then, Isla, unless you're honest with me," and he went to walk towards the door.

"Malleven," she said on a sob, rolled onto her side and dissolved into tears that wracked her whole body. Pain that had been held deep inside for years and with all the months of abuse, came tumbling out.

Dante sat back down on the edge of the bed and lifted her into his arms to comfort her.

"He's too strong," she said, between sobs.

He began to rock her to and fro like he did the children. "Shh."

"Malleven will kill him. It is better if he never sees me."

"Shh," Dante repeated, while his mind worked. "Tell me

everything," he said, and began to stroke her hair and kiss her gently to calm her. "Start at the beginning and tell me the whole story."

Gradually, her sobs lessened. "Or I can project it?"

"In the way the Murrs do?" Dante said, surprised.

She nodded. "Darres taught me."

Dante smiled. "It would be a lot quicker."

"Shall I start from my childhood?" she said, sitting up and sniffing.

"That would be grand," he said.

Isla knelt up on the bed and held the sides of his face with both of her hands and flashed him picture after picture and feeling after feeling. The hurt, the loss, the loneliness, the despair, the replacement of one abysmal life after another, culminating in Malleven's use of her and their mate's attraction to enslave her, and then, to exploit his best friend and cousin to win a kingdom for him.

When she finally finished with their last sordid meeting in the servant's stairwell, Dante sat back, exhausted. *Fuck.*

"Please don't tell Cesaré … I don't want to hurt him," Isla pleaded.

Dante held both her hands in his. "He already knows a great deal, Isla. But don't worry, remember you did not do this to him," he said, firmly. "I'll help you make him understand."

Isla lay back into the pillows, worn out and relieved. "Thank you, Dante … it is like a weight has been lifted."

"Good," he said, tucking her in. "The worst is over now." However, in the privacy of his mind, he was thinking, *Fuck! Malleven, my greatest enemy, is her true mate. She must never bond with him at all costs, because if she did that, Malleven would have a seat in government, and a link through him to all the Sirens.*

He left the room when she finally dropped off into a sound sleep.

. . .

ELENA STOOD straight as a school marm with her hand on her hips and an expression like she'd been chewing a wasp. "Malleven Mancini, how dare you play fast and loose with my son's mate," she said into the telephone.

"Elena … Elena … calm down," Malleven's voice placated from the other end. "What have you heard?" he asked, in his best patronising tone.

"That you have a relationship with Isla … Cesaré is heartbroken. I am so disappointed in you."

"Ah, fuck!"

"Swearing will not get you out of this …" she continued.

"Where are you, Elena?" Malleven interrupted.

"We are in Ireland. The official presentation is tonight."

"Has Cesaré bonded with Isla yet?"

"No, not to my knowledge. This has rocked him, Malleven."

"Shit … I will come immediately."

"Yes, come and sort out the mess you've made, before Cesaré does something stupid!"

"Before you go, Elena?"

"What?"

"Who told him?"

"Petra … Petra told him."

The line clicked dead.

CHAPTER 27

Tia and Lacy slipped into Isla's room, whispering and giggling like a pair of schoolgirls, while Isla was running a cold bath. She'd been desperate to submerge herself all day. They started to rummage through her wardrobe.

She came out of the bathroom and faced them with a blank face. She didn't mind Lacy, but Tia had been positively hostile at their first meetings. "I need a bath," she stated flatly. "What do you want?"

When she realized the girls weren't going to be warned off easily, she sighed, turned off the tap and slid back into bed, defeated and feeling ill all over again.

Lacy came and sat with her. "What have you been up to?" she asked, her eyes glittering with excitement at the hint of juicy gossip.

"Nothing."

"Ah come on … the place is like someone kicked a hornets' nest," Tia said, grinning. "The Florianna lot won't come out of their room, Axyl's called Murrtaine for back-up and Dante is talking about postponing the presentation."

"Come on, tell us?" Lacy said.

Isla put her head in her hands. *Oh god, how would she get herself out of this mess? Why couldn't she have just kept her mouth shut?* "Is Cesaré okay?"

"I think so," Tia said. "Although there's loads of shouting in Italian coming from their room."

"Oh no!" Isla threw herself face down on the bed and covered her head with a pillow.

Lacy walked around the bed, sat down next to her and stroked her hair. "You can tell us, Isla. I know you don't know us yet, but neither did me and Tia at first. We just got to know each other and saw how alike we are."

Isla slowly came out from under her pillow, sat back up and looked distrustfully at Tia.

Tia shrugged and looked insolently back. "What?"

Isla had come this far, so there didn't seem to be a lot of point in keeping quiet now. "I can't tell you it all, it would take too long." She took a breath and let it out raggedly. "Cesaré isn't my mate, and a Murr bonded with me ... I didn't know what it was at the time."

"Fucking hell," Tia said, plonking down on the bed to join them. "You have been busy ... what's his name?"

"Who?"

"The Murr."

"Darres."

Tia put her hands up to her mouth and giggled. "Oh shit!"

"What?" Lacy demanded, looking between them, not following at all.

"Axyl's brother."

"Who? ... Oh!" Lacy said, falling in.

"So is he your mate?" Tia said.

Isla shook her head slowly, dreading the next question.

"Who then?" both sisters said at the same time.

Isla closed her eyes and the word came out as a whisper, "Malleven."

When she allowed her eyes to open, the girls were staring at her, stunned. Then they looked at each other, then back at her.

"Bloody hell," Lacy said, shuddering.

Tia frowned. "So why are you lying in bed?"

Isla had to think about that for a minute. "I don't know ... Dante sent me here. He said he was getting Axyl to call Darres ... I was afraid. It's been a long time."

"Who's the scariest?" Lacy said, like a co-conspirator.

Isla had never thought about that before and was taken aback. She looked around while she thought about it.

"I don't know about Malleven," Tia said. "But that Darres is huge."

"Bigger than Keenan?" Lacy said, sceptically.

"Yeah, he actually is," Tia said, nodding enthusiastically. "I only saw him in water, but he's got all this brooding presence about him." She wiggled her eyebrows at Isla. "Sexy."

Isla scowled. That someone else could have a sexual opinion of Darres bothered her and she had never felt that before.

Tia stood up, her attention span gone. "Look, are you going to lie here and wait for the shit to hit the fan like a victim, or are you going to come out with us and get shit-faced?" Tia said, pausing, with her eyebrows up in question.

Isla wasn't sure what shit-faced was and looked at Lacy for some clarification. "It's what I'd do ... it is Saturday night," Lacy said, nodding.

Isla came to a decision and started to get up out of bed. "What's shit-faced?"

"Don't worry, we'll show you," Tia said, already throwing stuff at her from the wardrobe.

"We'll have to sneak out," Lacy said, eyes wide. "We'd never be allowed out unescorted."

Isla was pushing her legs into some trousers, looking at each sister with trepidation.

"We're never allowed out," Tia added, ruefully. "God, you need some jeans, girl."

"Worry about that another time. We've got to get out of here first," Lacy said, all business.

"Where are we going?" Isla said, now dressed.

"There's a little club not far from here. It's not the Ministry, but it'll do. Dante hired it out once. We'll go there … Shit … money?" Tia said, suddenly remembering. They wouldn't get far without it. "We'll have to go via my room … ring a cab, Lace. Get it to pick us up at the end of the drive … And, oh yeah, make sure you shut out Dante and Keenan, okay?"

Lacy nodded, totally seeing the sense in that.

"They are in your heads?" Isla said, horrified.

"Yeah, Dante checks in with me about every ten minutes these days."

"Won't he think something's up?" Lacy said.

"Nah, I'll make out I'm jealous over her," Tia bobbed her head in Isla's direction. "He'll leave me alone like the plague then."

Lacy grinned.

They were soon all dressed, sneaking through the servants' quarters and out of the castle through a trade entrance.

Isla felt exhilarated. She'd never done anything so exciting in her life.

PETRA PRESSED the digits on the wall phone in the kitchen. "Malleven … it's Petra."

"Ah, my little canary … I've just landed."

"They've gone into town."

"Where?"

"Not sure, but they looked like they were going out dancing."

Malleven laughed; he simply loved rule-breakers. It just so appealed to his dark side. "There can't be many places in that backwater. It's already late, so they won't go far … Now, if you want Cesaré, Petra, keep your mouth shut."

"Okay." She quietly replaced the receiver.

THE BOUNCERS outside the club took one look at the trio and ushered them straight inside. The head guy even waived the cover charge. "My treat, ladies." Then he pointed them in the direction of the bar.

Isla's heart was racing with excitement. The noise, the people, the bombardment of the senses, she'd never been anywhere like it.

"You like?" Tia said, her eyes glittering. "Welcome to our world."

Lacy grinned, already moving to the music while they waited to be served. Isla was mesmerized by the way she moved her body.

"What are you drinking?" Tia said, already rummaging in her purse.

"I've only ever had wine or vodka and I didn't much like either … what do you have?" Isla asked.

"I drink whisky … she drinks beer," Tia said, pointing at Lacy who was singing along to the latest track, and taking a swig straight from her bottle, quickly served by an eager barman.

Isla grinned. "I'll try beer."

Tia laughed, ordered herself a scotch and coke and a bottle of 'wife beater'.

Isla's face was a picture.

Tia and Lacy laughed at her shocked expression. "It's just a nickname for the beer, don't worry, we'll stop you before you get aggressive," Tia said.

"Let's down these and get on the dance floor," Lacy said.

Tia nodded, already gulping hers back and nudging Isla to hurry her along. "All of it, Isla, then we'll get another."

Isla did as she was told. The 'wife beater' was easy to drink and going down a treat.

Tia laughed, delighted with her, and finished hers with a final gulp. "I'm getting a double!" She ordered another round.

Soon the three of them were in the throng of dancers in the centre of the room, penned in by hot bodies, lights spinning over their heads and dry ice buffeting up from the floor.

Isla squealed with excitement.

Lacy and Tia, deciding it was a sisterhood moment, linked arms with her and they all jumped around in a circle, throwing their heads back and laughing.

Isla lapped up every feeling, every sensation, every nuance in the music. She made them explain everything. "I've never enjoyed myself before," she shouted.

"Never as good as this, eh?" Tia shouted back.

"No, never enjoyed myself … ever. It's brilliant!" Isla spun around and almost fell over.

Tia almost didn't catch her when she registered what Isla had actually just said.

She soon snapped out of it when several people on a raised dais started to pull them up to join them.

Isla didn't hesitate, climbed up and copied the way her sisters moved, effortless and sexy.

"What do you think?" Tia shouted over the music.

"I love it!" Isla shouted back.

Lacy had slipped down to go to the bar and come back with more drinks – shots this time. "Come on, drink up!" she shouted up to Isla.

They all knocked back their drinks, pulled faces and then danced and laughed together.

Isla was warming more and more to her sisters. It was as though they were making up for all the years they'd spent apart.

Another driving beat started and everything began to become blurred and dreamlike when a mixture of strobe lighting and dry ice enticed them into their own little worlds. Isla gyrated and swayed and even let a man pull her towards a dark corner. Before she realized what was happening, he had pulled her into his body, pushing her hands up around his neck. Holding her tightly around her waist, he began to move with her. Through the whole process, she hadn't even opened her eyes, but just absorbed through her other senses. Wow, it was bliss.

As soon as his lips came next to her ear and she smelled the crook of his neck, she knew who it was. She screamed in shock.

"Hello, Snowflake."

She gasped and looked up, but he held her fast. "Mal-leven!" came out more like a strangled yelp.

He smiled down at her. "How sexy you look, letting your-self go … does anyone know you are here?" he said, looking around.

Her mind was sluggish and she struggled to think straight; she knew she was vulnerable. "Yes," she lied.

Malleven looked into her eyes, amused. "Mmm, they let three Sirens go out alone these days? I shall have to say something about that." He continued to move with her as he spoke.

"What are you doing here?" she finally dared to ask.

"Cesaré's mother called me and asked me to come and sort out your mess, Snowflake."

She squinted and frowned. She knew what he was saying was wrong somehow, but she couldn't quite get her head around it. Instead, she went into petulant child mode. "I don't want to go, I want to stay," she said, sulkily. "I'm enjoying myself."

He nipped her lips with his. "That you are … and I approve."

Isla felt a tap on her shoulder. It was Tia. "Excuse me …" she said, looking at Malleven. Her eyebrows went up when she focused on his face. "That's my sister, and we're on a girls' night."

Malleven smiled, let Isla go and took a step backwards. "Pardon for the intrusion. I will admire the three of you from afar."

Tia was looking at him long and hard, despite how pissed and bleary-eyed she was, and she said a little too loudly, "Is he taking the piss?"

Lacy joined them, but averted her eyes from him. It struck Isla as weird, even through her drunken haze. Lacy handed them each a drink.

"Who's he?" Lacy asked, taking a huge gulp of her drink.

"Mall … ev … en!" Isla mouthed.

Tia put her hand to her mouth. "Shit! I never knew he was so hot!"

Malleven laughed aloud, delighted with them.

Isla looked around her, suddenly aware that they were completely surrounded by a ring of the meanest-looking men she had ever seen.

Lacy clocked it at the same time and dug Tia in the ribs. "We've got company."

"Ah, can't you tell your lot to fuck off and let us have a night out?" Tia said, disappointed.

"They're not my lot. I don't know who they are either," Lacy said.

Tia turned to Malleven, who was still smiling benignly, and shook her head while she spoke, "Not Santalini?"

He copied her, grinning. "Not Santalini … these are my guards, come to escort you home safely."

I don't want to go!" Isla shouted. "I want more wife-beaters!"

Tia and Lacy shrieked with laughter and put their arms around her when she floundered and almost fell over.

Malleven nodded his head and his men began to herd them towards the exit and out to the street.

Just as the cold air slapped their faces, several cars screeched to a halt and Santalini guards sprang out from all directions. Isla looked frantically around her. Malleven had vanished. *Had he even been there?*

Keenan grabbed Lacy and tutted in disgust at the state of her, then called out to his men to arrest the men around them. They weren't difficult to spot, dressed completely in black with dark-coffee skin.

The three girls, now a bit green around the gills – literally – were bundled into one of the blacked-out SUVs. Keenan and Reeve got in with them. The wheels screeched and they sped off back to the castle, streetlights whizzing past until they were in the total blackness of the countryside.

"Turn the music up!" Isla shouted and hiccupped.

Lacy and Tia stifled giggles.

Keenan was looking sternly at Lacy.

"Talk out loud, Keenan. My head hurts," she complained. "There is nothing you can say to me that you can't say to my sisters."

Keenan rolled his eyes and they all laughed again. "What's the point? You're all too smashed to listen."

Lacy scrambled clumsily onto his lap, so he had to help her. "Ah, come on, Keenan, don't be a killjoy."

He half-smiled at her, really trying to keep his stern face.

Isla sighed. She thought Keenan was lovely; their relationship was lovely. Nothing was forced or fake; everything seemed totally natural. She felt like crying all of a sudden, but didn't want to ruin the night and so swallowed it down.

It didn't take long for them to reach the castle. The girls were taken in first. The men who had been arrested would be taken to the catacomb level, where the cells were. The lift taking them down to the great hall was full of guards. She wasn't sure who started it, but they got a chronic case of the giggles, and every time they tried to stop, as they were in so much trouble, they would feel the shake of the body next to them and they would shriek with laughter again.

When the lift doors opened, the three of them fell out and lay on the marble floor in a giggling heap of tangled arms and legs.

"Get up," Keenan ordered. "You're in enough trouble as it is."

But when they saw he was trying not to laugh himself, it only fuelled their own and they dissolved again.

Isla, who was now in pain, tried to roll onto her stomach and crawl away from the melee. She looked down the marble steps into the cavernous room. She squinted until her eyes began to focus. There was a welcoming committee waiting for them and she began to struggle to her feet but failed and fell down again.

Big arms came under her and lifted her up. She wriggled and turned in his arms and looked into Keenan's face. "What's that in your ears?" she asked, like a small child deflecting a telling off.

He grinned. "Come on, lightweight."

Lacy held onto one of his arms while he carried Isla, Tia

held the other, and together they walked slowly down the steps into the great hall.

"Ah, fuck!" Tia said, sagging dramatically when she caught sight of Jay. "What's he doing here?"

Dante walked over to the three of them, draped over Keenan. "He came as soon as he heard the three of you were missing."

"We weren't missing," Lacy said, affronted. "We were clubbing."

"Yeah, clubbing!" Isla chimed in from Keenan's arms, starting to feel a bit sick again.

The girls giggled. Keenan slowly put her down to rest on her feet. She was grateful to have her head upright to stop the spinning.

A little shaky, Isla looked around her and squinted to get a look at who was there. Most of the faces she recognized, but there was one who stood out, bigger than all the others. His hair was black and long, down to his waist. She inched forward to get a better look. Her eyes weren't great at the best of times. His large arms were folded over his huge chest. He had a black T-shirt on and black army-type trousers. As she got closer, she realized that his exposed skin was covered in stripes – even his face. A face so high above her that she had to crane her neck to look into his coal-black eyes.

Then the world fell out from under her.

CHAPTER 28

*D*arres' arms moved lightning fast and caught her. She hung loose and floppy like a dead weight. *What's wrong with her ... is she ill?* he asked.

Dante shook his head, "No, mate ... she's drunk. She'll feel rough tomorrow."

Axyl explained to him what being drunk was and Darres frowned. *You do it to yourselves deliberately?*

Dante would have seen the funny side of the situation, had he not been so angry. To think what could have happened tonight, and all because of Tia's wilfulness. Again. He walked over to her with narrowed eyes. "Of all the stupid things, Tia."

She batted him out of the way with the shoes she held in her hand. "Oh stop going on, Dante. You're like an old woman."

Dante's eyes went wide and he pushed her towards the bedchamber corridor while she continued to swear at him.

Darres was still in exactly the same position, holding Isla under the arms, unconscious. *What shall I do with her?*

"Cesaré's still here, Dant," Jay said. Reminding him before he forgot and left Darres and Isla alone together.

Dante stopped and thought with his hands on his hips.

Tia slipped down the wall next to him to a sitting position on the floor.

He looked down at her, then at Keenan. "Are all the cells full downstairs?"

Keenan grinned, knowing where his train of thought was going. "Yeah, there were eight arrested tonight."

Dante was almost disappointed, but it was just as well. The next day was going to be hard enough as it was. "Shove the three of them in Isla's room and stick a guard outside. None of them are to leave."

Darres, having heard the whole thing, had arranged Isla in his grip and unceremoniously threw her over his shoulder. The movement seemed to rouse her and she groaned as her head went up and down as he walked. "I'm gonna be sick!"

At Isla's room, Keenan and Darres threw Lacy and Isla onto the bed and they both turned over and fell asleep instantly.

Tia, who had been undressing unsteadily down to her bra and knickers since she left the great hall, threw her shoes and shouted at them to get out of her room and give a girl some privacy.

Dante paused in the doorway in time to see her flop onto the bed diagonally, in her underwear, with her eyes smudged black like a Panda.

DARRES HAD IMAGINED a million scenarios for the time when he finally came face to face with Isla again. He'd built her up in his mind as this heartless, powerful sorceress. But never in a single one did he envisage the sight of her giggling and tumbling out of the lift to greet him as she did at that moment. In fact, it completely trounced him, like nothing else.

With every halting step as she neared him, he remained riveted while his blood ran faster, oblivious to everyone else around him.

His heart leapt when she held onto his folded arms to squint up into his eyes with a comical expression of concentration. Then his realization that her eyes were weak out of the water knocked any last vestige of anger from him.

Darres caught her, bewildered, when she collapsed in his arms. Again, this didn't fit with the image he'd created for her. As he held her small weight under her shoulders and looked over at the king for guidance, he resisted the urge to pull her to him, to hold her, breathe in her wonderful scent at her neck. His mind reeled. He had her again. He couldn't quite believe it. After months of loneliness, suddenly she was there.

Instead of wanting to kill her as he imagined he would, he found he wanted to care for her in her need, to be close to her. Instinctively, he tightened his grip around her.

That was until he heard the words, 'Cesaré's still here.' His heart constricted and hardened and he came back to his senses. Of course, she would have ensnared another. That was how she survived in this world, on the backs of the hapless men who crossed her path.

He bit down, threw her over his shoulder and carried her to her bedchamber.

The witch would not ensnare him again.

THE EIGHT MAGI brothers stood in their separate cells in exactly the same position, with their eyes closed. Dressed totally in black with only three gold stars on the left lapel to add any colour to their dark souls, they looked every bit the mysterious agents they were.

Their meditation had begun as soon as they'd been locked in and left alone. The hum had grown from nothing to a loud chorus that reached between them and communicated to their high priest and leader, and to their brother, Malleven, joining their magic from another location.

After several minutes of chanting, their bodies began to shimmer and flicker and became surrounded by a gold dust, but it emanated from within. The atomic particles of the cells in their bodies vibrated and pulsated in rhythm with their chanting until they swirled and flowed up into a vortex of glittering energy and separated and surged towards the bars of their cells.

The golden specks clustered around the bars and slithered through to the other side, where they reformed and shimmered, solidifying into golden human shapes, quivering until they at last reached a solid form.

They stood breathing for a few moments, gathering themselves and the chanting stopped abruptly. They looked across at each other, all standing outside their cells, to make sure they had all made it through the transformation.

Satisfied, they nodded a farewell to each other and disappeared to different parts of the castle where they would wait unseen until they were needed.

Across the parish, Malleven had rented a place to be near Ballygowan Castle. He knelt, meditating, at a portable altar erected in his bedroom. Antonio reclined on the bed, watching him.

He knew better than to interrupt him. Malleven was doing some hocus pocus with his spiritual brotherhood; stuff that Antonio didn't want to know or understand, but he was worried for him. Everything in Malleven's life had culminated to this point and everything was at stake.

Later, Malleven would claim his right as a true Florianna prince; an honour that Antonio knew Malleven never thought would be bestowed on him – the right to claim his Siren on behalf of the family.

Antonio was scared. He loved Malleven with a passion, but he knew how he felt about water, and he'd seen the tests enough times in his life to know what it entailed. Malleven had not.

Being a proven mate by divining ring didn't automatically buy you a seat on the council; it was acceptance by that mate.

Malleven exhaled loudly and adjusted his kneeling position to sit cross-legged. He opened his eyes. "I feel your fear from here, Antonio," his voice rumbled.

There was silence for a beat. "I'm afraid of losing you." He wanted Malleven to assume it was to a mate and not to drowning; his lack of faith would anger him, but it was pointless as he saw right through him.

"She cannot resist me, Antonio. Not in the flesh." Malleven stood and stretched out his stiff muscles.

"I am losing you nonetheless."

Malleven stood at the altar where a golden liquid waited in a glass. It glistened and shimmered and lit up his face as he picked it up and brought it to his mouth, then he knocked it back, gulped it down, and instantly doubled over in pain.

A film of sweat broke out over his brow and Antonio jumped up to help him sit down. "Why do you put yourself through this?" he said anxiously, but knowing it was futile to protest.

Malleven began to breathe deeply to work through the excruciating pains until he eventually opened his eyes. "It is my insurance, Antonio ... All you have to be concerned about is being at the meeting point to rendezvous with the priest … Is that clear!"

Antonio pushed the sweat-soaked hair from Malleven's brow. "I will, okay … don't worry, I'll be there." The words 'just concentrate on staying alive' went unsaid.

Antonio helped him lie down on top of the bed to sleep off the pain. In a few hours, he would help him dress to face his destiny.

TIA WAS the first to be ushered into Dante's study for the inquiry that followed the next morning. Dante waited, grim-faced, sitting behind his desk with Jay in an armchair to his right.

Tia sank slowly into a chair placed opposite them and put her head in her hands, feeling and looking positively green.

"Feel like shit, do we?" Dante said, but he wasn't laughing today.

Tia just let the hand that held her head fall and gave him a look that said it all. "Just get it over with, Dante, so I can go back to bed." She didn't even look at Jay. On a good day, she needed to be on top of her game to face him, so today there was no chance. She waited for the barrage, *one, two, three.*

"What the fuck possessed you, Tia?" Dante shouted suddenly.

Aaand there it was. "What?" she shouted back. "I was just getting to know her … like you told me … I thought you'd be pleased?"

"Don't give me that, Tia, you were unescorted, knowing I had a cluster-fuck of a situation here … and you yourself suspect she's pregnant," he said, shaking his head in disbelief.

Tia's eyes went wide. "Shit! … I totally forgot … my god." She felt terrible and sank even lower in her chair, if that were possible.

Dante stopped shouting but still had his no-nonsense face on. "I've had to call a Murr doctor to examine her, which is a nightmare if she knows nothing about it ... Do you even understand how tricky things are gonna get when Vionne finds out and there's a chance it could be his brother's?"

Tia's eyebrows went up, "Really ... shit ... which one? I knew she was a dark horse ... what's going on?" she whispered, inching closer for him to dish the dirt. *Bloody Hell.* She'd suspected Isla was pregnant because of her preoccupation with being in water, and Isla herself had told her a Murr had bonded with her, but due to gratuitous amounts of alcohol, she hadn't had the chance to put two and two together to work out that the delectable Darres could be the father. *Shit, who knew!*

She was saved from Dante's withering look for trying his patience when there was a knock at the door.

Dante ignored the question; instead, he called out, "Come in, Keenan."

Keenan came in, shoving a reluctant Lacy to stand in front of Dante and next to Tia. She looked down at Tia and gave her a wan smile.

"What exactly happened in the club?" Dante asked the pair of them.

Tia recounted the events as best she could remember, how Isla had been dancing with Malleven and they hadn't noticed his men surrounding them until they started to push them towards the exit.

Dante directed his gaze at Lacy.

"Don't look at me, I didn't see him, I only saw his men."

Keenan frowned but kept quiet. They'd all started to notice that whenever Malleven was around, she never, ever saw him.

"I'm going to the cells next," Dante said.

Keenan's radio hissed and he took it from his belt and put

it to his ear. "Have you searched everywhere?" He clicked it off and replaced it.

They all waited for an explanation, seeing Keenan's worried expression.

"What is it?" Dante asked.

"The cells are empty," Keenan said, shaking his head, not really believing what he was saying. "Malleven's men have disappeared."

WHEN DANTE HAD DISMISSED the girls, he went down to the catacombs to see for himself that the men had disappeared into thin air. The question of why Malleven had allowed them to be arrested in the first place played on his mind.

He stopped outside Isla's room on the way back and knocked. A psychic male voice filtered through to his consciousness from the other side of the door to come in.

Isla lay pale and small, propped up against her many pillows with a sheet across her.

Is she okay? Dante asked.

She is fine, the Murr doctor replied. *She still has a high concentration of alcohol in her blood, but it should return to normal in a day or so.*

Is she pregnant?

It's hard to say until she enters her gestation period in the water. Siren can carry a fertilized egg for years if necessary. It is nothing more than a collection of cells at this stage, the doctor explained.

But in your opinion? Dante persisted.

HCG is present in high concentration, suggesting that pregnancy is likely. But this is a Human indicator rather than a Murr one, so not conclusive, the doctor said, not willing to commit either way.

Dante nodded and sat on the edge of the bed.

Isla had been watching him the whole time and had guessed that some kind of internal conversation was going on. "What are you saying?" she asked in a croaky voice. "You should talk aloud if it's about me."

Dante studied her face for a few moments, deciding how to put it. "Okay, Isla," he said on a sigh. "I'll give it to you straight; you might be pregnant." He allowed the words to sink in.

Her eyes didn't move from his. "Might."

"You are lucky you are a Siren, because the amount of alcohol you drank last night could have been harmful to a baby. Yours won't grow until you spend time underwater."

She looked momentarily stunned.

"You want to be in the water a lot?" he asked.

"All the time," she breathed.

Dante nodded; he knew all the signs from when it first happened for Tia. "Look, there is no sugar-coating this question, Isla, but who is in the frame for being the baby's father?"

Isla slowly closed her eyes as if she were in pain. "What does it matter?" she whispered.

"I'm trying to help you, Isla, but you gotta help me. I got all kinds of shit to sort out … The Florianna are here as well as the Borge. All of them want to know what's going on. And after speaking to Cesaré's family, they want a seat on the council, whether it is Cesaré or Malleven … a child makes a hell of a difference as to who that is," he said.

"It can't be Cesaré's," she answered, her face bursting red.

"Okay," Dante said, feeling like he was getting somewhere. "Darres was here last night?" Dante hedged.

Her eyes darted to his in alarm. "He was here?"

"You don't remember? You collapsed in his arms."

She groaned and rolled onto her side.

"Is he your Murr, Isla?"

She covered her eyes with her hands and nodded behind them, too mortified to look at him.

"Could you be pregnant by him?"

"Yes," she sobbed.

Dante moved closer and stroked her hair. "Shh ... we'll sort it out, okay?"

"You don't understand ... when he finds out who Malleven is, he'll hate me."

DANTE'S DAY was going from shit to worse. Cesaré was in bits over Malleven's betrayal, and Vionne was no fool and not willing to accept any old bollocks now he knew that Darres had been involved with Isla and doctors had been called. He wanted clear and concise answers, and Dante couldn't blame him. He hadn't even had the heart to tell Cesaré that part yet.

For the inevitable meeting that followed, Dante kept Jay with him as well as Keenan, Alfonzo, Sebastian and several of the Santalini guards. Emotions were high, and it was highly likely that things could turn nasty. The truce between the families was always tenuous at best and everything had to be witnessed and recorded.

When he interviewed Cesaré, out of the Borge family, he only allowed Vionne and Axyl to be present. He could only deal with one situation at a time. Cesaré's father, Ronaldo, and eldest brother, Sandro, entered the room with him. Vionne arrived with Axyl soon after.

"Why do they need to be here?" Cesaré's father, Ronaldo, said angrily.

"Calm down, Ronaldo. Vionne has brought a replacement divining ring to settle things once and for all," Dante explained. He didn't state the obvious, that when a prince's position as mate was brought into question, all the families had a right to attend the hearing.

Cesaré looked at his father as if he was expecting a further argument and then stared at the floor again.

"You know why we have to do this, don't you?" Dante said to Cesaré. He loathed what he had to do. If he could hand-pick the Siren's mates, Cesaré would have been his choice for Isla, but he was as tied to tradition as they all were.

Cesaré just nodded his head and kept his eyes downcast.

"Call Isla in," Dante said to Keenan, standing by the door.

He opened it slightly and she slipped in, looking pale and small.

"Come closer, Isla," Dante said.

Isla couldn't bear to look at Cesaré. He didn't deserve to be treated like this. He was completely innocent.

"Hold up your hand, Cesaré," Dante said.

Cesaré did as he was asked, but his head remained low. He held it aloft long enough for all present to be satisfied that they had witnessed his ring being the colour of deepest purple.

Alfonzo recorded the outcome on parchment.

"Take off the ring, Cesaré," Dante said.

There was no playfulness in Dante's eyes today, only steely focus, Isla thought. He was being the king.

Dante held out his hand to Vionne, who passed him a dark-blue velvet pouch. Dante pulled open the cord and took out another ring, identical to Cesaré's but pearl white. "Put it on," he ordered, swapping the one Cesaré held out to him for the new one.

Isla watched closely as Cesaré pressed the side and a long spike sprang out. Then he put it at the end of the middle finger of his left hand, closed his eyes, and pushed it down hard. She jumped, horrified.

The room was silent but charged with electricity. Everyone waited with anticipation.

Cesaré slowly opened his eyes. Blood started to drip from his hand onto his worn jeans. Smoke began to swirl around the ring until it settled a rich turquoise green.

Murmurs and grumbles spread among the spectators. Dante held up his hand. "Have patience."

They gave it a few more minutes, but nothing further happened. Dante sank back into his chair, obviously disappointed. He liked Cesaré, so did Isla, come to that. She swallowed down a lump in her throat.

"Hold up your hand, Cesaré," Dante said in a defeated voice.

Cesaré obeyed with his head still hung low.

"The ring conclusively reveals the status of the bearer," Dante said, clearly. "Did you, Cesaré Florianna, tamper with your ring to gain the Siren, Airla Leukosia Artemisia Bonaci as your mate?"

Isla watched Alfonzo scribble down the outcome, the charges, and her official birth name as it was spoken.

"I did not!" Cesaré said quietly.

"Speak up for the record, Cesaré," Dante said, more kindly.

"I. Did. Not." Cesaré said loudly.

Alfonzo continued to scratch away on his parchment with an old-fashioned fountain pen.

"Thank you, Cesaré … you may leave the room," Dante said.

Cesaré lifted his eyes for the first time. The merriness in them had gone, replaced by bloodshot hopelessness. "What now?" he said.

"We'll speak later, okay?" Dante said, nodding.

Cesaré rose slowly and, without looking at her once, left the room. His father and brother remained to witness the next test.

Isla wanted to run after him and beg his forgiveness, but he wouldn't listen, not now, and she couldn't blame him. She dragged her arm across her wet eyes.

"Call Darres," Dante said.

Isla's heart pounded. She felt faint again and grabbed onto the edge of the table. A guard quickly came forward and helped her into the chair that Cesaré had just vacated.

She couldn't look, but heard the door open and close again behind her. She had a vague memory of looking up into the eyes of a striped face last night, a face that reminded her of a Native American.

A powerful presence came and stood next to her. It was as though he radiated heat to her, warning that he was there. Still, she didn't look at him.

"Pass me the ring," Dante said.

Vionne passed him another pouch. Dante took out the ring as he had the last time and passed it to Darres. She felt rather than saw when he pushed it onto his hand. She heard the mumbles and the whispers and couldn't resist a glance. First to the ring, which was turquoise, and then up into the cold eyes, looking straight into hers.

Oblivious to the ring and what it meant, and the blood dripping onto the floor, his gaze penetrated her as if no one else were in the room.

Isla wished she could say it was with love or passion, but it was not. His eyes were deep, black and emotionless. His face was an empty screen, and gave nothing away about how he felt underneath, if anything at all. It was her turn to look at the floor in shame.

"That is it then," Dante said, exhausted. "Let it be

recorded that neither the Florianna prince, Cesaré, nor the Borge prince, Darres, is proven mate to Airla Leukosia Artemisia Bonaci … You may leave now, Isla."

Isla felt utterly lost and looked at Dante as if to say, 'Is that it?' while she rose from her chair slowly, but he was quickly distracted. Reeve came forward to escort her from the room.

Ronaldo and Sandro both stood up quickly, satisfied with the outcome and, ignoring her as they walked past, went to plan their next move.

WHEN THE ROOM HAD EMPTIED, Dante was left with just Jay, Keenan and the Borges.

Vionne didn't beat around the bush. *Is it true you sought out our doctors?* he projected, so all could hear.

"It is," Dante said.

And what was the outcome? Vionne said.

Darres frowned and looked between them.

"Inconclusive," Dante said.

Come on, Dante … be straight.

"I'm telling you all I know. The doctor was non-committal either way."

Is she showing any signs?

Dante shook his head. "Only a wish to be in water, but that doesn't necessarily mean she's pregnant."

Darres stood stock still at those last words – not so much as a blink.

ISLA RUSHED OUT of the lift and down the steps to go through the great hall to the bedchamber corridor and skidded to a halt when she spotted Cesaré waiting in one of the armchairs. She wasn't sure whether to turn and run back the way she came, but decided not to be a coward. He'd never been a violent man and he deserved an explanation. "Cesaré," she whispered.

His eyes flashed up to hers and he stood slowly. *Shit!*

"Are you okay?" she asked, cautiously.

"I've been waiting for you," his voice rasped like he had a hundred-a-day smoking habit.

She exhaled and nodded. "I understand."

"The whole time … you knew?" he said, his brow furrowed in pain.

She swallowed and looked down. "Yes, I did."

His body seemed to sag even lower with her frank admission, as if he wanted her to deny it.

"You have to understand, I don't love him. I needed to get here any way I could." She shook her head. "It was the only way."

"So you played along to escape him?" he said, flummoxed.

"You don't know what he's really like."

"You don't get it, do you?" he said, amazed. "Where all this is going now."

She stared at him, not comprehending what he was getting at at all, waiting for him to explain.

"Our uncle is pushing for Malleven to be recognized to keep our seat. My family will be forced to go along with it for the good of the Florianna."

She continued to frown, still not grasping his meaning.

"Malleven is coming to claim you legitimately … It is him, isn't it, Isla … He is your true mate?"

She grabbed onto the nearest available chair and sat down while she thought frantically.

"Why didn't he do that in the beginning?" Cesaré said, staring down at her.

She was still racking her brains. "He said he'd done some bad stuff … they would have killed him on sight." She looked up at him, hoping he would know the answer.

Cesaré shook his head and shrugged. "I don't know about any of that, but the whole family is getting behind him now because he has the backing of the Magi."

Isla frowned at him.

"They were here last night … the men they arrested when you were brought home … They are very powerful men from an ancient order of mystics."

"Are they Florianna?" she asked.

"I'm not sure … some maybe. Not all are Atlantean."

They were both quiet for a minute.

"I never meant to hurt you, Cesaré … What will you do?" she asked, wanting to comfort him, but it seemed inappropriate now.

"I'll wait for Malleven. I need to speak to him … and then … I'm not sure … go back to California, maybe." He put his hands in his pockets and looked up at the ceiling.

Isla's hands came up to her mouth. "Be careful, Cesaré, he is ruthless."

He smiled at her ruefully. "You're worried for me?" He laughed and shook his head and walked off towards the bedrooms.

Isla curled up in the armchair Cesaré had left for quite some time after, feeling miserable and alone. She heard the lift doors and raised her head slightly to see who was coming. Darres descended the marble steps with large, purposeful strides and made his way towards the fountain. He stood with his back to her and pulled his T-shirt up over his head to reveal his well-muscled body.

She could watch him all day, the way his muscles rippled, moving with his now barely visible stripes. It seemed that even his faded the longer he was out of water. He stood still as if he were waiting for something.

Her heart was hammering in her chest. She stood up very slowly, not sure what to say or do.

You have recovered, little one? he projected, without looking at her once.

Darres! she replied, reaching out with her mind to him as she used to.

He slammed down his mental barriers, making her flinch. He slowly turned to face her. His eyes narrowed with suspicion as he studied her.

Isla approached him slowly. Half of her wanted to run and leap into his arms, and the other half was terrified he would reject her. In fact, he hadn't shown any signs of missing her in the few brief glimpses she'd had of him.

She walked into his personal space and craned her neck to look up into his face. She tentatively reached up a hand to touch his cheek. Before she could make contact with his skin, he grabbed her wrist, lightning fast, and held it hard.

He looked at her quizzically, with his head at an angle. *We're not in the pool any more, little one?*

She frowned, not understanding. "I've missed you so much," she whispered. A tear escaped the corner of her eye. "You escaped," she said, trying to smile.

He narrowed his eyes again. *I didn't wait a year.*

"Good," she said, swallowing hard. "I'm glad." This reunion wasn't going how she'd imagined it.

How did you do it? he asked.

"Do what?" she said, trying to pull away slightly, but he held her still.

Your intentions, he said, bearing down on her, hurting her wrist. *How did you obscure them from me?*

"My intentions? … You're hurting me," she winced.

The commander came to see me after you'd left and took great pleasure in telling me you worked for them. That you had now been reassigned as you had tamed me. He grimaced as if he hated her.

She whimpered and her eyes widened with every shocking word.

I worked for them after that, until I could take my chance and escape to find you.

Every word dripped with venom, like he would kill her any second.

"You couldn't see those intentions because they simply weren't there," she said, desperately. "I wasn't reassigned, I was released to the Florianna. I spoke to the Duke Delissi … I told him about you." She couldn't believe that he had twisted what she'd told him to use Darres in her place. "I thought he would help you. Everything I have done since was to escape to find you," she pleaded, openly crying now.

He pushed her away from him harshly and looked contemptuously at her. *You would destroy me like you did Cesaré, and all for your true mate.*

"I wouldn't, Darres," she sobbed. "I don't want him. I wanted to escape him, I promise you."

You lie, little one. You cannot tell the truth. He waved her away with a hand and turned and resumed undressing.

Desperate, she flew at him and went to batter his chest with her fists, all her training lost in her madness.

Darres grabbed her arms and pushed them behind her back, easily gripping them in one hand, holding her by her hair with the other.

Isla remained still, looking up into his black, fathomless eyes. He bent his head and covered her mouth with his. There were no protests; she just dissolved into him and immediately relaxed and kissed him. Like she'd never kissed anyone in her life.

He seemed to wake up and pushed her away from him like she'd beguiled him for a moment. She felt a mental push at her barriers. She frowned. "No, Darres … you said never again."

How convenient. How else will I believe you?

"You didn't find anything the first time you did it, when you forced yourself on me … so why would you need to look again?"

His face contorted with contempt. *You are a witch.* He pushed down his trousers and stepped out of them and over the fountain wall.

"Darres … don't!" She leapt forward, as if to grab him, but changed her mind.

He paused before he disappeared and looked back at her.

"He's coming for me tomorrow," she said, as one last futile attempt to get through to him.

He nodded. *The dark man!*

There was no point in hiding the fact any more. She just nodded hopelessly and watched him turn back and step into the deep hole in the centre of the fountain. The innocent male she'd met all those months ago had gone for ever.

Perhaps she *was* Malleven's ideal mate. She seemed to destroy the people she got close to as surely as he did. She sank to the floor. It was no use fighting it and she rose, turned and went to walk back to her room, tears streaming. She stopped sharply in front of the two people she knew loosely as her parents.

Their faces were pained, as if they'd witnessed the whole thing with Darres and felt it all with her.

"What?" she shrieked bitterly. "I'm not in the mood right now. In case you hadn't noticed. It hasn't been a great day." They'd had only the briefest introductions upon her arrival at the castle, then they'd visited her in her room, but then circumstances had taken off like a whirlwind and she hadn't had a chance to get to know them more or even develop a little curiosity

Naomi looked briefly up at her husband, Sebastian, then looked back at her with soulful eyes. *We wanted to see how you were faring, child,* she projected straight to Isla's mind.

Her Murr speech, reminding her of Darres, only served to sting her all the more. "Well, you've seen now. If you don't mind, I need to go to my room." And Isla went to walk off.

Sebastian touched her gently on the arm as she went to pass. "Airla … wait," he said in his quiet Italian voice.

"What could either of you possibly have to say that I would want to hear this late in the day?" Isla said, in a rare outburst of anger.

Naomi stepped forward and, ignoring her hostility, touched her hand gently to her face.

Isla felt the warm vibration buzz through her at the contact and it instantly calmed her as it had done before. She continued to look into the large, deer-like eyes of her mother, the colour of deepest mahogany.

Do not worry, child, the male of your heart cannot keep his anger.

Isla took a step back, snapping herself out of her mother's thrall. "That's easy for you to say. How can you possibly know what Darres feels?"

"Because he has bound himself to you," her father added.

Isla looked between their smiling faces, confused. "What difference does that make? Malleven, my true mate, in case you hadn't realized, is coming for me at any moment." She wanted to stamp in her exasperation at them for not grasping the hopelessness of her situation.

Whoever claims you now makes no difference to the bond, child; he has still claimed you … whatever the outcome of the test.

Remember that and hold onto it, her mother projected, her eyes insistent.

Sebastian led Naomi away, in the direction of his quarters, but she continued to look back at Isla over her shoulder.

Isla watched them walk away, wondering what the hell she meant.

CHAPTER 30

*D*ante had taken no chances. Proven mate though Malleven may be, he was still his enemy and Dante would never forget that. Santalini soldiers had swarmed into the castle from all around the globe to protect him, his kingdom and his family from a possible attack. A show of strength and solidarity was needed in front of the delegations from the other families invited today.

Keenan was a worry, though. He'd been quiet ever since the news hit him that Cesaré was discredited and Darres was ruled out, and that any prince now had the right to present themselves to the court in the presence of the eligible Siren, Isla Snow. He had a massive score to settle, as many of them did. Keenan's life mate had been ripped away from him, imprisoned, drugged and brainwashed for almost a year. The calm facade of the controlled soldier was ready to crack open to reveal the jealous animal needing revenge prowling beneath the surface.

Dante's heart was heaviest for Isla. He had really hoped she'd be for Cesaré. He liked him. Darres was an unknown quantity. He was strong, he knew, but Dante couldn't help feeling that a life like Darres had led would forever make him a loner, and out to serve no one but himself. So the poor cow waited with dread, like the rest of them, for the appointed time when she would be led to the altar and sacrificed to the devil himself. That was how she was feeling; he could feel it deep inside him in that part she occupied, and he was sure her sisters could feel it too.

A message came down to Keenan to warn them that Malleven had arrived. Dante sat in a throne-like chair with Tia, Lacy and Isla standing next to him. Naomi and Sebastian, the girls' mother and father, sat in similar chairs on either side of him, with Alfonzo next to Sebastian.

Keenan hovered next to Lacy, determined to keep her near him. The threat Malleven posed did nothing to ease his overprotective nature. The rest of the room was divided in two, with Cesaré and the Florianna family on one side, and the Bonaci and Borge, including Vionne, Dax, Axyl and Caan on the other. Darres was noticeably absent.

Dante's own family – the Dubonnettis – were sparse. The Duke Ormond Delissi (Dante's father), surrounded by a heavy guard, made up for the deficit. Dante still wasn't sure whose side he was on or whether he would jump sides at any moment.

Keenan leaned down to Dante's ear. "He's arrived with eight of those blokes we arrested the other night."

Dante nodded. *Only eight.* "Send them down." It was enough men for an impressive entrance, but no match for the Santalini presence now at the castle.

The room was deafeningly silent while they all waited the agonizing five minutes for the lift to descend. Only the odd cough or shuffle of feet could be heard.

With the loud ping and clank of the doors opening, everyone seemed to crane their necks to get a first glimpse at the famous Florianna prince who'd caused such a stir. Many had heard of him, but few knew his face.

Isla was mesmerized while the eight men and Malleven walked down the marble steps into the great hall. They moved as one unit, like a super-tight, well-drilled division of soldiers. It was eerie. Not a hair, not a blink, or so much as a twitch was out of synch with another. It was hypnotizing.

They were all dressed totally in black right up to their chins. Just the three gold stars embroidered on their left lapels stood out as the only colour on them. Their hair was black and long to their shoulders, except Malleven's, whose hair was always kept impeccably short. But the creepiest thing of all was what looked like a black Sanskrit symbol etched on each of their cheekbones on their dark skin.

Every one of them was tall and handsome. Isla tried not to look at them as they neared, but her eyes were drawn to Malleven, whose magnetism exceeded them all.

"Fucking hell…I couldn't call this." She heard Tia say next to her. "You are fucked, girl."

Isla threw her an annoyed look. She really wasn't helping.

They were almost in front of them. Isla's heart was thumping and she closed her eyes. Then, as if she were being saved at the last minute, she heard Cesaré's voice. Her eyes flashed open to see he'd broken ranks and stood barring their way.

Malleven's men stepped in front of him to halt his progress and protect their brother.

"Who are they?" Lacy asked.

"The Magi," Dante said quietly.

Malleven held up a hand and his men stood down a little so he could speak to Cesaré.

Isla had never seen Cesaré look so full of simmering anger. He half turned and pointed towards the panoramic window behind him. "When you get out of there, I challenge you for my honour and full Florianna rights," and he spat on the floor.

The room seemed to murmur at once. Isla looked at Dante to see what he would do, but he watched with shrewd interest, letting the show play out.

Malleven's brow creased as if he were hurt by Cesaré's outburst. "Cesaré … I have no wish to fight you. You are as a brother to me. I gave you my own Siren, my love for you was so great," Malleven said, dramatically.

Isla thought Cesaré would combust on the spot; his face was contorted with such disgust. "Love?" he spat. "You pimped out that dear sweet girl like some kind of common prostitute, and all to get where you stand today," he said, pointing at Isla. He spat on the floor again. "My challenge stands."

Isla couldn't resist a glance at Elena, Cesaré's mother, whose chin rose with pride at her son's words. But Isla's heart sank. She knew Cesaré didn't stand a chance against Malleven. He was just too strong, mentally, physically and psychically, and most people around the room thought the same thing, judging by the furtive looks they all gave each other.

Malleven's expression turned to pity, which insulted Cesaré more than any words. "I hope you will change your mind before that sad occasion, Cesaré."

Isla felt a shove as Keenan pushed between her and Tia to stand in front of them and face Malleven. A low buzz of whispers and gasps erupted while people became nervous, knowing that trouble was imminent.

Isla thought it was from Keenan's aggressive stance alone, but when she noticed all their gazes went past Keenan, she glanced behind her and saw another eight of Malleven's men all standing to attention right behind the royal family. They had simply appeared from nowhere.

Dante, Alfonzo and Sebastian all stood up, feeling the threat. Menacingly still, they awaited their next command. Everyone knew now what had happened to the men who had disappeared from the cells.

An uneasy silence crept over the hall before Malleven spoke. "You have something to say to me, Prince?"

Keenan squinted and looked momentarily confused. "You … I have met you before?"

Malleven smiled, as if they were passing time at a social gathering. "Why yes … at the last presentation, I believe."

Keenan's face seemed to blacken when he remembered him. Then he pointed at Cesaré. "I will champion him … if you get out alive."

"What's happening … what's he saying?" Isla asked Tia frantically, not following what was going on.

"Shh," Tia said, frightened to miss a second of the show. "He's going to fight for Cesaré, I think."

"I can fight my own battles," Cesaré said angrily, turning on Keenan.

"Believe me, the battle I fight is my own," Keenan said, ominously, and he turned his gaze back to Malleven.

Isla looked fearfully over at Dante, who was now completely surrounded by Malleven's newly materialized men, totally cut off from his guards. It seemed that Malleven was now in the position of strength. She swallowed down her rising panic and willed Dante to do something.

Dante appeared calm. He narrowed his eyes with contempt at Malleven. "Stand down, everyone. The Florianna has sent its designated son to be tested in the old tradition. Let him take the test." Then he smiled at Malleven with no humour. "Let the Siren decide whether he is worthy or not," and he rested his eyes on Isla and gave her the distinct impression he was trying to convey something to her. *Why didn't he speak straight to her mind?* She stared back at him for a long moment.

The rules, Isla ... It's the rules, Tia projected from next to her.

Isla looked at her sister anxiously. *Why couldn't anyone help her when so much was at stake?*

Tia smiled apologetically at her.

Isla faced front again, not knowing what the hell any of them meant.

Her attention was dragged back to Malleven when he walked towards the fountain. One of his men came from behind her and steered her by the elbow in the same direction. She looked into his face, but his eyes appeared empty and unseeing.

Already in a robe with her swimsuit underneath, she clutched it to her as some sort of protection while she was led to the gateway to the sea.

ISLA'S KNEES were shaking when she let the robe fall to the floor and stood with her body revealed to the whole assembly, dressed in just a plain black swimsuit.

Malleven took off his clothes carefully and meticulously, folding them and placing them over the arms of a servant placed there precisely for that purpose. As always, Malleven's expression was one of confidence, while a slight smile played on his lips and danced across his eyes as they watched her throughout the whole process of undressing. He didn't seem to care that he kept the whole hall waiting – he seemed to enjoy it, in fact.

Eventually, he stood in just his black Calvins. His black tattoos perfectly accentuated the muscles on his toned chest and abdomen and tapered into his slim hips.

Malleven caught her studying his physique and smiled arrogantly, as if he expected nothing less. He stepped into her as he always did, knowing it set her off balance. "Come, Snowflake … it is time," he said, as casually as if they were about to enter a party.

They both stepped over the wall of the fountain and she watched his face closely for any sign of nerves, but there were none. *Was he really scared of water? Perhaps he had overcome it.*

Her heart thumped with foreboding as they inched towards the deep hole in the fountain's centre. Her life as she knew it was about to end again. She took a glance over her shoulder at the last minute and met Dante's eyes. She smiled apologetically for what she was about to do and there was nothing anyone could do about it.

Dante seemed to understand and gave her the smallest of nods to let her know it was okay.

"She doesn't stand a chance," Tia said, too loudly.

"Shh," came from Lacy, standing next to her.

Then she stepped into the cold water in the hope the bubbles would consume her.

HER LUNGS OPENED AS SOON as she submerged in the water. No blissful oblivion awaited her. Her eyes quickly found Malleven. She would have had to be heartless not to acknowledge the bravery it must have taken for him to take that last lungful of air and plunge with her into the tunnel.

Instead of betraying himself, he took her hand and they swam together through the roughly hewn tunnel that led out to sea. Watching his face, she had to keep reminding herself what a thorough egomaniac he was, and how he took pleasure in dominating and humiliating her, because under the water she had the upper hand and he knew it. They were now in her world.

Malleven still tried to breach her barriers periodically, in the hope she would accept him and give herself to him in some sort of complete submission, but she would die first. But didn't the access he sought come with the bond anyway? She shuddered.

She wasn't totally submissive to Dante, though. Maybe because that wasn't what he wanted from her? Maybe an unscrupulous king could take it all if he wanted. A glance sideways at Malleven assured her that he was exactly that. She thanked god then for the rules Tia had spoken of so that both of them came into the water in ignorance.

Malleven wasn't a good swimmer, it was obvious. He moved stiffly and with great effort. It wouldn't have taken much to project words of encouragement to him, but somehow she had to remain aloof. Perhaps he'd hurt her one too many times. The crushing of Cesaré's spirit was the last straw.

They arrived in front of the large expanse that must be the window of the great hall and Isla reminded herself of the hundreds of pairs of eyes watching them. She let go of Malleven's hand and turned to face him. Even out of his comfort zone, his eyes held a cocky confidence that he owned her. Perhaps he'd just learned from a young age to brazen and style everything out. The tactic had certainly brought him far.

He bent and picked up the chain and manacle and attached it to his ankle. It was necessary to hold him still, she guessed, as they were in the sea and not in a pool. Then he straightened up to face her again.

Unbidden, her eyes skated over his perfectly proportioned body with dark skin that was lightening before her eyes, revealing his dark bands that formed in the patterns of the Florianna family. Hers were so much thicker and darker, like the Murrs'. An image of Darres came to her and stabbed her heart. She put such pointless thoughts to the back of her mind.

Malleven took her hand and pulled her towards him so his arms came around her waist and hers were forced around his back. She was conscious of every inch of him brushing up against her while he brushed her lips with his.

When she opened her eyes, he was smirking as if he knew every bit of the power he held over her. God, her life with him would be miserable.

Isla closed her eyes as if in prayer. *Dante, I don't know what to do. Do I have to do what I did with you? I feel that if I did it, I would be dying a slow death.*

She swallowed hard when no reply came. *He must have heard.*

She jolted when Malleven slanted his mouth over hers again and licked the seam of her lips to encourage her. She pulled back slightly to look into his eyes. The overconfidence had gone. In fact, his eyes had narrowed and his face creased in pain. She panicked for a second until she realized it was because he was running out of air. He had already held his breath way longer than any Human.

My god, this was the test, wasn't it? The reason for the chain. He was meant to drown. There had been no need with Dante because his test had been with Tia.

Malleven's head came down on her shoulder and he shook it as if to wake himself up. His whole body was becoming heavy and uncoordinated.

He grabbed her roughly and pulled her in close to him again. What she wasn't prepared for was the despair that leeched out of his eyes. He was imploring her. It was that final look of devastated resignation that crept across his face and he knew what she would do.

. . .

DARRES WAS SUPPOSED to accompany his four brothers to the official presentation of Isla to the Florianna prince today, but he couldn't face it. Axyl understood, as he always did. It wasn't just the sheer number of people with their fancy manners and polite conversation he knew nothing about, but that Isla would be giving herself to another man in front of everyone. He couldn't watch that.

He'd replayed the memory of the time they'd spent together at the airbase over and over, and even now, when he'd dissected it a thousand times, he still couldn't see any hint of Isla's duplicity. She was a clever witch, he'd concluded, nothing more.

That aside, his long strokes in the water still took him to the shallower choppy waters around Ballygowan Castle, where the ceremony was to take place. Except he didn't go inside where his senses told him his brothers were. They had enough witnesses on behalf of the Borge to satisfy the scribes, so he stayed outside and watched, hidden amongst the seaweeds and rocks. There in front of him played out the mesmerizing performance.

Isla was with the dark man. The one he'd seen in the recesses of her mind – her mate. His hands nearly crumbled the rock he held onto when he thought of her giving herself openly to him. It had been him all along, always him. She had betrayed him and Cesaré to get back to this male.

The urge to swim like a seal and smash the pair of them and rip the male apart became almost impossible to resist. *But wait*, the male was not breathing the water. He appeared to be fading, pulling her to him to complete the exchange of themselves, but she was holding off.

Darres remembered what that felt like. It had been the most liberating, loving, most natural thing in the world to do, but she had turned her face and expelled hers into the water. And here she was, avoiding it again. *Was she aware of what she was meant to do?*

The male began to shake his head and grab onto her shoulders to roughly pull and push her as if to wake her up. She remained limp in his grip. All she did was watch his face and wait for the life to ebb from him.

CHAPTER 31

*D*ante felt the most helpless in his whole life, and he'd certainly experienced some crap. Isla's mental pleas were like a stab to his heart, and he felt the worst kind of bastard to ignore them.

He closed his eyes and used all his willpower not to ruin everything and tell her just to fucking kill the bastard. Instead, he had to hope and pray that her good sense and ability to think of the bigger picture would win through. And, of course, the stone-cold-heartedness he knew she possessed as a killer.

What's the matter? Tia projected to him, feeling his misery.

She keeps on asking what she needs to do, he thought. *I can't interfere.*

But she knows what she needs to do, Tia thought, frowning.

Feel her through the bond, Lacy projected to both of them.

The three all closed their eyes and concentrated.

She is terrified of him ... Lacy thought. *More than that, she's terrified of how he makes her feel.*

Isn't that the way with mates? Tia thought, squeezing Dante's hand.

She doesn't feel him like that, Dante thought, getting what Lacy was driving at. It was fascinating to him, as he assumed that mates couldn't help falling in love with each other.

Imagine being mated to someone totally evil. Someone you know is rotten but still can't help yourself with, Lacy thought, her eyes far-off and distant. *It would be like torture.*

Then there is only one thing she can do, Tia projected.

Let's hope that she thinks the same way, because none of us can sway her, Dante thought.

Tia exhaled loudly. *Let's see if she's got the balls*, and she looked stony-faced at Dante.

THAT LOOK, that final plea, that little-boy-lost look of utter disappointment, was nearly her undoing. She was about to cover his mouth with hers when Tia's mental voice, of all people's, came through.

We aren't ignoring you, Isla, but for this test to be legal, we can't intervene. But what I will say to you is what was once said to me; it is up to you, Isla, do you hear me? ... Up to you whether your mate comes out of the water again.

Then Tia was gone.

It all seemed to happen in a split second and in super-fast time. *Was she actually saying that she could kill Malleven?* Maybe she could; she was certainly capable. She could choose to breathe for him like she did Dante. Sharing herself was everything Malleven had always wanted. Then she remembered the conversations about breathing underwater she'd had with Cesaré. He had told her that he hadn't been initiated. It had troubled her at the time what that meant. Now she guessed that was what would happen when she breathed into an Atlantean male for the first time.

God no, Malleven would be unbearable then. He'd become as strong underwater as he was on the land. Never could she do that. And yet she looked at the beautiful male in front of her, who was a small boy once, pushed from pillar to post, with no one to care for him until he pulled himself up into the position he was in today, and she felt she couldn't kill him. She couldn't maliciously end him like that.

Malleven's eyes were now slowly closing and the life force was leaving him. It was then that it came to her. His arms and legs hung bent in the water and he floated with his head drooping forward and downwards when the memory of her mother's reminder echoed through her head like an epiphany. She simply would not accept him as her mate. Another had already claimed her.

Malleven may be her most compatible person in the world, according to fate, but she didn't have to accept him as such. She was Airla Leukosia Artemisia Bonaci and she refused this male and she refused the Florianna.

Isla took a last look at Malleven's face and, eerily, there was still a hint of a smile on his lips as if he had already second-guessed her. She pushed herself away from him so there was a clear space for the spectators to see. *I refuse this male,* she projected as loudly and as clearly as she could, so that all those with a psychic ability could hear. *I belong to another.*

Malleven's body hung lifeless and suspended in the water for the whole Atlantean world to see.

DANTE, Tia and Lacy closed their eyes and breathed a huge sigh of relief when Isla's words rang clearly in their heads; *I refuse this male.*

"She did it. I don't believe it!" Tia said, throwing her arms around her sister's neck.

Then pandemonium seemed to break out all around them as the Santalini wasted no time setting about the magi, and the Florianna began to argue with everyone about the legality of the test and how it had never been heard of for a royal prince to be rejected.

Dante glanced behind him and saw Keenan brawling with several magi, even Vionne was fighting and he didn't think the Murrs were like that?

He faced back to the window. He couldn't help staring at the poor little brave girl still treading water out there, moving slowly away from the lifeless body of Malleven.

Dante was about to join in the fray when, out of the corner of his eye, something darted so fast in front of the window that he almost missed it. A large striped male stopped abruptly behind Isla and grabbed her around her waist. Then he turned with her in his arms to face the window as if he knew Dante was watching, and a powerful mental voice filtered through despite the distance and thickness of the glass.

Other people started to notice what Dante was witnessing and stopped fighting. The Borge brothers and Alfonzo and Sebastian, to name but a few, all stared with amazement out of the large window.

I, Darres Borge, son of Darl, son of Murrtaine, of the pure race of Atlas, do claim this Siren for the Borge.

All the while he spoke, Isla stared up into his face from within his arms, not struggling or moving at all.

Tia came up to Dante's side and he instinctively put his arm around her. They both watched through the window.

Isla wrapped her legs around Darres' waist and threaded her fingers into his long black hair. They made a spellbinding couple, striped in heavy black bands with his long black hair and hers blonde, curling and fanning out all around them.

Darres touched Isla's cheek, then she linked her hands around his neck and he swam out to sea as fast as he had appeared.

Dante and Tia were left with their mouths open. Then they turned their heads and looked at each other, not believing what they had just seen.

"Where is he?" Keenan said, stepping over an unconscious body to reach them.

"Where's who?" Dante said absently, still looking into Tia's face.

"Malleven."

Dante looked at Keenan, frowned, and then back out to sea. "Fuck!"

"What?" Tia said, following his line of vision.

"He's gone."

Antonio stood with Nasr and two of the magi, being buffeted and tossed on a small boat on the choppy sea just off the coast around Ballygowan Castle. He was terrified, and not just because he felt he'd be pitched into the drink any minute, but because of the reason they were there.

They were Malleven's insurance policy; he always had one just in case something went gravely wrong. He'd gone off to the ceremony full of confidence in Isla. The truth was, he underestimated her greatly, but not so much that he didn't bother with a safety net.

Antonio's wary eyes drifted across to Nasr, standing on the bow of the boat with hands outstretched over the water, chanting. Low at first, but it was building in speed and volume. He moved closer to him, waiting anxiously for what would happen. Malleven had reassured him that nothing was impossible with the magi.

The other two men closed their eyes and held their heads down as if they were praying, then joined Nasr in the chanting. They seemed to be saying the same thing over and over like a mantra.

The wind whipped up around them and the boat seemed less stable than ever. Antonio crouched low and grabbed the sides of the wooden boat, but he was closer to the surface and could look down into its depths.

There was just a small glow at first. He nearly didn't spot it. But it grew brighter and larger and it was rising to the surface. It looked like a ball of light in the water.

Antonio checked Nasr's face. He was concentrating hard through his hands onto the water. Antonio squinted when it seemed to halt and then watched gold droplets of water leave the surface and rise to Nasr's hands. There were sparse beads at first, until they buzzed and vibrated and separated into a fine gold mist. More and more rose up out of the water until they formed the shape of an unconscious man. His head lay back limp, and his arms and legs hung like heavy weights down to the molten sea's surface.

Nasr inched backwards and the other two men came around to his sides and pushed Antonio back out of the way. Then Nasr slowly turned and the men placed their hands underneath the body and guided it down onto the floor of the boat. The three stood and chanted over it.

Antonio watched nervously, while the gold particles stopped moving and appeared to solidify and set into the solid features of a man. His skin darkened and Antonio breathed a sigh of relief when he recognized Malleven. But he wasn't breathing.

"Turn him over," Nasr ordered.

The men flipped him over to his front and Nasr crouched and pushed his palms into his back to massage the water out of his lungs.

"Do something!" Antonio shouted over the din of the waves when nothing seemed to be happening.

Then, when Malleven eventually coughed and retched, Antonio snatched him up to rest on his lap, smoothing his sopping black hair from his brow and rocking him to and fro.

Antonio sent a silent prayer up to the heavens, then kissed his forehead. "It's okay … it's over … You're with me now … I've got you."

WHEN DARRES APPEARED FROM NOWHERE, grabbed Isla to him and announced to the whole Atlantean world that she was his, her heart stopped beating. She felt like she wanted nothing more than to spend her life with this male and couldn't believe he still wanted her.

All she could think of was clinging to him with every fibre of her being when he swam off away from the castle with her. There was no way she would let him go now. With her legs clamped around his waist, arms linked around his neck, and her cheek pressed against his chest, he swam effortlessly, covering miles in no time at all.

She felt a stab of guilt when she thought of Dante and those she would leave behind and she fortified herself with the reminder that it wouldn't be for ever, just until she and Darres were settled.

Then, as if he'd felt her, Dante's voice traversed the distance to her mind. *Thank you, Isla, for what you did. I know how hard it was for you to do … Be safe and be well. Good luck with the babies.* His voice began to fade, possibly because they were moving further and further away.

I'm sorry, Dante, she replied while she still could. *But I have to go with him … it's my chance, you know?*

I know, and you have my blessing. Just bring the babies when they're born and give me your pledge, okay?

She was overwhelmed with such gratitude. *Thank you so much.* She held onto Darres tighter still as they had reached an underground tunnel

I'll see you soon. Your sisters send their love... And Dante's voice disappeared.

She buried her face into Darres' skin to stifle her emotion; the mention of her sisters' love made her miss them already – even the mother and father she barely knew. She would never forget their part in her freedom. It would seem it's okay to show your love to members of your family.

Darres slowed down when he navigated the narrow tunnels of the underwater caves. She could see very little until they entered a large circular space illuminated by green and orange sea plants that emitted a subtle glow. This place had been fashioned into a bolthole – Darres' place. He slowly released her and backed away, as if he was unsure what she would do now that he had her.

Wait a minute – babies! The word suddenly struck her – plural. Did Dante know something she didn't? She inadvertently touched her stomach.

Darres never missed a thing and watched her closely. *You are pregnant?* His face looked so vulnerable and unsure. He was like a small boy in so many ways and very much a man in others.

She swam hesitantly towards him. *I think so*, she said, touching her palm against his face.

She didn't want to think about the implications of whose babies they might be. For now, they were his. All she wanted was to feel him close to her and not to hate her, even if it was for a little while. *You claimed me for yourself?*

He nodded. *For the Borge and for Murrtaine.*

It wasn't a declaration of undying love, but it was a start. She'd work with that for now. She came closer still so her lips were millimetres from his. He didn't close the distance but remained still, waiting for what she would do.

I claimed you, but I am a Murr; I cannot be tested in the way of the Atlanteans.

She understood what he was saying; he was goading her. The way of acceptance for a Murr had to be a full bond, as they couldn't drown. She began nipping at his lips with hers to melt him. He was all hardness and unyielding, as he'd been when she'd first met him. He parted his lips slightly. *Progress.*

You want to be tested? she projected, kissing down the column of his neck, biting and sucking as she went.

Darres pulled her back up to his mouth. *How else would I know if you accept me?* he glared through narrowed eyes. *You leave a trail of destruction in your wake.*

Isla ignored him again and pushed her tongue into his mouth. His resolve weakened slightly and he met her with his, where he circled and stroked. His arms came around her and he pulled the straps down from her swimsuit and it disappeared from beneath her.

It was a submission of sorts and she melted into him and kissed him passionately as his hands roamed over her sensitive body. His thumb stopped to rub over the pebble of her nipple, causing her to throw her head back and expose her neck, which he sucked hard.

Isla allowed him, this time, to explore her all over again. She also knew he was trying to resist her and failing.

Her legs linked behind his back and she felt his hardness nudge at her behind, straining to escape the sheer Murr cloth of the trousers he wore. He read her mind and the barrier was gone.

My god, he was so large. She'd forgotten the scale of him, it had been so long. She positioned herself over him and gave herself over to the blissful pain of the feeling of fullness and worked herself over him, pushing down a little at a time.

Darres became impatient and held her hips to give her the precious leverage she needed. He was still only partly inside her and she thought he was an impossible fit. Her heart was beating and she was mindless with want while she moved on him, still inch by inch.

He stopped moving, held her still and asked again, *How do I know you accept me, Isla?*

Her mind unclouded for a second when she opened her eyes and saw his pained, beautiful face looking down at her. She guided his mouth to hers and paused while she remembered the one and only time she'd shared herself with Dante. It had not been the end of the world as she knew it. He had not taken advantage of the bond but had helped her all he could and now she had a bond with her sisters and a family at last.

Surely Darres was worth the risk? It was something he needed from her. He needed proof that she cared for him. Darres would never intentionally hurt her. And she was convinced that she carried his babies inside her.

Wasting no more time, Isla kissed up to his waiting mouth again and covered it with hers completely. And when he invaded her mouth with his tongue, she sucked and held it. *Hold still, Darres.*

She felt him stiffen, waiting.

Then she blew very gently, even and steady; a stream of everything within her. He yielded to her completely when the overwhelming pleasure hit him, and she projected the words he was waiting for. *I accept you, Darres Borge ... as my mate. I never wanted another. You are the one I chose for myself. I love you.* And while she blew her essence into him again, he thrust deeply inside her, making her break the seal of their lips.

Her muscles clenched and pulsated around him while he bit down onto her shoulder and he began to move and surge deeply within her. She floated back in the water, boneless and limp, when her climax crept over her. Holding her to him by her hips, showing her no mercy while his own orgasm swept through him, his face became a picture of blessed torture.

I love you, Darres, she whispered, while she luxuriated in ecstasy in the green glow of the water that felt like a velvet cocoon. Her muscles held him, prolonging his climax for the longest time.

His movements gradually slowed and he opened his eyes to gaze down at her.

Share yourself with me, Darres. He pulled her up against him again and, without hesitation, breathed effortlessly into her. It was total and complete; a joy. His spirit filled her and his body entered her again and stroked her intimately. Her climax was immediate and all-consuming, over and over. Pulling her to him, he ground into her and joined her. She bit him and scored his back with her nails and accepted every part of him, body and soul, and returned it so he was in no doubt they were completely connected. Their spirits communed; they soared, clinging to each other psychically while their bodies rippled, joined in the water. Together for hours, they enjoyed and shared each other, over and over, so no one, whoever they were, could ever pull them apart.

EPILOGUE

*H*illside overlooking Higashi Village, Japan
　　"Keep up, you two," Isla said, trudging up through the lush vegetation.

Darres, who followed behind the two children, bent down from his great height and scooped the twin boys up into his arms as if they weighed nothing.

Isla stopped for a breather with her hands on her hips. "There it is … Higashi Village." She closed her eyes, breathed in the scents and was transported back to when she was eight years old.

Darres held the boys easily in one arm and stood behind her with a hand on her shoulder and looked over her head at the view. *It is as beautiful as your picture.*

She turned into him and hugged him while he kissed the top of her head. *Shall we go on?* he projected.

She nodded and they continued to climb the many steps to the monastery that sat almost at the top of the hillside.

Everything looked exactly as she remembered it; peaceful and clean avenues of red-timbered tori – everything pure and right with the world.

An old monk shuffled by with a cane and stopped when he sensed them there. He looked over a long while, so Isla thought perhaps he couldn't see.

"Is that you, Snow-san?"

Isla recognized his voice immediately and laughed. "Sensei Masahiro!" She ran over and just stopped herself from hugging him. She bowed at the last minute in the way the monks had taught her.

"You have grown into a beautiful young woman, Snow-san. We've been expecting you."

"Thank you … really?" Then she remembered that to a monk he probably meant in his lifetime, as time meant very little to him.

He began to walk to the shade of the temple. "Sensei Daichi is no longer with us," he stated simply.

She shook her head and swallowed down the emotion she always felt when she thought of her sensei.

Darres gave her hand a squeeze.

"He was with you till the end?" Masahiro said.

She looked into Darres' eyes. "Yes, Sensei … just as he promised," she said, blinking away her tears.

Masahiro nodded and she wondered whether he knew she held back so much. He quickly changed the subject. "And you have a family, Snow-san," he said, smiling brightly, delighted with the two boys staring up at him. Both had long, dark hair to their shoulders but their mother's clear blue eyes.

"There is no doubt whose these sons belong to," Masahiro said, smiling to Isla and then to Darres in turn. *Weird, he seemed to know instinctively so much, or was he just being polite?*

He was right though. There was no doubt that Darres was their father. A paternity test taken as soon as the boys were born confirmed it. But Isla and Darres knew, it was more of a formality in case it was challenged later. The doctors had said it was likely she conceived because she had been under-water with Darres, but she preferred to believe the boys had been conceived out of love, and she pushed unpleasant thoughts out of her mind.

"This is Dannon," she said, pulling one boy to stand in front of her. "And this one is Keefa," she said, touching the shoulders of the other.

Masahiro's eyes travelled up the long distance from Darres' feet, all the way up the trim, toned body to his jet-black eyes. His hair was still long to his waist like a Native American brave (Isla wouldn't let him cut it) and, thankfully, he had Human clothes on. "And this is your man of the sea," Masahiro stated, as if it were nothing more than he expected.

Isla snuggled into Darres and he put his arm around her. Her hand rested on his stomach. "Yes," she said, smiling up at him. Darres looked down at her as if she amused him. "This is my husband, Sensei … my chosen mate."

"Ah, yes … a true man of the sea was always for you, just as Daichi said."

They followed Masahiro further into the temple. She was surprised at how relaxed Darres was here. He wasn't usually comfortable around people, and even less so around Humans.

As usual, he read her mind. *It is tranquil here, little one. I can see why you love it.*

The boys came scooting up to them, pointing at the hundreds of brightly coloured wooden plaques hanging on the wall.

"They are wishing plaques," Isla explained.

"You may choose one each and hang them up to make a wish," Masahiro said, laughing at their energy and enthu-siasm as they both ran to the little display.

"Just one!" Isla called over.

"Come, let us take some tea," Masahiro said. "Then you can tell me of your many adventures."

***

Click here to: https://books2read.com/u/b5KNdk to read book 4, Tiger Lily, right away!
And to receive your two, 21st Century Sirens Novellas, and be the first to know anything relating to T's books, leave your details here: https://mailchi.mp/d18c89c14f50/tstedmannovellas
And please don't forget to leave a review, I really appreciate the feedback.
Much love
T

ACKNOWLEDGMENTS

A special thank you to my children and my lovely NHS ladies for being there through the dark times, and to my proofreader, Diane Burke. RIP

GLOSSARY

Characters in family groups

Bonaci

Alfonzo Bonaci – Head of the Bonaci royal family and uncle to the Sirens

Sebastian Bonaci – Brother to Alfonzo and father to the Sirens

Luca Bonaci – Half-brother to the Sirens

Dino Bonaci – Full brother to Luca and half brother to the Sirens

Tia Storm – Siren – First wife and most compatible to Dante – queen – bonded to Jay

Lacy Rain – Siren – Mated and most compatible to Keenan Santalini – second wife to Dante

Isla Snow – Siren – Mated to Darres Borge, third wife to Dante. Most compatible to Malleven

Royal Children

Xavier – Son of Dante and Tia

Alexia – Daughter of Dante and Tia
JJ – Son of Jay and Tia

Borge
Darl – Lord Advocate of Murrtaine and father to Vionne,
Dax, Caan, Axyl and Darres
Vionne Borge – Murr and eldest son and successor to Darl
Dax Borge – Son of Darl, brother to Vionne
Caan Borge – Son of Darl, brother to Vionne
Axyl Borge – Son of Darl, brother to Vionne, Dax, Caan,
twin of Darres and ruler of Murrla
Darres Borge – Son of Darl, twin of Axyl, brother to Vionne,
Dax and Caan – Mate to Isla Snow
Naomi – Wife to Sabastian Bonaci – Mother to Sirens

Royal children

Keefa – Son of Darres and Isla Snow
Dannon – Son of Darres and Isla Snow

Dubonnetti
Dante Dubonnetti – King and most compatible mate and
married to Tia Storm and Lacy Rain
Duke Ormond Deliss – Biological father to Dante and
Ambassador for the Atlanteans in Washington, DC
Christian Dubonnetti – Stepfather to Dante and head of the
Dubonnetti royal family
Marco Dubonnetti – Half-brother to Dante
Paulo Dubonnetti – Half-brother to Dante
Antonio Dubonnetti – Half-brother to Dante – Lover to
Malleven Mancini
Stephan Dubonnetti – Youngest – Half-brother to Dante

Florianna

Cesaré Florianna – One of the five sons of the Florianna and cousin to Malleven Mancini
Sandro Florianna – Eldest brother to Cesaré
David, Roberto and Mario – Brothers to Cesaré
Malleven Mancini – Cousin to Cesaré – most compatible with Isla
Ronaldo Florianna – Cesaré's Father
Elena Florianna – Cesaré's Mother
Rodrigo Mancini – Uncle and benefactor to Malleven

Santalini
Andreas – Elder of the Santalini royal family and uncle to Keenan Santalini
Keenan Santalini – Most compatible and mated to Lacy Rain
Ruby Santalini – Sister to Keenan
Marius Santalini – Eldest brother to Keenan
Adriano, Drago and Louis – Brothers to Keenan
Reeve Santalini – Fellow guard and cousin to the brothers

The Humans
Jay Gardiner – Protector/Lover bonded to Tia Storm – Best friend to Dante
Max Brunswick – Advisor to Dante for Atlantean history and language.
Mrs Ross – Cash's housekeeper
Nasr – High Priest of the Magi

Protectors (Appearing in this book)
Sean McPhearson – Protector to Tia Storm
Cash Reynolds – Protector to Tia Storm

Terms particular to the Atlanteans

Divining ring – worn by all princes and forged particularly

for them. Can only have one wearer. Forged from the Orb itself. Determines whether a Siren is nearby and the wearer's status to her by its color
Opaque white – default resting color
Turquoise/green – a Siren is nearby
Purple – the Siren nearby is the wearer's most compatible mate

Elixir – Potion taken by princes and those humans in contact with a Siren to prevent an extreme reaction or even death in the event of breathing her essence.

First Breath – The breath passed from a Siren for the very first time. Her power passes to the recipient only on the very first exchange. Usually reserved for the king.

The Magi – Ancient order of magicians and alchemists of which Malleven belongs. Mainly Human in origin, but have worked alongside the Atlantean nation since the beginning of their colonization.

The Orb – the ancient power source of Atlanteans. Believed to rest beneath Murrtaine and came with their ancestors from Atlas.

ALSO BY T STEDMAN

21st Century Siren Series

Soul Breather

Blood Sister

Shield Maiden

Tiger Lily

Night Goddess

Darkly Begotten

* * *

The Dark Valentines Collection

Diablo

* * *

Non-Fiction

My Migraine Story

9 780099 330 983 0